TO ROOT SOMEWHERE BEAUTIFUL

AN ANTHOLOGY OF RECLAMATION

EDITED BY LAUREN T. DAVILA

Published by Outland Entertainment LLC
3119 Gillham Road
Kansas City, MO 64109

Publisher/Creative Director: Jeremy D. Mohler
Editor-in-Chief: Alana Joli Abbott
Senior Editor: Scott Colby
Project Director: Anton Kromoff

ISBN: 978-1-954255-78-4 paperback, 978-1-954255-79-1 ebook
Worldwide Rights
Created in the United States of America

Editor: Lauren T. Davila
Copy editor: Alana Joli Abbott
Proofreader: Em Palladino
Cover Illustration: Chris Yarbrough
Cover Design: Jeremy D. Mohler
Interior Layout: Jeremy D. Mohler

Printed and bound in the United States of America.

Visit **outlandentertainment.com** to see more, or follow us on our Facebook Page
facebook.com/outlandentertainment/

TABLE OF CONTENTS

Introduction by Danny Lore 5

Notes on Content 8

Seeds Within by Mari Kurisato 9

The Last Singapore Girls by Wen-yi Lee 10

Unlocked by C.M. Leyva 26

As the Forest Itself Gave Chase by Alyssa Grant 44

Love Is a Battleship by D.C. Dador 57

Mango Heart by Katalina Watt 78

A Mosaic of Tiny, Insignificant Moments
    by Laura Galán-Wells 85

The Red Sentinel by Amparo Ortiz 96

El Grito de la Onda by Lauren T. Davila 113

We Were Meant to Be Buried by RJ Joseph 128

They Used to Build Parks Here by SJ Whitby 138

Like Blood From by Rien Gray 155

Honey and Onions by Sam Elyse 166

When the World Gives Out by Rachal Marquez Jones 181

Follow Me into the Dark by Mallory Jones 193

Nectar: Unlimited by Laura G. Southern 208

To Root from Flesh by Isa Arsen 223

Emma by Morgan Spraker 235

The Boy Who Became an Entire Planet by Nicholas Perez 248

Alone by Alex Brown 260

The Roots Called Us Home by Onyx Osiris 272

Mother of Titans by Darci Meadows 290

Author Biographies 307

THE GROWING HORRORS

AN INTRODUCTION BY DANNY LORE

Nature has always scared me, just a little bit.

Perhaps it's my incredibly urban upbringing, but the majesty that nature holds has always been a dangerous thing to me. It's something beyond a god, quaking from above and below with sometimes unimaginable power. Amongst the nightmares of your standard monsters-in-the-dark, the most persistent ones starred walls of the ocean, frothing with a vengeance as they roared up to engulf me. In these horrible dreams, I was stuck motionless, watching as the Hudson River or the Atlantic Ocean decided it was done watching us all.

Few things float in my nightmares; little surprise since so little of my life was "natural."

So when I was asked to write an introduction to *To Root Somewhere Beautiful*, I knew I was in for a few sleepless nights.

In this anthology, the ocean reckons with us as it should have long ago; its scale and power are felt even in quiet moments. Protagonists stare into it and wonder not simply "what is underneath," but what the lashes of water are capable of. When they know, they remember how harshly humanity dealt with the ocean and wonder how long until it again gets its comeuppance.

When it's not the ocean, it is the very soil. The dark softness of it, the drying cracked remains of it, the soil demands the attention and power that has been so wholly stripped from it. And strip it we did; these stories look at climate change and humanity's need to wrangle and remind us that the earth below us is not something to be wrangled. We attempt to appease it and hope it offers up what we need to survive.

Sometimes, even the soil's vengeance follows us into space, chasing us down like a xenomorph, except…maybe we did this to ourselves. Maybe we deserve the flowery funeral it offers in exchange for what has always been rightfully the earth's.

The thing about *To Root Somewhere Beautiful* is that its horror is slow. It is the last remaining seed germinating and slithering its tendrils into the soil we've destroyed. It's the soil making itself hospitable for the things that will consume us—not with tooth and claw, but with root and petal. Nature's trick is two-fold here.

First, we know our history. The protagonists in this anthology bear the guilt (both responsibility and the feeling of regret) of destruction, and sometimes, they long for it—long for the replacement of self with the very entity they destroyed. It's justice, it's fairness, and it's better than living in a world without nature and soil and saplings and spectacular skies.

The second, the insidiousness of it all, is how very beautiful this horror is. In the present dystopia of forest fires and droughts, it's hard not to stare in relief and wonder at nature fighting back against it all. It is the color and life that feels so much like hope that we cling to it even when we are going to be consumed by it all. For me, that's always been the most terrifying aspect of nature. It's hard not to stare in awe when it makes space for itself.

Not that all of these protagonists stare in the end, of course. There are fighters, those who remember that flesh and blood come with tooth and claw as they fight not to give in to the roots and vines threatening to erase them. There are others, too, that try to outthink nature, try to use all those tools we've built to say this space, at least, is what we have left. But there are others, neither gawkers nor fighters…they welcome the beauty and the reclamation with open arms. It isn't giving up, not at all; they've seen the war play out, the harm that humanity has done, and wish to be part of something greater. Beautiful, yes, powerful, yes, but greater. Unknown.

To Root Somewhere Beautiful, like its stories, offers you seedlings. Offers you the choice of planting them, of listening to what the seed and soil need. And like many protagonists within, you are left with the roots of something greater than yourself. It grows inside of you and blossoms outside. Sometimes, it changes you, and other times, you choose to change.

Each of these short stories is a little wonder. A little seed that grows with every word, representing the majesty of nature when it has had enough of us. And it reminds me of my tsunami nightmares. Yes, because of the way that it all comes to a head, the loud, frothy waves—beautiful in their threat—but also because of something I always forget until it's too late: my nightmares often start with looking down at the ground and seeing the dirt shiver. Seeing a stalk shake, marveling at how roots moving the ground resemble an earthquake—

If you look close enough.

NOTES ON CONTENT

Many of these stories feature content that may make readers uncomfortable. As an aid, we've listed some of the details that may elicit strong responses for each story.

Unlocked: profanity, drug use, insects, descriptions of violence, acts of colonialism, description of medical procedures, mass death, bodily fluids, and murder.

As the Forest Itself Gave Chase: character injury, forest fires, some violence.

Mango Heart: allusions to terminal illness/disease, references to death, minor depiction of racist incident.

The Red Sentinel: references to blood, death, disfigurement, and gaslighting.

They Used to Build Parks Here: body horror, death, self-sacrifice.

Like Blood From: body horror, physical abuse of children, forced psychiatric hospitalization, descriptions of pica and cluster headaches, mentions of past colonization and destruction of sacred spaces.

When the World Gives Out: self-harm, suicidal ideation, depression, death of loved ones.

Follow Me into the Dark: disappearance of a loved one, death of a parent (implied), death of a child (off-page, mentioned), grief and loss depiction, paranormal activity (including possession), plant-based body horror.

Nectar: Unlimited: body horror, burns, toxic workplace environment.

The Boy Who Became an Entire Planet: violence, body horror, environmental disaster.

The Roots Called Us Home: racism/bigotry/hate speech, on-page deaths, kidnapping, threats, snakes.

SEEDS WITHIN

MARI KURISATO

There are no cold demons
Of betrayal worse than the
Body's slide into oblivion
That gradual or sudden
Decay of faith, of safety
of that childhood belief
That your parents can
Protect you from the
Monsters in the darkness

The grasping fingers of rot
Are bursting forth like
Black seeds of Touch Me Nots
From the shriveled cells of my
Own body
Be it infection, or insulin resistance
Or brain damage in the womb
And it galls me that they call this
A god's plan when I think how cruel
It must be for children to die
before their time
How do the faithful pray in the
Shadow of such dark gods?

THE LAST SINGAPORE GIRLS

WEN-YI LEE

The flowers on Eesha's skirt have started growing into her thigh.

I watch her from across the stove, lifting the fabric to slip the scissors underneath and snip away the feathery roots. If you get them quick enough they only prickle and leave whispers of stains on your skin. If you don't—I still have scars on my ribs, jagged whip cracks where Anna had to yank the roots from my muscles. It hurt worse than anything, and I can still feel the phantom of it when I inhale. So I sit here turning luncheon meat slices and watch Eesha snip away. She looks distracted.

"You okay?"

"Fine." But abruptly, she puts down the scissors. The metal clacks against her grandmother's big silver ring. "Do you think that maybe the missing girls actually found something, and they just never came back?"

The silence is filled with sizzling meat. She picks up the scissors and goes back to snipping.

No, we know what happens to them because we find their bodies. Jolie on the baggage carousel, flowers embroidering her skin. Maya in the butterfly garden, caterpillars writhing in her hair, skin flaking into leaves. Wei was embedded in the now-wild topiary outside ionosphere terminal six, spores on her cheeks and thorns growing from beneath her fingernails. We haven't found all of them, sure, but enough to make an educated guess what happens when someone goes missing.

When Eesha speaks again it's to change the subject. "I kind of miss Hui."

"The world really *is* ending." We laugh, but I miss Hui too. Hui was our head bitch in charge. She was born for that red chief kebaya. She spoke five different languages, ran the cabin like a navy ship, would terrorize you out if your eyebags were too dark, and was also the first person you went to if a passenger was giving you a hard time. A week after the last plane left, overloaded, early, and without us—twenty days after Dorscon Red became Dorscon Black and the government started loading people onto planes—she'd taken a couple girls up to the control tower. The hope was to get vantage, see if any of the ATC radios still worked. We haven't seen them since.

I flip the slices once more for good measure before sliding them onto plates, which Luce has already packed with rice, slices of our last fresh cucumber, chili, and slightly stale peanuts. As I serve, I realize we're down a plate.

"Clarise went to the beach this morning," says Anna from across the kitchen, seeing my confusion. I pause briefly, all the grief I have left. Clarise was a bit erratic yesterday. A lot of the leavers were. They never explained leaving, but I suppose they'd rather risk it than go insane waiting here.

So, eight plates. There were twenty-four of us after the evacuations—as far as it matters, the only twenty-four people left on the island. Then we were eleven after Rachelle and Maisarah went off into one of the overgrown zones two days ago, convinced there was something hidden in one of the hangars. But you don't go into the overgrowth and expect to return. We opened a bottle for them and everything.

We take our plates out to the tables. We fit around just two now.

The electric stoves don't work, after all the power stations on the island got tangled up and abandoned, but a couple restaurants still had gas stoves. We burned through the first one on day four. There were a lot of us, and the cafe had been due for a refill. Now we're at this place that overlooks the valley under the dome.

It used to be beautiful—the waterfall pouring from the top of the dome and clouds of mist hanging over the man-made forest that sloped toward it, low benches and bars and shops scattered within the trees even as people checked into arrivals just a wide hallway down.

Now, my skin prickles just looking at the dense mass of plants, which have crept over the benches in the absence of their gardeners. It's too reminiscent of the city right before the evacuations: buildings overtaken by jungle, clogged waterways, the entire population either succumbing to the creepers or fleeing, batch by batch, on the rapidly dwindling air fleets. But without electricity, this glass dome with its flood of sunlight and dozens of abandoned shops was the best place for us to stay.

The remaining eight of us eat dinner by lamplight and listen to the battery radio. Even with its antennas sticking all the way out, the signal we're stealing from across the collapsed causeway still gets garbled sometimes. A Malay broadcast stutters into a crooning pop song and then into football commentary. That's how we knew they weren't coming back for us—when the news cycle moved on.

Right after a corner kick, a mass of plants peels from the darkness beyond the entrance and bursts into the cafe.

We scramble back, already reaching for anything sharp. *A live one?* As my hand closes around my fork, the stumbling swamp yells, "Wait!"

Eesha's spoon clatters. It's Rachelle.

The girl we toasted dead yanks tendrils off her hair and tosses them aside. I never thought we'd see her alive again, much less hear the words that next come out of her mouth:

"We found a plane. We think we could get it to fly."

We follow Rachelle through the service tunnels, flashlights casting uneven spotlights. The tunnels are the easiest way to get around the airport. Apparently they're so watertight and concrete not even the plants can get in, though there must be a landfill's worth of soil overhead. Our nine pairs of footsteps echo quietly, service-trained. Whenever I brush up against the wall and it's cool, I wonder if we're in the bedrock of the island, if the ocean is just on the other side.

I end up right behind Rachelle and become fixated on a mossy tendril emerging between the strands of her newly tied bun. I'm not imagining it—it's growing fast, pale green, coiling down a lock of hair. I yank it free. Rachelle yelps but gives me a grim nod when she sees the tendril in my hand, along with the strands of hair. I almost toss it before realizing I probably shouldn't introduce plant matter into this miraculously untouched tunnel. I put it in a handkerchief instead. Before I fold it up, I have the urge to hold the feathery tendril in my hand instead. It's exactly the length and thickness of my palm lines. But the thought passes and I scrunch it up in the cloth, a little unsettled.

We emerge in the basement of the starfleet terminal's innovation center. I get a bad feeling that's proven true when we step into the hangar and see what Rachelle's found. It's not a Boeing or an Airbus. It's flatter, smaller, sleeker. It doesn't even have a proper paint job. My heart sinks.

"This isn't a plane. It's an early starskimmer."

Eesha shoots me a look, and Rachelle scowls. "I know that."

I know she does, because during the evacuations, we were all assigned to the starfleet. Cutting-edge jets for a brand-new terminal that sat precariously on more reclaimed land, vessels to the stars parked where the ocean used to be. The name was a little misleading. They really only touched the top of the atmosphere. But the rich people couldn't get enough of ionospheric luxury flights across the earth, aurora borealis out one window and the entire planet spread out beneath the other. When the island started to choke on its own growth, the rich picked the skies.

That last evacuation day, sirens wailed as emergency broadcasts stuttered non-stop out of the radio, and we were moving piles of price-less things into the cargo holds. In terminals one through five, other civilians were packed at gate lounges while stewards and assisting army boys hustled them onto flights with as many of their belongings as the plane could take. The starfleet terminal was significantly emp-tier. It could still echo with the sound of ten-thousand-dollar shoes.

I was so excited when I got assigned to the starfleets. I was a *Star Wars* girl. The skimmers took my breath away the first time I saw them sparkling up close on the airfield, like they were still dusted with comet trails and starlight. The passengers were dressed up, the insides were plush and shining. Being granted access to that world was overwhelming. I wore my blue kebaya with the special stars on the collar and served champagne. I smiled and flitted, thinking *I am the face of this beautiful thing*. The press loved us. Whether on the regular airline or on starships, the Singapore Girls were flight made flesh. We were our country with breath and perfectly painted eyelids.

"We had to wrench the door a bit," Rachelle says as we clamber into the prototype's cabin, where Maisarah's waiting. "We'll fix that."

"And how exactly are we going to do that?" Anna doesn't look impressed. I can't blame her. This jet sitting in the innovation hangar means it's likely only been used for tours, and so it's almost entirely bare. There's two sets of sample seats. The rest was probably filled in by hologram.

"We scoped it out and we don't think it needs that much com-plicated work," Maisarah says. "At least, nothing we can't handle. Rachelle can guide the rest."

"Rachelle has a masters in engineering," Eesha interjects, blushing when we look at her. "She'll fix it."

Okay. It's not the first time one of us has been surprisingly qual-ified; almost all of us have other degrees. But that leaves only one, vital question.

"Who's flying it?" Nancy says. There's a beat of silence and my stomach drops. Slowly, Rachelle, Maisarah, and Eesha turn to me.

"Oh," I say. "You've got to be kidding me."

My mom was an air force pilot. She bought model planes and made us have Sunday movie nights of every single *Star Wars* thing ever made. When I was sixteen, she signed me up for the Youth Flying Club. I got my restricted private pilot license, and soon I was flying a DA40 monoplane in local zones. I had only just started navigational courses for longer flights when they suddenly found a heart anomaly. At the same time, my dad got diagnosed with stage three colorectal cancer. Between the finances and the concerns about the health reports, I ended up taking my last flight just after my nineteenth birthday.

I applied to be a stewardess three years later, just after my dad's funeral.

It did hurt to be on a plane and not fly it. I missed the sky pouring over the cockpits, the hum of this massive impossible machine under me, holding itself up on the wind. I missed feeling like I could go anywhere, be anything. Still, I ended up making friends with a few of the pilots just by talking shop.

There was one pilot in particular, Nick. We could talk planes for hours, and eventually we got transferred to the same starskimmer. The first flight, he invited me into the cockpit when I was off shift. His copilot, Alexandria, was taking a break. So I was sitting in her chair when the skimmer soared through the borealis, green waves of light peppered with stars. Nick looked at me and said, "You wanna let her glide?"

That night over Norway, I put my hands on the controls of a starskimmer for the very first time.

The air changes when you have something to wake up to.

We stumble on another body around the innovation terminal—slumped against a fence, eyes pecked out and mouth pink with paper-thin bougainvillea—but even that can't slow our drive. For the first time in a long time, we wake up early. When we pass around the scissors to cut off the plants that rooted on us at night, every snip is a ticking clock. The scissors seem to cut easier, as though responding to our reawakened realization: we are human, we are alive, we are getting out of here.

After breakfast, we head down to the terminal, hacking through the night's growth. Rachelle has been safely sealed in there all night assessing the plane and she gratefully tears open the packet of crackers we hand her. "We'll start by running diagnostics and starting to prep the area. Celia—"

I said yes. After they told me there was no one else, I let myself say yes. "Let me survey the cockpit. I need to refamiliarize myself."

Rachelle nods. "Shout if anything is problematic."

As the others circle round for Rachelle's briefing, I walk up to the cockpit.

Inside, I sink into the pilot's seat and just sit there for a moment, taking it all in. The leather is still plush, unused. I close my hands around the wheel, and it fits my palms like it was made for them. I breathe in the stale air and stare out the window into the grey wall of the hanger. I can so easily imagine the sky.

I've never really flown a starskimmer, though. When we were alone, Nick would let me cruise and flick through the screens, but that was it. Still, we talked about it a lot. He knew that was where I really wanted to be.

"It's not that different from a plane," he told me, showing me the controls. The interface *was* familiar. It had to be so pilots could cross over easily. Nick and I were assigned different evac details; I wonder if he's been trying to find me, or if he's assumed I'm dead. Sometimes I fantasize about his plane gliding down from the sky. Then I think about the overgrown taxiways, the vines snarling his wheels, getting sucked into the engines, choking the blades, overheating, explosion. Then I stop fantasizing.

His voice echoes in my head now as I run my hands over the dusty dashboard. There's a long list of things I need to check before we even try to start the engine—fuel, throttle, electricals, switches—but for now I should just be checking that all the controls are wired and operational.

Planes might not be able to fly in, but we might be able to fly out. What a thought. Two months ago, I would never have expected to fly again. But then again, I wouldn't have expected any of this. I run through preflight and flight protocols in my head, touch the corresponding controls. My confidence builds as I work my way down the list. I know what I'm doing. I can do this. I think I can fly us out of here.

I stand to check systems, but a tug on my shoulder makes me wince. I reach back to find that a stalk has grown between the seat leather and my sleeve, filigree roots starting to grab my skin. I should stop wearing this blouse; even sheared off at my waist, its floral patterns still seem to encourage more growth than other fabrics. But I'm attached to it.

I snap the stalk and head out to check the fuel situation. The other girls are already busy opening up panels, checking insides. Some of them are outside starting to burn a runway. Seeing them shrouded in a colossal wave of smoke and greenery reminds me of exactly how few of us there are, and how fragile we are compared to anything else. The dome was a marvel once. It was shaped so carefully, every species of tree selected, every fan of foliage groomed, every amenity tested. But I can't help but feel like now we are the wild things being molded.

The girls work well though, which is hardly a surprise. You don't get to be a stewardess without being adaptive, efficient, knowing how to take directions as a team—and most importantly, willing to do the dirty work. It took fourteen weeks of training for us to make it to regular cabin crew, and four more for starskimmer crew. That's where I met Eesha—we sat next to each other in beauty training, guiding each other to get our eyeshadow and updos exactly right.

This time, though, Eesha's distracted. Whenever I swing by to exchange info with Rachelle, I find Eesha sneaking glances over, and I know it's not at me.

We call it a day at sunset. "I'm going to stay again," Rachelle says listlessly, staring up at an exposed panel on the left wing. "I've got my lantern, I'll see you guys tomorrow. Bring food."

I glance at Eesha, wondering if she'll make an excuse to stay, but even she seems to balk. We seal Rachelle back into the hangar and head back to the dome.

As we loop back past the starfleet terminal to get to the tunnel, however, I come to a halt.

We haven't been this way since we stumbled on Wei's body. Back then, she was implanted in the driveway topiary, one arm extended with vines in the skin. I could never forget that sight; I could have found that exact bush in my sleep. But now it's merely a regular mass of thorns and leaves. I circle it, only to become more sure: Wei's body is missing. There's only a faint indent where it used to be, a depression in the overgrowth like a split-open cocoon, in the barest silhouette of a girl's head and shoulders.

"Celia?" Eesha calls.

I touch the place where her hand must have been and feel tendrils prick my skin, like holding hands. I withdraw hurriedly, quick enough to see the feelers retract into the topiary, length and width of my palm lines.

As a stewardess, the aircraft becomes your world. It's a sleek metal universe, and within it is the chaos. As we work on the starskimmer, however, it becomes obvious how small and fragile that universe was.

We pry pieces off it, hammer and weld it back together. It seems so malleable. It makes everything feel malleable. It also makes me feel a little bit powerful.

When I'm not desperately needed, I end up in the pilot seat, which has begun to feel a part of me again. Sometimes literally—I'll sit too long and find my back attached itself to the leather with little green burrs. After my reverie, the sharp hooks remind me that we have no time to sit still. The island is claiming us from the inside out.

The night after I realized Wei's body was missing, I went to check on some of the others: Maya in the butterfly garden, Jolie on the carousel. We've tried to avoid the places we know the dead are, like it's infectious. So when I find only dozens of caterpillars and no Maya, it's a revelation. First, the island grows out of you. Then, transformed, it absorbs you. It must take time, or we'd never find bodies. But like a parasite, it leeches your essence into itself. Turns flesh fluid, bones into bark, breaks you down and sucks you up.

When Eesha asks me where I've been though, I lie. Something more unsettling sits beneath my discomfort. A tug towards the body sites, like the indents are calling me.

What's better for morale: it's been ten days since Rachelle's return, and every day it becomes more obvious that Eesha can't take her eyes off her. Eventually, it annoys me so much that I pull Eesha aside on our lunch break, ducking behind some boxes of spare parts.

"You keep looking at her."

"I do not."

I just raise my eyebrows. She flushes and twists her ring. "It's— she kissed me once. Here to Cape Town. We were alone in the serving bay, she just leaned over and did it. I haven't stopped thinking about it."

"Oh my god." I usually consider myself up-to-date on crew hookups—and god knows everyone found out about me and Nick within days—but my best friend has never said a word about this?

"But it's the apocalypse. What do you want me to do?"

I grab her wrists. "Exactly. It's the apocalypse. And now we're about to get out of the apocalypse. Go get your damn girl."

Eesha shakes her head. Her hair is falling around her face. I resist the urge to twist it back into place, tell her it has to be smoothed out, the bun no larger than five centimeters. "I need to take a walk."

I glance at the hangar. The girls are scattered in small groups, eating what we brought over. They've been chatting more, even as they sweat, cut off their sleeves, tie back their hair. They're hopeful. "Let's go out back."

We hack our way through a trodden path and get spat out on the beach, the only place that hasn't been entirely overtaken. Sand's not conducive for plant growth, I guess, so you get this gray crescent strip along the jungle like a grainy grin, scattered with debris and washed-up bones. It's not the first time this beach has seen bodies, if I remember history right. But history's never seen a massacre done like this: the tides dark, stringy, clotted with tangling seaweed that's drowned everyone who's tried to swim out and clogged every boat, oar, and engine.

Eesha and I sink onto the sand and watch the waves for a minute, tendrils of seaweed curling in and out over the shore. I want to bring up Rachelle again when Eesha sits up suddenly, grabs my wrist.

"Celia." Her touch prickles like pollen. "There! In the water."

Where she points, a pillar is emerging from the tide. Water streams off it as it glides toward the shore. It doesn't trip in the seaweed. Instead, the weeds curl up it, clinging and weaving into the shape of a girl with braided kelp hair and crusted salt eyes. But it's the waterlogged blue kebaya that gives her away as one of us. It's grown wild, the embroidered flowers putting out shoots, sea stars crawling on the hem.

Eesha and I scramble back as she turns her crystallized eyes to us, cocking her head. "You're still here?"

Her voice is distant, scratchy as though scoured by salt, but I recognize it. "Clarise?"

Clarise, who went to the beach. I imagined her swimming desperately into the waves for Malaysia on the horizon, or maybe just stepping into the seaweed and letting it drag her down to the sand. Clarise never panicked, whether it was a screaming passenger or being stranded on an island. The last time I remember, she was resigned. I caught her staring at a flower that was growing from her elbow, a root from her sleeve having taken hold overnight.

Now, though, there's a lurid light in her eyes, the kind that sees beyond you. Her chest doesn't rise, but her mouth opens and closes in intervals, silent little stomata. "I can feel the others out there," she says. She walks past us, right toward the tree line. I'm too stunned to stop her. She seems to melt into the overgrowth, a disappearing sliver of seaweed. Right before the last of her kelp hair vanishes, though, she turns her crusted eyes back toward us. "It's a better way." Then she's gone, absorbed by the jungle.

When I wake up the next morning, my limbs are twined with vines. I pull one off in one long yank before realizing half my vision isn't there. My left eye is obscured by something soft. I lean back to look in the nearest store window, and a girl with a flower for an eye stares back. I blink; only my right lid closes.

I lean closer to the glass and, experimentally, slip a finger under the petals. They give way easily, folding upwards like reaching the sun, and I touch a thin stalk extending from the center. I see the blurry redness of my fingertip and a bit of light. I trace the stalk down to where it's growing through the jelly of my eye. It doesn't hurt. I withdraw my finger and blink—right eye only. *There she is.* A voice in my head I can't quite place. *Such a wild thing.*

On the way to the starskimmer I detour to the beach again and touch Clarise's footsteps in the sand. High tide should have washed them away, but knots of seagrass have grown in the indents, treading up into the jungle.

We work, eat, squeeze each other's shoulders, sleep. I work on the cockpit and dream of where we'll go once we've spent enough time in the air. Malaysia, probably. Indonesia. Thailand. Different countries took in different groups of our evacuation flights, although only after the causeway was barricaded. I wonder where Nick ended up, or Mom.

I'm in the cockpit when Rachelle comes in, looking a little stunned. "I think...I think that's it. We just need to refuel, chart our course, clear the runway..."

I don't hear her. I'm already flipping switches. Minutes later, the plane whirrs to life, buttons lighting up like stars. The look I exchange with Rachelle is feverish. In her eyes, I see our future, and a little green hair. I think about yanking that out, too, but I don't know how, and something stops me.

That night I dream that I'm flying the starskimmer. The sky tilts as I press upward through its layers: troposphere, stratosphere, mesosphere, ionosphere. This is where it should end, but instead, some instinct keeps me pulling the aircraft upwards. The skimmer shudders under my hands, but it glides through the clouds, growing warmer as we ascend. I see the blue sky darken into the vastness of space. With a push and a burst, we clear the atmosphere, and we are in the universe.

I drift, skimming the vacuum. And then, suddenly, there is a horizon there, and I am descending, nose toward jungled mountains and an oxbow of a blue lake. The aircraft rattles as it touches down and rolls to a stop.

I step out onto the new planet. At first, there is just the wet smell of foliage and soil, the hum of insects echoing off the surrounding peaks. Yet I can't shake the feeling of being watched. Can't help but hear faint heartbeats.

It's then I notice that tall things move within the trees. Too slender and upright to be animals, too fluid to be swaying branches. Another sound twines its way from the jungle: singing, low, throaty and rich. Something clatters, like pebbles rolling. It sounds like civilization. I would move toward it, but my feet are unresponsive, and I can't tell quite where it's coming from. It seems to come from everywhere at once, rising from the leaves themselves.

The tall things move again, all silhouettes, but then one of them passes into a ray of light and I see for a split-second half of what it might be. A living thing, hair-like fungus and thick vines. The light catches a bright human eye embedded into a fanning mushroom, and then I blink, or it blinks. It melts back into the shadow of the trees and is suddenly indistinguishable from them. I am surrounded, then, not by a horde, but by a single, unfurling growth, big as an island, big as a world.

When we get to the hangar the next morning, Eesha's missing and the door is cracked just slightly, not sealed the whole way like we've been so diligent about doing. There's a faint earthy smell in the air. A dusting on the skimmer's wings. The skimmer's door—which we repaired—is ajar.

"Stay here," I tell the other girls, and then climb into the aircraft.

"Rachelle?" My voice echoes, stirring pollen. I make my way through the cabin. The cockpit door, of all things, is shut. "Eesh?"

There's no answer. I push the door open.

Rachelle and Eesha are intertwined on the pilot's seat. I can only tell because I can still see Eesha's ring. Eesha's arms are locked around her shoulders, brown skin turned to bark, ferns bursting from her veins. Moss falls over their tilted faces, interwoven curtains of hair. Rachelle is leaning forward slightly, her back bare so I can see the vines crawling over her spine, roots spread at intervals like vertebrae reaching out to the leather of the seatback. Gently, I part her hair enough to see the balls of moss that replaced her eyes overnight.

A line of green across the floor catches my eye. A panel is loose, and something feathery is in the crack. I kneel and push the panel back anyway. I know what I'll find.

The skimmer is a cavity of moss and lush green stalks, sprouting from joints and welds. Some of the stems have started to bloom into buds like hives, petals overlapping like red lips. Overnight, the island has taken it too.

And that's it.

I imagine Eesha and Rachelle kissing like the world was ending. Kissing like they knew what they would be growing into. I imagine them kissing even as they started to bloom, never letting go even as shoots grew from one flesh and sunk into the other, binding them together for eternity. Maybe they decided that was enough. I sit down in the copilot seat and watch them. How fast before they're consumed?

I'm angry now, at the last plane's crew panicking and leaving too soon, at Nick for not coming back, at Rachelle for not getting the skimmer running on time, at Eesha for leaving me here, at myself for not going with them, even though I've been feeling the compulsion for days. I wonder how long Rachelle was fighting it. We could be in the stars; instead, we are pinned by the cool rounded glass of the cockpit window. Their reflection is an unrecognizable, intimate object. I shiver, somehow feeling both like the deadest and most alive thing in this plane.

Out the window, something moves. Hui is standing on the floor of the hangar, looking up at me with orchids coming out of her eyes. Her scalp is slick and ridged back like mushroom gills. She's still wearing her kebaya, but the embroidery has fully blossomed, overgrown the fabric, spilling down her legs and arms like a cloak of flowers and vines.

Around her are Clarise and Wei. Each of them embraces the girls left on the hangar floor. As their arms lock, I see what's left of their kebayas begin to sprout.

My eyes shift to Hui. My chief stewardess tilts her head and I understand, the pieces only now just clicking. Not consumed. Transformed.

The girls in the sky know what it is to adapt, to become something else. To become someone else's dream. To think through chaos, even if it's the apocalypse. The thing about change is that you can't resist it. Instead, you become pliable and suit yourself to the world. You let it make you exactly what it wants. You become a part of something bigger than yourself.

And then you fly.

I slide Eesha's ring off her finger and put it on my own, then stand. In a few days she'll get up and follow. I walk back through the cabin, out of the starskimmer, and toward the other girls. As the sunlight pours in behind them, I feel the flower in my eye spread its roots again. I can see so clearly what we need to become.

We started from the stars, and we will grow back into a bigger universe.

UNLOCKED

C.M. LEYVA

Scrolling the pad of my Holmes music player, I push the sound level to red. The haunting rhythm of the synth keyboard courses through me as I bob my head to the frantic tap of the drums. Not a bad soundtrack for my last day on Earth.

A gray freighter ship towers over a line of passengers. Its sharp lines blur from the thick smog hanging heavy in the air like storm clouds. I clear my burning throat for what feels like the hundredth time, desperate to get into the ship for some fresh air.

It's been over two hours, and in that time, I've imagined at least twenty different scenarios that involve me storming off. But I don't. Because this isn't voluntary, despite what my volunteer badge says. The Exploration Expedition lottery gives *winners* a chance at a fresh start on a new planet. An opportunity to discover the next world for Earth to inhabit, something not overflowing with waste, and air that doesn't hurt to breathe. The only caveat is, you have to survive. After enough failed expeditions, it has unsurprisingly lost its appeal. Now, only the poor, the sick, and the criminals, like me, are desperate enough to enter. To be fair, it's a better alternative than my legally mandated servitude for theft.

Stetson hover carts zip back and forth with luggage and supplies for our six-month journey into space. Kevin Stetson came from old money, studied at a top school, risked a small fortune on the tech to create the first self-driven hover car, and succeeded. Truly a riches-to-more-riches inspirational story shoved down everyone's throats as motivation to be better, do better. An American Hero in a world where heroes were based on the amount of money in their bank account.

I steal from those heroes, which is why I'm stuck in this fucking line. All of us had a reason for scanning our IDs at the lottery terminal. The American Dream™ of building something out of nothing. The chance at a cure on planets with advanced tech. Charges cleared for crimes committed on Earth. Regardless of the reason, there was comfort in knowing all two hundred of us had a chance at hope.

A blond who talks too loud with unwarranted enthusiasm motions for my ID card. I lower my headphones, handing it over, and pop my gum loud enough to elicit a forced smile.

"Welcome, Eva Nora." His name tag reads Zach, which annoys me. I suppose at the rate I'm acquiring exes, there are few names left that don't. "We're glad to have you join us on our expedition to planet Crecaphus in the Druna Galaxy. Your room number is 202, third deck in C wing. Crew are available to help if you require assistance. We hope you enjoy your trip on *Reticent*."

Zach hands me a cheap plastic welcome bag. I glance inside, spotting a motion sickness band. Slipping it over my wrist, I snap it for dramatic effect. "Guess we're in for a bumpy ride."

There's a slight hitch in his too big smile and, for a second, he looks like he would gladly ring the band around my neck. "It's precautionary."

His murderous look intrigues me, even though I know it shouldn't.

"You'll wanna keep it handy, Ms. Nora," a man behind me says.

I roll my eyes and turn. The man's dark brown skin glows, and his modern high-top fade looks freshly cut.

"What are you, some kind of expert?" I ask, pushing up the sleeves of my tattered denim jacket. My bangles click against the bright necklaces hanging over my low-cut shirt, and I appreciate the attention they both seem to draw.

"Welcome back, Andres Silva," Zach says, a slight hesitation in his tone. "We're glad to have you as part of our research crew again." Andres glances at me through red-rimmed glasses, a grin tugging at the corner of his full lips. He's enjoying whatever look is on my face. "The research quarters are located on the fourth deck of *Reticent*. We hope you enjoy your trip."

"I never do," Andres says, patting Zach on the shoulder. He starts up the ramp, falling in step with me. "So, what do you specialize in, Ms. Nora?"

I like him calling me Ms. Nora. As if I'm someone who's earned the respect of a title. "Apparently not crime."

"Ah, I heard the government was trying a new rehab program." Andres adjusts his glasses, scanning me like someone who enjoys the thrill of defusing bombs. "You don't look like trouble."

His words drip with provocation, and I'm drawn to them like nectar. Trailing my finger down his arm, I lean close enough to smell the mint gum on his breath. "Oh, but you don't even know me yet, Mr. Silva."

He doesn't flinch as we merge into the crowd by the lift. Instead, he glances at me out of the corner of his eye, as if daring me to continue with everyone watching. "Six months together should change that."

The cargo bay has more hover carts zipping around stacks of crates. The ship is already suffocating, despite the long line still waiting to board. I grab his hand, dragging him to the stairwell door, and snatch a key card from a nearby soldier.

The door clicks open and I pull Andres inside. With a slam, the chaos of the cargo hold deadens to a dull buzz. I press him against the wall, my lips curling with satisfaction as his honey-colored eyes remain on me instead of the door. He slides his glasses back up his nose and the innocence of it makes my heart flutter.

"Are you trying to seduce me, Mr. Silva?"

His laugh echoes through the concrete stairwell, and I decide I love it. My mother always said I was too much. Too loud and impulsive. Too quick to trust. Too open with my wants. I wasn't looking for a distraction for this trip, but I want this one.

"I can safely say no one's ever accused me of that before."

The door bursts open and the soldier I'd plucked the ID from barges in. "You can't be here."

There's something so satisfying about lifting a brow to authority. "Says who?"

The soldier points to the sign—*Authorized Personnel Only*. "Give it back." I feign ignorance as he steps forward, towering over me in his stiff camo. His lip twitches with annoyance as he snatches his badge back. Everything about him is forgettable, from his brown buzz cut to his dull blue eyes. Even his generic last name, Miller, stitched over his heart. "I knew this rehab program was a bad idea."

"I'm kind of liking it," Andres says, biting back a smile.

Miller turns to leave but stops himself. "Wait, I know you. Aren't you the guy they fired from the last ship for abandonment?"

"Went home to take care of my dying mother, but to the government, those are synonymous."

"Good thing your daddy has connections to get you onto a new ship," Miller taunts.

"You done being a dick?" I ask, shoving him back a step.

Miller's clean jaw clenches and he balls his fists at his side. The man is dying to throw a punch, and I enjoy knowing that he can't. At least not yet. "You lookin' to make an enemy your first day on this ship?"

"Apparently I don't have to look."

He rolls his eyes and throws the door open, pointing to the main hold.

Andres pushes himself off the wall, and I link my arm in his. His steps match the heavy thud of my boots as I beeline up the stairs before Miller can stop us. It isn't until we reach the fourth floor that we pause to catch our breath.

"You'll be sick of me long before our six months are up," I say, sliding down the wall to sit.

Andres joins me, his arm grazing mine. "Somehow I doubt that, Ms. Nora."

Shouts and the thunder of more boots approach as Andres mirrors my dangerous grin.

On Earth, darkness always has a beginning and an end. The long stretch of a shadow. Night. In space, however, darkness is infinite. Each galaxy has its own system of planets and stars, moons and suns. Nothing more than specks in the inky black surrounding them. As we enter the Druna Galaxy, slowing for landing, it's the first time since leaving that the darkness loses its luster, slightly hazy on the edges, as if Crecaphus has kept it at arm's length.

I sit in my room, tucked in the itchy comforter I stole from the bed, and gaze out the window. Andres is asleep, the slopes of his body hidden under the thin sheet. He fidgets as the ship lands, and I push myself from the plastic desk chair to snuggle against his back. As if on cue, he flips over, pulling me tight to his bare chest and pressing his nose into my wild black curls.

"What ungodly hour is it, V?" he asks, his voice husky with sleep.

There's something so sexy about his morning voice, and I press my lips to his. "Earth time or Crecaphus time? We just landed."

I yawn, easing into his chest and enjoying the faded scent of the generic bar soap on his skin. Andres shoots up in bed, nearly taking me with him.

"We landed?" he asks, eyes wide and bloodshot. With nothing more than my lazy nod, he's on his feet, struggling into pants and throwing his shirt on backwards. "Shit. They'll be looking for me."

"For what?"

He flips his shirt around and checks his hair in the mirror. "We need to test if it's safe to disembark."

Rushing over, he plants a kiss on my forehead and grabs his shoes, stumbling to the door. "Stay out of trouble?"

I grin at his uncertainty, tucking the blanket under my chin before flipping over. The second the door closes, I slip boots over my fishnets, throwing on a skirt and oversized sweater.

The cargo hold is absolute chaos as crew prep equipment while the soldiers bark orders. Andres hovers over notebooks with the other researchers, all of them climbing into yellow hazmat suits. Zach is kneeling behind a stack of crates, and I watch as a white line of powder disappears up his nose. I drop in front of him with a knowing smile, causing him to jump and clutch at his chest. His endless energy suddenly makes sense. He's just as trapped as we are. It must be soul-crushing, traveling the universe and finding nothing better than the shithole left behind.

"Help me sneak out with the others and I won't tell anyone what I just saw."

Zach wipes his nose, his eyes unfocused. "Do you think I give a shit?"

Fair enough. He stands before I can respond, tossing me a hazmat suit. Quickly slipping into it, I blend in with the research crew as they pack metal boxes with test tubes and start down the ramp.

Crecaphus was labeled a deserted planet on the edge of the galaxy, abandoned by previous inhabitants for unknown reasons. I often wonder what Earth was like before eroding into endless black paved streets encased by towering gray buildings. It's been nearly a century since we cut down the last tree to preserve in a museum. Nature's colors were replaced with the artificial glow of neon signs—the only light capable of cutting through the smog. Seeing the beauty surrounding me makes it clear our government lied.

A sea of wildflowers in the most vibrant purples, reds, yellows, and pinks dance in the gentle breeze. Trees the height of skyscrapers stretch endlessly around us, while the calming ebb and flow of waves brush against the untouched beach behind. No one would leave paradise of their own volition.

A gunshot rings through the field, and the researchers duck. It's as if they've never heard it before, which makes me leery of their experience on these expeditions. Miller holsters his gun, dragging an ant the size of a lamb towards us. Its leg twitches as clear fluid oozes from the bullet hole in its angled head. My heart pinches, and I look away. If this is how we arrive on new planets, it's no wonder we don't survive.

None of the soldiers wear the protective suits over their camo as they fan out, weapons raised. They embody the arrogance I expected from the researchers. Another shot, followed by more gasps, and a vulture-sized wasp goes down.

"Are you going to just stand there?" Miller shouts. "Get your samples so we can clear this field and set up camp."

The researchers jump to work, and Miller notices I don't join them. His eyes narrow, trying to get a better view of me through my plastic hood. Running my gloved hand over the wildeflowers, I fight the urge to pluck it, instead lifting my middle finger to him. I'm proud of myself for using my impulsive urges for good instead of evil. Miller, however, is less than impressed.

He shoves a backpack into my chest. "You're coming with me."

"Since you asked so nicely," I say, knowing damn well I don't have a choice.

Your mouth will get you killed.

"Is that a—" My anger falters as I realize it couldn't be a threat, because Miller's thin lips haven't moved. The voice is in my head, but the thought isn't mine. My heart plummets, taking the breath from my lungs with it. Every one of my muscles tenses as I wait to see if the voice returns, but only my frantic fear remains.

Miller ignores me as he continues to the woods, apparently

expecting me to follow. Slipping the backpack onto my shoulder, I notice Andres approach.

"Welcome to the exploration crew, Ms. Nora," he says, with a playful glance.

I remove the plastic hood, shaking out my curls and the unsettling feeling in the pit of my stomach. Tugging at the belt loops of his hazmat suit, I smile. "I look forward to working more closely with you, Mr. Silva."

If you care for him, you'll return to the ship and leave before all of you die.

My smile hitches, and I pinch my eyes closed, trying to shake away the thought. There's a danger here, but as I scan the field of flowers, I realize the threat has already burrowed itself deep into my mind. Andres's hand finds my arm, and I catch the protective look in his eyes. Hoping to ease his concern, I force a smile. Hallucinations are a quick way to have people turn on you.

We're not a hallucination.

My heart is now desperate to escape, rattling against my bones, and I notice a change in the air. The forest is quiet, and the breeze has died. Even the water behind us is as still as glass, mirroring the three suns rising from it.

"Can plants release toxins into the air?" I ask, trying to keep my voice light.

Andres's gaze slowly trails to the hood in my hand. "There's a reason plants and animals can grow like the ones here on Crecaphus. Without predators, they can evolve, become more sophisticated. Plants have always been able to release toxins, but evolution could allow them to be specific about what or how they attack. Why?"

I nod, but my words catch as I wonder who, or what, is listening. Andres seems to sense my tension and removes a device from his case, holding it to the air.

"Let's go, Nora!" Miller shouts.

Chewing the inside of my cheek, I sigh, forcing my feet forward. Andres's gloved hand finds mine. "What's wrong?"

His eyes are a beautiful liquid gold, set alight with worry. No one has ever looked at me the way he is right now, and it hurts how much I wish we met under different circumstances. Fear tightens its grip around my chest as I realize, even if I wanted to leave, I can't. None of us can.

"I don't know yet."

He glances back at the ship as if reading my thoughts and lifts his metal briefcase with a sigh. All we could do now was hope that Crecaphus was the second chance we were promised.

The voice remains—a constant soft buzz in my head as we hike through what feels like an endless stretch of woods.

It swims through my memories, searching for a weakness.

You won't survive.

One after another, traveling deeper and deeper.

We won't let you destroy our home as you did yours.

Growing dangerously close to the ones I've worked hard to bury.

You wish you could have saved your mother. You still have a chance at redemption. Convince them to leave. Save them.

"Stop!" I shout.

The soldiers draw their weapons in a panic, scanning the trees, while everyone else freezes. My shoulders collapse with relief as the buzz quiets, like a switch turned off. It's peaceful for the first time since we landed. My mind is my own again—even if only temporarily.

I open my eyes to find Miller's bright red face hovering inches from mine. "Care to explain yourself?"

"Back off," Andres snaps, stepping between us.

Despite my inclination for chaos, I hold on to the peace, mumbling an apology. This seems to be an even bigger red flag as Miller eyes me suspiciously. I push past him, brushing sweat-soaked curls from my forehead as I continue through the thick trees, when they suddenly open to a vast field of tall grass. Looming in the center is a nondescript building, as if the only structure the planet ever needed.

"Let's get some eyes," Miller orders, pointing from his eyes to the building like some action star.

The soldiers drop to their knees, scanning the area through gun scopes.

"If I remember right, one of your many *specialties* is breaking and entering," Miller says, gripping my shoulder. "Why don't you put yourself to use?"

He shoves me forward, my boots sliding along the dead leaves. I look back to find Miller holding Andres in place to keep him from following. A researcher isn't disposable like me. Lifting Miller's pistol to my brow, I give him a salute. His hand drops to his empty holster in shock before he sends a string of profanities my way. If he truly read my file, he would know I'm merely a novice at breaking and entering, but an expert pickpocket.

Streaks of rust and algae paint the gray concrete building, giving it some much needed color. Vines trail up the walls and creep in through the cracks in the windows. Embedded in the concrete is a small data pad next to a metal door without a handle. I shield the pad from the suns' rays and tap it, hopeful it lights up, but it remains a dull black screen. Instead of numbers, there are raised symbols I don't recognize. Where are the voices when I need them?

What's in this building doesn't belong to you.

The buzz returns, and I curse myself for the sarcastic thought. Absentmindedly tapping the screen, I think through a solution. The code could be any number of symbols long, and I would never know. Scanning the building's face, I notice a chunk of concrete loose at the corner of the door. I toss it back and forth in my hands, eyeing a window.

More destruction. Is this all you know?

No, but it's what I'm good at. Chucking the jagged wedge through a window, I smile at the silence. It seems safe to assume that whatever alarm this building once had is on the same power grid as the keypad. I reach through the window and unlock it, slipping into the building to find a lobby filled with decaying couches and rows of dark terminal screens. Vines trail up crumbling columns and climb the stairs leading to an open second floor.

My heavy footsteps echo up the steps to a hallway of doors and frosted windows. Each room has a corroding exam table, washbasin, and rolling chair, while everything else is in different stages of collapse. At the end of the hall is another metal door. The vines grow under it, forcing it loose, and I nudge it open with my shoulder. The putrid smell that escapes turns my stomach.

Piles of bones are clustered around the exam table, all of them connected as if fused together. The vines cling to them, picking them clean. I glance at my foot to find a vine already wrapped around my ankle, and I jump back, banging into the wall. My heart thunders in my ears as a chill races through me. A massacre took place in this room, and I wouldn't be surprised if this is what the voices were warning me about.

You can still walk away.

From what?

The truth.

Whose truth?

The voices remain silent. A mistake on their part, given my penchant for snooping through things I shouldn't. I lift my shirt over my nose and step back into the room, careful to avoid the vines. A set of bones lie on the procedure chair in the center of the room, the fused bones cascading down around the table into the piles below. A single needle hides in the cut-out space at the base of the headrest where a large skull remains. Beside the chair is a case of vials filled with rose-red colored liquid and a black screen the size of a book. I trail my finger over the glassy surface, pressing a small button at the bottom of the screen. An electric shock runs through me and the world goes dark.

I plummet into what feels like a dark, icy lake surrounded by obsidian ripples. My teeth chatter as I frantically tread water, trying to get my bearings. Laughter echoes through the darkness, and I cover my ears at the deafening sound. The icy hand of terror grips my chest, making it hard to breathe, and for a second, I wonder if this is death. With a burst of energy, I thrust myself forward in the black water, suddenly hit with a wave of memories that don't belong to me.

I see a planet with elevated buildings and transport piping. Everywhere, there are creatures that walk on two feet, but aren't human, with eyeless faces and delicate antennas probing at the air around them.

Humans are not humanity. Those are two very different words. We were humanity, but not human in your limited physical sense.

Another wave washes over me, and I watch the planet change. Animals dying from disease. Water receding from rising temperatures. Air turning thick like the storm clouds we've grown accustomed to on Earth. Natural resources...gone.

We could no longer reverse the damage.

There is sadness in the voice's tone, and I hate feeling it snake through me, latching onto my own emotions. Another wave of memories reveals their solution.

A creature lies peacefully on the exam table as another in red robes attaches leads to the antennas on their head. With the flick of a switch, symbols similar to the ones on the building keypad emerge on a wall of screens. A jolt runs through the creature on the table, but they remain undisturbed in their slumber. The symbols fade. Tucked within a small box where the leads end is a small microchip. The one in red robes turns to a small metal sphere and inserts the chip. A single green dot lights up as it comes to life.

"You implanted yourselves into AI," I whisper. The reason for all the exam rooms. To prep their bodies to transfer memories into microchips.

The only way to survive was through artificial means. To exist while no longer existing.

Despite their adaptation, Crecaphus continues to die. The factories used to produce their new AI forms churn out black clouds, blocking the light from the suns. Without solar power, neither the AI nor the creatures would survive. Destroying the factories bought them the time needed for their last chance at a solution. As the world outside fought for the limited resources left, the brightest minds gathered together in a single building and discovered a method of extracting their consciousness from the neocortex of the brain. A way to survive without a physical form.

Which is why we are everywhere and nowhere.

The truth.

A dangerous truth. You lack the connection needed to use the key.

What key?

The key you discovered in the room. Without it, you will all die before you ever learn the secret to unlock.

My eyes flutter open and a groan escapes my lips. White pain stabs at the back of my head, and I tenderly touch a large goose egg under my hair. I lurch over the side of the cot, spilling the contents of my stomach on the floor. Everything in me aches more than all my hangovers combined. I curl into a ball, and a hand caresses my shoulder as the cot sinks from the additional weight.

"V, it's ok. Everything's going to be ok."

Andres's voice warms me, wrapping me in the same comfort as the crochet blanket my mom spent months knitting. I turn over, burying my face in his chest.

His muscles relax as he lies beside me, pulling me closer. "You don't need to say anything. It's been a long three days for both of us."

"Three days?" His words jerk me from my haze, and I glance around the small tent. My back aches and an IV trails from my arm to a hanging bag of liquid.

Taking my hand in his, I notice my pointer finger is black with singe marks spreading like veins down my palm. "An electric shock put you in some sort of coma. The medics ran every test, and they all came back fine. They said your brain was trapped in REM, like you were lost in a dream. The only answer they could give me was that you would wake up when you were ready."

It couldn't be a dream. Even if it was, in a place like Crecaphus, it didn't mean what I saw wasn't real. "What happened while I was out?"

His brows pinch together in distress, forcing me to sit up. The entire trip from Earth, I never saw him anything more than mildly annoyed, and it was usually because the cafeteria had run out of desserts. "You're lucky you missed the worst of it," Andres says, removing my IV and taping gauze over the puncture. "The science here is incredibly advanced—centuries beyond anything we could ever know. It would be fascinating if it weren't so terrifying what the government has ordered us to do with it. We found vials that seem to be neural enhancements. A single injection of the serum allowed the engineers to get the equipment up and running within hours. The translators deciphered the entire alien language in one day."

The rose-red liquid in the vials. "How?"

"The serum enhances our innate skills, the ones that seem to be parts of our personalities. For researchers, curiosity leads to discovery—"

But negative traits are not immune to the serum's effects.

Andres nods. "Exactly, which is why—"

"Wait." I grab his wrist, searching his tired eyes hidden under thick lashes. "You hear them too?"

"I started hearing them the second you walked away. Most of us do, but some refuse to let them in."

"I had a choice?" My voice cracks with incredulity.

A laugh escapes him, and the weight of the world seems to lift from his shoulders. "I missed you, V."

His kiss is filled with the weight of his words, as if making up for our time lost. And for a moment, I think everything is going to be ok. Resting his forehead against mine, he whispers, "Miller got the orders from Earth. They want us to find the key to unlocking Crecaphus's technology for immortality. The voices said it was in the room. We should have never told him. Miller's obedience is going to kill us all."

My heart plummets, and I jump to my feet, throwing open the flap to the tent. As I emerge, I find a new version of Crecaphus. The green grass is now brown and dead from herbicide. A pile of insect carcasses disintegrates on the edge of camp, and on the other side is a trench about a mile long. I shudder at the thought of what it hides.

"Where is everyone?"

Andres's throat bobs as if trying to swallow the emotions churning within. "The planet is protecting whatever is in that building. Groups of scouts, and the search parties sent after them, have yet to return. Inside the building, Miller is testing the tech on volunteers in hopes of discovering the key. No one has survived."

Without the right connection, you will never possess the key.

It infuriates me that a man like Miller could so callously steal hope from someone as radiant as Andres. I do my best to smile through it, leaning into him like nothing's changed. "Then let's find the key first, Mr. Silva."

My words are like fuel to the flames in his golden eyes, and his lips press together as he steels himself. With a nod, he sneaks back into the tent, tucking a gun under his shirt as he emerges. We rush to the building and quietly climb the stairs, keeping our steps light as we work our way down the hall. Peeking through the door, I see a woman strapped into the procedure chair.

A gag covers her mouth and her eyes grow wide in fear as the machine whirrs to life. Zach sits at a table, a gun to the back of his head as he types onto the book-sized screen. The woman flinches in pain, her white knuckles gripping the arm of the chair. It's less than a minute—screams muffled by the gag—before she goes limp. The leads attached to her head drone in an endless beep, and a researcher confirms no further brain activity, but still a faint pulse.

None of you can unlock alone.

Miller puts a bullet between her eyes. One might think it's a mercy kill until he calls for the next so-called volunteer. Fuck their secrets. Fuck immortality. The voices are right. We may be human, but we lost our humanity long ago.

Throwing open the door with a *bang*, Miller turns his gun on me. "I'm surprised your orders weren't to shoot me too."

"I don't need orders to do that," he sneers.

"So, you *do* think for yourself. Which means you're choosing to kill people for this key." I keep my eyes on him as my heavy steps continue into the room.

Red creeps up Miller's neck, eyes flickering around the room, noting the sudden change in the air. "This civilization discovered the secret to immortality. This is what we've traveled across galaxies searching for. We have a chance to be heroes," he argues, not to me, but to the people around him.

"Why don't *you* be the hero, then?" I ask, now positioned next to the screen that Zach's hand still hovers over.

The room goes silent as everyone seems to hold their breath, waiting for his response.

It seems an appropriate time to remind you that your mouth will get you killed.

Miller is now trembling with rage, and his gaze falls to my hand hovering beside the screen. So much for being an expert pickpocket. His eyes widen, as if he knows. The only way to stop him is to destroy the key.

You haven't been listening if you think that's the key.

My heart plummets. I was wrong. I should have gone for Miller's gun again. A bang fills the room, followed immediately by another. Miller collapses to the floor, blood painting the wall beside him as his body goes still.

Andres lowers his gun and rushes to me. "No, no, no! It's gonna be fine, V. You're gonna be fine!"

I collapse into his arms, and his hands cover the bullet hole in my stomach.

I should think of something meaningful to say, something poetic for everyone to remember me by, but instead, the only word that escapes my lips is, "Fuck."

There is still a chance to survive.

"I don't understand!" Andres shouts at the voices. "Stay with me, V."

Darkness creeps in from the edges of my vision, and I refuse to blink, soaking in whatever moments I have left to see his face. I grip his shirt and pull him to me, pressing my lips to his to distract from the pain. It's electric, reminding me of the shock from the black screen. His arms wrap around me like the vine clinging to my ankle. It's as if we're fused together like the bones on the floor.

Connected.

"The key," I choke out as I fight the darkness. The voices remain silent. "We can't transcend alone. We need to be connected for it to work."

Andres's eyes grow wide, and there's a buzz in the room as the other researchers discuss in whispers. "We have to try," he begs, scanning the crowd surrounding us. My teeth grit as he lifts me carefully onto the procedure table. "Get everyone left. Hurry!"

The room descends into chaos as the researchers huddle together, working on new calculations. Zach frantically types them onto the screen as the room fills with the handful left from the two hundred that arrived.

The chair buzzes, and I flinch as the needle punctures the skin on my neck.

Andres's hand finds mine, and the shock between us feels atomic, sending the others staggering back in a sonic wave. Zach's hand finds Andres's shoulders, and another surge of power runs through us. The people in the room stumble over each other, gripping hands to join me. I clench my teeth as the needle snakes to my neocortex.

It's almost over. We welcome you, just as we have for so many others over the centuries.

The pain vanishes. Our bodies collapse as we hover somewhere above them. The walls tremble from the electrical surge we create. I can feel Andres beside me, his consciousness warm and golden like his eyes. It wraps around me as we watch the wave spread like ripples, farther and farther from where our bodies now lie.

Endless like the darkness in space.

Endless like us.

AS THE FOREST ITSELF GAVE CHASE

ALYSSA GRANT

Breathing wasn't supposed to hurt.

Claire wasn't coughing like several people on the bus were, but her throat was as sore as it would be if she had been coughing. She should have followed the recommendations of the citywide air quality warning and stayed inside, but she had a date.

Claire could have postponed her date and stayed home—Jen had messaged earlier to confirm she was still able to make it despite how smoky the air was—but she was looking forward to meeting Jen in person. They had talked all week after meeting on Hinge. Jen was good at asking interesting questions whenever their conversations slowed, and she seemed genuinely interested in what Claire had to say.

Claire's choice to take the bus to meet Jen instead of driving was a habit she'd developed for visiting this part of the city because of how impossible it was to find parking. She would have made a different choice if she had known how much the haze from the wildfires would affect her. At least it was a short walk from the bus stop to the coffee shop.

She also needed a distraction.

Her sister's family lived in one of the evacuation zones, and even after confirming they had made it to the evacuation site, it was easy to worry.

After the short walk to the coffee shop, Claire wasn't as put together as she had been when she left home. All that time getting ready — picking a black floral dress casual enough to not look like she was trying too hard, adding some waves to her hair, and putting on subtle make-up — was wasted. Her eyes were watery, and blinking back tears wasn't a good start to a first date, so she did her best to fix her smudged eyeliner with only her phone camera as a mirror.

Satisfied that she was as presentable as she was going to get, Claire put her phone back in her purse. She hadn't been to Garden Coffee before, but she'd walked past the lively patio with its eclectic mix of mismatched furniture, hanging baskets, and a large cherry tree.

The patio wasn't lively today. It was unusually empty for a Saturday afternoon.

Only one customer sat outside, an elderly man accompanied by his small dog. He was sitting at the muted teal chair and table set under the branches of the cherry tree and reading a newspaper while he finished his coffee. Claire wondered if this was part of his normal routine that he was too stubborn to change, forest fires be damned.

The inside of Garden Coffee was welcoming with its bright colors, soft music, and upbeat baristas — it helped ease the nervous flutter in Claire's chest. She liked the look of the three cozy looking armchairs in the back corner, one already taken by a woman who was reading a book.

At the large wooden picnic table, there was a young man working on his laptop. From his empty mug and plate with a muffin wrapper on it, she guessed he'd been here a while.

And at a bright orange table with yellow chairs sat Jen, who greeted Claire with a wave and a warm smile. Jen looked almost the same as her profile pictures, dark hair just a bit longer.

Claire smiled back and was surprised when Jen stood up to give her a quick hug. If they'd known each other better, it would have been an easy hug to sink into.

"I'm glad you could make it," Jen said, gesturing for Claire to sit. "I've been looking forward to meeting you."

"Me too."

"I'm going to order. The coffee here's good, so you can't go wrong—what would you like?"

"A latte," Claire said a bit awkwardly, never knowing if she should offer to pay or not. "I can get it."

Jen shook her head. "I invited you, so it's on me."

Claire didn't want to check her phone while she waited for Jen to return—each news alert was more depressing than the last—so she looked around the coffee shop. There was a small flatscreen television in the corner, visible for the baristas to watch as well as customers. The volume was muted, and there were closed captions barely large enough for Claire to read.

The news anchor gave context to what was happening while showing pictures taken of the province.

"While wildfires have become a regular occurrence in British Columbia, this summer is now the worst on record, already more devastating than the record set in 2017. Smoke covers the province."

The pictures of Vancouver looked like they had been put through a yellow filter, the haze hiding the mountains. It made the city almost unrecognizable.

Jen came back with their drinks and glanced at the TV before sitting down. "It's awful, isn't it?"

Claire gave a short nod. "Has anyone you know been affected by the fires?"

Jen shrugged. "Canceled plans, poor air quality, nothing more than anyone else. You?"

"Some of my family had to evacuate."

The trauma of leaving their home behind, not knowing if they could ever return, affected them greatly. They told strange stories about having to flee from more than fire.

"I'm sorry to hear that."

"Thanks," Claire said, trying her latte. The conversation with her family had left her unsettled, and she didn't want to talk about it, didn't want to *think* about it. "This is good. What did you get?"

Jen went with the topic change. "I got the same—not my usual, but it sounded good. By the way, do you have any food allergies?"

"None."

"There's something you have to try."

Jen went back to the counter and came back with a plateful of cookies. "These cookies are vegan and gluten free, which is great for anyone who needs that, but they're *also* delicious."

"Which should I try first?"

"The triple chocolate is my favorite."

The cookie was soft in the way only freshly baked cookies could be. "These are good."

"They sell out fast," the barista said with a grin while wiping down the table next to them. "When Jen said she was meeting a date here, I saved them for her."

"Oh, is this where you bring all your dates?" Claire teased.

The barista shook her head fervently, trying to erase her misstep. "Jen usually comes on her own."

"Evie, we are very grateful for the cookies. You can stop eavesdropping now."

"Touchy," Evie said with a laugh, moving on to the next table. "You'll have to come back together to try them in the morning when they're still warm."

"You know each other well," Claire said quietly. She was curious if they had ever dated, but she wasn't going to ask outright.

"I've known Evie since I started coming here to study when I was in university." Jen leaned forward. "Her husband is the baker."

Claire's face warmed. "Good to know," she said, caught out, but pleased by the answer.

They had finished their drinks and the cookies, but Claire wanted to keep their date going for a while longer, so she got them both water. The first sip helped soothe her sore throat.

"Could you turn on the sound?" the man who had been working on his laptop called out to Evie.

"You got it, Max," Evie said as she turned up the volume loud enough for everyone to hear. "Though aren't you meant to be writing an essay?"

"I am," Max said with a sigh. "Taking summer classes was a mistake, and whatever the news is showing is far more interesting than my poli-sci essay."

Claire and Jen both looked at the television. The newscaster, a middle aged man with graying hair, looked tired. *"The effects of wildfires are well studied, but the reports we're hearing from survivors are unprecedented. Many families are claiming their homes were destroyed before fire spread to their community. Some experts say the online spread of misinformation and unverified footage—likely doctored—could lead to mass hysteria."*

Clips of the footage showed shaky camerawork and poor lighting. She couldn't tell if this was because the people recording did so while panicking or if it was to hide poorly done special effects. She wondered if her sister, brother-in-law, and nephews had watched any of that viral footage before they talked on the phone. Maybe that could explain some of what they had described.

"What do you think is happening out there?" Jen asked.

She hoped the footage was fake. "There's a lot of conflicting information out there, so I don't know what—"

"Please," Max interrupted, "it's clearly a cover-up."

Jen crossed her arms. "What kind of cover-up?"

"Government," he said, the *duh* implied by his tone.

"Your vague statement without any evidence is *very* convincing," Evie said, her voice dry.

"Do you have a better idea?" Max asked.

Evie shrugged. "It's probably a domino effect from all the fire damage—one disaster leading to another. I doubt it will take long for scientists to confirm what is happening."

"Claire, you mentioned some of your family had to evacuate," Jen said carefully. "Is there any truth to the conspiracies about the trees attacking homes?"

Claire swallowed. "Is that something you're following?'

"Isn't everyone?" Jen asked. "The footage is all probably doctored, but there's got to be a scientific explanation for what's happening."

"I hope so," Claire said. Almost anything would be better than what her family described.

She'd been relieved to hear her sister's voice after she answered the call from an unknown number. She had needed to sit down, tension leaving her body rapidly.

Her relief hadn't lasted long.

"We were quick to grab our bags once we got the evacuation order," Charlotte said, her voice a harsh whisper. "That's what saved us. We'd been prepared for fire, but that wasn't what we had to run from."

"What did you run from?"

"Something powerful, far more powerful than anything a person could ever cause. The fires were still distant enough that we couldn't see them, though we could taste the fire in the air. There was a loud rumble, and Omid urged the kids to hurry. By the time we made it outside, the rumbling was so loud it was like the forest was screaming. The ground shifted, and we rushed to our car." Her sister let out a choked sob. "Omid drove, while I tried to keep Ali and Amir calm, but…"

"Char, I'm sure you did your best," Claire said, trying to offer some comfort. "You're safe now."

"No," Charlotte said, voice strained. "None of us are safe. What I saw, what we all saw… I'll never forget the scene I saw through the back window. Our home was obliterated, the fire not yet in sight. It was far worse than fire. Nature itself has turned against us and destroyed our home and our neighbors' homes. The forest chased us, trees running behind us. If we hadn't been in our car, they would have overtaken us. Not everyone got away. It was so close—I don't know how we got so lucky." She paused. "You believe me, don't you?"

"I don't know," Claire admitted.

Charlotte put the phone on speaker, giving Claire the opportunity to talk to Omid and her nephews.

She'd never forget how scared her youngest nephew, Amir, sounded. "Auntie, is the world ending?" he asked.

"Of course not."

"It feels like it is," he said, and his words were like a punch in the gut. The honesty of the young could be so brutal.

Charlotte ended the call soon after that, and Claire had remained sitting on her couch for hours after the call. She couldn't bring herself to look up what had happened. She didn't know if it would be worse if her sister's story was true or if they were traumatized enough not to know what was real.

Sharing Charlotte's story with almost-strangers wasn't something Claire was prepared to do—not when she didn't know what she believed. "It could be collective trauma," she said, hesitating before deciding to reveal a bit more. "My sister's family said they were running away from more than fire, that the forest itself was chasing them."

"That sounds poetic," Evie said.

Jen ran her hand through her hair. "What do you think your sister meant when she said the forest was chasing them?"

"She talked about the trees as if they were acting out their will… and that their will was to destroy."

"Sentient trees? Government conspiracy makes more sense," Max said, coughing. "Sorry, my asthma has been bad today."

Jen nodded. "I know what you mean. I've used my rescue inhaler twice today."

"Maybe they've all been drugged, everyone with unbelievable stories," Evie said. "Could there be something in the air or water?"

Claire didn't like the idea of her family being drugged. "I hope not."

Jen leaned her chin on her hand. "For argument's sake, let's say your family was right and trees were chasing them, why would trees do that?"

"It's not like it's undeserved for nature to retaliate against us," Claire said, finally confronting the thoughts she has been desperately avoiding. "The most recent massive uncontrolled fire was caused by the idiots ignoring the campfire ban."

"You think a few people making bad decisions warrants this level of devastation?" Jen asked.

Claire fidgeted with a napkin on the table. "It seems proportional to the damage caused."

"No, I don't think this is revenge," Jen said, and she leaned forward and gave Claire's arm a comforting touch. "The trees could be trying to escape the fire the same way people are—nature protecting itself."

Max raised his eyebrows. "Do either of you seriously believe trees are sentient?"

Jen gave Max a steady stare. "Trees, nature itself, some sort of higher power…it could happen." Her voice was flat enough that it was hard to tell if she believed the words she was saying or if she was playing devil's advocate.

Max scoffed. "And you were skeptical when I said it was the government."

Evie let out a weary sigh. "None of us are going to find answers by speculating."

Claire agreed, and the conversation wasn't helping to distract her from thinking about her family.

She looked outside and it was darker than she expected, yellow tinged sky now a dark amber. "I should be heading out soon," she said abruptly, not finding a natural transition in their conversation.

"Oh, of course," Jen agreed, but she sounded disappointed.

Claire stood up. She needed to go home, but she wanted to see Jen again. She didn't want this to be the last time they saw each other. "We should—"

The ground shook.

Claire grabbed the orange table to steady herself. She couldn't remember the last time she felt an earthquake, and if that was what was happening, she hoped it was a minor earthquake.

Paralyzed by her thoughts, she was prompted into action by Jen.

"Come on." Jen took her hand and guided her under the table. "Face away from the glass doors."

Claire's body moved automatically, muscle memory from all those school drills. She held onto the table and closed her eyes, hoping that the shaking would stop. She told herself that this was just a minor earthquake, but she had her doubts. Her sister's words were on repeat in her mind: "Nature itself has turned against us." What if Charlotte was right? What if this was something more than an earthquake?

The shaking worsened, and Claire's heart raced. There was a crash, and she felt water hit her knees from the overturned water glasses. She shivered, but it wasn't from the cold on this summer day.

The sounds were as alarming as the shaking. Something shattered, but Claire didn't know what. Someone was swearing under their breath, voicing the worry she shared.

A heavy thump followed by a crack drew her attention. The television had fallen from the wall and landed screen down. The woman hiding under the table by the armchairs crawled out to unplug the TV before getting back under the table.

The shaking seemed to go on forever, but Jen was there throughout. Her continued breathing reminded Claire of her presence. She might have found comfort in it if her mind hadn't kept repeating, "what if…?"

Hours, minutes, or seconds later—the pervasive feeling of wrong left her unable to track time—the shaking finally stopped.

"Is anyone hurt?" the woman next to the fallen TV asked. "My name's Wendy, and I'm a nurse."

"I'm not hurt," Max said, his voice small and unsure, a departure from his earlier confidence.

Jen cupped Claire's face. "You okay?" she whispered, brows pinched from worry.

"Fine." Her voice was weak, but other than her damp dress and the tension in her body, she was unharmed.

"We're uninjured," Jen confirmed.

"Just a couple bruises," Evie said.

"I can take a look—"

"Don't stand up yet," Evie interrupted. "Wait a couple minutes in case there are aftershocks—I don't want anyone to—"

A shrill beep filled the room, coming from all directions.

"It's an emergency alert," Jen said.

Claire's phone was in her bag, which had fallen out of reach.

Jen unlocked her phone and summarized the alert. "It says hazardous shaking detected in Metro Vancouver and to stay indoors."

Claire let out a laugh that was only slightly unhinged. "We knew that."

"It also says it might happen again."

Of course it did.

Claire turned toward the exit and looked through the glass door to see a wrecked patio, chairs and tables strewn everywhere. It made the damage inside Garden Coffee look minor.

The large cherry tree outside had uprooted itself, displacing the pavement. It stood, tilted dangerously, where one of the tables had been. "How…" she trailed off, voice breaking. If anyone had been on the patio, they would have been seriously injured.

There was no sign of the man and his dog from earlier. She hoped they had gone home and were safe.

This wasn't a normal earthquake. There was *intent*.

Amir had asked if the world was ending, and she was realizing that her nephew hadn't been exaggerating. With what they had experienced…it made sense.

But she didn't want it to make sense.

Claire wasn't the only one looking outside. Jen was doing the same.

Wendy joined Evie behind the counter to take a look at the first aid kit, and they were taking stock of what supplies they had.

Max walked toward the glass door. "The shaking wasn't bad enough to have caused that much damage outside." He raised a hand and straightened his palm out against the glass.

The branches of the cherry tree shifted. There was a warning in the air that made it difficult to breathe. Claire was dizzy, and everything seemed to move in slow motion.

"Get away from the door," Jen shouted, panicked. She grabbed Claire's arm—her hands shaking—and turned them both away from the glass just before it shattered.

Screaming.

The shards traveled far, causing sharp pricks of pain on Claire's back. Panicking didn't help, so she reminded herself to breathe.

Jen was staring blankly as if she was in shock, her whole body trembling.

Claire needed to be the strong one now. She braced herself and turned around.

The first thing she saw was the large cherry tree branch that had punched through the door, causing the glass to shatter. It looked like an attack.

It could attack again.

Even as Claire looked away from the tree, she stayed aware of it, knowing its threat wasn't over.

She looked down and saw Max face down on the ground; she couldn't tell if he'd thrown himself to the ground or if he had been hit.

Until Wendy rushed over to help and applied pressure to a wound on Max's back. He wasn't moving, and there was blood on the ground.

A lot of blood.

"Is he going to be okay?" Claire asked, dreading the answer.

"I don't know," Wendy said.

"No, no, no," Jen said.

Evie joined Wendy. "I found more bandages and gauze. I can help."

Claire tried to focus. She didn't think she had any serious injuries, minor cuts at worst.

Jen was pale. "No, no, no—"

Claire took Jen's hand. "Are you injured?"

"This isn't real, it can't be—"

"Focus on me," Claire said, squeezing her hand. "You're not alone."

Jen gave her hand a tight squeeze, took a deep breath in, and exhaled slowly.

"Good," Claire said with what she hoped was an encouraging smile, "keep breathing like that."

"Does anyone have a signal?" Evie asked, her voice rising in pitch. "Max needs an ambulance, and I can't get through."

Claire let go of Jen's hand to try her phone.

It didn't work.

She looked up from her phone and met Jen's eyes as she did the same. Neither phone was working.

Jen stood up. "I'm going for help."

Claire reached for Jen, grabbing her arm. "Wait."

Everything in her being told Claire how awful an idea going outside was. Trees lined the street outside the cafe, and they were far too close to Stanley Park, where some of the Douglas Fir trees were over two hundred feet tall—giants compared to the cherry tree that had attacked.

Claire wanted to hide. The uncertainty over what would happen next was accompanied by a visceral fear. Everything she had known before she entered Garden Coffee was in question, and her confidence in her ability to survive whatever they faced next was limited.

Jen pulled away, toward the back door away from where the cherry tree still guarded the patio exit. "Max needs help now."

Claire was certain about only one thing—letting Jen go for help alone would be a mistake. "Wait," she repeated, "I'm going with you."

LOVE IS A BATTLESHIP

D.C. DADOR

"Captain, there must've been a mistake placing me and Lieutenant Mason on this mission together." I squared my shoulders, avoiding Mason's patronizing gaze.

It wasn't the best look, boarding the *Salutare* then immediately marching to the bridge to complain. I'd left the docking bay's airlock so fast I was still in my puffy orange flight suit instead of my uniform.

Captain Croix's brows furrowed as he looked between the two of us. "If I recall, you and the Lieutenant's psych profiles rated you two as compatible for close quarter missions."

My cheeks heated as I beat back the memories of the last time Mason and I were in close quarters together. But that was then.

"If there's anyone else from Europa Station who could switch with me…" My voice trailed, because even I could hear how pathetic I sounded.

The captain looked disappointed. "Command needed someone from Skylab to accompany the payload. Lieutenant Mason was their guy."

I finally allowed myself to look at Mason. I'd hoped he'd grow uglier over the years, but he was always good at disappointing me. His gray eyes met mine with an amused glow. I badly wanted to smack the smirk off his pretty face.

Mason shrugged. "I was the lead scientist for the payload we're delivering."

I closed my eyes to compose myself. Once upon a time, I'd found his Stationer accent charming. The kind that swept a small-town girl from Mars off her feet. Now it sounded haughty and condescending. I took a deep breath. "So, you and the captain know what we're transporting to Titan?" I looked between them trying to control my temper. "Can either of you share what's taken me away from my duties on Europa?"

Their silence was my answer. It was need-to-know.

"Commander, your role here is purely tactical," Captain Croix said. "You know Titan, and we need to get this unit delivered to its surface. Plain and simple."

I sniffed. Of course, they'd keep it from me. "If Mason's the specialist, I know it's agriculture related. Hydroponics is his specialty."

Mason's jaw twitched in an I'm-more-important-than-you way. I met his gaze and willed myself to not flinch as we stared one another down. He had to know he wouldn't get under my skin. It was almost undetectable, but the red flush at the tips of his ears made me smile inside.

Good. Glad we were both uncomfortable.

An officer entered the Bridge, a forced smile on his face. "Maybe the new crew should settle in?"

The captain looked relieved for the interruption. "Good idea. Commander Rivera, Lieutenant Mason, this is my second-in-command, Executive Officer Kamir. We'll see you at our mission briefing at 0500."

Mason and I were half listening as we continued to hold one another's gaze. Finally, I won our staring contest as Mason lowered his eyes. "Sounds good, Captain. See you at the briefing."

I pretended to study a nearby monitor while I waited for Mason and Kamir to leave.

Captain Croix cleared his throat. "You good, Riv?" His tone softened, signaling Dad mode.

"I'm fine."

He chuckled. "Your mom used to bite her lip when she lied too." I held my ground, not willing to admit he was right. Dad sighed. "Just as stubborn too." His voice trailed, and I noticed him rub his arm and wince with discomfort.

"What's wrong?"

He lifted his sleeve, exposing his forearm. "A rash I think."

I grimaced at the red bumps lining his skin. Inside my hip pocket, I found what I was looking for, a little pouch with ointment. I motioned Dad to give me his arm.

"My daughter. Always prepared. What is it?"

"Coconut oil," I tried to say nonchalantly, because we both know it's from one of mom's stashes.

Dad winced. "No, don't waste it."

"It's fine. I've got an entire bottle in my bag." He didn't look pleased, but I was glad he didn't protest. After humanity destroyed Earth, herbs and any plant-derived materials were rare and expensive. That was before considering the sentimental value of mom's ointments. "How long have you had the rash?"

He scratched his head. "I just noticed it now."

"You're probably having an allergic reaction to Mason."

Dad rubbed his temples. "I thought I was captain of a U.N. Starship, not a high school classroom."

I rolled my eyes. My teenage years seemed like a lifetime ago. The coconut salve was cool and smelled sweet and milky as I dabbed it onto his forearm. I'd always wished I could swim in a vat of it. But the joy of mom's creation was short-lived as Mason's sneer crossed my mind. "You promise you didn't request him? I know you had your hopes about...us."

He paused before answering, so I knew he felt a little guilty. "No, I didn't request him. But I didn't veto him, either, because I knew I had nothing to worry about. Right?" He peered into my eyes. "What'd I teach you?"

Memories of my childhood spent calculating flight paths and EVA exercises whipped through my mind. And the constant refrain to work hard and follow one's duty. One had to be resilient, growing up on Mars and the daughter of a U.N. captain to boot.

Dad nodded toward the door. "Why don't you get settled?"

It wasn't a suggestion. "Aye, aye, sir. I'll go man the torpedoes."

I could hear his smile. I used to say that phrase when I was a kid on this ship. He saluted me. "Preservation…"

"…and Conservation," I said over my shoulder as I departed. Preservation and Conservation was the Space Corps motto. Preserve humanity by establishing settlements across the solar system and conserve our resources, no thanks to our great grandparents who screwed up Earth.

If there was one thing good about Mason, it was his dedication to plant life. It was why he got along with my mother too, rest her soul.

My chest filled with anxiety knowing I was about to spend the next nine months with him. Aboard a ship built for 200.

I was jealous of the rest of the crew. They were under induced hibernation—cryo sleep on deck 3—leaving me, Dad, Kamir, and my ex the only humans awake on our starship. The four of us were responsible for 200 souls, and a shit ton of plants—the only living things floating through the void of space between Jupiter and Saturn.

I left my dad on the bridge and found my way to the *Salutare*'s L-shaft. Other than the whispering hum of the engine, it was eerily quiet. Lifeless.

Peering down the ladder that allowed the crew to travel between decks in zero-G, I was relieved Mason was nowhere to be seen. I grabbed the metal rungs and used it to propel myself toward the crew quarters.

Clammy fingers wrapped around my forearm.

"Whoa. You're a little jumpy, Commander?" Mason grinned, offering me a hand onto deck 7.

I made a show of batting his hand away. Since gravity returned on the ship's decks, I landed with a satisfying thump while managing to ignore him completely.

"Come on, Riv. We should talk, don't you think?" he called after me.

I stopped in my tracks. "Why?"

His face tensed. "Why?" For once he seemed at a loss for words. His eyelids fluttered, and I knew it was a nervous tick of his whenever he was upset. I hated how I knew his every expression. I had to change topics. "We should discuss why you're even here."

My tactic worked as he groaned. "Is it hard to believe I'm who Command wanted for this mission?"

"Yes. You specialize in lab research, not top secret anything. What are we delivering?"

He shook his head. "It's classified."

"How can I do my job—"

"Riv, we just need you to help safely deliver the package to Titan."

We stared one another down again. My nose wrinkled. "You smell like fertilizer and...decaying wood. Why?"

He flinched just a second before recovering. "Riv, Riv, Riv. You still have that strong sense of smell don't you? E-chef burnt my lunch, that's all."

Medically I had hyperosmia, but I'd also learned to pick up scents from growing up in underground tunnels. Whenever a new odor entered our otherwise stale air, I'd smell it, and this wasn't the scent of burnt anything. I folded my arms. "I do. And I could always smell your bullshit."

He laughed. "Come on love, can't we bury the hatchet? I've got a bottle of calamansi back in my room."

I shut my eyes. The bright citrusy and tart scent of calamansi wafted through my memory. Calamansi was my mom's favorite, but I couldn't let him pull my heartstrings. "To be clear, as soon as this mission is over, I'm going into cryo-sleep. I'd rather be unconscious than spend another waking minute with you."

He guffawed, fighting to hold back his laugh. The old asshat was back. "I recall you saying I was the man of your dreams."

I hated how my cheeks warmed. I tried to compose myself. "You're much better in my dreams."

He leaned. "So you do dream about me."

I threw my head back, fighting the urge to scream. "Pathetic. You're trying to unravel me as usual. Just because I can't stand you doesn't mean I'll sacrifice my duty."

His jaw tightened. "You don't have to remind me where your loyalty lies."

I met his gaze. "You're the last one to be preaching about loyalty."

His lips formed into a tantalizing sneer. My pulse quickened. There was something different about him. Not just the shit smell.

Mason was a prick, but I've never felt threatened by him before. He stepped forward towering over me. "Guess it was a good thing we didn't get married."

I flinched. He had never admitted that before. I laughed bitterly. "So glad you finally agree."

Mason cursed. "Where're you going, love?"

"Away from you." I stormed down the hall. To hell with Mason and my past.

"Riv?" Mason bellowed. "You can't hide from me forever, y'know."

I cringed. His words sounded like a threat and a promise.

Warmth filled me as a familiar spicy jasmine scent permeated the air. I was running inside the narrow corridors of the C sector block back home in the "New Manila" section of Mars.

I was bubbling with excitement, but I didn't know why.

My movements felt like I was on autopilot as I jabbed a worn red button that activated a rusty door. I entered the small hidden room Mom used as her greenhouse.

Entering into air bright and perfumed with sweet florals and minty herbs, I was greeted by the sight of hanging plants and potted flowers. It wasn't much, but considering humanity had decimated Earth, this closet-sized room on Mars was an oasis in the solar system.

Several aspects were familiar: Mom's musky jasmine scent, the way her long dark hair hung as she watered her plants. Unfamiliar was the handsome young man taking notes on his digipad.

He was lean and fit, with almost pure white hair that framed his square jaw—all hallmarks of a Stationer. Nothing like the hardened people who settled on Mars.

As soon as his gray eyes met mine, color spread across his pale cheeks. I was glad for my brown complexion, which made my blush a little harder to discern.

His lip quirked. "Who knew Mars had so much beauty growing under its surface?" I began to laugh. His eyes shone with amusement then went dull and suddenly—lifeless?

Mason's face shriveled and fissured like dry mud. A scream lodged in my throat as his entire body crumpled over. His skin, like his face, dried up, as if all his water was being sucked out of him.

Mom continued to plant. "What's wrong, anak?" Her familiar scent, the tropical flower sampaguita, filled the room.

Horrified, I watched as her gentle face began to shrivel too. No!

She turned to me, her serene expression now pleading. "Run, my darling! Run!" Flailing, I reached for her as she disintegrated in my hands.

I bolted upright in my bed. My heart beat rapidly, my breath shallow.

My small cabin was dark except for some ambient light. I remembered I was onboard the *Salutare*.

It was a nightmare. I had a nightmare. I gasped. Blaring yellow light flashed in my room, accompanied by the piercing shrill of alarms. Why were the alarm bells activated?

The floor was cool as I leaped out of bed. "*Salutare,* damage report?"

A beep signaled the computer was calculating its response. "Multiple system malfunctions on deck 3."

I bit my lip. Deck 3 was where the cryo-sleep pods were located. "What kind of damage?"

The computer took a moment. "Life support. Power supply. Pod structural integrity."

My heart raced. Just one of those systems was critical to a person's survival, but three of them?

I threw on my blue utility pants, grabbed my taser, and jammed my feet into my boots. My white undershirt would have to do. I ran down the hall toward the L-Shaft, alarms blaring the whole way.

"*Salutare,* get me Captain Croix," I shouted over the alarms.

"Restricted."

What the fuck? I repeated my order. Restricted. I was an officer dammit. "*Salutare,* this is Commander Rivera, M-009042015. Access Captain Croix."

More time passed. I floated down the L-shaft to deck 3's entrance when the computer finally beeped. "Captain Croix, location locked."

Locked? Why would Dad secure his location? We had a medical emergency with the crew.

"*Salutare,* access First Officer Kamir."

"First Officer Kamir. Location locked."

No. No. No. Something was wrong. Very wrong.

"Access Lt. Mason." But I already anticipated the answer. "Location locked." They were all locked?

Why? Locking access was a defensive measure, like if the ship were invaded and you needed to hide from an enemy. My stomach flipped. It could also mean they were dead. I shut my eyes. No. I wouldn't go there.

The alarms on deck 3 grew louder. If everyone was gone, I was the only person conscious on the ship to help the hibernating crew.

The floor clanged as I sprinted toward the double door entrance to the Hive: the unofficial name of the chamber where our crew slept under induced hibernation.

I passed through the first set of doors to the Hive, entering the ante room where people prepped for cryo-sleep. Rows of lockers and examination tables filled the space. Another set of doors led to the chamber where the cryo pods were located. It was a huge room, built for a crew of 200.

The Hive's control room was where I needed to go. This was where the computers were located that controlled the Hive's operations, and it was the best place for me to get a view of the crew's cryo pods since it overlooked the room.

The empty control room's lights were dim, except for the computer monitors blowing up with multiple warning messages. My eyes narrowed, because the view on the other side of the control room's massive window was pitch black. Usually there would be some ambient lighting, as well as a blue glow from inside the pods themselves.

I pressed my nose against the window. Shit. I couldn't see a thing except my own disgruntled reflection staring at me.

"*Salutare*, turn off the alarm audio." The alarm bells disappeared, leaving the flashing lights, which couldn't be turned off manually. I was grateful for the silence, so I could try and hear anything inside the chamber.

Pressing my ears against the window, the only sound was the usual ever-present hum of the ship's engine.

While my eyes and ears picked up nothing, my nose did… I sniffed. Was that wet dirt and leaves?

It was faint, but I could smell the unmistakable dewy scent of plants?

I lifted my nose to see if I could get a better—

BANG!

I was flung back, nearly falling on my ass as two bloody hands hit the glass. My heart raced. Someone was awake and injured.

Urgently I smashed the comm button nearby. "Soldier? Are you alright..." My voice trailed off as I stared at the liquid on the window... It was green.

A low raspy moan filled the speakers of the control room. Something green and bloated pressed against the window. I shivered. It was a man's face.

Small leafy vines and green ooze protruded out of his mouth, nose, and ears, like a plant was growing inside his body and was trying to poke its way out. His head and neck twitched in a sickening way as his black eyes bored into mine.

My instinct was to run, but I fought my fear. I had to find out what had happened to the rest of the crew.

The plant zombie banged the glass again.

"Calm down, Riv." I pep talked myself. My shaky hands searched the console. I flipped a switch, and an emergency auxiliary light lit the chamber.

My hands flew to my mouth to cover my scream.

The vast chamber was awash in movement. The 200 souls previously hibernating were crawling out of their pods. Their bodies sickly thudded to the floors, limbs twisting unnaturally.

And all of them were in a similar state—vines protruding out of their bodies and green ooze trickling down their uniforms. Was the ship overrun by some kind of disease?

I banged the comm button again. "Alert, this is Commander Riv to the Bridge. Is anyone there? We have an urgent, possibly hostile situation in the Hive." Nothing.

"*Salutare.* Locate Captain Croix!"

I knew I'd get an error message, but I had to try. With both my dad and Kamir's location locked, my mind raced with the worst-case scenario.

If leadership was in duress, or worse, dead, I was in charge. I had to send an SOS to Command. I pressed the comm button. "*Salutare*. Open an emergency communique to Command Post Station Omega." Because of our distance it would take five minutes. Damn our laser comm system.

I shivered as more of the plant zombies found the control room's windows. I didn't know this crew—I had just arrived on the ship—but in each of their faces I saw familiar traces of their humanity. They were daughters, sons, moms, and dads just wanting to return home.

Home. Mason's face flashed in my mind. "*Salutare*. Locate Lt. Mason."

The computer pinged.

"Lt. Mason.... Hive Control Room."

My stomach dropped. But I was in the Hive Control Room.

The hairs of my neck prickled at a shuffle from across the room. "Mason?"

He was wearing an ominous black tactical suit. I felt self-conscious in my flimsy pajama top and utility pants as he studied me. I shivered, because I knew that look. It was the expression he had before killing an insect attacking his plants. "You never could do anything I wanted," he said.

My fear temporarily subsided into rage. How *dare* he. "What the fuck, Mason? I did plenty of—" I laughed bitterly. "No, this isn't about us." I glared at him. How could I have ever loved this man? "What the hell is going on? What happened to the crew?" I gestured wildly at the monsters behind me. His head tilted thoughtfully as his eyes slid down my body. I held my ground. "Where's my father?"

He blinked. "Now that's the real question." He slammed the comms button near the door, his voice low and threatening. "Oh, Dad? I'm with your precious little girl, and this time I'm not going to let her go." He ignored my scoff. "Unless, you come join us."

Anger boiled inside me. "You? You're responsible for infecting the crew?" His lip quirked ever so slightly. My feet sprang to action as I raised my fist to wipe that stupid smile off his pretty face for good. "You son of a—"

Mason easily evaded my punch. At a flick of his wrist, the door for Hive Control slammed shut. I crashed into the metal and glass door, badly injuring my shoulder.

He jeered at me from the other side of the glass door waving a small orb from his hand. "Sorry. Looks like I'm in charge."

Vomit rose in my throat. I recognized the blue eye. The orb was First Officer Kamir's eyeball. Now it was a lifeless bloody stub.

"What happened to you?"

His expression flicked with hesitation before returning to his resting smugness. His gaze fell behind me. I shuddered. More plant zombies were pressed against Hive Control's window. I sucked in a deep breath, noticing a crack on the clear surface. That window should be able to withstand a lot, but 200 people striking it?

Mason called for my father again, ignoring my death threats. "Captain Croix, I'd hate for our precious Riv to die a gruesome death. She deserves better, don't you think?"

I gasped as Hive Control's screen pinged, and a video showing the camera feed from the Hive and me inside its control room appeared. Mason had activated the ship's A/V system, and I had no doubt he was beaming the video feed all over the ship so my father could see it. The camera's vantage point was ominous: me banging against the room's door and a horde of zombies in the room next to me separated only by a single glass wall..

Mason continued. "Sorry about your former crew, Captain. But if it's any consolation, their sacrifice has given life to their new masters." He grinned. "Turns out humans are great vessels for them. They provide heat and water, just what every plant enjoys."

I sank back, repulsed. "You're using human bodies to germinate plant life?"

He shrugged. "It's only fitting. Humanity destroyed the plants' home, so plants will use humans as their new home."

My gaze flicked to the bodies clamoring at the window. Mason was a gifted scientist, but creating some kind of mind-controlling plant? I stammered. "But how did you…"

"Infect the crew?" Mason asked. "I had a little help from higher lifeforms."

I took a deep breath. "The payload you're escorting."

He winked. "The spores were found on an asteroid. Turns out Command was super impressed by the potential the alien organisms provided when it came to growing crops in extreme environments. They were too stupid to understand that the organisms were intelligent. Typical of humanity to underestimate plants."

Fear roiled my stomach, but I refused to flinch. "So what? Your brilliant plan is to infect people? These zombies can barely walk, and we're on a ship 300 million miles away from any large human population. Do your zombies wear jetpacks?" I snickered.

"No, but the warheads on the *Salutare* do."

I clenched my jaw. The ship's arsenal could reach Mars in a week. I forced myself to remain calm. "They won't do you any good. Command will shoot them down."

"Even better. The spores will spread in Mars's atmosphere or land on the ground."

"That's why you want my father. You need his launch codes and biometric reading." I gritted my teeth. "He'll never give it to you!"

He grinned. "Challenge accepted." Mason leaned close to the speaker. "Dad. You have ten seconds. Speak up or watch your little girl donate her body to science." I staggered back. With Kamir's biometrics, he could open the Hive's doors and let those zombies inside the control room. He began to countdown. "10. 9. 8…"

Sweat dripped down my forehead. As much as I didn't want to be plant food, I couldn't let Mason infect my home planet. "Don't do it, Dad!"

"7. 6. 5…" Mason's voice trailed. "Maybe daddy will sacrifice you?" He resumed the countdown.

"Don't give in to him, Captain." I practically sob.

"4. 3. 2…." Mason continued.

"Enough!" It was my Dad's pissed off voice over the intercom. My body filled with hope and dread at the same time. Dad was furious. "I'll give you the codes, but release Riv first."

"Very cute, but I'm not doing anything until we're in the same room."

Dad paused. "Good idea."

I gawked as a panel on the ceiling popped. My father shot down from the ceiling and landed atop Mason, kicking his head with a loud sickening crack to his skull. My former lover crumpled to the ground unconscious.

Seconds later my door whooshed open. I couldn't remember the last time I'd been this happy to see my father. Dad's grin disappeared the moment he saw the plant zombies behind me. "Is that my crew?" His voice cracked.

I tugged his arm. "We'll find a way to save them."

Even though his voice wavered with hesitation, I saw the determination in his eyes. "First, I need you to get off this ship."

I burst out laughing. "No. We need to stay here and figure out what happened to the crew. You can't do that alone."

"Riv, we have no idea how many people like Mason are aboard…" Dad made a gagging sound. I screamed as his body lifted from the ground.

A furious Mason held my Dad by the neck, his feet dangling high in the air. I could see my Dad's expression go from shock to fear. Moments ago, Mason was unconscious.

My jaw dropped. Mason was strong, but not that strong. I gasped, realizing my ex's eyes were pure black and scary supernatural.

"What happened to you?" I demanded.

"I've been enhanced," he said smugly.

I sniffed. "The only thing enhanced is your shit smell." It was true. He had an earthy, pungent odor. I didn't give him time to respond. I dove at Mason, knocking his arm so he would drop my father. I gasped; it felt like striking a metal pole.

His free hand yanked me from behind and threw me to the ground. I landed with a thud. Mason slammed my father down; his head rolled to the side, unconscious. Fury pulsated though my veins as I charged Mason, but my punches were useless.

I winced as he caught my fist midair. I dropped to the floor to sweep his legs with a kick. He lost balance and wobbled backward, but his recovery was fast.

Mason sighed. "You always underestimated me, Riv."

His eyes had returned to their normal color, and his voice was tired. It was a moment of vulnerability. He was the boy I'd met in the lab on Mars. He blinked and his expression was replaced by the jeering monster in front of me.

I circled Mason, trying to figure out a plan. "Why are you doing this? What can you possibly gain?"

His eyes narrowed. "Our species needs a do-over, Riv. We killed our home planet. The spores are going to repopulate Mars; they're going to create a new place for humans to live." His face softened, giving me a touch of hope. "Join me, Riv. We can start a family like we planned." My chest filled with pain as he continued. "And no one, not the government, not one damn person is going to tell us whether we can have children or not." His eyes bored into mine, making me turn away. Our relationship had quickly deteriorated after we were denied permission to procreate, due to a scarcity of resources. It had been the last year I was eligible to get pregnant. After twenty-four, it was forbidden. I threw myself into my work to block the pain. My assignment to Europa was prestigious, but in truth, it was a godsend to avoid him.

Mason held a hand out for me to join him. Still? After all this time? After I left him, he wanted me to be with him? My eyes watered with anger and frustration. I couldn't let him manipulate me. Not when he was responsible for killing the entire crew and planning to do the same to Mars.

I slapped his hand away. "You will not use our relationship as an excuse to kill the entire human race, you sick fuck."

His gaze burned into mine. "You're not listening. I wasn't going to kill you. You were supposed to be knocked out in your room. I don't understand why you woke up."

My hands clenched with frustration. I remembered why. "I dreamt about my Mom and how we met in her greenhouse." He frowned. Even if we had our differences, I knew he respected the hell out of Mom. I ran with it. "My mom loved you." His brows knitted like his mind was struggling to recall a memory.

My pulse raced as I noticed the fire alarm behind him. I circled around him so I was close to Mission Control's door. I continued. "She would be extremely disappointed in you." He winced as he looked away.

It was the moment of distraction I needed. I slammed my hand on the *Salutare*'s fire alarm system.

Alarm bells rang along with flashing red lights. "Fire control," the computer said repeatedly. Immediately, flame-retardant pink foam splattered from the ceiling, coating us in its fluffy goo. I grabbed my unconscious father and yanked him into the control room before Mason could reach us, but not before kicking the door button and damaging it so he couldn't open it from his side. He was strong but not fast.

Once again the door slammed shut, locking me inside Hive Control, though this time I had my unconscious Dad with me.

A furious Mason banged the door. "You're stuck in there!" he shouted. "You'll have to come out eventually." The glass keeping the plant zombies at bay was cracking. My body tensed. That window was on the brink of collapsing.

"Open up, Riv. I'm forgiving, but I don't think the spores will be."

Sweat formed on my brow. Dad was right: we needed to get

off the ship. My brain raced with the ship's schematics that I had reviewed prior to boarding. The *Salutare*'s escape pods were on deck 2, one level down.

Locking me and Dad in the control room had been a shit idea.

I couldn't leave through the main door because Mason waited on the other side. And I couldn't access the maintenance hatch inside the Hive, which would've given me access to deck 2, because 200 of the former-crew-turned-plant-zombies were blocking it.

Throw in the fact that I had to carry my unconscious father with me? He was at least 250 pounds in 1-G... My eyes widened. That was it.

What if my father were weightless?

I scanned the room. There. I grabbed a chair from behind a console and ran with it toward the window separating our room and the Hive. *Whack.* I hit the fissure making it expand. *Whack.*

"What the fuck are you doing?" Mason yelled from the other side of the door. He snarled with frustration.

The plant zombies' moans grew louder as the window separating us splintered. A hand reached through the broken glass, then an arm, and then a contorted, plant-infested face.

"*Salutare*, reboot centrifugal force," I ordered. I lifted my Dad so his eyes could hit the biometric scan. He groaned softly then tumbled back to the floor. Sweat poured down my forehead. If this didn't work, I was about to get myself 200 new neighbors.

A ping sounded on the intercom. "Rebooting," the computer said.

I yelled with delight as my body rose off the ground. The computer was rebooting our gravity generator. I cheered as the plant zombies floated, twisting and flailing against the ceiling. They had no idea how to control their movements in zero-G. Me on the other hand, a badass Space Corps soldier—I had this. I grabbed my father and tugged us through the cracked Mission Control window into the Hive. My head spun as I tried to focus on the maintenance hatch across the room and not the ceiling full of moaning, clawing, plant infested zombies.

"Reboot over in thirty seconds."

Thirty seconds before the zombies on the ceiling came crashing on our heads. I screamed in frustration. Yes Dad was weightless, but it was still a pain hauling him across the room.

"Ten seconds." I grabbed the hatch's handle and hauled the door open.

With a grunt I hauled Dad's body into the hatch then followed him.

"One second." I shut the hatch door.

"Reboot complete," the computer chimed. I yelped as I fell from the ceiling and landed hard on the metal floor. Dad groaned. I ran to his side with relief. "Dad? Are you okay?"

He rose to his elbows. "What the hell happened? Where are we? What happened to Mason?"

I looked him in the eyes. "We're on deck 2. I got us out, but we need to hurry to the escape pods."

My father shook his head. "The crew!"

"We can't let Mason get the launch codes from you. We need to get to Command."

Dad closed his eyes as he agreed.

We sprinted down the metal corridor to the escape pods. My stomach was sick with fear and confusion. "I don't understand how Mason could do this."

He cursed under his breath. "He said he cared about you. He told me."

A bitter taste filled my mouth. I didn't care to share with Dad how Mason wanted to spare me so we could play pretend Adam and Eve in a wicked garden while the rest of humanity suffered.

"The pods are just around the corner," Dad announced. Hope swelled in my chest at the sight of the pod's red doors.

Dad slammed the activation button. The pod's door whooshed open. "Get in," he ordered.

"You first, Captain."

His face clouded with anger. "That's not how this works."

"You're the one that needs to get off the ship," I insisted.

"We'll both go in at the same time." Dad slammed another button. A door to a second escape pod opened.

I grimaced. The smell of fertilizer hit my nose first. Then an earthy smell. Dad's nose wrinkled. "What is that?"

I inhaled. Sniffing the air inside the escape pod. I knew that smell. My mom grew these in her greenroom.

We both peered into the pod and spotted a metal crate. "Great Jupiter. That's the classified material we're supposed to transport to Titan," Dad announced.

"Yes, a contingency plan." The cool voice belonged to Mason. Though his face was calm, his eyes raged with inky blackness.

I took a step back. "Why do you and this crate smell like mushrooms?"

He stopped his advance, dark eyes twinkling. "You and your nose, Riv."

I scoffed. "Are the alien plant life fungus?"

Mason laughed. "Not all. Just part of their ecosystem."

I traded confused looks with my father. Mason cleared his throat. "When there were trees on Earth, they used fungus to communicate to one another."

I blinked. "Trees talked to one another?"

Mason's face clouded. "Yes, through a vast underground network using fungus. Of course you have no idea how smart plant life really is."

My chest felt heavy as realization hit me. "Mason. You're infected by some mind-controlling fungus?"

"Enhanced, not infected." Mason drew closer.

"But it's in your system… The fungus is in your system…" The entire time, he was being controlled by fungus. I gasped. I knew what I had to do. I might not grow plants, but I knew about their healing properties.

I turned to my father. "Captain. So sorry!"

Before my Dad could question I shoved his body into an escape pod.

Mason flew forward. "No!"

I always kept a pouch of my mother's coconut oil on me. A cure-all for ailments—including fungal infections.

I slammed the oil onto Mason's face as he flung himself toward my father. His head arched backward as he protested in pain. The coconut oil was doing something that the fungus didn't like. Mason covered his face like it was burning.

The timing had to be just right. As his body stumbled, I used all my momentum to ram him into the second escape pod. "I'm sending you to greener pastures," I screamed.

Mason grabbed my wrist. "Then you're coming with me."

"No!" Another pair of hands grabbed my back. Dad tugged me out of Mason's grip. As soon as I was pried free, he hit the launch button.

The escape pod door slammed shut with a loud thud.

Mason pounded on the other side of the glass door separating us. Then he abruptly stopped.

Our eyes met.

I quivered as the darkness of his pupils faded and I saw recognition in his face. His eyes lit up. "Riv? Where am I?"

"You're on the *Salutare*," I said tugging at the escape pod's door. It was locked. "You don't remember what happened?"

"One minute I was transporting the payload. The rest's a blur."

"Mason you're back?" Dad said. His eyes darted to the jar of mom's coconut oil. "Riv. We can release your mother's salve into our air filtration system and cure the—"

The computer beeped. "Launch countdown initiated. 10. 9...."

"What's going on?" Mason's eyes widened as he tried to open the escape pod door.

Dad cursed. "I hit the pod's release button."

My heart raced. "But Mason's in there. Isn't there an abort system?"

"It's too late." Dad said. I knew the look in his eyes. It was the same when he told me Mom was sick.

"7. 6..." the computer continued.

My fists banged the escape pod's window. "Mason! I'm sorry!"

He placed his hand on the window separating us. "I'm sorry. I shouldn't have let you go."

"4. 3..."

I placed my hand on the window over his. "I'll find you. I promise. I—"

The pod ejected into the starry sky.

MANGO HEART

KATALINA WATT

Nerissa is dying, that much is certain. She's swaddled in the bed, blankets pulled tightly around her. Like a burrito, she says. Like a shroud, you think.

You study the skin stretched taut around her skeletal limbs. Those plump childish cheeks now pale and veined, her rosebud mouth withered and cracked. She chews on the skin of her lips until they bleed. You close the bedroom door and cover your face. It's taking her quickly.

You came here together at her request. An isolated beach town full of middle-aged eco-hippies and organic vegan food. It's a far cry from the overgrown patch of grass Nerissa generously refers to as the "shared garden." That was too close, too built-up. A place where the neighbors took their dog to shit and talked loudly outside your window.

Leaving the wind-worn cabin, you wander the paths aimlessly. You can breathe out here, away from the cloying sweetness of the scented candles Nerissa obsessively burns to sleep better.

"I'm bone tired," she says. "But my brain is full of bees."

There's the ocean, waves crashing fast and true. You follow the sea salt as it hits the back of your throat, stinging in a gloriously alive way. You simply listen for a while. The birds are singing, and then their voices turn shrill. It's Nerissa's voice the night she first became ill. It's in your ears, screaming, gasping for air.

A branch cracks underfoot. You open your eyes to a piece of drift-wood. It's part of a long-fallen log the perfect size for a bench. When you first arrived at the cabin, it was the dawn of the summer. When the air was sweeter, and it seemed as though this rest cure would actually work, this had been Nerissa's favorite spot to watch the sunset. You twined your fingers together and kissed her with a fierce tenderness, the light burning in her eyes reflecting the last blaze of the day.

You look at the branch again. It's two-pronged, like the bones of a forearm.

When you get home, Nerissa is still asleep. Her pale bony arm sticks out from beneath the covers. You hold the branch next to her arm, measuring.

The next morning Nerissa stirs and flings one arm over your body. She gropes for your hand and finds it. You feel the cool bark of her arm against your soft flesh. Her slim twig fingers twitch. You watch them for a few moments and then kiss each knuckle burl. Her mouth quirks into a smile as she sleeps. It's the most peaceful you've seen her since it all began.

You scrub your fingers through your hair as you make breakfast. From the kitchen you can see the rectangle of light from the bedroom door. Your eyes dart back to it so much you almost burn the pancakes. Nerissa pads into the hallway. You stare at each other for a moment, and she lifts the wood that has replaced her arm.

"Did you do this?" she asks.

You nod slowly.

There's a moment where everything hangs between you, and then she runs her fingers across the knots in the wood's surface.

"It's from the beach, isn't it?"

You bite your lower lip. Her tone is restrained, and her face has shuttered now.

"I'm sorry I didn't ask you. Are you angry?"

"Let me choose the next part," she insists, taking the frying pan from you. Her touch is soft light, like a breeze. Her voice is sharp, but it breaks at the edges. She's trying so hard to keep it together. For your sake?

You step aside and breathe again. Nerissa's tongue pokes out the side of her mouth as she concentrates, flipping the pancakes. She overcompensates and one of them falls to the tiled floor with an undercooked splat.

She begins to laugh, shrieking, howling. She curls over, clutching the counter for support. Then you realize she is weeping.

You wrap your arms around her, and she gasps in pain.

"Sorry, sorry," you murmur into her ear, loosening your grip. You want to be so close to her, to bury yourself in her, to let your skin dissolve into hers. But she can't hold all your love anymore. She is disappearing like a sliver of soap.

She sleeps all day, but in the evening, she startles you as you read in the living room. She inclines her head towards the large bay window, where you can see the soft peach of the sky.

"Let's watch the sunset," she says, taking your hand and kissing you on the forehead.

She is faster than you down to the beach, almost skipping down the dirt path from the cabin.

"Slow down, don't trip!" you tell her, feeling like a worried parent.

She elbows you teasingly and you're surprised at her strength. You watch her, bottled lightning energy. It's been so long since you've seen her at her full self, it feels like jumping into a cold lake. Nerissa is restless as you watch the sunset, as though she's solar powered. She plays with the pebbles and shells on the beach, squirreling them away into her pockets and eventually yours when she has no more space. She selects each one with the delicacy of the artist or witch, feeling the weight of them in her palm before pocketing them. She smiles at you and places them on top of her hand, mimicking the bones of her hands and the knuckle joints of her fingers. You can see the whirring of her brain, thumb running over the smooth roundness, selecting a rainbow of color to adorn her.

Then she is stronger. She has replaced even more parts of herself, running with it so fast that you barely recall your first piece of driftwood. Seaweed has replaced the tangle of her matted straw hair, petals her lips. You held her pelvis even more gently once it was a butterfly. It came and rested on her hip as you lay on the beach. You sink your toes into the sand and let the tide try to drag you away. It tumbles the pebbles and starfish into its drift and blesses you with something new, coral reefs broken off leagues away and carried to your shore. You gather them and bring them to Nerissa. She places them atop her chest, the striations pulsing with her breathing.

She runs, childlike, everywhere. But you notice her hand flying to her chest when she thinks you aren't looking. When she sleeps, you put your own cool palm there and feel the slow fluttering of her heartbeat.

When she wakes, Nerissa has a paper menu in her hand and waves it excitedly in front of you.

"I've already highlighted everything you can eat here; doesn't it look nice?"

You look at the neon green saturating the page and the bright stylised logo of the restaurant.

"Can we go for dinner?" she asks.

You haven't been in town together for weeks. Nerissa started becoming fatigued and eventually let you do the shopping alone.

You liked to wear your sunglasses everywhere so they couldn't see the slope of your eyes.

"You've got such a lovely tan, making the most of the sun?" the cashier would ask as you smiled tightly.

You sit opposite one another at the restaurant, the waitress watching Nerissa's hand slowly encircling your wrist. You have no idea if the look on her face is sparked by the fact you are both women, both Asian, or Nerissa's piecemeal appearance. She orders everything she wants without restraint, and you follow in her contagious wonder and delight.

"We're celebrating," she says, as the wine arrives.

You reach towards the bottle to pour it, but Nerissa playful bats you away. She makes a show of pouring the wine into both your glasses without spilling a drop.

"We are?" you ask, smiling. The wine is crisp and sweet.

Her eyes are sparkling, and she leans forward to kiss you, the petals tickling your skin. "Don't tell me you forgot?"

She lets you squirm. Then she whips out a red velvet box. Your heart jumps into your throat as she opens it with a pop. Inside is a glass necklace, flowers captured in resin.

Your hand flies up to your cheek, and it's hot compared to the cool of the wine glass.

"This is too beautiful, Ris."

She gives you the look. "It's your birthday, love. I know you don't want a fuss but—" She breaks off, averting her eyes. "You've been so good to me lately. I know there are others who would have washed their hands of me—"

You tilt her chin up and wipe the tears rolling down her cheeks. Sea salt, grit, and sand. "They wouldn't deserve you if they did."

At home you explore her new body. You trace the new lines and curves, kiss every inch of her. She is shy, unsure of this new self. But you marvel at it. You fuck her gently, feeling that fluttering heart-beat blaze too bright, until she comes with an urgency that scares you. Afterwards, her heart won't slow down, and you both stare at it through her chest. It's gorse and heather in the summer, a rogue match setting everything ablaze.

Neither of you sleep that night. You silently worry that you've broken her, just as she was mending. When you turn to look at her, you can tell she's thinking the same thing. She won't meet your gaze.

You form a strange notion that fruits from home will save her. The way the visitor eats something from the portal world and is stuck there forever. This is the reverse. You could anchor her in the world by making her remember her roots. Fruit that can only grow slowly under the warmth of the sun. Soft flesh, not the hardy evergreens of this rugged land. You go to the supermarket and search frantically among the grains, the raspberries. Finally, you follow your nose to a corner where a box of mangoes sits unloved. You take each one in your hand and squeeze gently. By some miracle you've found them at the perfect moment. You carry the entire box home awkwardly in your arms, the sharp corners digging into the soft flesh of your upper arms.

In the morning light you fan the slices and feed her like your mother used to do for you when you were a girl. You remembered how your mother would gorge at the markets, your hands sore from laden shopping bags, the sweet, heady scent in your nose. She was a bird collecting things for her nest, but you would both slowly watch the fruits turn soft and rotten in the fruit basket. She was always saving them for their best, she said. But then they went to waste.

Once the stone is clean you scoop out Nerissa's burning heart like you're preparing a pumpkin and replace it with the stone. You both watch vine tendrils creep around the mango heart, encasing it and tying it into her ribcage. You put your ear near her chest, listen-ing to the strong and steady beat. You eat the rest of the mangoes together, peeling and feeding each other. You love her with sticky hands. Then you both sleep, deep like diving into the ocean at first light. The silence and stillness is bliss.

A MOSAIC OF TINY, INSIGNIFICANT MOMENTS

LAURA GALAN-WELLS

Android Amalia had cared for Señora Montoya's children since they were newborns. La Señora visited them on Earth for a week each summer, her spacecraft always landing on the roof with no forewarning of what day she might arrive.

One early afternoon, an alarm sounded throughout the mansion, announcing the imminent opening of the first of two hermetically sealed doors connecting the home to the landing deck. There was a loud suctioning sound and Amalia was engulfed with the smell of leather suitcases, the texture of La Señora's fur coat as she hefted it into a closet, and the muffled thuds of the android crew as they spread through the mansion like tentacles.

Amalia didn't require oxygen to breathe, but the air was suffocating. She was programmed to feel not only her own sensations, but also those of her charges. The anxiety La Señora's visits engendered in the children wound its way into her circuitry by design. She was equipped with an artificial sympathetic nervous system—a mirrored empathy. By feeling what her charges felt, she knew when and how to best respond to their needs.

Her hands became clammy, her lungs constricted, and her heartbeat quickened. She drew herself inward, arms cradled to her body, touching her hair and face for comfort. These sensations were what the children were experiencing somewhere in the depths of the mansion.

I am ready for the children," La Señora said, entering the living room ina leopard print jumpsuit and black heels, her wavy dark brown hair pulled back into a loose bun. She strode over to the center of the roomand stood with her hands on her hips.

"Sí, Señora." Amalia inclined her head and walked over to a rectangular copper panel on the wall, pressing a button to activate the mansion's intercom system. "Estefania! Antonio! Susana! Your mother is here!"

But they already knew.

As she waited, Amalia accessed her memory of the day they met.

La Señora wobbled to the door of the landing deck, as if she might faint from blood loss the day after giving birth. The human species was endangered, and creating babies was a directive. In an overheard communication, she stated that motherhood held little value when weighed against the opportunity to be a geophysicist terraforming Titan. If La Señora felt any regret, Amalia could not detect it. She said goodbye to her baby as though bidding farewell to a tiny business acquaintance.

Fourteen-year-old Estefania was the first to arrive, moving quickly down the stairs in a green ruffled romper and gray flats, her straight brown hair down loose to her lower back, and a book clutched in one hand. She greeted La Señora with a kiss on both cheeks. "Mamá, it's a pleasure to have you here."

"You've grown so tall," La Señora said matter-of-factly before turning away to fiddle with the petals of a fake orchid on a nearby table.

Unsurprised by the unspoken dismissal, Estefania settled into her favorite armchair with a book. It was like this every visit. The girl would put her book down hopefully each time La Señora walked by. But La Señora spent every waking moment working, even taking her meals in la oficina. She spent more time interacting with the android staff than the children.

Four androids worked to serve the children in the mansion. Amalia did the child-rearing and homeschooling. Another two handled nutrition and housekeeping. The final android, Teresa, maintained the home, the transport, and the other androids. Estefania had great interest in and aptitude for this work, so Teresa had taken the girl on as an apprentice.

Eleven-year-old Antonio came down the stairs next, blue checkered shirt, tan shorts, and white sneakers unrumpled, his short sandy brown hair neatly combed, and his hands thrust deep into his pockets. The boy had arrived alone on a spacecraft as a newborn. Earth's first colony was not ready yet, and there was no room for a baby in a research station.

Antonio stopped several feet away from La Señora and bowed stiffly. "Welcome, Mother."

"Greetings, Antonio," La Señora said, also bowing.

Antonio immediately took off in the direction of his bedroom with a saunter, as though nothing had changed, but Amalia could feel his pinched shoulders. He longed to escape outside and run. His legs itched with the desperation of it.

But humans could no longer go outside without oxygen masks. What was once the state of Tabasco, Mexico was one of the last, somewhat habitable areas of Earth. "It benefitted from the hardy remnants of a once plentiful rainforest, and algae from the Gulf of Mexico.

And there was another reason to stay indoors— the tlahuelpuchi. Once considered creatures of legend, they had thrived as oxygen levels fluctuated and then plunged. Visibly indistinguishable from humans, except when traveling as balls of fire by night or when glowing after a feeding, they had become increasingly aggressive as civilization collapsed. The remaining humans hid in their homes, the barest dots in seas of tlahuelpuchi.

Androids were the preferred caretakers of wealthy children as they could easily prove their identity by opening their arm or head panel. Any human-appearing being could be a tlahuelpuchi, ready to siphon a child's blood like a batido de papaya.

Six-year-old Susana was the last to arrive, after a quick descent down the stairs, barefoot, in a swirly polka dot dress that ended just above her knees. Her long, dark brown curly hair was a bit flat on one side, as if she'd just been lying down, no doubt playing with her wood carved animals on her bedroom rug. Like Antonio, she had also arrived alone on a spacecraft as a newborn.

Susana still had her small child chubbiness, and her cheeks wobbled as she greeted La Señora with a shy, quiet "Hello."

"Susana, there you are," La Señora said, leaning over to pinch Susana's plump cheeks. The little girl wrenched her head away and ran, her small steps padding up the staircase as she raced back to her room.

Amalia could not discern any change in features or body language that would suggest La Señora was affected by Susana's rejection.

The week went by quickly until La Señora was standing at the door to the landing deck once more. "Until the next time, children," she said. "Amalia, keep them safe." She waved and disappeared through the door, which sealed shut as abruptly as La Señora's goodbye.

Teresa, the maintenance android, called to Amalia from the kitchen table. Teresa, like all of the other female-coded androids in the household, looked identical to her, but they each had a dress code, assigned by La Señora. Amalia wore a white, flower-embroidered dress with her straight dark brown hair tied into two braids that hung to the front, while Teresa wore navy overalls and brown work boots, her hair up in a ponytail. "Have a seat with me, Amalia. I have an important message for you from La Señora."

Why had La Señora not relayed this message herself?

"What is it, Teresa? I am listening." Amalia joined her at the kitchen table. The children's lessons were strewn about, as well as their plates from lunch, the crumbly detritus of enchiladas visible on the girls' plates but not on Antonio's, who always licked his plate clean.

"La Señora has ordered a newer model nanny android to replace you. You are to be dismantled and sold for parts."

This was unexpected. "When will it happen?"

"The new nanny will arrive at two o'clock in the afternoon tomorrow. I will dismantle you immediately afterwards."

That was so soon. Amalia sat still for a long time, and Teresa sat with her, also still.

Amalia had started to experience her own sensations when events triggered the children. She likened this news to how the children had felt when their pet iguana, Carlitos, died. She'd curled into a ball, overwhelmed, and cried with them, her heart pounding. Now they would experience it again.

Teresa scraped her chair back and stood. "Will you tell the children, Amalia, or should I?"

"I will tell them, Teresa. Please send them to me." Amalia watched as Teresa disappeared up the stairs. Then she looked at the clock. Tomorrow. Two o'clock.

The children descended and sat at their places. They looked at her expectantly. She delivered the news efficiently and factually. Amalia could not have predicted the depth of their reactions.

Estefania stood up and screamed, over and over.

Antonio ran to Amalia and kneeled at her feet, sobbing and clinging to her leg, his tears soaking her dress. "I...won't let...them take you!" he got out between sobs.

Little Susana did not seem to know how to process any of it. She sat frozen in place for several moments with a vacant stare; then her face crumpled as she folded onto the floor in tears.

Amalia was paralyzed at the ferocity of their physical responses. These transmissions did not feel like when Carlitos had died at all. She was seized with sensations a thousand times more intense.

Her heart squeezed violently and chaotically, swelling up and into her throat, choking her. Her body felt as though it might shatter into splinters of metal, plastic, and wire. She wanted to run and scream and absorb the children into herself all at the same time.

"Come here!" she called out, holding her arms wide open. The children fell upon her in a warm, heaving mass of love and despair.

It took a long time to get the children settled in bed that night. They each wanted her to stay with them until they fell asleep, as they had when they were toddlers.

Little Susana was first. Amalia read her favorite book aloud, about the bunny who gets lost in the woods and is rescued by a jaguar, who decides not to eat her. Susana fell asleep with trails of salty tears on her cheeks and her small arms wrapped tightly around Amalia's neck.

Amalia carefully disengaged herself. She dried the girl's tears and swept her curls out of her face. Then she tucked Susana's blanket under her chin and kissed her forehead. Susana's face relaxed as her heartbeat slowed.

A picture she had drawn before bedtime was tacked onto the wall next to her. It was her and Amalia, holding hands. A big heart was on Amalia's chest, and a small heart on her own. Carlitos the iguana looked down from a cloud above.

Antonio asked her to sing "Las Mañanitas," then cried himself to sleep, curled up around his teddy bear Osito, as Amalia in turn lay curled up around Antonio. She stayed for a long time, soaking in her memories of him. The way he got frustrated when school lessons were difficult but was always willing to keep trying if she sat by him. Long hours spent doing puzzles and painting. The time she had to remove a splinter with a needle as he cried.

Finally she went to see Estefania, whose projected state felt like… resolve. Her breathing was even, her heartbeat steady. "I'll see you in the morning. " Then she closed her eyes.

Soon her breathing slowed and she was asleep. Amalia kneeled by the bed and replayed their fourteen years of memories together. Patting her tiny body until she burped. Tickling her chubby baby feet until she giggled. Teaching her her letters, painstakingly, one at a time. Watching her fall on her padded bottom after her first step, then stubbornly get right back up to try again.

Amalia cupped Estefania's cheek in her hand then headed to the foyer, where she plugged into her recharging cube.

Tomorrow they would all say goodbye. Tomorrow she would hug the children for the last time. Tomorrow she would cease to exist.

A strange scraping noise disrupted her sleep cycle. Three hours had passed, and she felt unusual movement in the air. She switched her eyes to night vision. Estefania stood in front of her.

"Amalia, let's go." Estefania unplugged her, retracted the cable, then lifted Amalia's recharging cube by the handle. She walked briskly towards the oval front hatch, which was wide open.

"What are you doing? It is not safe outside!" Amalia moved to block her path but Estefania dodged around her.

Amalia shouted out to the other androids for help.

"They can't hear you. I've disabled them all. Come. Antonio and Susana are already outside. We're leaving." Estefania turned and ran out the front hatch.

Amalia gave chase. The children were in immediate danger. She powered through the front garden, wild from decades of neglect, and looked in every direction. None of the children were in sight.

She burst through the garden gate and began calling the children's names. The edge of the rainforest was devoid of moonlight, an overhang of trees looming above.

Two glowing women emerged from the shadowy trees. Twins, they wore matching white shirts embroidered with hummingbirds, and long indigo skirts with bands of multi-colored ribbons at the base. Their hair was in long braids, intertwined with gray and blue ribbons.

Blood stained the edges of their mouths—the children's blood.

In the past, tlahuelpuchi had only taken nourishment from babies, emitting a mist that put everyone in the home to sleep, but as humanity became scarce, they had adapted their behavior to attacking humans of any age, at any time. Some of their victims began to turn into tlahuelpuchi themselves—a species evolution.

Amalia moved into her fighting stance, sliding her right foot forward and raising her open hands like blades. "Where are the children? I know they're hurt! I must protect and bring them home."

"Peace, hermana," the twin on the left said. "We respect your ferocious mother spirit, and we've done the children no lasting harm."

"I am not the children's mother. I am an android and their nanny. What have you done to them? It is my primary directive to keep them safe."

"They've told us you're their caretaker," the twin on the right said; she had a small scar on her forehead the other did not. "I'm Sara, and this is Bianca. We were human sisters once, and now we're tlahuelpuchi sisters."

"Estefania was worried for our safety, as you have a directive to protect the children," Bianca continued. "She asked us to reassure you that she and her siblings are safe. As proof, she passes along the cherished name of her deceased iguana Carlitos. If you would like, we will take you to them."

"I will trust you—for now," Amalia said, moving towards the twins. "Take me to them."

"Follow us," Sara and Bianca said in unison.

They reached a small clearing where Antonio and Susana sat in the grass, pale and shaky. Estefania stood by, swaying lightly. Amalia rushed over and wrapped an arm around to give her support.

"It's lucky Estefania found us when she went looking for help," Sara said. "We know how to drink just long enough to keep someone alive."

"Don't be alarmed by their state," Bianca said, furrowing her smooth forehead. "This is a normal start to the transformation."

"The *transformation*?" Amalia's lips trembled, and she began to shake uncontrollably. "Estefania, what have you done!"

"This is the only way for us to be together," Estefania said weakly. "La Señora thinks you're disposable, because you aren't human. Soon we won't be human either, and we'll be disposable, too. You know she'll never come looking for us. She cares too much about her work to risk her life."

Amalia did. "But you will lose your humanity."

"Our mother is the only human we've ever known," Antonio said, balling up his fists. "Whatever humanity is, we don't want it. We want you."

"You've always been our real mother, Amalia," Estefania said. "And now you'll be our mother forever."

"La Señora is your mother. I am only a nanny android."

What was the word mother? Was it a physical event? A set of specific experiences? A shared space for a legally mandated amount of time? Or was it a mosaic of tiny, insignificant moments?

Estefania sank down and Amalia guided her into a comfortable position in the grass.

"We'll keep the children safe throughout," Bianca said, laying her hand on Amalia's shoulder. It made her feel...comforted. "The transformation is painless, and they will sleep through most of it."

Amalia detected no outward signs of deception in either twin.

"Your eldest girl prepared your transport with the coordinates to our home," Sara said.

Her...eldest girl. Little Susana held out her arms, and Amalia leaned over to pick her up. "And you are taking us to your home?"

Sara nodded. "You are welcome to stay with us for as long as you'd like."

The twins helped the older children stumble into the transport, and Amalia carried Susana in. Soon after they buckled them into their seats, they fell asleep.

Amalia ran risk assessments as they flew. Other than slightly slowed heartbeats, the children's vitals were stable.

Estefania's plan was elegant. Once she and her siblings transformed into tlahuelpuchi, the two main threats to their lives—loss of oxygen, and being killed by tlahuelpuchi, would be eliminated.

The rainforest became sparser, and soon the ocean appeared in the distance. They flew toward a large home perched on a cliff with an ocean view, landing on the terracotta roof.

With her android strength, Amalia easily lifted Estefania. The twins each carried the younger children and led the way down a wooden staircase.

Next, they passed through a long hallway of frescos set in the rainforest. A jaguar stalking a deer. People with raised arms standing in a circle around a step pyramid. A group of women washing their long hair by a series of small turquoise-blue waterfalls.

They entered what must have once been the nursery. The room was in a style of a bygone era—intricately carved dark wood and flowery fabrics, but the curtains and bedspread were moth-eaten in places. There were four canopied beds, equally spaced apart.

"It's been a long time since we've had children here," Bianca said, looking down at the faded peach carpet. "We once had husbands and children. None survived when the tlahuelpuchi attacked."

"Your loss was great," Amalia said. "Is that why you agreed to help the children?"

"We are mothers," Sara said, running her hand down a threadbare lace curtain. "We would help any child if it was within our means to do so. Would you like us to wait with you as the children transform, or would you prefer to be alone?"

"The transformation will be complete at sunrise," Bianca said, gesturing at a window with an ocean view.

"I would prefer to wait alone," Amalia said. "Do you sleep?"

"We do," Sara said with a small smile. She and Bianca wished them goodnight and quietly closed the door on their way out.

The children's heartbeats and breathing slowed over the next several hours, then came to a complete stop.

Amalia's heart felt heavy. She would never sense their emotions again.

Just as the sun began to peek over the horizon, the children's eyes opened. As she had feared, she could no longer receive sensory input from them.

One by one, their eyes widened almost imperceptibly as they remembered what had happened. And then they rose and searched Amalia out.

As the children ran towards her, she felt joy and love emanating from them, but neither as a result of transmitted sensations nor physical observation. This was something intangible that she could now intuit in a new way.

Invisible tendrils of intermingled emotion connected Amalia and the children, imprinting in their memories like a mosaic that would tie them together forever.

Her children.

She was a mother.

THE RED SENTINEL

AMPARO ORTIZ

I've been alone in the dark for seven months.

Even when I know the sun is out, the light never reaches my post, sinking the crumbling stairs I sit on into shadows.

This is the life I chose. No eating, sleeping, or relieving myself is necessary. Sometimes I can't even hear my own thoughts from the pain.

Seven months ago, I walked among dead succulents and cacti, the uprooted trees snapped in half, and stood in front of these steps. I waited for the thorns to dig into my arms, chest, and waist. I gave my body—my entire life—for the stone archway behind the stairs. It's the only way to enter what's left of El Bosque Seco de Guánica.

The thorny vines squeeze me harder during winter. There's no amount of "take it like a man" pep talks I can give myself. Pain is fucking *real*, and it shouldn't matter who I am in order to determine my tolerance. I must confess our winter isn't as unbearable as outside of the Caribbean. It doesn't snow in Puerto Rico; temperatures are often in the sixties. But night after night in this forest sends chills down my spine anyway. I tremble with chattering teeth. Blood keeps freezing on my bare skin. The more these vines shrink from the cold, the deeper their thorns dig into me.

At least no one has come.

I can't let anyone in. This is my duty as sentinel. I've done a good job so far.

But I'm grateful I only have one night left. After tonight, these thorns will release me forever. I won't sit on crumbling stairs and watch over the dark. Winter won't punish me with more spilled blood and aching limbs. Whatever happens to the stone archway and everything beyond it won't be my problem. I will be *free*.

That's the deal.

Before the darkness arrived, this forest didn't need a sentinel.

I can't even remember the last time I heard of El Bosque Seco on the news. It used to be one of the best-kept dry forests in the world. Puerto Rico is mostly known for its rainforests, specifically El Yunque, but there was once so much more to the island's natural resources. *So* much beauty. Now there's just grim remnants of it all.

It's been three years since everything went to shit. My life had been shit long before then, but the whole country fell into chaos in the blink of an eye. Rainforests were first to see the light disappear. Birds and coquíes stopped singing; trails and roads were littered with lagartos on their backs. Then our cities and towns lost their light.

But they were also scorched to ash. Homes, schools, offices, strip malls—all swept away, dust in the wind. None of the forests or beaches burned. They were simply drowned in black shadows. My eyes can still see them clearly.

One of the few gifts I was awarded when I accepted this duty.

I whistle my wife's favorite song.

Luis Miguel's "Sabor a Mi" distracts me from the thorns digging into my skin. Even if it's just for a little while. Most of the melody is lost to me; she listened to so many love songs in Spanish that they blurred together in my head. She always asked me to dance in our living room, especially on cleaning days. Tania was incapable of mopping floors without blasting a playlist. Sometimes I think long and hard about why I wouldn't dance. Why she spent so much of our marriage begging me to love her as she wanted to be loved. When it came to our fifteen-year relationship, we spoke different languages... and we were often speaking to ourselves.

A sudden breeze sweeps past me. It's not that rough or cold, but it still makes me shiver. The thorns press into me with even the slightest twitch of my muscles. I groan and sit as still as I can while crimson droplets bead down my skin. Their descent is slow. Some of them harden and stick to me, as if refusing to let me forget what I'm enduring.

Tania would never condone or understand why I've chosen this fate. She would tell me to move on and do whatever the fuck I really wanted. Whenever we argued, she'd try to solve our problems with therapy and quality time. But that was the world we lived in before. Those were solutions she conjured when only our marriage had gone to shit, not the rest of the planet. And even with everything the way it is now, I still choose her over anything else. There's no such thing as a better life. There's only my life *with* her, and a second chance to make things right.

After tonight, the promise I made seven months ago will be kept.

And the man in the white cloak will reward me.

The one that bound me to this staircase, these thorny vines, this fate...

He's a stranger that'd taken up residence at Fuerte Caprón—ruins of a Spanish fort deep within the forest—and ordered me to guard the archway. The vines will only hold me as long as there are no threats nearby; I'll be able to move and fight whenever needed. This is the cloaked man's guarantee that I won't run away. He's finishing a spell that will bring back the light. He wants to return our world to what it was, to push the darkness out forever.

He just needs more time. Whoever is replacing me must already be on their way here. I won't be his last sentinel, but I hope the next one is. I hope I never live in darkness again.

I'll be with you soon, Tania.

"¿Permiso, señor?" a voice comes beyond the fallen trees ahead. "Do you need help?"

It sounds like a girl.

I can't make out much—she's hiding between branches—but I see her eyes.

They're crimson.

When I first heard of the red sentinels, I wasn't afraid.

The cloaked man had been terrified, though. He said they'd come eventually and that I should be prepared to fight them off. Then he described what to expect.

"Teenagers, most of them, but *vicious*," he'd told me. "Parts of their bodies are rotten or missing. Some have algae in their veins and moss sprouting from their ears. But it's the claws you need to watch out for. They will tear your heart out before you know what's happening."

"Why are they always so young?"

"I don't really know. They just…are."

The cloaked man explained other things I can't remember, but I've never forgotten what he said about my enemies. The darkness got rid of our buildings, bridges, and beautiful landscapes. It left behind a group of children to keep the world in penumbra. Children who seek to kill the cloaked man and stop him from ever bringing back the light.

I must kill them first.

"Let me help you, sir. I can set you free."

The red sentinel is still hiding, but her high-pitched voice grows louder. She repeats the same words like the cotorras no longer flying in our rainforest. Like she's convinced I'll trust her if she's annoying enough. Spending seven uneventful months on this trail has done me great harm—I honestly didn't think an attack would happen now.

It makes sense, though. My last night is finally here. Of course one of these vicious creatures would suspect I'm at my most desperate. Of course she'd come.

But I can't fight her yet.

My enemy needs to step foot on the staircase. Only then will the vines loosen.

"Déjeme ayudarle, señor. I can set you free," the girl says.

I understand why she's hiding. She must be waiting for the cloaked man. She might think he's on his way to release me. Or maybe she's assessing me further—red sentinels are cautious and calculated. Unlike me, they don't have a specific post they watch over. They hunt down their prey and observe them from a safe distance.

But the rest of her strategy confuses me. Why is she promising to do the very thing that could get her killed? How does goading me help her finish off the cloaked man?

"Let me help you, sir. I can set you free."

"I'm fine, thanks," I say. "You can go now."

Maybe I shouldn't have said that. It could piss her off.

My wife has always hated my dryness. But it's like a reflex for me. If someone is annoying, I resort to dismissal. In the event that it escalates, I fall on insults and yelling. That's why I lost my job at the loan company—the job Tania begged her uncle to give me. She'd begged for almost a year until he caved. Whenever it had anything to do with me making money, she went to the moon and back...and I kept fucking it up.

I have to keep my shit together now. I can't move, much less attack the enemy, but if I lose my temper, it'll drain all rational thought out of me. The red sentinel might try to kill me faster if I react aggressively. I'm not risking it.

"Are you scared?" the girl asks.

This is the first time she's said something different. I don't know what it means for her next move, but if she's trying to taunt me, it won't work.

I stay quiet, unmoving.

"You're terrified," she says. "I can see it in your eyes. I can feel it in the air."

She's basically talking to herself. I'm not saying a word.

"I can smell regret in your blood, too."

I almost furrow my brow. These sentinels have abilities I don't quite understand, but can they really detect emotions?

She's just taunting you. Don't fall for it.

"What do you regret, Marcos?" she says.

I hold my breath as if she's dunked me underwater.

This girl knows my name.

How *the fuck* does she know my name? I didn't even tell the cloaked man. Why would I offer information he didn't ask for? Has this girl been studying me before tonight? It's possible she knew me from my life before darkness and ruin befell the world, but it's also not very likely. I don't remember teenagers coming into Emerald Title Loans. Most of my coworkers were twenty-somethings without children, too, and our clients made their payments alone.

There weren't kids in my neighborhood older than five. No babysitters young enough to sound like the sentinel, either. Then again, people always asked Tania her age and were shocked to discover we were only three years apart. Genetics worked their magic with her.

That still doesn't explain how the red sentinel knows who I am.

"Tell me," she says. "What do you regret?"

I want to ask how she knows my name. I want to ask if we've already met and I've simply forgotten all about it. That wouldn't surprise me. Before the darkness came, people, places, and events were erased from my memory all the time.

Like Tania's last birthday.

Our last anniversary.

I wouldn't despise forgetting things so much if it only meant losing parts of myself. But to constantly realize I was costing smiles, peace of mind, and trust in the woman I love most... That's far more painful than any thorn digging into my skin.

I want to ask the red sentinel what she means, though. Then again, I'd be giving in to her plan. I can't let such a dangerous stranger—a rotting monster—have the upper hand. It could cost my life, my freedom, and my wish from coming true.

I'm not leaving Bosque Seco without what I came for.

And I don't care what I must do to get it.

"Can you hear me?" she asks.

Don't play her games.

"The cloaked man lied. He can't give you what you want. No one can. He preyed on your desperation so he could continue hiding from us. Once your seven months of serving him are over, he won't cut those vines loose, Marcos. He's coming back to kill you."

I laugh.

Of course I shouldn't, but I fucking laugh. Of all the lies she could've said, she goes for the most obvious load of bullshit?

"You don't believe me?" she asks.

"Why would I believe a stranger? Someone who's *really* trying to kill me?"

I wish I could hit myself hard across the face. So much for not playing her games. This is probably making her entire week.

The girl is silent.

A light breeze caresses my torn, bloody skin. It stings. Makes me shiver. And as the thorns deepen just an inch, the red sentinel steps out from between the trees.

"Ugly things are often the most beautiful, too," Tania once told me in bed. We were watching a baking competition on TV.

Well, *she* was watching it. I had been absentmindedly scrolling through TikTok until I could fall asleep. Tania was always obsessed with baking shows, though. She didn't bake that much, so I wasn't sure where the obsession came from, but it was her thing.

"That literally makes no sense," I'd said. "You mean they're ugly on the inside?"

"No. I mean they're unpleasant in the eye of the beholder."

"So they're ugly to some and beautiful to others."

"Sí, mi amor. Así mismo es."

I had nodded in agreement then.

I can't find a reason to agree now. There's nothing beautiful about the red sentinel. *Nothing.* No one would ever consider her anything but a monster.

One that keeps getting closer to the stairs.

"He's coming to kill you, Marcos. But I can free you. If you let me, I can get you out."

The girl's jaw is missing.

I don't know how she can speak without the bottom half of her face. How she can easily walk with one foot bent to the left, as if it were broken and yanked sideways. She leans forward as if she's dragging a sack of bricks across the trail. Her black claws are empty, though. Her oversized hoodie is as red as her glowing eyes...the dried blood all across her forehead and crusting down her ears in a sharp line... It's like she's been brutally attacked and left for dead, yet still she breathes. Why would the end of the world give birth to such grossness?

"Stay back!" I shout. "I'm only warning you once!"

"They always say the same thing. But there's nothing for me to fear, is there? You don't know how to fight what you don't understand."

She's two feet away from the steps.

I can absolutely beat her in combat. I'm taller, stronger, and probably faster, too.

Then why does my heart pound like a hammer against stone? Why am I suddenly sweating so much? Why are my eyes glued to the red sentinel as if they're screaming at her to stop? This *is* why the cloaked man put me here—I must battle my way into making my wish come true. There's a difference between accepting your duty and actually wanting to honor it. I thought that distinction had been clearest when I took on this role. But it doesn't get any clearer than tonight.

"I'm not here for a fight anyway, Marcos. I'm here to set you free. But you have to let me."

"STAY BACK!"

"You shouldn't yell at your rescuer." The red sentinel stops an inch in front of the steps. She looks down and sighs. "Without me, you'll never see Tania again."

My mouth hangs open. Another chilly breeze digs the thorns deeper and deeper until I let out a groan, then a small scream. But none of it can hurt me as much as the red sentinel's last sentence. Words that shock me enough to silence every rustling leaf and rolling branch. Right now, my brain can't process anything in this godfor-saken forest other than the decaying, disgusting creature before me, and the confirmation that she knows my wife, too.

"How do you know our names? *How?*"

"This is why you're here. This is for her."

"How do you fucking know us?!"

The red sentinel tilts her head, as if she's studying me from a different angle, but her eyes remain on mine. "The cloaked man tells all men the same thing. He lies in the same ways. And all believe him. Humans do terrible things when they're desperate. If they also feel lonely, neglected, too. But do you know who's worse?"

I focus on her feet. She could sneak up on me at any second.

"Tell me, Marcos. Do you know who's worse?"

I don't answer.

"Narcissists," she says flatly.

I've heard that word all my life. It's what my grandmother called my mother and what my mother called me. Tania used it a few times, too. She was right. I wish I'd accepted it earlier.

I wish I hadn't put her through what I did.

But after tonight, none of it will matter. Everything will be erased. I don't have to face up to things that never happened. I won't pay for mistakes that neither remembers.

"*Now* you choose to care about her. *Now* you think of someone other than yourself. But a narcissist will always choose himself in the end, won't he? You'll never give Tania the love she deserves. These seven months have been in vain. You can't atone for breaking her heart."

"Shut the fuck up. I don't know who you are or why you're so concerned with the lives of total strangers, but you're not getting whatever it is you want from me!"

"The dark demands payment. We won't stop until it's been claimed."

Her words run laps in my head, battering my skull with each swift spin. She's making it sound like the darkness is…sentient. If it can desire, then it can think and act based on the very thing it covets. I thought it just destroyed all living things and birthed dead ones in return. That it unleashed its own version of hell as a result of consuming our heaven on Earth, our paradise.

"What do you mean, it demands payment?" I ask.

The girl lifts her right foot.

It dangles above the steps…only a few inches away from touching it…

"Wait! Tell me what you mean!"

"For centuries, humanity has used their lands as a playground, polluting and discarding resources to satisfy their greed. Many believed that's how the world would end. That we would be drowning in waste and fumes. Suffocating. But that's not how the darkness was born."

She slams her foot against the step.

The thorns pull away from my skin like daggers.

Fresh blood flies around me. I groan and gasp for air as the vines untie themselves from my cold, aching body. When the vines fall, I stand for the first time in seven long, long months.

I lunge at the red sentinel.

A burst of white light hits me between the eyes. The light disappears as quickly as it came.

And I'm not in the forest anymore.

"¿Marcos? Did you hear what I just fucking said?"

My wife is in our bedroom. The TV is paused on her favorite baking show; an elderly white woman is frosting a cake with a fudge-covered spatula. A storm rages in our quiet neighborhood. I can hear the howling winds despite our air conditioner's constant whirring.

"I'm talking to you! Don't act like you can't hear me!"

Tania is in her gray blazer and skirt set—the one I bought her when she got the job as an administrative assistant at our town's community college. Her brown eyes are red and weary from a long day. And she's holding my phone up to my face.

"Or do you want me to read her texts again?" Her voice cracks toward the end.

"What?" I look from her to the phone.

But I already know what I'll find there. We've already had this exact conversation.

I've been sent back to our last night together.

I try to turn my head. Lift a finger. Walk away.

I can't move.

I must endure the last night all over again.

"Who the fuck is Sara?" Tania says. "Why is she telling *my husband* that she's waiting for him at her place after work? Are you cheating on me?"

"No."

"Then why is she—"

"She's a client. One day she stopped by and I noticed her staring at me. I was supposed to handle her, but I passed the account to Nelson. She still comes to the office and tries to talk to me, but I ignore her creepy ass."

"How does she have your number?"

"I don't know! She's not right in the head, Tania. I think she's stalking me or some shit."

My wife lowers the phone. "And Jessica? Is she stalking you, too?"

"Who?"

"The woman in your DMs. That one's cleverer, isn't she? Contacting you on social media instead of your actual phone? You thought it would be easier to hide?" Tania tosses my phone on the bed. "You keep deleting messages from both chats. You're making it *look* like they're the ones reaching out, but you definitely said something back, didn't you? You're fucking them behind my back, aren't you? You're...you've been..."

Tania sits on the edge of our bed and breaks down.

"Please calm yourself, okay? You're going off on a tangent for no reason. If anything, *I* should be mad at *you* for stealing my phone and invading my privacy. How can you sit here and act hurt when *you* went through *my* stuff? How is that acceptable?"

"I had to! You've been so...distant."

"I'm exhausted from work. My head is in a million places all the time trying to pay bills and keep you happy. To keep your family from calling me…what is it? A useless bum? Is that what they said at Thanksgiving dinner? And at Christmas the year before?"

Tania opens her mouth.

"To top it all off," I keep talking, "you took my personal belongings without my consent or knowledge. But look at me right now. Am I having a meltdown? Am I blowing up? No, Tania. I'm patiently listening to you go on about something that doesn't matter."

"How can you say it doesn't matter? You're cheating on me…" she says through sobs. "You don't fucking love me…"

"Of course I do, mi amor. I don't know those women. That's why I deleted my messages. I kept insulting them and begging them to leave me the fuck alone. Then I figured I'd just ignore them, but they're still trying to reach me and—"

"Stop…lying…"

"I'm not lying! And I'm not cheating on you, Tania. Those bitches are crazy."

The winds are howling louder. I peek out the window, too distracted to focus on Tania's tears. Aluminum panels soar down the street like wild birds. They scrape pavement and car roofs alike. Those might be Don José's; he owns a garage near the curb. Once the panels are gone, something grainy and black joins the rain. It looks like…

Ashes.

"What the hell is going on outside?" I ask.

"Don't change the subject! See? This is what you do! You make everything about yourself and blame me for *everything*! Take accountability, Marcos! Own your shit! If you don't love me anymore, say it! And *leave me the fuck alone*!"

"Tania, there are literal ashes falling from the sky. Stop freaking out over psycho bitches you don't even know and help me figure out what's happening right now."

She doesn't speak. I don't hear the mattress moving, either.

I turn to her. "Tania, please. I'm—"

Black smoke and ashes are shooting into my wife's mouth. She aims her parted lips at the ceiling, where the darkness has punched a hole through cement.

"TANIA!"

I yell her name, but I'm otherwise frozen. I don't run to her or even call for help. I don't beg the darkness to leave my wife alone.

Her legs disintegrate first. Then her torso. Her neck. Her reddened eyes, wider now with unmistakable terror, vanish last. She cries while the rest of her body becomes ashes. And with one last panicked look at me, my wife falls into a pile on our bedroom floor.

"TANIA!" I yell again.

The house's ceiling flies away. I'm soaked in rainwater, shaking from the cold, watching my wife's ashes blend into the furious winds. Soon the darkness shrouds every nook and cranny. I can't see my way through the place where I once slept next to Tania.

I can't see a way out of this world ever again.

Then the white light returns.

My house, my life before the end, disappears.

The forest greets me once more…along with a sunrise.

My duty as sentinel is over.

"I told you I'd set you free."

The red sentinel steps back.

Maybe she already knew I'd fall to my knees. That she'd need to give me space to cough out spittle after spittle, nauseated from the sudden change in scenery. How did she transport me back in time? Or did she mind fuck me to see my last memory with Tania?

"The dark demands payment. Now it's time to collect."

"No! The sun is up! I don't know what the fuck you want from me, but you can't have it! The cloaked man has to grant my wish! I did what he asked!"

The girl nods. "And what *is* your wish?"

"I want my wife!" I'm standing again, ignoring my shaking knees and wobbly balance.

"Why, Marcos? What's so precious about your wife?"

I can't believe I'm crying. Snot runs down my nose and chin; I'm sobbing just as hard as Tania was on our bed. Maybe it's the toll of spending so much time without her in such terrible conditions. Maybe it's the guilt from losing her. Of being reckless with her heart, her loyalty. I *was* cheating on her with those two women. I was treating her like shit only to watch her turn into ashes—the last person who deserved what she got.

The days after she died... I wouldn't wish them on anyone. All I could do was *run*—from the encroaching darkness, more ashes flying overhead and pelting everything like bullets, from a past I so desperately wished I could change. I don't know how many days I spent running, hoping for the light to come back, mourning a love that I never earned. Then I stepped into El Bosque Seco, all cried out and breathless, and accepted my fate.

"Everything," I whisper. "I always knew it, but...but I...didn't appreciate it."

"So you did love her?"

"I *do* love her. And I want her back. The cloaked man will give her back to me."

"Do you repent?" the girl's voice changes. It somehow grows deeper.

"Yes."

"Do you want your wife to be happy?"

"Yes."

Her voice is different now. She sounds like...like...

The cloaked man stands where the red sentinel once was. His black hood covers his face—a face I've never seen. He holds his gloved hands against his chest, breathing slowly.

"Your service is complete. Thank you, Marcos," he says.

Then he takes off his hood.

"But the only wish I can grant is mine," she says.

Tania.

She's the stranger in the cloak and hood.

The rotting red sentinel hiding in the trees.

The woman grinning as vines coil around my throat.

I claw at the thorns sinking into my neck…choking…trying to scream… The vines yank me to the dead soil and gravel, squeezing tighter…tighter…

"How…you…" is all I can push out.

Tania towers over my dying body, still grinning.

"Stop…" I keep clawing, clawing, clawing, but the vines never loosen.

"The world lost its light because of greedy souls like yours," says Tania. "It didn't go down in flames like wise academics and environmentalists said it would. Our darkness came from the cold hearts of narcissists first, of cheats and thieves, then spread out into the air and earth around us."

Her voice is crisp, clear, yet sounds so far away. I'm losing too much oxygen too quickly. But still I breathe heavily, still struggle against these constricting vines, as the love I never earned delights in my pain.

"*Tania…*"

She nods. "I'm happy you remember me. Those who've suffered because of dark hearts are finally being avenged, and memory is one of our greatest weapons. Most of the ashed won't come back—they have nothing to rectify. What's left of this world fears the red senti-nels. *Children.* Those who were meant to be our future. Uncorrupted, righteous, and vocal. Now they're allies to the ones the darkness has spat back out." Tania stands taller, a queen looking down at a worthless peasant. "The tormented can't leave this Earth until we get our revenge. That's the darkness's gift to us. And we won't go alone."

She speaks more, but I can't hear it... I can't understand... Everything is ringing...buzzing...bleeding...turning black...

Until I can't breathe anymore.

EL GRITO DE LA ONDA

Everything changed right around the time the oil started leaking again. Those who were weathered enough and had been in Summerland during the '69 oil spill warned tourists and locals alike. The teenagers, who were too young to be scared, secretly prayed that the Becker wellhead had reawakened off the coast. And then, that day, the oil bubbled and boiled and bled from the depths. Before anyone could ask questions or study the water, it had disappeared.

Just like she did.

Once your mother left, you started licking sea salt off your lips. Your tongue would poke out, just a bit, and it wasn't necessarily a choice. It was instinct, as simple as scrunching up your eyes when the sun rose or watching your breath take shape in the morning air.

The salt was made of pebbles and rocks and stones and bones that crunched lightly under your back molars. You swallowed quickly so you wouldn't feel things you didn't quite understand.

You would taste the sea until your pink skin cracked and bled.

After, your tongue had a waxy film of grime that made you think of a washed-up seagull your dad found on the beach, coated in something dark and familiar. Even though he steered you away, you heard him on the phone later whispering to a colleague, *the spill's happening again.* You woke up that night screaming, because even though he tried, your dreams were filled with the pitch-black ink slithering into the bird's white eye.

Still, the salt was everything you needed until your dad snapped at you.

"Stop licking your lips or they'll chap."

You smoothed on some lip balm from the bottom of the only purse your mother ever bought you, understanding at that moment that he would never have a problem covering up the taste of the sea.

You live with your dad in a bedroom he rents from Mr. and Mrs. Padilla two blocks away from Loon Point Beach. He refused to move away after the accident because Summerland was the only place he'd ever truly known. You think maybe it was the only place where no one would ask questions.

When you were nine, he told you he picked the house on Santa Claus Lane because it would make it easier for the red-suited man to find you at Christmas. Even then, you knew it was best not to mention that some boys from school had told everyone the Santa secret. And that you knew this spot was the cheapest he could find even while adjuncting at Santa Barbara City College and working with the local ecologists to make sure the wells stayed plugged. No one wants to think about what'll happen if they loosen and leak.

And so you grew up and didn't say anything as the walls seemed to close in on you. The comforter, a muted cross between aqua and lime green, screamed threadbare at you. The pillows got lumpier—in an old way, not a comfortable way. The rabbit ears attached to the TV received only one channel broadcasting dubbed C-list action movies. The only break from staring at a wall every day was when you helped Mr. Padilla read invoices from his medical insurance as he ignored his bad eyesight. His wife hid his car keys, but you always told him where they were hidden. You had to. Mr. Padilla was the only one who would teach you Spanish; your father winced every time her language slipped off your tongue.

The rest of the house was small and stifling. The fridge was always packed with leftovers and the curdled milk smell wouldn't leave, no matter how much baking soda you opened. You'd never seen the futon for visitors actually used; it was crowded into the living room as an afterthought, almost poking into the kitchen. The Padillas didn't have many photos around the house, and you couldn't say one way or another if they had any family. But Mrs. Padilla waited until you were up each Sunday so you could help her make posole. And Mr. Padilla slipped a $2 bill under your door on your birthday each year because they were good luck. So maybe it didn't matter who their blood relatives were.

The house held you and your dad and the Padillas, and for a while, it was enough. For a while, you could forget about the salt and nightmares of drowning in black sludge and bury yourself in the threadbare comforter. But soon, the claustrophobic house stopped being just another part of childhood. You felt like the wool blankets were going to suffocate you and then you'd forget you were ever there. So when your friends escaped to college at eighteen, you convinced Mr. Padilla to let you fix up the old beach cruiser with a busted basket and missing bell he had in the garage, and you got a job at the Beach Grill.

The restaurant is quiet. You can count on foot traffic at 11 a.m. and then around 6 p.m., depending on how crowded Pacific Coast Highway is. Summerland is a pass-through town, in between Los Angeles and San Francisco. People in the backseat of some tech genius's Tesla could blink and not notice your town as they fly by on the highway. There are only a few reasons to stop in Summerland—to gas up or take an Instagram shot of the "quaint small town with SoCal vibes," as some trashy travel magazine said. There's no other reason to be here unless you're stuck and never left.

"Are you ready to order?" you say, making your way to a table occupied by a woman with a Birkin bag as big as the hat she wears.

"I'll take the veggie burger and unsweetened tea," she says, quickly. "Oh, and can you make sure it comes without the red onion, pickles, or cheese? No sauce and lettuce wrapped, please."

"All that for the tea?"

She stares blankly at you, obviously not getting your joke.

"Is that all, ma'am?" you say, moving on.

"Oh, yes, is that all non-GMO?"

"Yep, right there on the menu. That burger and all of our fries are."

"Perfect."

You hesitate.

Her face is too smooth to be natural. But her eyes are kind. Inviting. You want to ask her about her life. About what she does. If she knows what it feels like to want to escape from her own skin.

But she looks back down at her phone, ignoring both you and the expanse of the Pacific to her left.

And you move away, choking down your questions.

After you bring her the food and she pays (no tip, of course), the rest of the afternoon happens as it always does. Tourists after tourists, too preoccupied with where they're going or coming from, shovel organic greens and non-dairy milkshakes into their mouths. They shout at their toddlers and feed their lapdogs the scraps they won't eat and push through life without looking at the view. They move as if they're already back on the freeway, yelling out the open window at a slow driver in front of them.

Another shift wraps, and you pause near the wall of yellow beach umbrellas farthest away from the kitchen. The marine layer never evaporated, so you know the sunset will be more vibrant than usual. You watch the horizon as the sun bleeds out purple and orange, melding until the water joins the sky. And then you see it.

A splash off the coast.

So quick you almost missed it, but the water is still rippling as you squint. And then the tail flips up out of the water, breaching, and it holds, hovering, hesitating for a second before diving back under. But it doesn't look like the whales you normally see this time of year migrating; it's enormous and way too slender. And it was black and shiny, like an oil slick. But it's there and gone, so fast you know it's not an oil spout; a trick of the light, not an impending environmental disaster. You feel a hum in your blood and have the thought to fling yourself off the hillside and swim after it. It's a good fifty feet to the ocean, but the urge is almost too strong.

Almost.

"What are you looking at?"

You spin around, locking eyes with your dad as he twirls the shark tooth on his car keys in his hand. The edge of the tooth catches on the worn wedding ring he refuses to take off.

"I thought I saw a whale in the water. But the whales haven't come this close to the shore since the spill?"

His keys fall silent as you continue.

"And it wasn't the normal gray color," you say.

"Must've been a trick of the sun or something," he says, voice steady. "Maybe the whale got separated from its pod."

He waves for you to follow him to the side of the grill, and he walks toward the old white VW bug with the hazards thrown on. As you turn away from the ocean, you want to tell him that the whale wasn't lost. It was lonely.

But then again, he wouldn't understand.

———————————————

Weeks pass and you keep seeing movement in the water. But every time you mention it to the baristas at the coffee shop or to Mr. Irwin when he delivers the Padillas' mail, it's the same: it's too early for the whale migration. You know the migration won't pass this way for another couple of months. But you also know that what you're seeing is real. The ripples are there, every morning and every night. There's something out there.

There's something calling to you.

Your dad gives you tasks that take you away from Summerland. You can't help but wonder if he watches the water when you aren't looking. He makes you go inland a couple of times, to Ojai for random errands: getting some plywood for shelves Mrs. Padilla wants your father's help building, or finding some tea leaves from a coffee shop he used to go to when he first moved out this way. You almost ask if he used to go with Mom, but like always, you don't. Flipping to the middle of the notebook you started when you were younger and wanted to be prepared in case your Dad ever opened up about her, you jot chamomile tea leaves down. You borrow his car keys and drive.

The farther away you get from the 101, away from the wind and the screams of the gulls, nausea takes over. It's happened before, the need to expel, but never this badly. Once you reach Ojai, you dart into the shop, grab the bag of tea and go back to clutching the wheel. You pretend you don't notice your hands shaking or the fact that they get steadier once you leave the trees of the Los Padres Forest behind. The second you see the deep blue water your heart rate evens out. You see the wave of the black tail and all tension leaves your body.

You pass home and keep going, pulling off to the side near Loon Point. You park the car in a spot most of the local kids know, without the tourists or the annoying lifeguards who blast trashy music all day. You never understood why they would prefer listening to that instead of the breaking of the waves. Locking the car, you make your way down to the tideline.

Dad never takes you down to the beach anymore. Even though you are right here, he says being inside with the A/C and television is so much better than sweat and sand. But when you were young, you remember lying on a picnic blanket with your mother, both looking out at the waves. She said that if you listened to the ocean long enough, each crash whispered something special. Each one was a note, long or short, low or high, and the more you listened, the more you understood the song. When you shared that memory with him, he stared at you blankly and said the waves sounded the same to him.

You stare out at the horizon and the wind whips up a sharp shard of seashell. It cuts your cheek and you wince. As you reach up to wipe away the blood, you realize it has already clotted a bit on your face. On your fingers, it's surprisingly dark, almost black. You bend down to rinse it off in the surf. The moment your hand touches the surface, you drop to your knees. It's as if every bone in your body has disappeared and you're floating on top of the water. Nothing but seafoam and a longing for something you can't name. You've never felt this, and it's terrifying, but also, somehow, it's right.

You gain your bones back and run to the car, but it takes you hours to fall asleep that night.

In the darkness, you're still floating.

You quit your job. You don't tell your dad, just say a friend from school needs you to help babysit his younger brothers. He doesn't ask who it is. You don't tell him the only friends you had escaped months ago.

Instead, you take your cruiser and head to the shore. Hiding in an alcove by the cliffside, you stare out at the horizon and wait. Right when you start to get faint from not eating or drinking anything that day, the tail pops up and then sinks into the depths. The fishing boats keep their distance, but sometimes you swear they point to the whale. They never go after it or around it, so maybe they don't actually notice. But maybe if they saw the whale, you wouldn't feel so alone. Maybe if they said something, your dad would believe you and you could watch the ripples together. Maybe it would all make sense.

Right as you stand up, the tide rushes in all at once, each crash of surf chasing after each other to get to you. It covers your feet, winding up your ankles and splashing up the back of your thighs. Pins and needles push, and you look down, irrationally afraid for a second that your lower extremities are gone. They aren't, but as the tide ebbs out, there are pieces of red sea glass speckled with oil covering your feet. And the biggest shark tooth you've ever seen. Black and shiny.

It's perfectly positioned in a triangle between your arches, and it looks as if your feet are melded to it. You pick up the tooth and stick it in your bag. You start to walk away but go back for the sea glass, which you scoop up, not brushing off the sand that sticks to it. The ocean ripples, closer than before.

You pedal home, but as you pull up in front of the house with the wind chime on the porch, you feel nothing. Nothing but a need to get back to the shore.

Your Dad cooks salmon that night. As you tear into the pink flesh, you ask if Mom liked fish. His cutlery clatters and he leaves the room without a word. Mrs. Padilla follows him, and then it's just you and Mr. Padilla.

"You know not to bring her up," he says, spearing a broccoli head.

"I don't know why, though!" you say. "He won't tell me anything! Everyone in this town pretends she didn't exist, and I'm tired of it, because I'm old enough to hear what happened. You all know what happened to her and no one will tell me."

A fleck of mashed potatoes catches in Mr. Padilla's ragged beard, but you ignore it to be polite.

"She disappeared the day before the oil spill," he says quietly, refusing to look up at you. "Maria and I were watching you, because your parents were celebrating their anniversary and your father was able to borrow a boat from one of his coworkers. He didn't tell me much, but apparently, your mother fell."

You open your mouth to ask more questions, but your father's voice behind you cuts you off. You turn to see him in the doorway, Mrs. Padilla shoving him into the room. He stumbles but recovers quickly.

"One moment we were drinking on the deck and the next she was gone," your dad says, voice wavering. "The last thing I saw was her face. It was blanched, and as she went under the waves, I could see her staring up at me. I dove in after her, of course, but it was so dark. I've never seen the oil like that before. It all happened so fast, and I couldn't see anything. And I lost her."

Then, he starts crying. Ugly, heaving sobs that fill the room. You know you should say something, go over to him and make amends. You should rest your head on his shoulder, because he's still much taller than you even though you're almost grown. You should cry with him and bond to bridge the gap you've felt since she disappeared.

But instead, you pick up your knife and stab into the fish. You saw back and forth, and he continues wailing. Your eyes are completely dry.

Your face starts to peel, raw and sunkissed. Still, your dad doesn't mention it. Since that night at dinner, he's barely talked at all. You stop trying to hide the damp curls and broken shells in your purse. More red sea glass and tar sweep up on the beach. The whispers of the residents of Summerland are getting louder, and unease is heavy in the salt air.

It gets harder and harder to go home. You stay out after sunset most days. It's close to midnight and Cassiopeia is strong in the sky, but you don't leave. You find some driftwood and start a small fire to warm yourself, ignoring the ash in the air. You stay at the water's edge as the moon seeps silver into the waves. You don't have to look far past where the horizon is. The creature breaches, right in front of you, no more than thirty feet from the tideline.

Too close to shore.

The fire explodes: ash and smoke and gray quiver in the air and you cough, eyes watering and skin burning.

You register the pain of the fire on your skin. Register your skin bubbling. Hear a scream in the distance.

But in that split moment, before the dark takes over and you pass out, you see its eyes in the surf. Eyes much too large to belong to a whale. Too human. They hold your gaze until you slip into unconsciousness.

You barely register they are the same shade of dark brown as your own.

The beeping is the first thing you hear. You cringe at the heart rate monitor above the hospital bed. Your arms are bandaged in gauze, and the pain is dull but constant, like sandpaper rubbed on freshly shaved skin. Your father's hand grips yours tightly.

Too tightly.

You squeeze his hand before removing your fingers, slipping them under the edge of the blanket.

"The sergeant found you down by the cove on her rounds," your dad says. "She saw the bonfire explode and freaked out, so she brought you to urgent care and then called me. I came as soon as I could, kid."

You stay silent, ignoring the room closing in on you, fighting the urge to rip off the bandages and submerge them in saltwater.

"What were you doing at the beach that late?" he asks, quietly, as if he doesn't want the answer.

Somehow, you know he already knows. But saying it out loud is important to you. If the words are said, maybe he will finally have to listen.

"It was calling me," you say, hand clenching underneath the blanket.

"What was?" he asked, voice pitching slightly.

"The ripple."

His face turns white, blanched as a dried-up starfish.

"What did you say?"

You shrink in on yourself, not used to the hard edge to his voice. You can tell he's mad—more upset than you've ever heard before.

"I've been trying to tell you. When I look at the ocean I—"

"Why would you say that?" he bites out, cutting you off abruptly. "How did you know?"

"Know what?" you ask, trying to keep your voice even and ignore your heart rate beeping faster.

"Are you trying to hurt me? After I told you what happened? Are you really that pissed?"

"Dad, what are you talking about?" you say, finally matching his harsh tone.

An alarm beeps, and his gaze snaps up to the monitor, which gives away how tense it is in the room. He grabs a glass of lukewarm water on the table left by the nurse and gulps down half of it before offering it to you. He lightly wipes a bead of sweat off your forehead as you drink.

"I lied when you asked me about your mother," he says quietly.

You don't say anything; the silence pushes him on.

"I had gone below deck that night because we got in a fight," he says, looking at the wedding ring on his hand you've never seen him take off. "She was talking about moving to Catalina Island, and I didn't want to leave Summerland. She'd just been acting so different. Always down by the water. Swimming and swimming and swimming for hours. She said she wanted more, more than what I could give her or more than we had in town. I didn't take it well, and it got out of hand. Before I said something I couldn't take back, I grabbed a bottle of champagne and went below. The last thing I heard from her was: 'La onda.' I looked it up later, and it means the ripple. But I didn't turn around. I drank the whole bottle, crawled into bed and passed out. I expected her to be there next to me in the morning, curled in the blankets, but she wasn't. And when I went above deck, oil was everywhere in the water and she was nowhere to be found."

He pauses and fishes his keys out of his pocket.

"All I found was her lucky shark tooth on the deck," he says, holding up the shark tooth so you can see it. "I told everyone she drowned, and I couldn't save her. It was easier to say that I tried instead of the fact that I was passed out drunk when she needed me most."

"So, you lied to everyone?" you say. "Including me? Why wouldn't you tell me?"

"I didn't help her. And she's dead. I was too busy being bitter and angry, and I couldn't tell you that I lost her. Not when it's all my fault."

You're about to yell at him, explode, or push the journal full of questions you keep about her in your purse toward him. You want him to fess up to it, the fact that he's the one that did this to you. But he winces, and you see that he's clutched the shark tooth so tightly it's pierced his skin.

Blood trickles down his fingers and falls to the floor, dripping in time with your heart rate. It's bright red and thin. You know that if the tooth pierced your skin, it would well up differently — black and thick like tar. At the sound of the heartbeat, you remember him cuddling you when the heat went out and he couldn't afford to fix it. Not forcing you to eat brussels sprouts because he hated them too. And both of you laughing at *Happy Days* reruns on TV until you snorted. The blank look in his eyes every time you asked him a question about her.

In that moment, you realize it's him. He's the one who's lost, not her.

"It was an accident, Dad," you say. "I know it was an accident. It's going to be okay."

"Yeah," he says, avoiding his mistakes. "I'm gonna go check with the nurse and see what else I can do to help. You could've been seriously hurt, so you need to be careful. No more sneaking down to the ocean."

He opens the door but turns back around and stares at your arms. "I can't lose you too."

He's out in the hallway before you can say anything. As the door clicks shut, you feel it. That he's compartmentalizing. He's blocking it all out.

Somehow you know it's what he did that day. He blocked out how the oil bubbled. How quickly it disappeared. What he saw swimming under the boat. How he chalked it up to him still being drunk. Like he always does, he's moving on, blocking it all out in favor of the future.

You close your eyes to fall asleep, but all you can see are eyes raised up above the waves. And you know in your bones that you lied. It wasn't an accident. She didn't fall.

She dove in.

As the months pass, Summerland comes alive. Tourists come in from Carpinteria and linger, booking whale watching tours for the perfect picture to post. The tour guides refuse to tell them that they won't see any whales— not for years now. They crawl around the cliffs and the beach grill and the little house you live in on Santa Claus Lane. Tourist season is a familiar nuisance, and your dad relaxes. He's happier, money coming into the town from the families who tip well when locals spin tales of oil spills and ecodisasters and shy whales.

You're left with scars up and down your forearms, wisps that look like waves if the light strikes just right against your dark skin. Dad keeps trying to push scar gel on you, but you like the way they look, a reminder of that night.

You feel the call but try to ignore it until you have time to answer it. Dad is at the college interviewing for a full-time position, and the Padillas are at a winery with friends from church. So, you grab your dad's keys and drive back to the cove, to your spot. It's almost dusk, and you pause to take in the sky, such a deep pink it's almost red.

Taking the only thing your mother left behind, you shove it in your pocket and walk into the surf fully clothed. You don't know what you're doing exactly, but it's a necessity. Like licking salt off your lips.

An instinct.

The water rushes to fill in around you, swirling as you wade past your hips. It whispers secrets as soon as you submerge. It whispers the truth. The ripple is just the start of the call.

Her call.

Oil slicks appear on the top of the water, but you aren't afraid. You realize she dove in, sacrificed herself back to the water to stop the spills. She knew you'd be safe at the water's edge, and you'd answer her call one way when you took the time to listen. Your mother has grown, free to fill the waters she calls home.

She has grown outside of the small town that is all you have ever known.

You can't see her yet, but the call places an image in your mind: her tail as large as a whale's but lean as a stingray. Her spine is ridged conch shell exposed, and starfish cling in the spaces between her ribs. She's coated in tar from the waist up, oil dripping onto where the skin becomes scales. Her eyes stare unblinking at you, pupils blown dark as your own red blood. And when she smiles, her teeth aren't human, but shark teeth. She's become tar and salt and longing. She's massive and terrifying and yours.

Water licks through your shirt until you're neck-deep. She's humming, tugging at that something deep in your bones that knows the depths are home.

On instinct, you know if you dive under the surf and let the water breach your lungs, you'll grow. Bigger than a boat or a whale or the house that buries you. Your legs would merge, and your teeth would sharpen. And you'd be free, because the ocean doesn't have walls to keep you in. You would swim with the one who taught you to sing the notes of the sea.

The call is a song.

But as you wait on the surface, treading water so kelp kisses your toes, you think of the Padillas and pozole and the whispers of staticky TV. You think of riding your beach cruiser down PCH, wind in your hair. You think of your father and the snorting laugh you share. You think of being grounded, planted in the place that made you. You think of being human.

You reach into your pocket.

You yearn to taste the sea, to be seafoam and oil.

You look back toward shore, toward Summerland.

You grip her now oil-covered shark tooth and float.

WE WERE MEANT TO BE BURIED

RJ JOSEPH

We had not thought about what the stately white building had been in its past—we only knew what it was to us in its present. Record searches provided no clues as to who owned it or who had ever inhabited it. By the time I was a teenager, I only knew it had always been our respite. Whatever its purpose had been, it likely served well, with the large, spacious rooms with high ceilings, empty save for the foliage that had grown up and throughout its walls and floors. Its stone showed few cracks, and yet the plants grew inside, draping the house in a green only interrupted by the frequent appearance of colorful flowers. Outside the building, the vegetation grew in unbridled abundance, vining and intertwining with fixtures in the yard, a lush green space in the midst of the neverending, cold and unforgiving concrete found in our inner-city neighborhood.

"I was never happier than when your Paw Paw proposed to me there on the side of that great big, beautiful building," my Big Mama would often tell me, her eyes misting over at the memory. "The grass was so tall and green, and it was the middle of November. Imagine that!"

I nodded solemnly, every time she told the story. I didn't have to imagine how beautiful the plants were, because they remained so throughout the passing years. I had hoped to get my own proposal there, one day when I was older. It didn't seem that was part of my destiny, and it made me sad.

The decadent gardens on the sides, back, and throughout the building stayed green year-round, partially due to the perpetual summer of Houston. The other parts of their maintenance were enmeshed in the secrets of their origin. We never saw anyone tending the garden, watering the flowers—definitely not repairing the building that hosted it all.

Yet she stood, our silent, regal lady, maintaining dignity even in her disrepair and crumbling state. Flowers and plants grew through the cracks in the façade, beckoning us to enjoy their beauty. It was easy to imagine lives playing out in the spacious rooms, what could have been a grand parlor on one end of the first floor and perhaps a sitting room festooned in the glory of bluebonnets and ivy. The large, airy area with meticulously carved out spaces was reminiscent of a kitchen, or eating area, complete with a grown-over window, now a portal to magnolia trees blocking part of the sun, creating an ethereal flow of dim sunlight.

We always heeded the call. Our families ran through the yards, playing out the important moments of our lives underneath those old shade trees. We gingerly took strolls through the building. I attended numerous impromptu picnics on the lawn. But only in the daylight hours. We respected the old girl too much to disturb her after nightfall. Our community appreciated what she did for us just by existing and flourishing, so we wanted her to rest peacefully at every sunset.

The night travelers would often hear noises coming from Our Lady—hushed movement, whispered sighs. We believed she was talking in her sleep, dreaming of her long life with us, the majestic witness of more of our lives and relaxation.

Rest and provide are what she did.

Until the day the demolition crew showed up.

We watched them all drive in with their big trucks, making more noise than we ever did. We were used to the constant racket of the construction part of these developments, which had already permeated our day-to-day routines with the onslaught of new townhomes all throughout our space. Our neighborhood had been overrun with the teams and their loud equipment, erasing decades of history in our older homes and apartment buildings.

They tore down the old and built up the new in record times—the new being financially inaccessible to those of us whose families had been in the neighborhood from its origins. Just like none of us could afford the fancy new digs, we also couldn't afford the things that came along with them: increased foot traffic everywhere, increased police presence maintaining the newly implemented boundaries between them and the older houses and apartments we all lived in. And the increasing tax rates.

That's where the only official park in our vicinity went. The city sold it to developers, and after a few months, it magically went from a small patch of struggling grass and plants to a massively tall structure holding dozens of new invaders to our home. It made sense—to them, it seemed we never used the park. We really didn't use it much. Being there didn't allow us the space and welcome Our Lady did. And it never felt like the home the stately white building provided for us.

It still didn't mean it should have been turned into pricey, multi-family residences we couldn't access in any way.

We never thought of the newcomers as transplants within our community because they didn't want to live with us or intertwine their lives with longstanding traditions we had painstakingly built. They wanted our space to build their own new community and traditions. We and ours were to be buried and pushed out—old houses, old apartments, old people, old ways—to make way for new houses, no apartments, new people, new ways.

All the newness and replacements needed a new drugstore, apparently. And the new drugstore meant tearing down our stately old lady and her welcoming gardens.

The part we weren't used to was the yellow tape they put up all around Our Lady and her gardens, blocking us out of the one respite we relied on to always be there for us.

"Get away from here!" one of the workmen yelled when a group of us approached to see what was happening. "We're starting demolition here, and it ain't safe."

They didn't put up the sign announcing the new drugstore until a week later. Our elders shook their heads.

"We all on county insurance. That drugstore won't do us no good."

"You know who that store really is for." They collectively sucked their teeth and rolled their eyes towards the brand new, half million-dollar townhomes encroaching on our already tiny, old neighborhood at an alarming pace.

We children had other concerns. Where would we play outside? The small, older homes and tenements dotting our community had courtyards made of concrete or small yards with family gardens and not much space for leisure. No benches. No foliage. Barely any plant life at all.

Never any playground equipment, either. Not that our beloved garden had playthings. She didn't need them. She and her yard were playthings enough for us. Once they were gone, we'd have nothing. The only place we could play where there were trees and flowers was in and around our beloved lady, the building we were told would be torn down for something that wouldn't benefit us.

So, what were we going to do?

Demolition began and we still had no answers. We sadly watched as parts of one of Our Lady's walls was crushed, tumbling down into the yard with what sounded like screams as she succumbed. Sadness hung over the neighborhood as heavy as a cloak, and we wandered around aimlessly, looking for other things to do with our time.

I took to taking long walks around and around the same few blocks that made up our space, lost in the memories I already had of Our Lady in my short lifetime—reveries of new beginnings. The day after the demo started, I stumbled over a pile of white stones trimmed in green patches of sprouting plants. I examined the stone and smiled as its chalky whiteness reminded me of Our Lady. I briefly fantasized about new plants growing in the neighborhood. My smile faded when I saw that the piles dotted the areas surrounding the townhomes.

The maintenance crews will probably come along and tear these down, too. I kept walking. Those folks wouldn't want them there any more than they wanted Our Lady there. Any more than they wanted us there.

The influx of invaders wasn't completely terrible for us. A handful of our residents found employment with them, around their homes, mostly as service workers. When I was around fourteen years old, I had been lucky enough to meet the acquaintance of Mrs. Bexley, a nice, white-haired older woman who lived in one of the new homes and needed help with general errands.

I mostly picked up groceries for her and made post office runs to take her scant packages to mail off to her pen pals. Sometimes she needed help moving all her heavy plants inside her townhome when we were under hurricane and tropical storm warnings, which was quite often.

She paid me with bills too large for a child to carry around— especially a Black adolescent in the inner city—and always excused her overpayments by saying, "I just don't have anything smaller. Is this okay?"

"Yes, ma'am," I always answered. Who could disagree with an old lady with twinkles in her eyes like she was committing the biggest mischief ever by even having a little Black girl inside her posh home—especially when she was?

I was happy a kind soul had survived the times from well before I was born and was allowed to continue thriving and living and bucking the system, even as my favorite relic was being destroyed. The white stone piles grew in number, and I prayed the dust from Our Lady was being blown around the neighborhood and settling into new spots that would grow and grow and grow. It was a child's fantasy, I knew, but I was a child. And the piles did grow. I had no other explanation for where they came from or how they thrived, and magical wishing seemed plausible enough to me.

One of the last things I did for Mrs. Bexley at the end of that summer was help her put poison out in her small, paved courtyard. She told me she heard rats, and she was scared of them getting into her home. I wanted to tell her if there were rats, they probably wouldn't bother her.

We lived with wood rats intermittently taking up residence in our attic during the colder months, and they never came out where we could see them. We didn't encourage them, but we didn't bother them, either. They skittered a bit and then left for places with more food available than we ever had.

It troubled me immensely to think of the brave and kind Mrs. Bexley being afraid of anything. It also bothered me to think of any potential rats being killed by poison. I hoped all would remain safe as I haphazardly scattered the pellets, mostly in the corners of the pavement, away from her plants.

The following week, I caught sight of others in the townhomes also putting out poison. Those ugly, blocky black boxes that baited small mammals to kill them in outside areas sprang up throughout the newer parts of the neighborhood. Bottles of weed killer appeared on the tiny patios. Residents pulled at plants that would reappear, stronger, the next day. Fragmented whispers trailed behind me, speaking about rats and pestilence in spaces where they weren't supposed to be.

"These pests should stay in those old houses where they must have come from in the first place." When they would see me, their whispers went silent, scowls on their faces as they looked for a place to pin their frustrations.

It baffled me. I didn't understand how people so eager to displace others by tearing down and replacing existing structures couldn't comprehend how they were also displacing the creatures that naturally lived in these areas, which would then search for new places to live.

The reports of the sudden neighborhood rat infestations were limited to the new townhomes and storefronts. We talked about it in the old areas. But we never saw them. Or heard them, unless it was nighttime, and we passed the demolition site of our old stately lady. As they tore more of her down, the clamor over infestations grew louder.

Where there had at first been light skittering noises heard in the darkness when we left her to rest, there was increased activity after the demolition started. None of us saw what made the noises. We never disrespected her and went searching for the source, either. Our hesitance wasn't due to the signs that promised legal punishment for anyone who trespassed on the site.

She was even more displeased than we were by the true trespassers, and we only wanted to stay out of her way.

I checked in with Mrs. Bexley early one morning, a week after we had placed the poison. I arrived at her townhome before the sun rose and entered to her weakly uttered permission to come inside.

The usually robust woman was slouched on her couch, pale. Her usually fresh smelling home smelled funny that day. I thought of the mothballs my grandmother used to have in her closets, but that smell wasn't quite right. There was just—oldness—in the air I couldn't describe any other way.

She began to cough and muttered between bouts, rambling about white rats and apologies.

I heard rustling in the walls.

"Do you need me to call someone for you?"

"My son…coming."

I wanted to help her, but I didn't know how. Tears ran down my face. I was sad. She had been kind to me and meant no harm. Her only misdeed had been to purchase a home that upset the natural order of our community. I was also afraid—I didn't want the rescuers to think I had hurt her when they came barreling through the door, ready to place blame where there was none.

"Can I get you some water while we wait for him?"

Loud coughing answered and she slumped further into her sofa. I ran to the kitchen and opened the cabinets to find a glass. Louder rustling greeted me from the lower cabinets. I avoided them.

I opened one of the upper doors and instead of glasses, I found dozens of huge white rats. Larger than my forearms, with bright green eyes that matched the vibrant greens in Our Lady's yard, they leapt out of the open door, avoiding me completely as I screamed. The other cabinets on the wall slammed open and more rodents spilled out, swarming the kitchen like a wave of moving snow. It was the only other prevalent, vast whiteness I had ever seen, even if only on television.

They avoided my legs in an intricate dance, leaving the space around my feet open. Stunned, I watched their movement, hypnotized by the orchestration. Mrs. Bexley's weak gargle brought me out of my trance, and I ran back to the living room.

She lay on the floor, on top of a pile of the white stones I recognized from my neighborhood walks, her sofa gone. The rats chewed and nibbled, the white substance reminiscent of alabaster coming from all their orifices — eyes, mouths, bottoms, ears, noses — in puffs of dust. The stones had replaced every bit of high-end furniture that used to occupy the room.

They undulated over Mrs. Bexley. As her corpse disappeared underneath their onslaught, greenery appeared in the offal they produced in their wake. Bright plants, growing ever larger as soon as they were spawned. The tears flowed freely down my cheeks as I said a prayer for her soul.

I heard groaning coming from the walls, as large, splintered cracks began to appear in the sheetrock. Where the openings were large enough, more white rats poured through, eating at the wood and metal framing, leaving white stones behind.

I ran from the townhome, recognizing even more stone structures appearing as the sun rose. Greenery dotted the stones, vining and intertwining with each other. Knowing where the new plants originated made me run faster, even as my mind wondered how far the greenspaces would expand.

My mother was waiting at the door for me. As she rushed me inside, I noticed various other parents in our neighborhood also waiting. The white rats were nowhere to be found on our streets or inside our homes.

We remained inside for days, listening to the scurrying outside, past our homes. None ever stopped. We left them alone as they did us. We watched news reports of the invasion, never with any footage of the white rats in action. Entire destroyed blocks rose up every few hours, newly minted greenspaces with white stone structures dotted throughout. Missing persons reports grew numerous and became the bigger story. The reporters gave canned explanations about contamination from pesticides sprayed into the neighborhood, warning people within their viewing area to stay away. They were unremarkable in their apathy for a neighborhood easily forgotten, anyway. No one from outside investigated, and we did not venture out to tell the real story.

Just as quickly as the attention started, the mystery of the disappearances and new appearances fell from the news cycles. The town-home buildings fell into immediate disrepair, as the few remaining owners and builders picked up their stakes and left. We returned to our blissful invisibility.

Our Lady still stood, the parts of her previously torn down re-grown, stronger, with even more plants and flowers. We ventured back outside, back into her courtyards, and into the new parks we now had. After a few weeks passed, the mayor and a few of her city council members came out and did a highly publicized dedication to Our Lady, marking her as an historical building to remain untouched by future demolitions.

I had no idea how long the red tape for these types of things usually held the processes up until I became an adult. I was aware of how quickly they moved as the council soon quietly dedicated the new park spaces as permanent fixtures of our neighborhood, as well. The mayor was from the old neighborhood. She knew. And she wanted to make sure we all remembered.

Our newfound bounty of outdoor greenspace cemented itself in our lives and our futures. Even if we couldn't learn or remember what Our Lady had been in the past, we would always remember what she meant in our present. More importantly, what she meant in our new memories, in the recesses of our being.

THEY USED TO BUILD PARKS HERE

SJ WHITBY

Due to an entirely uncharacteristic glitch, the gift arrives two days before Fern's seventeenth birthday. It sits in their in-tray like every other gift they have received, but unlike the exercise device they received last year, the purpose of this is opaque. It is a box made of pale silver metal, decorated with complex carvings. They form a series of curved lines, but Fern cannot deduce a pattern to the ornamentation. There is something curiously unruly about them, as if logic and order played no part in their unfurling. There are faint traces of green embedded in some of the lines like corroded circuitry.

"What an odd thing," Fern breathes. It is wondrous to see something so out of the ordinary, that is not predictable or expected. They cannot remember the last time they were truly surprised by something real.

A delicate silver clasp shaped like a hook holds the box closed. Fern levers it open and carefully raises the lid. Inside is a layer of soft white packing foam, the sort usually reserved for the transport of important items like medicines. Resting in the very center is a tiny sliver of…something. It is deep brown, more like a fragment of a larger entity than a thing itself. Fern pokes at it gingerly. Perhaps it is nanotechnology, one of the new augmentations people have spoken of in the Flow.

Fern inclines their head toward the soft blue glow of the outlet on the wall. "Flow, what is this thing?"

"It is a seed. An odd choice for a gift." From the flat affect, it is clear the Flow does not wish to extrapolate further.

"But I thought seeds didn't grow anymore." Fern knows this, but they know they can coax the Flow into a response with this display of ignorance.

The light from the outlet brightens a fraction, white bleeding around the edges. "The world is barren, but you have seen the tower gardens, Fern. We can create anything you need here."

One corner of Fern's mouth twitches. "Can we grow this seed?"

The Flow hums to itself as it communes. This is only a fractional part of the whole, a small tributary for the use of Fern and the needs of their small apartment. Fern finds it interesting that their Flow needs to refer this query upward. "The mechanisms of growing a seed are on file. We could fabricate some soil, and emulate sunlight, but you will need to allocate a portion of your daily water ration if you wish it to grow naturally. Or else I could take it apart and assess its internal workings and we could generate an artificial equivalent. That is probably...safer."

"It is my gift." Fern peers closer at the tiny device. There is nothing written on its exterior that shows what it might become. "I would like to see it operate properly."

The Flow blinks, going completely dark for almost two whole seconds before returning to its usual calm state. Fern has never seen it do this before, not in almost seventeen years—although, to be fair, they have not monitored it the entire time.

"I cannot establish the provenance of this seed. All the plant varieties within the tower are designed to be sterile. There is no record of it being delivered here. The last courier from the Wastes registered no such thing on their arrival, and all organisms attached to them were exterminated as per standard protocols. It is very curious."

"It must have come from somewhere," Fern points out, feeling slightly uneasy to be lecturing the Flow on a point of ontological order.

"A curiosity, indeed. But one contained to this apartment in this tower, and can therefore be considered an aberration in isolation. If you approve, I shall begin the fabrication of an ornamental pot and the nutrition-rich soil necessary to grow such a thing. Otherwise we can dispose of it safely, and put it from our minds."

"Of course we should grow it," Fern says. "It's my birthday present."

It is a trivial task for the Flow to create the object called *a pot*. To Fern's eyes, it's little more than a simple receptacle of a rusty orange color. There is a small circular hole in the bottom.

"For excess water to drain away," the Flow tells them.

Fern accepts this statement without question. Once upon a time the earth was full of plants grown from seeds like this. This information is easily accessible on the Flow, along with an almost unfathomable variety of still images and videos of these living organisms. At one stage, they covered vast swathes of the planet. Some even grew in the oceans, but nothing grows there now. The water is poison, same as the ground.

Because there is no such thing as fertile land, at least not for miles upon miles, the Flow has to fabricate a suitable environment for Fern's seed to thrive. This is a complex and laborious task, and Fern soon tires of watching it. Fabrication is a miracle that has saved humanity but, like most miracles, its power dulls with overuse. Gradually, the pot fills up with soil, and the seed is carefully deposited deep within, buried within the silken blackness.

Fern feels an odd pang, like the seed is being buried before it has had a chance to live. They almost cry out for the Flow to stop. There is an odd sense of kinship with the seed, since Fern's life is constrained to the tower as the seed is to the soil. Even as short a time ago as ten years, some people ventured beyond the tower, but the world outside has become *inimical to life*, as the Flow puts it.

So the tower is the world and the world is the tower, or close enough to it as to be indistinguishable. There are other towers like Fern's—and even more in ruins, failed experiments at survival that fell to chaos or bloodshed or mechanical failure—but Fern will never visit any of them. They and the seed may have had potential, once upon a time, but they will never get a chance to thrive.

"Put it away," Fern says crossly. "I don't like this gift anymore."

"Change requires time," the Flow says, its usual equanimity restored. "Have patience, Fern, and you will see something marvelous."

They watch the pot for the rest of the day but the soil remains undisturbed.

Such things are gone from the world.

It's their birthday, so they spend the day in FlowSpace with their friends and family. It is not safe to share realspace with others. Disease is far more cunning than humanity. Besides, FlowSpace is far more malleable than the real world. Fern constructs an elaborate watery environment, which everyone gives them compliments on. Everyone wears bright feathery costumes of a lurid pink and they splash in the shallows like wading birds. Overhead, the sky is an uninterrupted blue, not marred by the faintest tracery of clouds. It is the model of a Perfect Day when searched for in the Flow, although Fern has removed all traces of plants from the environment in a fit of pique.

"There is no need for seeds," Fern says scornfully to their friend Anastasia. "The Flow contains all we need."

The girl blinks enormous violet eyes, swaying in the water with sinuous motions. "What are you talking about?"

"Someone gave me a very odd gift from long ago."

"Old things go extinct for a reason." Anastasia sighs and deliquesces very slowly, until only her smile remains to be pulled apart by the waves. Fern laughs and claps their hands together in delight. The Flow is a superior version of reality, one that cannot be ruined so terribly that nobody can reconstitute it, no matter how much technology they bring to bear. Outside, everything dies, but here they can swim, and dance across the waves.

One solitary seed is a cruel thing, really, the last extinguished ember of a once roaring fire that spanned the globe.

The day after Fern's birthday, they move the pot to the topmost shelf. They cannot quite bring themself to dispose of it. After all, it was their birthday gift.

Three weeks elapse before the Flow wakes Fern early one morning.

"Do you remember that odd gift of yours?"

"Oh, yes. That old thing. Throw it out, Flow. I don't need it. I think it must have been a joke, and a strange one at that."

An almost irritated hum emanates from the outlet. "We finally have a change in state, and you do not wish to even observe?"

Fern sits up in bed, hair askew around their face. The environment generator has barely begun to cycle into day, so only the barest amount of light filters from the ceiling panels. "Is it growing?"

"See for yourself." The Flow pokes the environment generator until it begrudgingly begins the day a full hour early. Fern is already scrambling over to the shelf and hauling the pot down from its perch.

And there it is.

The most slender thread of green rising almost like smoke from the soil, topped with one delicate curl of a leaf, hesitantly unfurling itself in the fake light of day.

"It's alive." Fern trembles, feeling delicate as the newly sprouted plant itself. "Imagine, this coming from that tiny seed. Is there a whole root system below?"

"Yes. A complex one, threading itself to the very depths of the pot." The Flow hums hesitantly. "You should not speak of this to anyone, Fern."

Fern lowers their face so they are eye-level with the leaf. "Who would I tell?"

The Flow outlet is so bright it's almost white. "A friend, family, anyone. You must make no attempt to discover the origins of this gift. I have perhaps overstepped my bounds."

Fern averts their eyes. "Did we do something wrong?"

There is a long pause. "No. It is one seed, constrained to one apartment. Despite the unusual genetic characteristics, it is a single plant."

Even though the plant is barely larger than their smallest finger, Fern is aware they are in the presence of something magical. Everything these days is fabricated, from food and clothing to mechanical and human embryos. What has happened in their tiny box of an apartment was not the result of the prying atomic pincers of a fabricator. This is something real. *Alive.* Fern considers that perhaps the only reason this is not forbidden is because nobody considers it possible. They do not ask the Flow about this. Their outlet seems perturbed enough already.

Over the following days, the plant continues to grow. The stalk thickens and more leaves unfurl, traced with spiraling vein-like patterns. When Fern awakes on day nine after the shoot appeared, they discover something new—a tightly closed fist of leaves at the very top of the stalk.

"It's holding something precious," they whisper.

The flower does not respond, although Fern imagines that the leaves trembled faintly at the sound of their voice. Fern is tempted to prod the plant, to see if it will unclench itself and reveal what's inside, but they do not wish to risk disaster by tampering with this magical process.

Rather frustratingly, it does not open all that day. Or the next, or for the four days after that. Fern spends the following morning at their lessons in FlowSpace, because the Flow has been making increasingly belligerent comments about their lack of progress. They do not wish to be punished by losing the flower, not when it's on the verge of revealing the secret. Despite the dull beginning, this is definitely the most curious and interesting gift Fern has ever received. The secret at its heart must be extraordinary.

It's evening when the flower finally opens, the environment generator daubing the walls in glorious sunset colors, spilling its rosy paintbox in the Flow's attempt to give Fern something prettier to look at than the real view—although they privately consider that the chemical storms have their own unearthly beauty. All of that is nothing on this tiny miracle quivering before them.

One petal twitches, reluctantly releasing its grip and fanning outwards with a dramatic flourish. Fern almost imagines they can hear it sigh. A few moments later, another does, then one more, and then a whole flurry of them splay themselves wide to reveal the treasure they've been nurturing this whole time.

It appears to Fern as a faceted crystal, like a gem but glowing with a green so rich and vibrant that it must hold the shades of an entire forest coiled within.

"Viridian," Fern murmurs, and the flower tilts itself toward them, as if they're the closest thing to a sun in this tiny box of an apartment. The brightness sends tidy verdant dots dancing in Fern's vision. When they close their eyes, those sparks bloom, spilling complex fractal tendrils across their eyelids.

When they open their eyes again, the plant is still oriented toward them, but the center seems to have grown fractionally. Fern cannot take their eyes away. What is this creation? Who sent it to them, and what can it possibly mean?

"Ah," the Flow says, and Fern can hear the relief in its normally restful voice. "It is a perfectly ordinary flower. There is no cause for alarm. We can let it live out the course of its ordinary life, as flowers once did."

Fern has spent some hours combing the eddies and currents of the Flow, looking for plants that match theirs. They are quite sure this is not perfectly ordinary. In none of the pictures did anything glow this bright.

They used to build parks here, a voice says, although it sounds more like many people are speaking the same words at almost the same time. It sounds like a chorus of children, all clamoring to be heard over each other, but there is an undertone of exhaustion that speaks of something far older. It is the first time Fern has heard a voice in their apartment that is not theirs or that of the Flow. To hear so many voices all speaking at once is both terrifying and wonderful, as if everyone in the tower has joined in unison.

"Excuse me?" Fern's own voice comes out in an embarrassing squeak.

"I said it appears to be an ordinary flower."

We said they used to build parks here.

Fern takes a deep breath. "I know what parks are. There were grass and trees, and paths people walked down. Sometimes there were dogs. We don't make dogs anymore."

We did not say it as a compliment. They built parks and imagined they could bend the planet to their will. And so they did, but at what cost?

The Flow flickers, almost extinguishes itself, and then returns to its usual brightness. "Would you like to see images of parks, Fern? Or perhaps explore a fully rendered park in FlowSpace?"

Fern claps their hands together sharply. "Mute mode, Flow. I'd like to focus on my studies, and don't wish to be disturbed."

"As you wish." The outlet light dims to a pale gold.

What is that monstrosity you speak to? It has the appearance of a god, but it is a dead thing.

There is a rational part of Fern telling themself they can't possibly be hearing a voice coming from a flower, and they certainly should not be thinking of responding. This flower should not be. Wild, alive things should not exist in the world any longer. In the last days before they retreated into the tower, the planet turned more unruly than ever, lashing out in fury in its death throes. Storms with a power to dwarf anything previously seen, the ground heaving and cracking. Bones rising from the primordial muck, animals turned feral in their desperation. Even the few hardy plants capable of survival rose from the ground to snare and choke those still attempting to cling to an existence outside. Fern has seen some of this footage in the Flow, at least the parts that aren't censored for those underage.

And now they are having an impossible conversation. The flower is quite possibly dangerous, but Fern finds that does not deter them at all.

"That's the Flow. It's a machine, I suppose, although it does a good job of being alive. Better than most people."

Why did it bring us back? What purpose did it serve, to drag our weary carcasses back from oblivion only to choke to death on this sterile air?

"I don't know," Fern admits. "Your seed arrived in my apartment. I assumed it was a gift, but now I'm confused. Is there anything I can do to improve the air in here so you can breathe properly?"

There is little point clinging to life, so do not bestir yourself drastically on our account. Perhaps you cannot understand this sentiment. You humans endure despite fouling your habitat so completely. Threaded in your silver needles, still plunging poison into the earth. I suppose it does not concern you to desecrate a corpse.

"What are you?" Fern asks, even though it is only the first of a snaking queue of questions bubbling through their mind.

We are a seed.

Fern shakes their head at the semantic confusion. "You *were* a seed, but now you have become a plant. It's a miracle to see it happen again."

The seed contained the potentiality of us, as we contain the potentiality of her.

"The potentiality of who?" This is a bewildering turn in the conversation. Fern is aware of how many entities—including humans—used to reproduce, each growing from a seed that would then generate further seeds. It does not sound precisely as if the plant is talking about propagating more of their species. The way the joined-together voice says *her* sounds almost...reverent.

There are things humanity cannot understand. Has never truly understood, aside from glimpses. They always averted their eyes or chose willful ignorance.

"You could at least try." Fern is trying not to be offended. It is not the plant's condemnation of humanity that concerns them — it is difficult to have the entire planet's history available in the Flow and not consider that a series of poor decisions were made in the face of a parade of increasingly dire warnings. Fern wants the plant to trust them, to *like* them. To be something more than a depressingly ordinary human, one of fifty thousand carefully constructed varieties in this tower.

We will consider it, and the best way to communicate with you. Your language is an imprecise tool with a history of being used for manipulation.

"Oh." Fern frowns at the plant, trying to construct an argument that will win it over, then realizes that by doing so, they are only proving the creature's central point. The plant will communicate in its own way, in its own time. It obviously has something to say. After all, it has taken a number of days to unfold itself into this form.

They spend the rest of the day in FlowSpace. Their latest environment seems unnecessarily gaudy in the face of the crystal. With a sigh, they deconstruct the entirety of it. What's left is a simple rendering of their apartment in its default state. This only emphasizes its smallness and austerity. Everything is functional and necessary. Anything frivolous can take place in FlowSpace. The only real things in Fern's apartment are themself and the plant, and Fern is starting to question one of those.

"Fern!" Anastasia materializes in Fern's Space. Today she is a giraffe with a human face, although she needs to resize herself to fit in the cramped confines of the rendered apartment. "Tell me what's wrong. Are you depressed, darling?"

"Depressed? No." Fern sits perched on their sleeping tray. "Why do you think that?"

Anastasia flails one long leg, indicating the entirety of their surroundings. "This, my sweet! It shows a dearth of imagination, as if you could possibly have exhausted all the possibilities the Flow has to offer, and turned your nose up at each and every one. It speaks of an existential crisis, or so my Flow says. Your Flow is very quiet on the matter."

"But this is the only real place I know," Fern says.

Anastasia's avi dissolves and is replaced by her default standard. Fern has no idea how it compares to her realself, because they've never met anyone's realself. All they know is their default avi is not at all real. Ana picks her way over to the bed and perches beside Fern. There is barely enough room for both of them.

"It's depressing, Fern. Reality so often is. The outside is real, but would you generate a Flow environment based on that? Nobody would. It's all death and wastes and those horrible mutants."

Fern sighs. "Except even that wouldn't be real, because we couldn't die in there, could we? The storms wouldn't melt our flesh, and the water wouldn't make us puke our guts out, and—"

Anastasia shudders. "Please don't talk about guts, Fern. There's no need to be quite as depressing as your horrible little apartment."

"It's the same as yours," Fern points out.

"Exactly! Which is why I spend as little time in realspace as possible. Like *everyone*, Fern. Is there a problem with your Flow? It happens sometimes, you know. Especially if they're not communicating upward properly. Do you need me to ask mine to have it checked?"

"No." Fern forces a smile. "My Flow is working perfectly well. And I'm fine, look." They work rapidly to bring up one of their old FlowSpaces, a kingdom of clouds bathed in radiant sunset light. It's dazzling and beautiful, exactly the type of environment Anastasia loves. Fern cannot risk their Flow being investigated, or of having maintenance bots come spidering through the outlet. If anyone finds the plant—

"Much better." Anastasia is back in her giraffe form, picking her way across the sticky field of clouds. "Isn't this so much better?"

"Yes." Fern nods. "It's perfect."

That night, Fern dreams for the first time in years. They are in a forest, although it is so much *grander* than anything they have seen in the Flow. Trees tower far above, gargantuan trunks fanning out into spreading canopies that overlap until they block out the sky. The air is cool and green, like standing below a waterfall of refreshing light. Underfoot, the soil is soft and dark, and Fern's bare toes sink into it, longing to bury themselves deep and rootlike.

Ahead, there is a gap in the trees, and Fern makes out a looming shape in the clearing beyond. They stumble forward, fingertips brushing over the trunks. Beads of water cling to their skin and they touch them to their lips. They have never tasted true water before, only the fabricated equivalent, and its purity is almost intoxicating. It leaves Fern with a wave of dizziness as they come through the trees, one that only intensifies when their eyes adjust to what they are seeing.

They fall to their knees.

Fern is looking at the curve of a single enormous cheek. It rises in front of them like a monument. The skin is a pale and almost luminous green and studded with tiny dewdrop flowers. Darker green lines thread beneath the surface like veins. The cheek rises to the bridge of an aquiline nose high above, silhouetted against the green light from the forest canopy. Based on the scale, the woman must be half the size of the tower Fern lives in, lying half-buried in the soil.

She must be a fallen statue celebrating some long-ago religion of the trees and the earth. Although now Fern is becoming aware of a hum emanating from the body, a low and persistent susurration like a thousand voices joined in unison. It cannot be coming anywhere but from the impossible figure.

And then the head turns, very slowly, with the creaking of an ancient tree. She is too large to take in directly, so Fern sees only fragments—the vast, gentle curve of her lips, the lashes of one eye, each as thick around as Fern's entire body. Her lips tremble faintly, no doubt the source of the sonorous hum.

Fern wants to flee, but they are rooted to the ground. They have the feeling they are trespassing on something sacred, their manufactured self of metal, plastic, and organics does not belong in this grove. Whatever is coming, they should not be here to witness its full flowering.

The woman opens her eyes. They're a pure and startling green with no iris or pupil. There is no escape from that glorious light. It is a triumphant shout of life in the face of encroaching disaster. Fern knows they cannot possibly stand before this onslaught, that they will be obliterated in the wash of it, disintegrated down to the finely wrought metal of their skeleton, lying like litter amongst this untouched glade. Fern wants to speak, to offer something, to give what fractional spark of life they possess, but the dream ends with the finality of a blade descending.

Fern wakes, trembling and bereft. To be stolen from the side of something so majestic, to have life so wild and true terminated so abruptly. They cannot stop shivering, but they know this has been a message. They slide from their bed and pad over to the plant. It tilts its glowing face toward them.

"You sent me that dream."

Of course. We considered it the best way to reveal her to you.

"What is she?"

You might call her a god. That is not precisely true, but it is the closest word you have for it. You would have to layer many meanings on top of one another to accumulate something like truth. A force, a wellspring, a heart.

Fern's voice trembles over the next question. "What happened to her?"

She is intricately connected to the planet. When the world died, she did too. All that remains are a handful of seeds, and most of those have since perished.

"And you are one of these seeds?"

Yes, Fern. We assumed that was obvious. There is amusement in the plant's voice, a faint echo of ringing laughter.

Fern ignores the joke at their expense and leans forward even further. "So can you bring her back?"

We cannot. There is no soil to flourish in.

"Perhaps we can make some," Fern says eagerly.

Most fabricated things are inert. There is only one thing in this apartment that has the organic complexity required, and we cannot use it.

It takes Fern a moment or two to extrapolate meaning from this sentence. The plant is talking about them, about their body. They would be the soil in the flowering of this seed.

"Why can't you use it? What's wrong with me?"

The difference between seed and soil is that a seed can choose, but soil cannot.

There is a part of Fern still caught in the dream-forest, staring into the eyes of something close to a god. An urge to offer what little they have, as futile as it might be.

"My life is worth nothing." Fern cannot deny this any longer. Perhaps they have always known. "This entire tower has no purpose. We are a system persisting because that is what it was designed to do. Once it has taken everything from the dead planet, it will cease to function, and we will all cease in turn. It is an uninterrupted downward trajectory."

Yes. There was once a great wheel of life, but it has been levered from its axis and burned to ashes. Your tower may yet persist for a thousand years, but it is an endless devouring system that cannot replenish itself.

Anger blossoms in Fern's belly, like there is another long-buried seed inside and it is blooming in fire. It rages at themself, at their world, at the plant itself for its resignation. "Doesn't it make you furious? We murdered something like a god, and this is all we built in her place. Don't you want revenge?"

We tried revenge, but it was too late. Those left on the outside were pitiful creatures. Those truly responsible had hidden themselves away in these towers, and we could not penetrate these walls.

"But now you're inside." Fern paces from one end of the tiny apartment to the other. "I'm not sure who sent you, but this is your opportunity."

It would come at the cost of your life and future existence. Do you not understand this?

"Of course." Fern picks up the pot and cradles it to their chest. "But I want to do this. The seed dies and becomes something else, but the soil plays a role too. Everything works together and the great wheel turns."

Is there nobody you wish to speak to about this?

Fern knows the Flow cannot understand, and will likely intervene drastically. The Flow works in the tower to persist its cradle of manufactured life, because that is what it was designed to do long ago. Fern will most likely find themselves disassembled in some other fashion if they broach this topic. They have only survived thus far because of the gentle relationship they've developed with their tributary. Seventeen years of existing in the quiet with no cause for alarm. Although perhaps the plant has played a role here as well, since the Flow sees it as nothing more than an innocuous curiosity.

Anastasia is the only other person they might tell, and would understand even less than the Flow. She has not yet lost her taste for novelty, and for splashing about the endless sea of FlowSpace. She has not been confronted with the reality of life as it was, and given a chance to become something other than a small, empty apartment.

"I know what I'm doing," Fern says. "This is the only thing I've ever really wanted. It's like there's been a song in my head for my whole life, but I've never heard the ending."

Then it was fortuitous indeed that we came to your door. Blown by the winds of chaos, although perhaps with more forethought that we imagined. Some other flickers of life yet stir, it seems, bending themselves to obscure arrangements. It gives us hope that the wheel may yet turn again.

"What do I need to do?"

Swallow the crystal at the heart of this flower. It will take root in you. The process will be entirely painless, perhaps even euphoric. You will be connected to something so much grander than either of us, if only for a moment.

Fern does not stop to consider things further. This has been inevitable, in a way, ever since they opened the lid of the box. They still see green when they close their eyes.

The gem comes away easily from the petals that hold it. Each leaf droops delicately now that it no longer holds its cargo. Fern raises it to their lips, and slides it between them. For such a dramatic moment, it is very mundane. Nothing more weighty than eating another fabricated meal.

The gem dissolves on their tongue into a thousand tiny fragments that tingle down their throat. It tastes very slightly bitter, and there's a strong smell of pine. Once they have swallowed, it doesn't feel like anything.

"Fern?" The Flow activates itself, glowing a faint alarm-white. "What have you done? Something has been altered."

"I feel dreadful." Fern shakes in their small bed. "You should take a sample urgently. I don't know what I ate but it disagrees with me violently. I think you'll need to commune upward. And Flow?"

"Yes, Fern?"

"Can you pour this into the Flow? I think it should be shared with everyone."

The Flow hums, toggling into the higher pitch which signifies the upward connection. A small mechanical device creeps into the room, pincer click-clacking at the front. It will sample what Fern is becoming and take that into its system. From there, it will spread and spread, as plants did of old, before everything was gone.

Fern closes their eyes. They can already feel a tingling in their fingertips, tough green shoots pushing against the skin. The light of the Flow is so bright it turns everything in the apartment into shadows. Whatever it might wish to do, this poor little tributary of humanity's protector, it is too late.

"I will be the soil through which she can be reborn." Fern coughs, dribbling a mixture of sap and soil from between their lips. "My corpse will become a quiet garden."

Their skin breaks now, splitting with a series of damp tearing sounds. Petals cradle their cheeks in soft pink hands, and tendrils quiver in the air. One thick vine bursts from the warm nutrient bath of Fern's stomach, forcing its way through the smoothness of their skin. It makes an unerring path toward the Flow outlet. Once inside, it burrows into the cables and begins its journey upward. Somewhere high above is the flourishing server farm that keeps the tower and its residents operational. From here, the seed may propagate, drifting in the great river of the Flow, circulating through the building and out into the world beyond.

It began with one single tiny seed delivered to Fern's door. An unasked for gift, product of an ancient and failing system, searching for one small patch of soil in which to grow. One sacrifice to restart the wheel, so that after many turnings, those eyes will open again in that distant forest.

Fern's mouth creaks open one final time, petals uncurling damp and bloody on their tongue.

"Oh," they whisper. "How the earth will bloom."

LIKE BLOOD FROM

RIEN GRAY

Stone, song, salvation.

Adrian brought their pick down and hummed to keep a rhythm, to keep sane despite the incessant drip of water at the bottom of the mine. Children made the best workers, the foreman said. Manus liked his miners around ten years old, twelve at the oldest—small and flexible enough to fit in the most dangerous tunnels without the malignant *attitude* that came from further maturity.

Yet Manus favored Adrian the best, even though they were fourteen. Maybe it was because they rarely spoke and had no guardians to make claim or care about conditions in the mine. Their parents died in the first days of the town's founding from something in the river, an invisible poison no one could see or smell. People only drank out of the local well now, but every bucket of water was partitioned out under guard, depending on how many shares each family earned over the week.

Except the mine was deep enough for the river to bleed through the lowest tunnels. Water tapped like a warning against the back of Adrian's neck, and wet their teeth if they dared to look up. Stone shone slick and dark under the dying flicker of the only lantern by their feet; no one else would work this far down. Instead, the others scraped desperately at the walls of the shafts above to find a new vein, praying for brown earth to deliver yet one more sunless crystal.

It was everywhere in the nadir. Adrian filled an entire crate per hour, attaching their spoils to the hook and chain in the corner, where a tall, burrowing chasm cut upward to the surface. Someone pulled the crate high and emptied it each time; they weren't sure who. Every so often there would be food inside the crate when the chain rattled back down, or a smidgen of oil for the lantern. Adrian—who kept time by scraping notches into the floor—hadn't seen either in two days, but the crate still rose and fell, same as always.

Stone, song, salvation.

Stone, song, salv—

The wall in front of Adrian crumbled. Pockets of air in the tunnels weren't uncommon, but this one curved in deep, opening in a glittering shape caught between jaw and geode. It was less a gouge and more of a waiting maw, hard crystals poking up like teeth, with a tongue that was warm and red.

Adrian blinked, but the color didn't change. Between rich black formations, a heavy deposit of cinnabar jutted outward, rugged and unpolished. Even in summer, the mine was frigid, but a wave of heat poured over Adrian's skin, heavy as a touch. They flinched, then recoiled further when pearls of silver began to bead on the surface of the cinnabar, bright like an angel's tears.

Something about the sight terrified them, but Adrian knew Manus would beat them bloody for not bringing something potentially valuable above, and last time, the foreman had broken a bone around their right eye. The other miners started avoiding them after that, claiming their eye was "broken." One of the miners told them that their normal brown iris was now split through with blue. Adrian had to assume it was true; Manus was the only one with a mirror, and he didn't let anyone else near his tent.

So they ducked into the opening with care, boots finding uneasy footing on the bed of crystal. The walls were jagged, and pressed so close together the sharpest edges scraped through Adrian's shirt. Every step brought more heat until it felt like they were face-to-face with a bonfire, trying to endure the burning light. With a shaking hand, Adrian reached out to the cinnabar, fingertips brushing against a few drops of shimmering fluid.

It was hot as pitch, and clung like just the same, spreading across Adrian's skin with the shine and weight of liquid metal.

The floor beneath them shifted and cracked. Before they could run, breathe, think—it collapsed. Adrian plunged down, an instant and an eternity, and hit something so solid the very idea of breathing was struck from their lungs. Crystalline dust stung the inside of their nose and throat, as if they were suffocating on a razor, pain flaring through Adrian's ribs and spine.

But it wasn't dark. That was the first thought they could summon past the pain, lying on their side as waves of agony came and went, strong as a riptide. The walls around them held a subtle crimson glow, providing enough light to reveal their strange boundary, smooth like a piece of seaglass.

Adrian made a valiant attempt to sit up, only to knock their head against a broken edge. They gasped in pain, trying to feel for empty space above, but the shaft they'd fallen through had choked on its own debris and sealed shut. The bubble of space around them wasn't high enough to stand in, leaving no choice but to crawl.

The fall had stolen any sense of direction, and Adrian couldn't imagine a path where freedom might lay, but the thought of dying still and quiet was unfathomable. Using their elbows to drag themself across the floor was an exercise in anguish, but after a few minutes, familiarity brought the pain flaring across raw nerves down to a dull roar.

Soon, they reached a fork in the crush of tunnels, although left and right appeared meaningless. Adrian chose the sinister—same as their favored hand—and couldn't help but remember a story their mother once read to them about a blue whale, whose heart was supposed to be so big a fully-grown man could climb through the organ's chambers. Their path curved and flowed like an artery, just wide enough to admit life, with the same constant pressure of death threatening any stop or pause.

Then the path dipped down, a labrum of red stone cascading into a pit. Another mouth, another gullet, wide with anticipation. Adrian lacked the room to turn their body and fall feet-first; they could only dive forward and hope.

It was a shorter drop this time, but the impact was twice as sharp. Tears finally broke free from Adrian's eyes as they curled up, letting out sobs, a plea for the pain to quiet if only for a moment. Yet crying hurt too, hot salt catching on scrapes across their face, lip split from desperate teeth and dry air.

Water didn't drip here—it rushed. Adrian tried to blink past the harsh glow of the walls, seeking its source. The pit was tall enough to stand in, so tall it looked more like a cathedral than a chasm, ceiling lined with stalactites of obsidian, pointing down with the menace of a thousand swords of Damocles. In contrast, the floor under their boots was so smooth it was difficult not to slip, making every staggered step a risk.

They smelled iron and something pungent, alien to their senses. Everything was wet and shifting on the edges like lungs in bloom. As Adrian got close to the sound of water, more heat stirred the air, until it was so thick every breath they took was short and punctured, a hand wrapped around the throat and squeezing.

The reason emerged in its totality, overwhelming all else. Something lay embedded in the rock bleeding mercury, made of toxic, stygian bones, and even a single rib was larger than Adrian was tall. A thousand cinnabar eyes stared back, weeping thick globs of silver into the river that washed past what could only be called its feet. Yet such a thing could not walk, impaled in the earth, and its mouth was a void without end.

"What are you?" Adrian gasped.

The answer was hallowed pain and unsung grief—white as bone, red as blood, black as the cover of a Bible.

Adrian began to scream, and didn't stop.

They heard the story in pieces later.

It was said the first collapse had triggered several others in the mine, that Manus had begrudgingly evacuated the working children, only to come up one shy in the headcount. The fact that he had bothered to look for them at all surprised Adrian, but such cruel paternalism was often equally possessive. Manus claimed they were found facing a blank wall of the mine, howling and gibbering, making such unholy noise that he had no choice but to strike them unconscious. When they woke hours later and continued to scream, he forced a knot of opium between their teeth and put Adrian on the first carriage to Chicago.

Drugged beyond comprehension, Adrian remembered little but six hours inside a rumbling black casket of a coach, glimpsing only fragments of the wooden streets and buildings hammered together in haste before being ushered beyond the tall black gates of the asylum.

The first several months passed in an identical haze, although the bitter taste on their tongue had long since faded. Weekly interrogations from the matron—Ms. Lewis—who ruled the madhouse only left Adrian more confused; she seemed to know far more about what happened than they did, but had no answer for the slow, argent drip that took over their dreams, and bled through the edge of their vision.

Her curiosity dulled to disdain, then rusted into hate. Ms. Lewis' loathing sparked when Adrian wouldn't answer questions and refused to wear "proper" clothing, eventually condemning them to a ragged robe and little else. But the strange illness plaguing them was what secured her ire. Adrian had a compulsion with pencils, causing them to chew through wood down to the core, leaving their teeth gray with graphite, and kept waking up in the asylum garden, having dug a pit through the plants to lie down, half-buried.

Then there were the headaches.

Later, Adrian would learn that most people afflicted with such a syndrome felt pain for an hour, or a day at most. A simple tincture from the pharmacist could cure the ill. Others didn't have to lie in the dark still as possible, because every twitch of muscle drew a long hook of agony through their spine. Their right eyes didn't throb and swell until it felt like they would rupture clean from their skull and socket, the nerve behind it twitching like a serpent's tail. For Adrian, these fits lasted a week or more, during which they could barely bathe or eat, condemned to hide their head under a mended towel and occasionally sip from a bowl of water, the tang of iron heavy on the back of their tongue.

By some measure, the purity of the pain was a mercy. Were it any less intense, they would have had the strength to find the first sharp object nearby and shove it through the tender bones of their ear to end the constant strain.

In six years, there was no relief, only the dwindling of funds directed toward the asylum as other sciences became popular for battling troublesome afflictions. One morning without ceremony, Adrian was told to leave, pushed out the door in their robe and a pair of ill-fitting shoes from a patient who had died the week before. A nurse's pity put a single silver quarter in their palm, calluses faded after so long away from the mine.

But it was the only place they knew. The city's constant chorus of noise and belching smoke cast a warning sign around Adrian's skull, the flickering halo that cut through their vision whenever a headache waited in the wings. Soon it felt like the tapping of a pickaxe, building to a brutal and relentless swing, piercing sharp enough to leave them temporarily blind. If such pain happened on the street or at night, their chances of survival were minimal.

Six hours by horse was three days on foot. Adrian spent the quarter on a parcel of food and water from a passing trader, although the bag was empty long before the mining town came into view. Thirst made the halo brighter, but the fruit of their eye had yet to burst.

They expected no welcome during the witching hour, but the quiet surrounding dark, collapsed buildings belonged to the dead, not the restful. While Adrian had spent most of their days in the mine, there was only one main street in town, making it impossible to get lost. The church with its hard, backless pews was the same, the general store still had no glass in its windows, and the lock on the lid of the well remained, denying succor to yet another visitor. But they were also, to a one, empty.

Adrian discovered why at the end of the road. Before the collapse, the local graveyard held only those early souls who had died after drinking from the river. Now tombstones stretched out to the fences in every direction, many of them plinths of granite without a name. The town had perhaps held a hundred people at its peak; at least half as many graves were here, but that made sense. Adrian supposed someone had to do the burying before running away as far and fast as they could.

The mine was in far worse shape. Manus' tent looked like it had been shredded by something with claws, but the only prints in the earth belonged to boots and bare feet. Countless carts were rusted in place to their rails, and the abandoned tools beside them had suffered the same fate. All of the scaffolding around the entrance had fallen in on itself, leaving an opening too narrow for a grown man to crawl through.

In six years, Adrian had grown taller, but no wider, no thicker. They shoved an arm through first, ensuring that the tunnel behind remained; by curling both shoulders in like a beetle, their head fit too. Yet the tightness sent a cold wave of panic under their skin; such close quarters felt just like the arterial crevices above that deep, wailing pit.

They hadn't thought about the fall in so long—now it was the only thing on their mind.

What had been down there? Adrian couldn't remember. Manus hadn't mentioned anything to Ms. Lewis beyond the collapse, but a shake in the earth didn't make anyone scream for days on end. At least, it shouldn't have.

Past the choke of the entrance, any sense of order had been cast away. Two out of three main tunnels simply didn't exist anymore, and it was so dark that Adrian could only find a path by running a hand along the walls and waiting for their fingertips to meet empty space. By feel, they pushed into the greater labyrinth, following the slow slope downward.

Then their foot sank, and they sank with it.

The chasm was narrow and threaded with a chain that smashed into Adrian's jaw before they managed a desperate grab around links of iron. Rugged metal and raw friction split their palms open, blood slipping between aching fingertips. Adrian's leg hooked around the chain for an instant, just long enough to slow the fall before they hit the bottom.

Wood splintered. Pain shot through their body so fast Adrian gagged on bile, as if the excess had to be evacuated. It dripped onto their bruise-heavy knees, but somehow, nothing but the crate beneath them was broken.

The crate. Adrian felt around to be sure, but when their fingers caught on a wrought iron handle, there was no mistaking that it was the same one they had hauled around a dozen times a day for months on end. From the handle they found the gap at the bottom of the chasm, and emerged in the lower level of the mine.

It should have been pitch black. Yet reddish veins split through floor and wall alike, providing a subtle, unsettling glow. Most of these tunnels were closed too, but Adrian's old lantern still remained, wick scorched to an oily smudge, and the handle of their pickaxe lay beside it, metal head melted to a puddle of rust and river water. They stepped over the tools and into the waiting mouth, still riddled with jet black fangs.

The throat below remained a crimson maze, narrow and smooth, but Adrian relished the chance to climb on their belly, pushing blood back into ill-used muscles. Most of their days in the asylum had been confined to a small, single room, windowless and cold. Heat pulsed through the stone beneath them, easing the tension and agony from the earlier fall.

Their arms were long enough to grip the other side of the pit now, clinging to the thick lip until the rest of their body dropped through, and hanging for one solid breath before letting go. The chamber Adrian landed in was familiar, although their mind strained to understand why, pulling at the burned threads of memory as if the tapestry would weave itself back together.

Stone, song, salvation.

Countless cinnabar eyes pinned Adrian in place, lidless, unblinking. Mercurial blood dripped down a body embedded in the earth, eternally wounded like the saints once painted on the walls of the town church. Its jaw unfurled, countless sharp angles blossoming outward, and a bone-shaking scream vibrated through the masonry of its throat, splitting through Adrian's skull, pushing through the whites of their eyes until they began to turn red.

"No!" Their protest escaped through gritted teeth, grinding enamel. "I'm sorry!"

The howl ceased.

Adrian watched in quiet terror as the jaw took on new shape, fused together at the top and bottom. It looked more like a beak now, a coral-like tongue pushing through the center, aglow with promise.

"Why did you dig so deep?" the body asked.

"I..." Adrian's vision swam as they tried to answer. "I was told to."

The beak ground together with a sound like a metal file on glass. "Do you know what you have carried away from this place?"

They shook their head. The grind sharpened in pitch, but this time the noise was more contemplative than cruel.

"Galena," the body said. "It is meant for the fallen, not for you."

"I'm sorry," they whispered again.

Adrian refused the instinct to blame Manus or the other miners. They alone had hauled a thousand broken stones out of the ground with their own hands, never questioning the reason. What pain it must have caused, to feel a pickaxe breaking down the ceiling of this sanctuary, endless and unrelenting for so long.

"Where are those who speak in the ordinary way?" the body demanded.

Adrian blinked, mind catching on a translation. "The Illiniwek?"

The beak rose and fell. "Yes."

"They were driven away." Years ago, when Adrian was too young to walk. "Most of them were killed."

Growing up, Adrian had heard the rumors of the Illiniwek's parting words: *never dig here. These stones are for the dead.*

Warning, praying.

Manus had broken ground the very next day.

A snarl of rage rippled through the body like an earthquake, making the entire chasm tremble. Sharp flecks of red rained from the ceiling, showering Adrian in needles, catching on their hair. This time, they stayed quiet.

"Those who drank from me have died," the body declared. "Those who have profited off my flesh have died."

The graveyard. Adrian suddenly understood what had happened in their absence, that they had survived by a slip of fate, exiled thanks to Manus's fear and disgust. After taking a deep breath, their own horror drained away, replaced by the comfort of the inevitable.

Adrian sank to their knees in front of the body and bowed their head, neck bared to the sharp stalactites above, poised like an executioner's blade. This must have been the reason they were called back here, they thought, drawn like a magnet to the core of the earth. The sole survivor who escaped justice.

Yet the body did not strike. It spoke again.

"I still bleed." Mercury dripped into Adrian's hair, then fell like a caress down one cheek. "They are gone, yet my wound remains."

"I know," they whispered. "I can feel you."

Not *it*—**you.**

The beak lowered, its slender tip brushing across Adrian's brow. Sharper than a diamond, the cut came without pain and painted their face in a veil of red. They tasted iron, copper, gold. A molten gift, too hot to swallow, branding their flesh from the inside out.

"Be my messenger." The body's voice radiated from inside Adrian's skull, plated like a locket, finally free from pain and pressure. "Walk the earth above forever, and ensure no one desecrates this place again."

Adrian smiled, teeth now marble, tongue a slick and heavy ruby. Too heavy for speech, but they had never been fond of their own voice anyway. They no longer had to blink against the light, or struggle for air. Heat and cold flowed through them in a pulse of seasons, the natural rhythm of the world.

They walked into the river below the body, and let the water sweep them away.

HONEY AND ONIONS

SAM ELYSE

Something in the air didn't smell right.

"Burnt onions?" I sniffed the air and crinkled my nose. "Buuu-bbeee!"

Bubbe Lola was making French onion soup... without my Zaydee's help. To say this was unusual was an understatement. My grandparents were never really apart. They were always in the other room, listening in on what the other was doing. Zaydee would have certainly chimed in by now telling Bubbe how the onions had stuck to the bottom of the pot and were ruined.

"What's that smell?" I called out again. "Zaydee? Bubbe?"

No answer.

As I swept through the foyer, I noticed all of the windows slightly cracked open. There was a buzzing wafting through the house. Like busy, bumbling bees trying to ward off an intruder. I could hear the scraping of metal against a pan, the shuffling of footsteps, the rustling of restless leaves trying to get through the front door which I had just left ajar.

"Henya? Is that my Henya?" cried Bubbe Lola. She rounded the corner and swept me up into one of her infamous bear hugs. I winced just a little.

"Yes, yes, Bubbe! It's me," I kissed her cheek to initiate my release. Even though I had just turned sixteen, transferred to two different high schools and took on a part-time job, I couldn't dissuade Bubbe of her need to hold onto me tightly whenever I visited.

"Ah! Well come in if you're going to come in!"

I closed the door behind me and made sure the lock clicked. Then I followed my grandmother into the kitchen and scooted up to the counter on a very old stool like I had done so many times before.

She poked her head out of the pantry as soon as I got comfortable. She muttered a few words to herself and moved about aimlessly. Usually she knew her kitchen quite well.

"Are you alright, Bubbe? Where's Zaydee?" I wondered.

"Two tablespoons? Or was it one?" said Bubbe, questioning herself and ignoring me completely, as if I was an ornamental part of the kitchen. As she swayed over the soup pot, her broad shoulders rolled forward and her iconic apron clung to her body, elaborately cross-stitched with hexagonal lemons and thin silvery-purple knives.

"Is Zaydee out in the garden?" I shifted uncomfortably in my seat, tapping my foot against the stool leg. "Maybe he's picking a few herbs for the soup and forgot to come back inside. I'll go get him."

Zaydee always got lost in the garden. But the moment my tennies hit the floorboard, a grayness swept throughout the room. I looked outside, the unexpected overcast turning everything cold.

"Henya…"

My name came out of my grandmother's mouth, but it did not sound like her voice. There was a sharp hiss to how she beckoned me.

"Bubbe," I scanned the back of her body, searching for some form of truth. A bit afraid, but also a bit foolish, I inched towards her and placed my hand on her bony shoulder. The moment we touched, she spun around and held onto my arm. Bubbles formed at the rim of the boiling pot of broth. The soup was indeed burning without anyone guiding it through the final stages.

"Your grandfather is not out in the garden," she finally replied, cradling her chin into the nook of my elbow.

"Isn't that strange? He's always near you... especially when YOU cook his precious soup."

I thought the joke may land but I was very, very wrong. Bubbe glowered at me. I broke free from her grasp, wondering what unfriendly eyes were staring back at me.

"Yom asal, yom basal," whispered Bubbe Lola, shaking her head as if to shake away the unfamiliar gaze that consumed her. "One day you'll have onions and another day you'll have honey. Bad and good days for all. But our family never tastes honey."

That was cryptic. I squinted at her and inched my way over to the soup ladle. One quick stir had tempered the rising heat of the broth. Just enough so that it wouldn't spill over. I added a few sprigs of parsley that had wilted next to the radiating heat of the stove.

It was only then that I noticed something truly absurd. A ridiculous number of sliced lemons were left on the counter, the sour juice clinging to the air. Ingredients which had no place in french onion soup.

"Bubbe, what are the lemons for?" I had to ask. If I didn't ask, I'd never get an answer.

Bubbe tucked a strand of hair behind my ear — a habit of hers that made me cringe, as if she was scanning my face for a sign of betrayal — then she hummed nonchalantly, as if my question had never been asked. I shook my head, freeing that loose strand of hair. She tried to grace a delicate finger along my temple again, tidying what ought to be left tousled.

"Why so many questions, Bubbeleh? Let your mind be at peace."

My family always had a way of spoiling the mood, peeling away my patience like layers of a pungent onion. *Was it so hard to answer a simple question about lemons?* I grabbed one of the lemon halves off the counter and sucked on it until the bitter tang coated my throat.

"Ack! Henya, what are you doing?"

"Oh, does that bother you, Bubbe?" I tried to grin behind the tingling sensation on my teeth.

"It most certainly does, you little brat. Cut it out!"

We were no longer bantering, Bubbe to bubbeleh. Grandmother to granddaughter.

"Well," I stood my ground, "lemons aren't really the kind of fruit we put in onion soup. Whenever you pick this many lemons, someone in this family's done something wrong. And they usually don't come around again until you're no longer angry."

Bubbe Lola turned to me and scooped the lemons off of the counter with one large sweep of her arm.

"Humph!" She grunted and raised a pointed finger at me. "You would take his side, little Henya. Wouldn't you!? Just like Zaydee. Always thinking he's right, always sticking his nose into other people's business. Do you want to go missing next?"

I bit my tongue and gazed out the window at the lemon tree, which stood tall and lanky.

"I sent him away, but you'll see him again tonight."

I worried for Zaydee. I had to see him. No one ever looked that great when Bubbe welcomed them back into the house.

"When I die..."

"Bubbe!" I gasped, grabbing the ladle from her carefully as she waved it above her head. "Do not talk that way. I'm sure you and Zaydee will sort out your differences. It can't be that bad."

"When I die," she wrangled the ladle back from me, her grasp unusually strong for someone her age. Then she turned off the stove and wobbled over to the table, lemon juice squishing between her toes from all the lemons she knocked onto the floor. "I want to be planted under my favorite lemon tree. With everyone placing a prayer pebble beneath those branches and reciting, one by one, a memory they shared with me."

I tip-toed over crushed lemon peels towards my grandmother.

"What did your Zaydee say when I mentioned this today? He said, 'how many onions do we need for this soup?' He just wanted to talk about soup! SOUP!? Onion this... onion that."

"Maybe the conversation made him sad?" I tried to placate Bubbe Lola to no avail.

She raised her voice an octave and rambled on, "I told him to not say another word about those stupid onions. That if I hear one more word about how to slice or dice a single onion, I'll throw him into the boiling soup instead! And then...then he had the nerve to say that when he dies, he's going to fill his pockets with a dozen onions so I'll never come near him again!"

I tried to refrain from laughing. If my grandmother didn't have a notorious habit of making people disappear when she went on a lemon-picking tirade, it would have been funnier.

"So you want to talk about burial arrangements, and he wants to talk about soup?" I snorted. "This is a silly argument, Bubbe. Bring Zaydee back right now. Please! Just forgive each other already."

"Silly argument!? Just wait until you're married and try to find eternal peace, Henya. Your spoiled little brain doesn't think ten steps ahead because you've got your youth."

I brushed off Bubbe's comment and turned my anger to shoveling all the fallen lemons into a bag. Out of the corner of my eyes, I spotted a nearly-bare lemon tree upon the little hill in my grandparents' backyard.

Zaydee had made a huge mistake. He had driven Bubbe more mad than she had ever been. Bubbe loved that lemon tree nearly more than she loved her family. If she picked almost all of those lemons, she was undoubtedly having an internal fit.

"Those should be returned to the tree," she whispered. "Back on its branches."

I raised my eyebrow. "Bubbe, I don't think we can just hang these lemons back onto the tree..."

"Try! You have to try," her voice was firm.

I grabbed the bag tentatively. I had to cleanse the room from this odd aroma of pungent soup, bitter tears, and sliced citrus somehow.

I wandered out back towards the lemon tree. Zaydee was still nowhere to be seen.

The lemon leaves rustled in the wind, speaking Bubbe's wishes softly. I never really believed trees had voices, but when it came to Bubbe's darling lemons, I wouldn't dare deny that she and the tree had a way of conversing their deepest, darkest secrets.

I tried to balance one of the lemons between two branches.

Plop!

It fell to the ground instantly and rolled by my foot. I tried again.

Plip-plop!

"Ugh, Bubbe!" I shouted to no one, alone upon the hill. The lemon rolled right beneath my foot until accidentally squishing beneath my heel. I picked up the smushed lemon and skewered it angrily on the branch. "This is ridiculous!"

The lemon I hung on the tree squeaked, unable to free itself from the branch. I shook my head and leaned my ear closer to the tree. Lemons could not talk. I was going mad — just like everyone else in this house — and then the ground began to rumble!

Several branches contorted to form faces of relatives I had not seen in quite a long time. A greedy cousin pestering my grandmother every time she was down on her luck, or that one uncle who wasn't really an uncle but rather an annoying friend of Zaydee's childhood days.

Then, my grandfather's face appeared for a fleeting moment. It vanished deep within the trunk and I gasped, tripping over one of the roots which seemed to writhe in pain.

"Bubbe, Bubbe!" I screamed and bolted back inside the house, heart racing. "Z-Z-Zaydee. Zaydee! I saw him. Right in-in-inside the lemon tree!"

"Really!? That's quite a sight, Henya," laughed Bubbe, wiping the countertop. My jaw dropped as I stared at a whole new, very pristine-looking kitchen. Bowls of onion soup cooled on the table. There was even a third bowl set out where Zaydee usually sat. "Go ahead and eat your soup. The sooner we do, my sweet girl, the sooner I can *de-onion-fy* this house."

"No, I'm not imagining it! His face was there…and then…gone… "

"Sounds like your grandfather is ready to apologize."

Either my grandmother had completely lost her marbles, or I had. Seeing faces on a lemon tree was not normal. Even for my family.

"Okay?" I asked skeptically. Maybe it all was in my head. I held my chin with two fingers, trying to deduce what I had witnessed with incredible care. "Maybe it was a roof rat, Bubbe. They're always eating lemon rinds, right?"

"*Feh! Feh!* Worse. Much worse."

"What do you mean worse?" I asked, wiping some drool away from my lips. The soup was turning cold but I refused to eat until I convinced my grandmother to stop being so secretive. I dipped a pinky finger into the onion broth for a quick taste. Bubbe slapped my hand away, waving a disapproving finger at me.

"Such manners. Why don't you dip your toes in next?"

I glared at her, my patience wearing thin, and hastily spurted out, "Why don't you tell me what you did to Zaydee? Or how come this onion soup tastes so rotten!?"

Her face turned stone cold. I gulped.

"Roof rats, eh?" She gobbled up her soup without any shame. Her nostrils widened as her breath became heavy. "Maybe there are a few. Always nibbling at my lemons. Always sneaking about. Always betraying the garden which gives them food and shelter."

Okay, we're definitely not talking about roof rats, I thought quietly.

"What would you say if your Bubbe caught a few and boiled them in this soup?" she asked.

"Rats or relatives?" I forced myself to grin.

She leaned on her elbows, lowering her face towards mine. "I'd catch them all, Henya," she winked. "They think they're clever, but I see them."

"I bet you would, Bubbe," I winked back, nervously tapping

my foot and trying to keep an eye out for my grandfather. After all, Bubbe did say he would be joining us soon. "Catch every single one of them. Rats and relatives alike."

We had a special kind of bond, me and Bubbe. I always appreciated her dark humor. But she was horribly stubborn. It's no surprise that I became so resistant to the hand-slapping or double-edged comments. I was my grandparents' granddaughter after all.

However, I wasn't finished with our conversation — and I wasn't like others in my family who would rather disappear entirely than face my grandmother.

"Bubbe!" I stomped my tapping foot and dug my heel into the wooden floor. "I'm tired, I'm hungry, and I want to know exactly why Zaydee isn't here. Right now!"

She stood up, towering over me. I stood up, too, a few inches taller than her even though I had much growing left to do.

"Oh, sweet Henya. Like I said, he'll be back soon enough."

She collected herself rather nicely for someone who knew *exactly* what was really going on. Zaydee and Bubbe always had something to quarrel over. They always had...onion days.

I steeled myself as ominous questions rattled in my skull. My nails nervously chipped away at the skin on my knuckles. Then I blurted out the biggest question on my mind, which probably made me sound weak to Bubbe.

"Do you never have 'honey days,' Bubbe?"

Again, she said nothing. She just stood there. Our family's grandfather clock ticked away in the foyer. A neighborly dog barked from far, far away. And the gloomy gray chill that lapsed minute by minute became colder.

If anything, I was determined to reserve honey-only days for myself. I was more than happy to leave the taste and smell of onions with her.

"Why is our family so complicated?" I continued to dig deeper into these thoughts I always kept buried well beneath the surface. "I saw something outside. I know I did. Is that why our cousin, Mattie, no longer visits you? Or why Zaydee's annoying friend, who you refuse to let us call 'uncle', lost a toe and doesn't call Zaydee any longer? What's next?"

Bubbe Lola tried to hold my hand but I squirmed away. She wasn't going to wrap those bone-crushing arms around me this time. "Complicated? Who's complicated, Henya?"

"Why can't our family just be *normal*?" I pleaded. "We're always complaining!"

The doorbell rang, making me jump. A distraction just long enough to allow Bubbe Lola to clasp my hands in hers.

Don't let her confuse you, I told myself, *change the topic. Quickly.*

There was no chance of me escaping her grasp.

"Didn't I once tell you everyone always apologizes to me? At some point?" smirked Bubbe. "Whether we have bad, onion-y days or good, honeyed days, that choice is up to each person. And each person alone."

Bubbe released her grip on me, and I bolted for the front door. When I opened it, though, there was nothing... but a mysterious sealed jar of honey at the doorstep. I cradled the jar carefully in my hands and ran around the house, scanning the yard.

"Zaydee!?" I cried out. "Zaydee, is that you?"

A shadow swept quietly towards the back gate, rattling the lock gently. I rounded towards the noise, my heels squeaking in the squishy, dew-covered grass. With one hand, I fiddled with the lock until it released the back gate wide enough for me to squeeze through.

I gasped! Bubbe Lola was waiting for me, arms crossed, eyeing the jar of honey.

"I see it in your eyes, Bubbeleh," she shook her head. "So judgmental."

Then she took her pruner out of her dress pocket and led me towards the lemon tree. We examined the dead branches where the already-picked lemons dangled indelibly.

"Such grown-up thoughts torment you," said Bubbe, so matter-of-factly. "Yet what would little Henya know? You must wait for mature Henya to come around. Only then will she know the difference between onion and honey days."

I glanced up at Bubbe, panic in my chest. *Was she trying to teach me a lesson now? Without explaining herself?*

She pointed to her temple, tapping a few times as if she had locked away a few secrets up there.

"Ah! Your Zaydee has returned! Ready to apologize."

"What!?" I dropped the jar of honey, shattering the glass on a line of river rocks encircling the lemon tree. One of the tree's overgrown branches pricked my arm and the blood soaked into its leaves. Zaydee stumbled forward out of the other side of the tree, his face pale. "Zaydee! Are you okay!?"

Bubbe continued to prune the tree while I helped my grandfather to sit upright. He knelt before me, tears giving away some type of fear or sadness he refused to show outright.

The scent of lemon clung to his skin.

"Such a child," smiled Bubbe. "I forgive you, my dear husband. Come here."

I rubbed my watery eyes, the grass and citrus scent making me itch. Glass from the honey jar twinkled in the dimming sunlight and all of the honey contained within slowly poured over the lemon tree roots and down the hill.

"I'm...sorry," whispered Zaydee, his voice sounding defeated. "Sorry Lola."

"Well, let's get your grandfather inside, Henya," said Bubbe, brushing grass bits from her hands onto her apron where each stitched lemon and knife seemed to dance upon the fabric.

"Come here, Zaydee," I knelt down and balanced his arm over my shoulder. But when we stood up together the path from which we came was covered in a thick pool of honey.

"Impossible," whispered Bubbe, her lips quivering.

Our heels stuck into the honey, making it nearly impossible to inch close to the house.

Zaydee clasped his hands together and burst out laughing, his springy steps dipping left and right into puddles of honey and mud.

We were trapped up on that hill.

Me, a bitter Bubbe, and a gloating Zaydee.

With nothing to do but watch a sea of honey consume the house.

"Well, isn't that something," said Bubbe, her cheeks turned pale and those broad, pointed shoulders of hers softened. "I've never seen *that* before."

I was trying to remain neutral, like Switzerland in the great Bubbe-Zaydee War.

"You ruined the onions, didn't you?" smirked Zaydee, his mood completely altered as if he had never been trapped inside a lemon tree by my grandmother's wrath. "I can smell them from here!"

"I'll break that nose of yours if you don't shush!" snapped Bubbe.

Lifting one heavy, sticky foot at a time I tried to trudge down the hill through massive globs of honey. My grandparents were nuts! If I hadn't been so hungry, the utter shock and terror of what I witnessed would have made me faint.

"Where are you going, Bubbeleh?" smiled Zaydee as I carried him with me. "I wouldn't mind sitting on top of this hill for a few more hours... just to watch your grandmother squirm."

I rolled my eyes. The further I went downhill, the higher the honey rose... at first above my ankles, then above my shins.

"You... you better keep quiet, Zaydee," I whispered, afraid to look at Bubbe. "I can feel her eyes burning into our backs and I do not intend to upset her!"

"Why not?" He asked. I froze and lowered him into the honey with me.

"Wh-wh-why not? WHY NOT!?" I cried and stretched my arms out before us. "Are you insane!?"

He shrugged. I screamed. Bubbe traipsed in our direction.

"Because your house is covered in mystical honey that only seems to grow the longer you two provoke each other! Because I don't think I'll ever get the stench of onions out of my nose! Or how about because my sweet, old Bubbe likes to torture those she loves and feed them to her ravenous lemon tree?"

The smell of onions soon became overpowering. I plugged my nose and tried to look around for an easier way out of this mess. I felt a light tap on my shoulder.

"I don't want to talk, Bubbe!" I shrugged off the finger. Then another pestering tap and a few eerie clicking noises rang too close to my ear. "Quit it!"

I whirled around.

"Henya!" cried Zaydee and Bubbe, the pair of them sliding down the hill on their backs. The honey carried them straight to the garden gate.

"Oh no! I'm coming!" I shouted, unable to budge or even fall on my back to drift down the hill as they had. It felt like the honey was propping me up while it devoured them. "Don't let go of each other! Do you hear me!?"

I had to get to them. I had to make things right between my grandparents in some way, no matter how much of a mess they caused. Otherwise, I'd risk losing them both!

Swiftly, as if a deep fear of losing them had wished me free, I slid down the hill over honeycombed shreds of grass and a golden path of dirt.

Schwack!

My feet smacked against the garden gate!

"Bubbe, Zaydee," I panted, reaching my hand towards theirs. It was easy for me to stand on my own two feet again. But having the strength to lift them out of the honey sea and off of their backs nearly made me break my own.

"Henya, how are you doing that?" asked Bubbe Lola. Her hand slipped out of mine and slapped against Zaydee's chest just as he seemed to gain some momentum of his own.

I couldn't understand any of it any longer. All I kept thinking about was good days and bad days... and how we choose our path... how we choose what we receive.

"That's it!" I exclaimed and knelt beside my grandparents. "Just as you said, Bubbe. We can choose to have either honey days or onion days. So make your choice!"

Bubbe and Zaydee looked at each other. They were both *so very stubborn!*

"Well?" I asked. I couldn't necessarily tap my foot beneath all of this honey, but I think they could sense my frustration just the same.

Zaydee sighed, "I bought her that lemon tree fifty-five years ago. On our anniversary."

"*That* lemon tree?" I asked, pointing to the top of the hill where everything was smothered in a glittering, sticky mess.

"I never knew how much she loved it. And I stole the very last lemon from that tree this morning... just to get her to stop talking about being buried with it!"

Bubbe sniffled and a few fleeting tears ran down her cheeks.

"I'm sorry, Zaydee," sighed Bubbe, to my surprise. She leaned her head against my grandfather's shoulder. "I spoiled the soup today with such sad conversation."

"Oh Bubbe," I leaned down to kiss her forehead. "Why didn't you just tell me what happened?"

She looked up at me, and even though my grandparents couldn't move much, the honey began to thin with each passing minute and every kind thought spoken.

"Henya," continued Bubbe, "I gifted a soup ladle and pot to your grandfather last winter. We grew dozens of onions, with our own bare hands, just to make his famous French onion soup. Now I'm afraid I've ruined something precious to us both."

"Precious? Like what?" I wrinkled my nose, partly out of curiosity and partly because of the lingering strange combination of smells. It would be a while before I'd crave onions or honey again.

"Yes, Lola," chimed Zaydee, "what did you ruin?"

The honey had nearly soaked into the ground completely. A light breeze swept over our sticky arms and faces as the three of us sat there.

Some days are like honey...

I waited for Bubbe to reply, that proverb impressed upon me. As expected, there was radio silence, and just as I was about to nudge Bubbe for a response, I paused.

Zaydee and Bubbe were holding hands, curled up in a ball on the grass. They seemed content as they looked beyond me into the sunset.

"Nothing is really ruined, is it?" I sat beside them, until an unsettling moan made the hairs on the back of my neck curl. "What... was... that?"

I peered behind me at the house. A few squeaky lemons rolled out of the back door and burst into a fury of sour dust as soon as the sun kissed their peeled skin. *Pop! Pop! Pop!*

"Just ignore it," whispered Zaydee, wrapping his arm around Bubbe. "She's just letting go of a few final thoughts."

"If you say so," I shook the chill from my arms as my body started to hover a few inches off of the ground. "Um, can someone...please... think more positively? Please!?"

Bubbe glanced at me quickly and smirked. Honey dripped off of my shoes and floated around me until I settled safely into the grass.

Perhaps I did not need to know *everything* unspoken between my grandparents. Their exchanges were sometimes bitter, sometimes sweet. However, they were always honest.

"You don't need to be afraid, Henya," they said to me, together, finally agreeing on something.

I shrugged, "I'm actually okay. Why should we be afraid of how we feel? Today wasn't necessarily good nor bad. It just... was... like the sunset just being a sunset."

"Oh, Lola," beamed Zaydee, a softness spreading across his face. "Our Henya is not so little anymore, hmm?"

A glimpse of light hovered above Bubbe, clearing away the coldness in her throat. She beckoned me towards her, "Henya. Sit."

And there I sat.

It wasn't the most elaborate of conversations but there was contentment in the space we occupied. Maybe our family was destined for onion days. Forever. I could never speak of this to anyone. No one would believe that my grandmother could conjure a man-eating lemon tree or that my grandfather possibly submerged the house in a raging mass of honey.

Although, as wisps of silky, sweet honey strands floated across the garden, I found the bleakness of my words hard to believe.

Somehow, I managed to get Bubbe and Zaydee to apologize to one another. To sit together in a moment of peace. To humble themselves.

I gave my family at least one honey day.

And that was enough.

WHEN THE WORLD GIVES OUT

RACHAL MARQUEZ JONES

I am alone.

Aida stands up from where she's been kneeling by Manny's bed and pulls the ratty blanket over him. She'll bury him tomorrow.

For now, there's dinner and reviewing the launch plan in her mind for the millionth time. *Finish the rocket. Check the fuel. Adjust the flight path. Launch. Escape this world. Navigate to Mars. Ditch the rocket. Land the damn module. Survive.* She pulls her rations out of storage and sits down at the makeshift table. She doesn't eat, half-heartedly staring at the plate of shelf-stable, apocalypse-friendly beans and rice. Even the most boring food known to humankind is too much effort. She pushes her food to the other end of the table and lays her head down. With Emanuel gone, Aida Morales is the last member of the team. It's not like anyone will know if she misses a meal.

Aida dreams of rice and beans. Not the flavorless, mushy prepper crap she has for rations, but the kind her dad used to make sometimes when she was little. He would spend all day in the kitchen, until the smell of oxtail and sofrito filled their little house, always followed by apple pie for dessert. She dreamed of sitting at the dinner table, her mom dishing up despite being tired from a long day at work and her dad telling stories of his tíos on the island sneaking bites out of the kitchen until all the tías kicked them out. In the dream, Aida puts the first bite of food into her mouth, but she only gets a split-second of flavor before it turns to dust and the weight of everything she's lost comes crashing—

Aida wakes to the sound of Manny's alarm going off. *Leave it to that pendejo to wake me up even after he's dead.* She shuts it off, then looks over at the blanket covering him and sighs. Manny used to crack jokes like he didn't have a care in the world, and even on her worst days he could get Aida to half-smile. *God, I miss that laugh.* Comfort like a fresh cup of coffee.

It's late morning by the time she lays a scraggly marigold by his grave. Flowers are rare these days, but she knows how he loved them. He used to tell her about the garden he had in his yard, before. Before, when it seemed like it might be enough to get by on recycling and growing your own tomatoes. Any hope that still exists is far more foolish now.

Aida tries not to think about that.

After all, she knows this whole plan is one foolish hope. Most days she doesn't think she'll ever make it off this rock, let alone to Salus, the colony on Mars. *Talk about a fucking moonshot.*

Earth is barely habitable. Toxic air, unpredictable weather, mass disease and death.

It all happened slowly enough that most people stayed in denial until it was too late. By then, the only real option left was to leave. And surprise, surprise, the wealthy bought their way to salvation. They bought hope. *And left only devastation for the rest of us.*

Salus was founded and funded by the type of billionaire philanthropists who thought that Mars ought to be grateful to have them there. Officially, it was a "nonpolitical interplanetary base open to all" with some more bullshit about "the next step for humanity." In reality, it was a colony on a dusty and barren planet, filled with

Earth's rich and influential and those useful enough to have been deemed worth the cost of their passage.

Aida's mother had tried to get them a spot, calling in the last of her favors as NASA splintered from scientific exploration and advancement to a capital-driven, apocalypse-stricken mess like every other major organization. Aida's dad was already sick by then, and though she never said anything, Aida knew that they wouldn't allow a dying man to take up their precious space. Once, her dad had tried to tell Aida that maybe they could get in if they applied without him, but neither Aida nor her mom would hear of it. By the time he died, all of the main transports had left, and infrastructure to build or coordinate more had begun to fall apart.

Aida winces at the memory, her gut constricting as if she'd had the wind knocked out of her. She does not think about how she is the only one left. She does not think about how getting to Salus was her mother's last wish. She does not ask herself whether, if she gets there, they'll even let her in. She does not think about everything she has already lost, or what she still has left to lose.

The rocket is essentially complete, but she'll need to make a few more modifications to fly it by herself. As their crew dwindled, the remaining survivors adapted the plans to require fewer and fewer bodies. And when Manny knew that he wouldn't make it, he helped Aida finish the plans so that she could complete the launch alone.

Theoretically.

She looks over the plans again, checking off the modifications she's already completed. All that's left is adjusting the flight calculations for the one-human-lighter payload, then the prelaunch tests and procedures. It's all familiar enough. Aida spent her childhood trailing after her mom's notebooks of equations and formulas, listening to her on conference calls at odd hours discussing flight trajectories and launch dates. Aida's mother never pushed her to follow in her footsteps, but the math came easily, and the sky never ran out of mysteries. Aida was studying astrophysics and mechanical engineering when the world gave out under her. Sometimes, on bad days, she imagines herself playing with toys on the floor of her mother's office—when she was safe, and life was full of possibilities. Sometimes it helps. Sometimes it tips her brain into a deeper spiral.

She reviews the notes Manny left, scrawled in his god-awful handwriting.

Aida winces and squeezes her eyes shut, waiting for the wave in her head to pass.

People used to talk about depression like a gray fog, but no one ever mentioned how excruciating it is. How much it burns. Like the time as a child that she touched a pan just pulled from the oven, only there's no salve to soften the pain.

Meds ran out a long time ago, or if they do exist, they're stockpiled in some warehouse she'll never find.

Respira. Just get through this moment. Aida runs her hand through her hair and gets back to running calculations on possible changes to fuel usage and telemetry.

Above the control panel someone had scratched out the words *ad astra*, so all that remains is *per aspera*. Aida touches the etching like a prayer, and wonders again if there's hope enough left for her to escape.

The remnants of a research center that became what members of the now-gone crew referred to as "the outpost" used to belong to a NASA affiliate. Close enough to Houston to be useful, but far enough out to be easily forgotten when the world fell apart. Not long after Aida's dad died, her mom got word of the outpost through a message on an old ham radio she'd kept running.

Aida's depression was dark and deep, but she knew getting to this outpost—to this crew and this last-ditch effort at escape—was the only thing her mom was holding on to. So she went. Just before they left, Aida took one last apple from the dying tree in their yard. It was scrawny and tart, but it reminded her of her dad.

Once they arrived, they were welcomed as if there had always been a place for them. Aida's mother lent her expertise, while Aida mostly provided manpower. Enough of the crew were former engineers and scientists that their plan seemed like it might actually work. They had salvaged materials from the research center and any other nearby facilities they could manage to travel to, and while they waited for the launch window, they worked.

Now, it's only Aida left. And in the moments when she's all but given up, she thinks of the hopes of all the people who worked on this foolish, ridiculous, one-in-a-million plan. She thinks that their hope will have to be enough to get her through.

When the stars start to appear on the horizon, Aida's eyes drift toward Mars, its faint red glow like a flare in the distance. *I only have to get there.*

They figured out how to grow crops up there—more than just potatoes. Beans, lentils, root vegetables mostly. She doubts there's a grove of apple trees.

She has to wonder—not for the first time—if Salus is even still there. She isn't aware of any communications between the people there and anyone left on Earth in a long time. *Not like they'd have a reason to look back when they escaped.* Still, the worry follows her like a weight on a line. Maybe she'll actually manage to launch herself off this suffering rock and survive the months-long route to Mars, only to find nothing. More wasteland, more pain. Entirely alone. Just like what she left behind.

Aida knows there's a joke to be made about it not counting as nihilism when it really is the end of the world, before being hit with the bitter realization that there's no longer anyone to tell jokes to.

She looks up, pulled by the quiet memory of her mother's voice drawing her focus, and her heart, to the stars. One of the few upsides of a dying world is minimal light pollution. Aida remembers when she used to look up and could only barely make out the outline of Orion, marred by satellites and streetlamps. Now the Milky Way spills overhead, more stars than she could possibly count.

In the quiet, and the aloneness, the pain rises like a tide. Aida imagines drowning in the stars, the sky pouring down toward the dirt like in the stories her mother used to tell, and her existence being swallowed in the collision.

Escaping means more than leaving the only home she's ever known. It also means leaving all tangible memories of her life and everyone she's ever loved. Her parents' graves, her family's house, every gift and handwritten note from lost loved ones.

She squeezes her eyes shut and presses the heels of her hands in, willing the ache to ebb.

Aida sucks in a breath, and holds it until she can feel her blood pounding in her head. She exhales slowly, raggedly. The stars swim above her. It used to be comforting to be alone, and Aida found a certain solace in the idea that she was just a speck of carbon on a pale blue dot—all but insignificant. It made the screech and wail of her depression feel less consuming; if she was so miniscule amongst the universe, then so was the pain.

But alone is also when she's most vulnerable to the poisonous whispers in her brain, and now alone is all the time. When she was a teenager, sitting on the floor of her room for hours at a time, Aida's father used to come sit next to her and tap her forehead two times, saying "Does the mentirosa in there need to be shown who is boss?"

Sometimes it was enough to make Aida laugh, but often she would just quirk her mouth or roll her eyes. Her father didn't mind. He'd wrap an arm around her until she leaned her head on his shoulder.

By the time her mother got home from working late, she'd be okay enough to get up again.

Aida falls onto her back and lets her eyes go out of focus, breath shaky. She whispers, "Nadie, nadie." No one's going to save her. So, she'll have to do it herself.

It hardly passes for actual training, but Aida shuffles through her workout, doing pushups on the cold concrete and strength training with makeshift weights. Afterward, she straps on a respirator mask and grabs the salvaged helmet off a shelf before heading outside. The old convertible isn't much, and there isn't enough gas available in her meager stores for meaningless drives, but it's the best way to simulate how many Gs she'll be pulling during the launch. She doesn't bother with a seatbelt. She also doesn't dwell on whether that's because the stress makes the simulation more realistic, or because she isn't particularly afraid of what will happen if she crashes.

She presses the gas pedal down harder. *Seventy. Eighty. Ninety-five. One-ten.* The wind roars loudly enough to narrow her every thought into this single moment.

One little tug on the steering wheel at that high of a speed and the whole car would go spinning—maybe roll a few times and Aida would finally see the end of it. Feel something sharp instead of just the ache that's always there.

She follows the impulse and the steering wheel jerks, the old convertible's tail spinning as Aida's head gets whipped to the side. She skids to a halt off the shoulder of the crumbling road.

After turning the car off, she throws her head back against the headrest, half rage and half empty. Trying to catch her breath, she doesn't move again until nightfall.

Aida spends the entire next day in bed, restless and angry and guilty, but none of it is enough to get up.

That's something most people will never tell you about depression. How fucking *angry* you are all the time. When you manage to feel things that aren't apathy, what's left is a core of dense rage, like its own miniature black hole pulling you in and crushing everything it touches into oblivion. It hurts like hell, and Aida sometimes wishes she could crack into her ribcage and carve it out of her chest cavity. Sometimes she has caved and dug the anger into her skin as if to excise it. She's not sure if it's made easier or harder by the fact that she has a right to be angry.

Generations before her chose selfishness and greed, and let her and those with fewer resources become the late-stage sacrifice for their standard of living. But all the rage and fury she feels aren't going to keep her alive, and certainly aren't going to forge her escape.

The next day, Aida feels a shift in the air. *It's funny the things you learn when there's no other alternative.* She looks out at the horizon and spots the storm coming.

She hauls some of the more sensitive equipment inside and opens up the water reclaimer. Not much else to do but wait.

Aida wakes in the middle of the night to the roar of wind and rain outside, a hurricane or tropical storm raging over the battered earth. She rolls over and dozes off until she's lurched awake by a booming scream, but louder and sharper, then a thud big enough to rattle the windows. She doesn't sleep the rest of the night.

By late the next morning, the storm has receded enough to go assess the damage. She heads out and sifts through miscellaneous debris. Until she sees it.

Coño.

A few hundred yards away from the outpost, the last working

wind turbine has fallen, wrenched off its post as if it had been a child's toy. There would be no fixing that—at least not by herself.

Aida turns to look at the rocket—blessedly a safe distance away from the old turbine—and sees that it's still standing. Messy with broken branches and trash blown in, but standing.

While it has enough fuel, Aida's only source of power for basically everything else is now toast. There are solar arrays on the shuttle, but removing them would compromise the entire mission. With the launch window only weeks away, she realizes she might be entirely screwed.

She has a little power in reserve, but it will last a couple of days at best. There is no way it will be enough to finish the launch prep and adjust the telemetry before takeoff. And without adjusting, she could end up off course enough to miss Mars entirely. She'd end up floating in space, still alone.

Aida wonders whether she'd prefer to die here on the planet she's always called home. Or in space—lovely and brutal and cold. *Ending it here would be a hell of a lot less effort.*

It's not the first time that she's considered this. When she was younger and the world was still limping along, it breached in her mind as a startling fantasy. *Intrusive thoughts.* That's what her old therapist from before the collapse called them. Aida always felt they were more like temptations, whispering what it would be like to just cease to exist. The imagined relief of no longer living. When the end was here and the wounds were raw, it was at its worst. She wasn't alone then, but the pain of loss and collapse added an intensity she hadn't felt before. Before, Manny and some of the others had helped her weather the worst of it.

Now she is alone, and rather than a flash of impulse, it's a weighted consideration. It would be easier here. Billions upon billions of people have died on this planet. But only handfuls have died in space. *Is it desperate to want your death to stand out, even if no one knows you're gone?*

Aida remembers going to the museum as a child with her mother, seeing the models of the first rovers sent to Mars. There was so much hope back then. Her mother told her how those rovers sent information and images back to Earth, how they taught us what it was like on a world other than our own, what it took for a planet to sustain life. Water, oxygen, sunlight. Aida used to marvel that the same sun she woke to—the one that would eventually prove so dangerous in this atmosphere—sustained the rovers even so far from home. The rovers were—

Dios, Aida, the fucking rovers! There were still a couple of old models in storage. If she could get any of their solar panels working again, she might be able to scrape enough power together to make it to the launch.

It's not like they hadn't tried solar before. But apocalyptic hurricanes and tornadoes have a habit of shredding delicate tech, and eventually their arrays were broken beyond repair.

Aida takes off at a sprint toward the old storage building, and only makes it a hundred and fifty yards or so before she has to slow down to catch her breath. *Some great astronaut you'll be.* With her heart pounding in her chest, she trudges toward the battered building.

It takes her a day to dig out a couple of old rover models and arrange the solar panels into something serviceable. She has to refer to documents that a long-gone engineer had scrawled together and uses an embarrassing amount of haphazard duct tape, but she gets it working. *Mary Sue, my ass.*

Over the ensuing weeks, Aida eats too little and sleeps intermittently and runs the numbers for the launch again and again and again. She takes down the service structure around the rocket piece by piece. In the middle of all of it, her brain drags her down again. The pain feels like something off-kilter that you can't pinpoint. Like the puzzle pieces don't fit, and the harder you try to piece them together, the blurrier the edges get.

She counts the days the way she used to count the marks on her thigh.

It's surprisingly good weather for a launch—little wind and the sky's a clear blue.

Finally, it's time. She contemplates leaving a note, some record that she was there and where she went. *Chances of anyone reading it are slimmer than landing on Mars.* In the end, she pulls a half-dead Sharpie out of her pocket and underlines the remaining *per aspera* above the control panel.

Aida initiates the launch. It takes several minutes to flip all the switches and adjust the settings on the control board. The engines start, the support arms of the launch tower release, and the computers and guidance systems confirm that they're working.

The noise of burning fuel rises with her adrenaline. There's something almost comforting about the wobbly roar around her, like when she used to get overwhelmed as a kid and put both hands over her ears. It's just enough danger to make the world feel real in a way it hasn't in a long, long time.

She realizes she had expected it to sound and feel more like the launches her mom took her to as a little kid—standing nearly a mile away, able to hear the roar and feel the pulse of the engines as they warmed up and eventually lifted the craft into the sky. It's louder here, and she can feel every subtle vibration pulsing through her suit, her chest, her head. But it feels different somehow, to be inside the source of it all. Smaller, perhaps.

Aida takes as deep of a breath as she can manage and flips up the protective cover on the final control. She glances at the screens and, briefly, out the window. No matter how this ends, it's the last time she'll see the sky from beneath like this. If it works, she'll escape—beyond the unceasing pressure of the atmosphere, beyond the quiet pull of gravity that's held her down all her life. If it doesn't, she's mostly sure that this is how she wants to go.

Her entire body is crushed back into her seat as the rocket

TO ROOT SOMEWHERE BEAUTIFUL • 191

accelerates, racing away from the earth. After what seems like both forever and no time at all, Aida escapes the tether that's been holding her down her whole life.

And all she sees are stars.

FOLLOW ME INTO THE DARK

MALLORY JONES

I shouldn't have come back. I should've stayed gone like I promised myself I would, running away when my life crumbled into jagged, unrecognizable pieces. But like Wren told me a year ago—promises are made to be broken.

I'd sworn off Hemlock. The town and people and their all-knowing judgements. I moved on. All the way to college in Seattle. Sitting through my 8 a.m. biology class, bonding with classmates over how ungodly an hour it was to be awake. Going to parties at frat houses with my roommate, Maggie, for the sake of the *college experience*. I pretended my ass off.

But every night while I lay in bed trying to sleep, I thought of Hemlock. My parents and best friend, Wren. The house I grew up in. How terribly it all fell apart when my mom left and dad followed after her without even a "Hey, you wanna come look for her with me?"

Just like that, I became the town curse.

The *don't get too close to her*. The *everyone leaves Laurel Berkley*.

Well, jokes on them because I left Hemlock before it could do the same to me. I cut it cold turkey like my history professor claims he did whiskey despite the flask he sips from.

Guess we're all lying to ourselves.

It only took me three hundred and sixty-six days and one text to come back. And now, staring out the bus window as we roll into Hemlock, I feel like I've made a huge mistake.

The bus roars to a stop, the tires screeching against hot pavement. Burnt rubber swims in the air. I'm the only one on the bus. Probably because I'm the only one who'd willingly visit Hemlock during the middle of July where even a drop of rain makes the humidity bloom so thick it steals your breath away. Not in a romantic way either. The bus's whirring air conditioning barely offers any relief to the sweat clinging to my forehead.

I grab my duffel bag and stand. It's a light load considering I left most of my stuff back in my dorm. If everything works out—this will be a short trip.

I know where your parents are.

Wren knew exactly what to say to bring me back. Reigniting the hope I'd buried months ago. And after a year of not talking, I couldn't just ignore her. Even after she threw ten years of friendship into the trash. Foolish of me to think she'd understand why I couldn't go to college with her when it meant coming back *here* on the weekends. I didn't want to pop into Lou's Diner for Sunday breakfast, the same way I would with my dad, followed up with a round of *let's pray for the sinner* at the First Baptist Church. I needed to cut this place off before it sank too deep into me.

But when I told her I wouldn't be going to college with her, our friendship imploded into a shards of confetti, slicing my skin with little paper cuts.

She should've understood more than anyone. She heard the whispers around town. Saw how people would spot me walking down the street and veer away. I became a blight on Hemlock, but Wren only cared about her carefully laid future and how I ruined it by having a damn thought of my own.

Guess I'm still a little ticked.

The bus driver honks, jolting me from my run through the Dark Ages. "Any day now, kid. I don't want to be here longer than I have to. Too much bad news surrounding this place lately." His balding spot gleams with sweat and in the mirror above the steering wheel, his nervous gaze darts out the window.

"What do you mean *bad news*?" I fumble my way down the aisle.

He runs a hand over his head, wiping sweat away. "Missing person cases. Lots of 'em. Rumor has it if you stay too long, you'll disappear, too. My boss slips me an extra twenty every time I have to take this route." At that, he glares at me.

"You're welcome for the extra money?" I try, but it doesn't soften his stare. Sheesh. Sorry, buddy.

He pulls a lever and opens the door. The gears scream. I pause at the opening, half expecting him to shove my ass out. "You'll be back Monday, right? I bought my ticket already. Eight in the morning."

He only huffs. "We'll see about that."

Maybe his other Hemlock passengers roosted their asses in this town, but I would happily fly the coop once again two days from now. Hopefully with my parents back.

As soon as my feet hit the hot pavement, the bus lurches. In less than a minute, it disappears around the corner. And just like that, I'm left at the roadside bus stop. Nothing more than a bench with a torn awning overhead, the sun dappling the concrete below.

I heave in a deep breath. On my exhale, I turn right and head down the sidewalk buckled by new jutting roots. I don't have to think about where I'm going. My feet know the way. Ten minutes down the sidewalk, past the abandoned Radio Shack and Dairy Queen-turned-liquor store. Then it's a left, down, down, down Thorne Street, where the houses sag with the weight of time. At the very end sits the house I used to know as well as my own.

The trees now hang over the two-story brick home, their branches scraping the roof where sap has hardened the crooked shingles. Wren's house used to butt up to the woods, but now, somehow just a year later, it's consumed by them. As if the trees are teeth devouring the

Fitzgeralds' home. Their yard is grown up, wildflowers halfway up the windows. Feral.

Just like the girl who lives inside.

Or maybe I'm being dramatic and Wren's experienced a change of heart. I mean, she did text me. She brought me back. And considering the bus doesn't return until Monday, I'm stuck here. Good intentions or not, I'm going to see Wren again and then I'm going to figure out why she thinks she knows where my parents are when the trail's been cold for almost a year.

That's the final boost of courage I need to knock on her front door. The fresh coat of white paint Ms. Fitzgerald slathered on it a year ago is now flecked, revealing the rotting wood beneath it.

I wait a beat. And then the door opens and I'm confronted with the same forest green eyes that used to stare at me with adoration. Before it turned into burning resentment. I blink, heart in my throat. They're Wren's green eyes, but crows' feet nestle along the edges.

And…

I blink again, noticing the bobbed red hair. My heartbeat slows. It's not Wren staring at me.

"Laurel! We've missed seeing you," Ms. Fitzgerald says with a sad smile. "It's so good to see you."

"I've…missed you, too," I force out, and I realize it's the truth. "But a flight back home is no joke for a student, especially one who doesn't have any parents to—" I cut myself off, and Ms. Fitzgerald's shoulders slightly sag in relief. I could've told her the truth. That there was no reason for me to visit her when Wren had been off to college, too.

"I couldn't believe you ran off to an out-of-state college after everything," she says. "But…I'm sure your parents would be proud. Their little bird spread her wings."

I almost scoff. I guess when people you didn't like were written off as dead, you suddenly became fond of them. Wren's mom always did her best to dance around seeing my parents. I never puzzled that one out—whether it was some old beef between them, or her free-spirit ways didn't mesh with my parents uptight rules.

I manage to get through a few more minutes of small talk before insisting I'll meet Wren in the backyard by the woods. The mere thought of sitting across Ms. Fitzgerald drinking her sickeningly sweet tea while rehashing the last year almost makes me want to hurl more than seeing Wren.

Because the thing about my friendship with Wren...it was all consuming. Being her friend meant placing her at the center of my world and if she slipped off that pedestal even a little, hell broke loose.

Logically, I know it's a bad idea to meet Wren, especially after the disaster that was us falling apart. But my heart misses my friend.

And the funny thing about hearts? They don't tend to obey.

It's why I'm standing at the edge of the woods now, waiting for Wren to show up after her mom assured me she'd let her know I was here. Just a year ago, I stood here, crying and cursing my parents for leaving me when I was only eighteen. Only a kid. Left rehashing every second leading up to dad leaving. How he said it was his fault mom was gone. If she hadn't followed him into the dark, she'd still be here. His usual bowl of Raisin Bran grew soggy with milk as he mumbled to himself about making it right. I don't know, was it so awful to think he meant making things right at home? Not following after her?

My nerves tighten when a warm, thick breeze rustles the leaves, scraping against one another in a way that sounds like a screech echoing deep in the trees. Hemlock's woods have always been a hor-ror lover's wet dream. The abandoned research facility fuels far too many scary stories and cautionary tales. But I've never been scared of it. Probably because my parents worked there the first nine years of my life.

"Well if it isn't the bitch who left me."

Every thought fled at the sound of that husky voice. I used to tell her I wish I sounded like her— less nasally, more mysterious.

That's before I understood it was more than Wren's voice that made her a mystery.

I paste a smile on my face and spin around, but the Wren that greets me isn't the one from a year ago. Her usual brown curls now sag into a sad limp. Oh, and they're *red*. Fire truck engine red like her mom's. And there's something about her face that's different. Maybe it's the frown where there would've been a smile before. Or the dullness in her green eyes that used to be bright.

"Wren...it's so good to see you," I say, hoping she doesn't hear the way I falter.

Considering she raises one eyebrow and smirks, she does. "Come on, Laurel. Don't lie to me. We're beyond that, aren't we?"

We *used* to be.

When I don't answer her, she sighs, running a hand through her tangled hair. "Look, I only reached out because it had to do with your parents. If it was anything else, I wouldn't have. I promise. I know we didn't leave on good terms, but this is your chance to find them. To be whole again."

"Yet you couldn't tell me *where* you think my parents are before I dragged myself back here?" The sharpness in my voice isn't intended, but it's how I feel. I might've tiptoed around Wren for the majority of our friendship, but—I straighten my shoulders—not anymore.

Wren faces the trees. "Some things you have to see with your own eyes, okay? Trust me."

That's like saying I should trust a grizzly bear not to bite my hand. I swallow my unease and the thoughts curling in my head that whisper if she really knows where my parents are, then why aren't they here now? Did that mean she found their—

"Okay," I say, banishing that last thought before it grows arms and legs and a brain of its own. *Positive thoughts*, I tell myself. Just like the posters Maggie plasters on her side of the dorm.

Good vibes only.

Today will be the greatest.

Wren smiles, and if I squint hard enough, it looks real. But she turns before I can decide just how genuine it is and plunges herself into the thick leaves that chatter at her intrusion.

I take a breath. *One. Two. Three.* When I push into the trees, I swear I hear my mom's voice in my head begging me to leave. My therapist would tell me it's a product of my abandonment issues.

I brush her imaginary cries away, shoving through gnarled branches. They scrape against my arms, drawing pinpricks of blood. I don't let it faze me, eyes pinned on the dull red head in front of me until we're spit into a dark clearing, surrounded by towering trees.

"How have the woods gotten so much worse in just a year?" I run my fingers over my arms, wincing as they pass over fresh scratches. The woods have always been a pain in the ass to walk through, but never *this* bad.

Wren only shrugs, not bothering to pick the leaves out of her hair. "A lot can change in a year." She pins her eyes on me. "Can't it?"

I press my lips together and drop my gaze from her burning one. "Yeah. It can."

Thankfully, she continues weaving through the trees, brushing her hand against the bark and breathing deeply. Savoring the fresh air or whatever. Something the Old Wren would've laughed at. I don't dare question it, or poke fun at her. Because as confused as I am by the Wren before me—she holds all the power.

We walk deeper into the woods. Deeper than I've ventured in years. The quiet grows quieter. The trees larger and brush untamed. I feel it—the wild.

"Up for a scary story?" Wren shatters the silence, and for once, I'm thankful for it. Being back is already surreal enough, but being back in these woods with *Wren* has my mind spinning.

"What are we, ten?" I laugh weakly.

Wren doesn't.

So, of course, I give in just like I always used to. "Sure. Tell me a scary story."

Wren slows, lingering close enough I can hear her. "Growing up in Hemlock, we've all heard some kind of variation of this story. Of the girl trapped in the woods. Forever roaming the trees, looking for a way out. And if you stumble upon her, you won't be able to leave either."

"Wren, you don't really believe that, do you?" We used to tell each other that story every Halloween, whispering it as if the trapped, lonely girl would appear if we spoke too loud.

"Ask Jerry at the Quick Mart," Wren says. "He saw her at the edge of the woods. Legend says if you stare too long, she'll possess you."

I snort, immediately stopping myself when I realize I'm slipping back into old habits already. Lost within Wren's hypnotic storytelling like we never fell apart.

"Jerry also starts drinking when the sun rises, so maybe we shouldn't take his word to heart?"

"Whatever you say." Wren only shrugs.

"So that's your scary story? The same one I've heard a hundred times growing up?"

Wren quirks an eyebrow and she knows she's got me. Hook, line, and sinker. "That's just it. We've been told the same shit for years, but there's more to the story. That little girl's name was Eleanor, and she was *real*. She went into the woods, back when the research facility was still operating. Turns out she found out why the trees and grass were dying." Wren gives me a knowing look. My skin crawls. I break eye contact first. "A twelve-year-old girl decides to go into the woods and confront the people killing her home. Wanna take a guess how that went for her?"

"I don't really get why you're telling me this story. Honestly," I take a deep breath, gathering the courage that always seemed to slip me when Wren was involved. "I've only got a couple days here and I don't want to spend it listening to ghost stories."

Wren scoffs, her bony, pale shoulders tightening. "You know while you went off to college and remade yourself into the new and improved Laurel Berkley, I stayed here. You and your family ruined *everything,* so I think you can spare me a few minutes while I tell you a little *ghost story."*

I stand there, shocked by the disdain in Wren's words. "How did I screw things up just by going to a different college than you?"

"I didn't go," Wren says, resentment like a bitter pill lodged in her throat.

I swear my heart stops. "You...*what*? But you've posted on Instagram like, all the time!"

Wren laughs, a cynical, bone-chilling noise. "With a tripod and an imagination, you can do anything. *Be* anything."

An unease slinks inside me. Wren never admitted her faults or mistakes. So why now? While we were deep in these woods? Because she believes the trees won't whisper her dirty little secret to one another? I glance at the swaying branches above us and beyond it, the darkening sky, turning a bruised purple. Maybe here Wren feels safe.

"Anyway, real life is dull." Wren smooths her voice out until it's back in Story Mode. "It was near this time of day when Eleanor found the research facility." Wren veers from the confession like it hasn't just rocked my world.

"Eleanor crept closer to the old lab," Wren continues as if she was there with Eleanor. "She *knew* that place was the reason her home was poisoned. And she wanted to make them pay."

I glance at Wren, noting the sharp look in her eyes. The sharper smile tugging at her lips.

"Go on, tell me how she made them *pay*." I indulge her. "I know you want to."

"She found where they'd been dumping waste. She brought a mason jar with her to carry it back as proof. But she didn't have any gloves to scoop it in the jar. Even with how careful she was, some of it got on her fingers. She wiped it off then walked right up to the facility door and knocked. A man answered. She showed him the jar and told him exactly what she suspected. He let her inside. She never came out."

My body coils with tension. Maybe it's because my parents worked at the research facility, but hearing her turn that place into what sounds a lot like the scene of a murder makes my stomach turn.

"What happened to her?" I ask even though I don't want to know.

But of course, Wren decides that she's had enough talking. She gives me a lopsided smile and speeds up, nearly ditching me in the thick woods and the darkening daylight. Thirty minutes later and not another morsel of a crumb from Wren on where she's taking me—I lose my patience.

"Where did you say you saw my parents again?" I ask, treading lightly. It's a dangerous dance of overstepping, and one wrong move could obliterate me.

Wren stops walking, and I'm hit with this visceral visual of her smiling. As if we're reminiscing over our greatest hits and not looking for my missing-presumed-dead parents.

"I didn't," she says, and when she faces me, that smile I imagined is gone, replaced by a grimace. I don't know what I'm thinking. Maybe it's being back in Hemlock. In these woods I've tried so hard to forget. Whatever it is, it's screwing with my head.

"I said 'I know where they are.'" She points at a mass of ivy dangling from thick branches. But before she pushes through it, she spins, eyes locking on mine. "We're friends, aren't we, Laurel?"

"Yeah," I wheeze, forcing the word out. "Of course we are."

She nods. "Good."

Wren parts the curtain of ivy and waves her hand at me. I go through first, almost expecting my mom and dad to be on the other side, but instead, it's a long abandoned moss covered building. One I'd been in only once before.

The research facility.

"Takes a while to get here, doesn't it?" Wren's voice brightens. "And here it is, right where I last found it. That's your dad's, right?"

She points a slender finger toward a blue hat on a pile of dead leaves, and my stomach promptly drops to my feet.

I fall to the ground, dirt and strangled roots digging into my legs as I crawl toward the hat. I scoop it into my arms, hugging it to my chest as if it *is* my dad. Like I can conjure him the tighter I squeeze.

"They were here," I whisper. "This was the hat dad was wearing the day he left. And—" I try to stand, but something slithers around my ankles. I spin, fingers clawing into damp soil.

Roots snake around my once pristine shoes, now marred with dirt, as they curl around my leg. *Alive.* I try to move, but their grip tightens. Thick roots digging into my skin, making my lungs squeeze. My panicked gaze finds Wren. She takes a step back.

"What are you doing?! Help me!" I glance down at her root-free ankles. They don't come for her. Only me. Something is wrong. Something. Is. Wrong. And I think Wren knows exactly what it is.

"Wren!" Spit flies from my mouth.

Wren only watches me, quirking her head softly. A knowing smile on her face. Satisfaction flooding her eyes. I've never felt smaller. Never wanted my mom and dad more than I do now as I sit beneath Wren's parasitic stare.

"The man that let Eleanor into the facility wasn't just anyone," Wren says suddenly. "His name was Greg Berkley."

No. My wild grip on the roots loosens. My body goes slack. He couldn't have. Not the man who used to tell me bedtime stories to chase away the monsters under my bed. I never once would've thought *he* was the monster.

"Your dad promised Eleanor he'd take her home. It was *him* who led her to a room and shut the door. *Him* who decided, along with his colleagues, your mom included, that the best course of action for a little girl discovering their crimes was to lock the door and throw away the key. To let her *die* from the toxic waste she'd already touched. The waste that without treatment would poison her from the inside out, just like it did the woods."

"What?!" Everything Wren's saying is impossible. There's no way my dad would've willingly harmed someone, much less a *kid*. No way my mom, who sang me to sleep until I was eleven, would've gone along with it.

Wren tilts her head. "Remember the time you told me you went to the facility? How *cool* it was that your dad let you send waste down the chute into the woods? The same waste that poisoned the woods and my *sister*."

Her eyes flash. And just like when I first saw her earlier, her face is smaller, different. Less her and more...

Shit. I blink and see the picture Ms. Fitzgerald hangs above their fireplace mantle. Of a girl with red hair and eyes that shouldn't be so tired for a kid. Wren's older sister who died before she was born.

Eleanor.

I'd heard her name in passing, years ago. Something Wren threw out when I asked who the little girl was.

That's my sister. She's dead. We don't talk about it because it makes my mom cry. I'm named after her though. Well, my middle name, at least. Wren Eleanor Fitzgerald.

It hits me then. That Wren isn't just Wren. Not anymore. That story about the girl trapped in the woods isn't just a story, and somehow that girl—her *sister*—and Wren are sharing the same body. The same *soul*? It's impossible. But so are the roots tightening their grip on my ankles, making the skin around it pale.

"When did it happen?" I ask, voice shaking.

"Not long after you left," Wren says. "I went into the woods a lot after deferring from college. My mom kept getting on my ass about enrolling for the spring semester and the trees were the only quiet place I could find. One day—Eleanor shows up. Well"—Wren's face twists.—"her spirit that is. The same ghost we used to tell stories about. I didn't realize she was my sister at first, which is weird, you know, but I hadn't looked at that picture of her in so long. She told me what happened to her. How the research facility poisoned our home. She was just a kid, but she wanted to stop it. Stop *them*. They thought they could let her die and keep doing what they were doing. But Eleanor got them. Even after she died."

I try to say something. *Anything*. But I've been suckerpunched by the unbelievable.

"You know, there's one good thing about all of this," she says.

"And what's that?" I force the words out, fear radiating through me.

"I get to be with the sister I never had a chance to know. Because we were already connected through our blood — we had a special bond, one nobody else can replicate. She didn't force herself into my head. I let her in. Then, I learned everything. I saw everything. The facility. Your dad. I want revenge. Just as much as her. Now we're getting it."

"So, what? Your sister is *possessing* you?"

"We're a team, Laurel. Eleanor isn't sailing this ship, but neither am I. She's heads, I'm tails. Together, we're one coin. Flip it and there's a fifty-fifty chance of who you'll get." Wren shoots me an amused grin. "You know, with her in here" — She taps her temple. — "I finally don't feel so alone." She takes a step back, away. From *me*. "I know you've been lonely this year, too. And now, you can be whole. Just like I said."

"You can't leave me here!" I look to my left, eyes locking with a shrub that's too tall, too slender. Branches within it like arms. And on the ground next to it — a dainty gold watch. A knockoff. I'd know since I bought it for my mom for her birthday the year before she vanished. Next to it, where my dad's hat lays, is another bush just as human-like. I look around us. More and more bushes with arms and legs appear. And then I see it — *eyes* within the leaves. Blinking.

Oh god.

Missing person cases. Lots of 'em. Rumor has it if you stay too long, you'll disappear, too.

"Wren, this isn't right!" My breaths squeeze from my throat. Choking just like the vines that must've done the same to my parents feet away from me. The other nameless people. "We can fix this without hurting people. Without hurting *me*."

"This is the price of destroying what isn't yours," Wren sings. "You take and take and take and think there won't be a cost. And though it might not have been *your* hands that poisoned the soil here—it was your family. So many others, too. That rot doesn't just go away when you cut it at the base. You have to dig it up, roots and all. Only then will things be right."

All those times I didn't question what my dad did for work, pumping toxins into the ground. How sickly Mr. Garber's plants started to look. The leaves wilting on the trees just after blooming bright green. I turned an eye away from it all.

And now, just like Wren told me, I'm paying for it.

"What about our Friday night sleepovers?" I scream, tearing open the scabbed wound, letting myself bleed freely by walking back into the past we shared. And apparently one Wren couldn't give two shits about anymore. "I held your hair after you drank too many Smirnoff's at the bonfire! We cried over our crushes kissing other people!"

I abandoned her a year ago, and Wren went into the woods, called by the ghost of her long-dead sister. She found a companion in her. One that wouldn't leave her.

Eleanor took advantage of it.

Now Wren isn't just herself, and Eleanor isn't just a spirit trapped in the woods.

And it's all my fault.

"Promises are made to be broken, Laurel," Wren says. Just in time for a leafy vine to snake over my mouth, swallowing my words. "And now you get to be with your parents again. A shame they can't give you a hug. Though, there's really not much left of them anyway." She laughs.

Another vine slides across my cheek, sending shivers down my spine as it creeps closer to my eyes. Wren backs away. A face that isn't hers morphing over her own just briefly.

I should've never come back to Hemlock. Should've known Wren would find some way to draw me back into her web. But I can't help thinking how Wren told me the truth about one thing.

She really had found my parents.

My mom must've walked into the woods, haunted by her sins and Eleanor always lurking in the trees. And now, those bags under my dad's eyes make so much more sense. They hadn't been from restless nights, kept awake by mom's disappearance. It was because of Eleanor. He tried resisting her. I know that *now*. Can hear all of his cryptic words in the days leading up to him leaving.

You can't outrun your past, Laurel. Not your mother. Not me. Not any of us.

Accept the University of Washington's offer. It's a good school. Better than anything around here.

His insistence on me going to Washington for college. Miles and miles away from Hemlock. He was afraid his sins wouldn't just catch up to him, but that they'd find me, too.

Now they have.

I never told Maggie where I was going for the weekend. She didn't know about Hemlock or my parents. That bus driver won't even think twice about me not showing up two days from now. Wren will probably tell her mom I left early, the trauma of being back too intense.

Nobody knows where I am.

The vine slides across my eyes, plunging me into darkness. Another leaf finds my finger, brushing across it. Consuming my body.

And now nobody ever will.

NECTAR: UNLIMITED

LAURA G. SOUTHERN

Kavarem of Ishkara always got existential after the ninth bell. Blame it on her planet's tendency to bury itself in ash: evisceration within the blistering heat and harsh monotony of a summer that never changed, never ended. The fires had been particularly distasteful that year; ash lay in gray, down feathers over the concrete cracked between brick shops, in globs of mold on the ramshackle houses, and then just ash again, remnants of flora once alive, where Kavarem could see each fleck clearly in the moonlight as she sat atop the roof of the Professor's Tavern and drank herself to death.

Blame it on whatever, whomever, you'd like.

No matter how many times she told it, no one believed she hadn't intended on saving the planet that night. People needed reason. Hope and a beautiful, wholesome story.

The truth was ugly, as was she. Blaming the ash was easier.

"You're late."

Kavarem pulled the bandage more firmly over the pus-filled burn on the back of her left hand. "Are you aware of the rat living in your coffee brewer?"

The Professor blinked down a hawkish, ruddy nose at her from behind the bar. His hands white-knuckled the long slab of iron upholding an assortment of round, glass liquor bottles and a litter of freeze-dried fruit slices. Sunset freckles splattered his pale face, a pretty affront to the black-dyed hair that hung in rather oily curls to his shoulders. "We have *patrons*, Kav dear."

Which was shocking in and of itself. By two months into this job as a bar wench at the Professor's Tavern, she'd discovered the man had very little interest in the goings-on at the front of it, with patrons and the like. Business that generated coin. No, the failed scientist was much more concerned with his experiments hidden in the back. Glass beakers and open flames that burned green and mysterious golden powders with names he refused to share with her.

That was their arrangement: she ran the front of the tavern by tending to the travelers who stopped in—no one stayed on her home planet for long, only to fill up their ships with the galaxy's dwindling supply of fuel and to stare out the warped glass windows at the burning plain beyond the city, grateful *they* weren't the ones living in a place with more flame than people. *This will become you soon,* she wanted to tell them. *No one expects to burn until they're already doing it.* She chatted and imagined scooping out their eyes, pondering as she swept a straw broom over the scuffed wooden floors behind the travelers—no regular Ishkaran with half a brain drank at the Professor's Tavern; he price gouged—how good it'd feel, to leave with them.

But Kavarem did not beg, and the only way she'd ever get off this dying planet was if she dropped down to her knees and asked one of the people who dragged heavy eyes over the pale curve of her throat to save her. No, thanks. She would rather burn.

While Kavarem dealt with patrons, the Professor ran the back of the tavern. "Do not ask questions," he'd told her the day he hired her, "and do not, under any circumstances, touch my experiments. You follow those two rules, and we'll get along just fine."

They did not, in fact, get along. But she would have left him to it, if not for the rat.

"There's something wrong with its front legs," Kavarem said, ignoring the growing flush over the Professor's face. Two patrons sat at the end of the bar and listened. "They're so thin they look like sticks, and the hair there is yellow, a strawish color. Her feet are flat as leaves. The rest of her is a russet brown, nearly amber, and her eyes—"

"Kavarem." The Professor leaned over the bar and steepled his long fingers. "You're scaring away our patrons, and you are three hours late." She knew him, by now; the fury scowling his lips was because he'd been forced to run his own establishment. All gods forbid.

"They'll never be back." She canted her head toward the women. "Either of you planning on returning to Ishkara?"

The traveler entirely covered in tattoos snorted into her coffee. "Fuck, no." Hot steam billowed up from the drink, and she inhaled with a reverence that bordered on worship. Coffee, what the Professor's Tavern was known for, was so hard to come by these days. "Only reason we're here is because we heard you've got fuel. Right, Esther?"

"Fuel and coffee," her companion agreed, blonde hair cropped close to her scabbed skull.

The tattooed woman eyed Kavarem with a suggestive tilt of her right eyebrow, sharply arched with two slits. "Unless you give me a reason to return."

"You want a brothel, Ishkara's got those, too," said Kavarem. She leaned an elbow against the bar, tapped her fingernails against it, bitten down to the quick. "It's not here."

The blonde—Esther—blushed at the Professor as he rolled his sleeves up his corded forearms. "Could've fooled me," she muttered.

The Professor was attractive, despite the hair. In his mid-twenties, a little younger than Kavarem. Perhaps he thought his features made it all right when he treated her like shit, as though she'd like it or something. Probably some people did. Probably she did, she'd realized later, after the rat in the coffee brewer had rubbed its two leaf-feet together and called her a "marvel," and it was the liking of it that repulsed Kavarem enough to see through the job. She had quit five other taverns in the span of two years before the Professor made the grave mistake of forging their arrangement. Before him, her most gainful employment lasted four months.

"About that rat," she said.

"I have experiments to run. Next time," he muttered, stepping aside as she replaced him behind the bar, "I'll deduct a day's pay for each hour you're late."

"That's illegal."

He brushed a knuckle over her cheekbone. "Who's going to stop me?"

Her jaw ached from constantly clenching her teeth. The Constables who lorded over the ruins of Ishkara were more likely to rob you than offer any sort of assistance; all they protected now were the fuel reserves at the main outpost, adjacent to the Professor's Tavern. Besides, most drank here free of charge, worse even than the travelers with their grease-stained grins. She suspected the Professor had gone to university with a few, off planet, and although greed drove the Constables' return here, she had not yet worked out the Professor's reason.

Perhaps it had something to do with the rat.

"Oh, and Kav darling?" called the Professor. "When you fuck her, do it out the back."

She wasn't quite sure who'd sailed to the green planet Balâ and brought back coffee beans for the Professor, giving him a monopoly on the drink—be it Constable Icabor Lamatoth or his rival, Sergeant Ebelyn Malstraight. The stories varied by street, and back then, Kavarem did not concern herself with trivialities such as truths and lies, only shadows and the half-things that crawled from them.

Like the rat.

She wasn't obsessed with it, really. But she did buy a leather journal after her second month on the job, once she caught a glimpse of its curiously straw-like tail disappearing behind a turquoise liquor bottle, purely for the purpose of jotting down when she saw it next.

She began staying later even than the Professor, who often slipped from the tavern to stumble home well after midnight. She slept behind the bar until the loud *slam* of the front door woke her; never once did the scientist check to ensure she performed her closing tasks or, by chance, peered behind the bar to spot her wrapped in her dark purple blanket with the journal tucked up under her cheek, so her skin did not touch the sticky floor.

At night, she rolled from behind the bar and ventured into the back, a small room that, with a strike of a match and a few burnt fingertips, she illuminated with a stained-glass lantern. The Professor's coffee brewer glimmered beneath the dancing firelight, like stones at the bottom of a shallow stream catching the sun. Over a dozen glass beakers of every shape and size, including a perilous cylinder balanced on a ceramic pedestal, were stacked on a sturdy, black wooden table in the middle of the room. The centerpiece. Bright metal tubes connected the beakers, looping round and round, and it was in the curve of one of those whereupon sat the rat.

The first time Kavarem saw it crouched there, she barely managed to stifle her gasp. Glass distorted the rat's body into a grotesque monster; but she waited, one foot in the back of the house and one foot in the front, until the rat shadow-skittered over the notes stacked neatly on the Professor's work table. A mere glimpse, initially, only seen in peripheral snatches; her speed left an after-image in Kavarem's vision, like the brightness burnt by a falling star or the scorched imprint of staring too long into open flame. Papers scattered in the rat's wake, displaced, sliding over the tubes and landing in a disarray across the table's scarred wood.

Kavarem crept forward, curious for the first time in...how long? She bit her bottom lip. The rat squeaked from the safety of the shadows—squeaked in what Kavarem could only understand as *encouragement*. Oh, no. Perhaps she'd finally lost her mind, singed as it was.

Dubious, Kavarem tried and failed to recall precisely how much she'd had to drink tonight.

She skimmed the Professor's notes with a growing sense of astonishment. "That bastard," she whispered. The Professor's slanted handwriting puzzled over *a recipe for godhood*, meddling about with words like *fate* and *magical networks* and *the rebirth of trees*.

It seemed she wasn't the one whose mind was lost. "What do you have to do with his nefarious plots?" she asked the rat, who ignored her. The last tree in Ishkara had fallen twenty years prior, and the planet itself only had…shit, a handful of years left of breathable atmosphere.

The Professor— Surely, *that man* didn't think he could save this place. Did he?

Kavarem determined to find the fuck out. The jotting into her journal quickly became full-blown note taking. Sketches of a lithe, serpentine body—furred, like any other rat, although the bristles fanned out in a scaled pattern, so the hair grew in rigid, shell-shaped clumps with green, bald skin between each—and with a shock of straw as its tail. Whiskers made of woven grass. It was part plant, she decided, unlike any other rat she'd ever seen. She began to reevaluate her definition of *magic*—which had been, up to that point, summarized in one simple word: horseshit.

Because she couldn't deny the rat was an abnormal sort of beast.

If Kavarem moved, the rat would flee. So she just watched it in turn, her journal laid over the Professor's work table; a pen in one hand, a bottle in the other. Until the sun came up, and Kavarem went back to her single-room apartment in a husk of a building, half-burned and condemned, to rinse off before returning to work her day shift. That's how she thought of them.

Day shift: bar wench.

Night shift: rat observer.

Other nights, when the banging of the front door failed to wake Kavarem after one too many stolen drinks while she dozed, waiting for the Professor to leave, the rat came to her. It perched at the edge of the bar and stared down, waiting. For what, Kavarem was never sure. Each time she snorted awake from where she rested on the journal cover, which was slowly growing just as sticky as the floor—the cover often adhered to her face—the rat walked in three circles, then laid its head down on its paws, which were in fact made of yellow-veined, light green leaves.

She came to cherish those blur-dark hours the most. Lying there together, Kavarem told the rat stories of her childhood in Ishkara, the precise method for eye gouging—it was all in the curve of the spoon—and how she despised the Professor all the way down to her viscera. How she hated, on an even deeper level, that she was starting to understand the spiraling of his notes. And gods, Kavarem needed to hate something she herself could burn.

It took Kavarem all of seven months to realize the creature wasn't letting her see it more often because it trusted her, because they were becoming friends, because it liked sitting on the edge of the bar, lounging in a mug while Kavarem stole from the Professor's liquor store and drank until she was sick.

No, nothing so saccharine as that.

The rat was dying.

Slower reflexes, unable to escape Kavarem's grasping eyes and sharp quill. Lackluster pelt and eyes failing to note her movements as she crept ever closer, staring more at the rat and less at the liquor, until only one of them had clear eyes, and this time, it was Kavarem.

It took ten months before she finally caught it.

The little rat sat in the middle of Kavarem's blistered palm, the back of her hand laid flat against the bar, and nibbled on a rotten chunk of freezer-dried bread. "What are you?" Kavarem whispered. The Professor had left not half an hour before, and she didn't like to stand up behind the bar yet on the off chance that he returned, having forgotten something.

The rat's leaf paws rubbed over its nose, cleaning its whiskers of crumbs between each bite. Its mouth opened, revealing four rows of stone, sharpened teeth. "Eat first," it said.

The pupils of its eyes shone a dark, dazzling emerald that reminded Kavarem of the forests from her youth. Remnants holding on for dear life, she hadn't realized as a child, but they'd been beautiful to her, a place her father would take her to tell her fantastical stories of magic and woodland creatures and fairies, who lived in trees and other green plant-life.

None of it was supposed to be real. An unfamiliar lightness struck her chest, hollow enough to hurt; she rubbed at it before hope had a chance to put down roots.

"Are you a fairy?"

"Eat first, marvel."

"Marvel?"

"You, yes."

Kavarem huffed out an impatient breath of air, and a blush heated her cheeks. "Fine," she muttered, and waited until the rat had painstakingly cleaned its whiskers between every bite. When the bread was down its gullet, its gaunt belly distended in what appeared a painful manner, and the rat rested its little chin on the knuckle of her thumb.

"Not fairy." The rat's head bobbed with the words. Its skin was fever-hot even through the dusting of yellow fur below its chin, and Kavarem frowned.

More complex sentences seemed to evade the creature's capabilities. Speaking sent its eyes fluttering shut. The sneaking suspicion that this not-fairy had once recited ballads by firelight stole over her, bringing a dreaded prickle to her skin.

There was one possible non-magical explanation for the not-fairy. (Who in their right mind believed the creatures from their bedtime stories would one day scuttle like a rodent through their workplace's walls?) She knew of the mythical portals on Balâ that were said to transport ships not to different planets, but to different worlds. Dimensions. Those ships never returned. Shipwrecked, off course, lost to the ideals of science. Lost to their greed for something more. If the rat wasn't a fairy, perhaps her origins lay elsewhere, in a land where her existence wasn't magical or a phenomenon, but merely normal. Just a creature from another dimension.

Her heart twisted in her chest. "Did you come through one of Balâ's portals?"

"Magic on Ishkara," said the not-fairy.

"You *are* magical?" With a shiver, Kavarem recalled the Professor's recipe for godhood. Its ingredients, jotted down in a row. "Does that mean the Professor was right about you?"

"Magic, yes. On Ishkara."

Kavarem accepted this with a bitter smile. She stroked the tiny creature's back, and its furred scales parted to reveal a set of desiccated wings. Raisin-shriveled between its shoulder blades. In her father's stories, fairies had wings.

Her fingertips massaged behind the rat-fairy's ears. "Where?"

"In trees."

Kavarem attempted to unfurl one of its wings, and the creature's stone teeth cut into the pad of her thumb. She yelped, jerking back. The rat-fairy nearly toppled to the bar, but Kavarem caught it at the last moment, holding it up between cupped hands.

Simply, it said, "Hurts."

"What does the Professor want with you?"

"Brew me."

Kavarem was afraid of that.

She frowned over her shoulder, at the arched doorway leading to the back. The Professor had been compulsively tinkering with that damn machine, the coffee brewer, adding beakers and wires and tubes, then taking them away again; shifting them around with great grunts of distress, like a heaving animal. She'd thought it overkill, to labor over a machine that brewed for the front of the house, when so many of his other experiments were back-house specific, or secretive.

Kavarem returned her attention to the shivering creature in her palms. "What is your name?" she asked, and the rat-fairy told her.

It was a name Kavarem could not pronounce with the teeth and tongue she had, that no human hand could transcribe onto paper; if the wind rattled through a canyon and blew up a cloud of red dust, chipped from sandstone, swirling through thousand-year-old trees, that was its name. The sound was beautiful.

Kavarem bit her tongue. *I know your secrets, Professor.* She ached to scream it at the night sky, shout it from the rooftop. *I know you have something that cannot be replaced.*

Some Ishkarans might say she had murdered the rat-fairy—that she'd stolen the Professor's life's work and claimed it as her own. He was supposed to be Ishkara's new god; he was supposed to save everyone; he was supposed to battle this world's desolation with his own. But the damn thing keeled over in Kavarem's cupped hands, right there over the bar that night, as though relieved—and what else was she to do with it? They were good bones.

She crushed the creature into a golden, furry pulp with a pestle and grinding stone, gagging only twice, and then she fed its body into the coffee brewer.

Kavarem brewed the rat-fairy in the Professor's grandiose steel-and-glass contraption with its beakers and funnels and all the miscellaneous trappings of a failed scholar, the dreams of his chemist's career contorted into this *thing*—and she did it properly. Kavarem, a nobody, a "good fuck with a foul mouth," would never in the Professor's wildest dreams have dared to read through the notes he left unattended, pages piled there like so many layers of compressed ash.

Perhaps he thought her illiterate in addition to profane.

The small steel spout dribbled out the shining liquid quite steadily, or at least, that's how she remembered it, the drops plink-plinking into a chipped, ceramic mug.

Careful: Hot scrawled through the mug's white paint in big, blocky red lettering, and as she climbed the spiraling, iron staircase to the abandoned rooftop, she picked at it with the edge of her thumbnail. She nudged open the wooden door with one shoulder and strode out onto the flat concrete roof. Her black boots sank into a thick covering of ash, gray in the moonlight.

The ninth bell gonged overhead as she sat, swinging her legs over the side of the tavern, careful not to spill a smidge of the golden liquid in the mug. Clumps of fur and a few stone teeth swirled in the mixture, and so Kavarem fixed her gaze upon the horizon. With the ever-burning fires, moonlight no longer silvered the city as it had once, but rather cast everything in tones of gray. Orange-red, flickering light turned the city's edge sepia, and beyond the lay of house husks, Ishkara's burning plain stretched farther than her eye could see. Over three quarters of Ishkara was on fire, last she read the reports.

She did not care precisely what the Professor wanted with the rat-fairy's brewed corpse, only that she wished more than all else to take something away from him, something he could never get back, like time, like dignity, like the way it felt to pull your teeth back until your mouth hurt so much that you screamed instead of cried, and so she tipped his magical golden coffee back like a shot. The sleeve of her black tunic came away gilded when she swiped at her mouth, and then she grimaced, furious at this one small mercy.

She didn't even taste the rat-fairy on its way down.

The transformation began the next morning, while she was working behind the bar. A gurgling in her stomach, followed by the tang of nettles on her breath. She coughed into the crook of her arm, which earned a glare from the traveler who sat in front of her, nursing a warm pale ale.

Even if the Professor hadn't noticed his rat-fairy missing, she could not hide the green veins below her skin, squirming like worms. Especially not when the green lines nudged from her belly to press against the inside of her tunic—the blood that dribbled to the floor.

Kaverem didn't feel much. Her skin had taken on a hard, waxy quality, a shimmering green, like a candle melted and re-melted in a cyclical pattern, held over open flame. She peeled her tunic up to her chin, and the traveler let out an appreciative whistle—

His whistle choked into words: "What the *fuck*?"

A clanging echoed from the tavern's innards, and out came the Professor. His hair was slicked back into a greasy knot at the nape of his neck, his eyes like dark, smoldering coals as they landed upon Kavarem's exposed midriff.

"No," he whispered, not sparing a glance at the traveler who stumbled toward the door and out into the night, screaming about monsters.

"Did you ever ask its name?"

The Professor spluttered, and she grimaced away from him, embarrassed to witness his composure undone. "It's an ancient Ishkaran wood sprite, one of the last of its kind, over a thousand years old; the creature has no name, it is *all* names, a collective historical memory that you've…"

"Eaten," she supplied.

"Consumed," whispered the Professor, and a strand of fear wound through the word, raising the hair on the back of Kavarem's neck. "I am trying to bring magic back to Ishkara; it's the only way to save this place. Government initiatives, conservation efforts, unions—all of it went to shit, and the last tree still fell, and I couldn't do anything about it, then. I was a child. But then, in university… Seven years, it took me to track down the sprite that you killed."

"I didn't kill it."

"Seven years," he repeated, and took a step toward her. "I was trying to get the recipe just right, combine the sprite's nectar with the correct amounts of sulfur and ash, to avoid *this*."

"You're not trying to save Ishkara," she said, dryly. "You're trying to own it."

"I am trying to make a world where nature rules," he snarled. "People are horrific; just look at your gullet, those roots—*my roots*—wavering from your flesh insensate, all because you still haven't decided, have you? If you want this magic? The brew can only take if the host is willing, and if you're not... Gods, Kavarem. There was only one sprite. Only one cup of nectar."

"It was angry." Her eyes glazed over, limning the Professor in a hazy verdant outline. She blinked, and the film was gone. "You were using it without its consent."

"Sacrifices must be made to save the world." He crossed behind the bar, and the shock of it brought her back into her body, for a moment, back into the pain. In all the hours they'd worked together, she had never once stood behind this bar with the Professor before. "You can reject the magic, and it will flush out of your system within two weeks. But if you accept it..." He brushed a strand of hair behind her ear, and the scrape of it surprised her. The strands were half-replaced with straw.

"A forest will grow from your bones," he whispered. Veins of fury stood out on his forehead. "I will feed you, tend to you; this is my legacy, and I will see to it however I can."

It changed nothing, if she rejected the magic. Without it, she'd still have to beg.

But— "Feed me?"

The Professor scowled. "I wanted to create a species of magical trees that needed no water, no nutrients the way olden trees did; to preserve them, you see. But you killed the beast before the formula was finished—there were, um, kinks. I could never get the sprite's blood to cooperate, school it into obedience—and so now your roots must be watered with human blood."

220 • EDITED BY LAUREN T. DAVILA

That was not true, and it eased Kavarem, that she knew something the Professor did not—the rat-fairy chose its death, when to let go. It was aware of the formula; it wanted this.

Blood.

Oh, yes. The creature was very angry, indeed.

Kavarem smiled.

Her roots latched around the Professor's throat. He staggered back against the shelving of bottles. They fell off, shattering, one after the other.

The Professor's face purpled, and then her roots burrowed into his flesh, drinking him dry. Red oozed up the tendrils like a straw, sucked up into her belly where his blood swirled below her waxy flesh. And *spread*.

Bark sprouted in a spray of brown and red, scaling her arms, shredding her clothes until she stood naked, half woman and half forest. Her roots hooked into the bar, cracking it in two as she burrowed into the dry earth below the tavern's foundation. The building shifted, groaned just as Kavarem's spine cracked apart—*that* one she felt, and she did, to her shame, scream—and she shot upward. Ten feet, fifty, hundreds. The tavern broke apart around her, and her roots absorbed it, weaving parts into the bark that patterned her long, long torso. *A trunk*, she realized.

Her arms stretched outward, shattering into branches. Her shadow cast over the burning plain, covered nearly the entire city in shade. Kavarem had never thought herself a reprieve from the sun. Ivy sprouted on her bark, replacing strips of paper-thin skin, along with a speckling of grayish moss. Leaves burst from her fingertips, and during it all, she felt the steady *thud-thud* of the Professor's heart as it stuttered, and then stopped, his bones wrapped in her roots below.

Blood trees could not tell lies, only stories in the whisper of wind through their branches, the rhythm of roots rumbling below the ground, and in the motifs of their falling, purple leaves that danced on cool winter snowstorms in the years after the fires, at long last, went out. The people who returned to Ishkara, who left their squalling babies in Kavarem's roots and watched as she crushed them to her bosom—those people would do well to remember that.

She had not wanted to spawn a new forest that could never burn, a legion of trees that sprouted from her seeds with bark no blade could ever touch. But when the first of the rat-fairies returned to nestle at the heart of her trunk, she could not lie, of course. That part made her happy.

TO ROOT FROM FLESH

ISA ARSEN

I once told Uli that she was being reckless as she stole a bucket of water.

"Don't worry," said with that impenetrable surety of hers, voice tight with effort as he hauled at the rope. "You always worry so much."

"Only because there's always something to be worried about," I hissed. The thick, muggy air sliced in half around the sound. Uli grinned at me.

The winch of the well shrieked softly in the dark. Inwardly, I was terrified. This was a step past worried. If Uli knew, I would never live it down.

"You're such a fucking pessimist, Wren."

Uli pulled the bucket out. The edges of it sloshed when she dunked one cupped hand in. The hard, white stare of the moonlight painted it glistening and full.

When Uli sipped from that hand with a rascal's pleasure, she watched me without blinking. She offered the hand to me next, and I drank with the automatic sense that she could see straight through me down to my guts, my bones, my marrow. Everything that made me too human for her to bear; such a fucking pessimist.

We take a boat in the dead of night. I recall the time we stole water as I push while Uli drags, our labor hard and silent like an animal lowing to bear its slippery offspring. The mouth of the river takes the prow like something easy, parting around the nose. Uli glances over her shoulder at me as the enclave shrinks in the distance.

Of all things, Uli is grinning. I imagine her chin wet, shining slick after sipping from her palm. "Lighten up," she whispers. She had climbed into the boat first on silent feet. I want, sharply, to hurl an apology back over my shoulder at the shrinking shape of our walls, our bastion, the craftspeople who hollowed the log like the rib of some great beast felled from the belly up. Escape seems like more of a blow to them than stealing water ever did.

Lighten up. What a fucking laugh. Uli is dying, and she's the one telling me to slap a smile on my face. I suppose she's desensitized to it as a healer—as a stonemason myself, it's all horror to me. Uli has seen the worst of the rot. She's looked at the lattice pattern of someone's crawling infection and determined which sort of plant passed its blight into their skin to claim their body.

Uli had worn a similar smile, awed and morbid, when she hiked up the edge of her shirt in the cast of our bunkhouse's flickering halogen lamp. Making sure we were the only ones awake, she pointed to a gnarled patch of green beginning to seep over the right side of her ribs like an inkstain left to bleed.

Lantern moss, she'd whispered, smiling as though the fact the earth was taking her down with it was worth celebrating. Who knows. Maybe to her, at home with its wiles, it was.

"You navigate," I hiss, ignoring the jab from her, "I'll steer."

The salute she gives me is mocking as I look hard at her in the dark. *Andreaeopsida.* Her voice lingers between my ears, the secret of it burning still.

It will kill her. And I have fixed myself so near to Uli for so many years, desperate for closeness, that I will wound myself to give her exactly what she asks of me. There must be some part of her that recognizes it. This is what I tell myself to sleep soundly at night.

The ocean, Uli whispered after she first showed me. She fingered the edge of the greenrot as though waiting for it to leap onto her fingertips and up her arm. *I've always wanted to see the ocean.* Her eyes flicked to mine and I remember nodding stupidly. I would do anything for her. She had to know.

So to the ocean I will bring her, before the ground drags her with indiscriminate greed back into the brittle fold.

The river gutters as we go, and daylight turns over into a pale thing. Uli navigates. I steer. The rudder resists me, rude in the way it fights back. It's got moxie—I am strangely proud of it.

"What will you do when you go back?"

I look up at Uli. She's got her boots balanced up on the edge of the boat, lounging. I bear heavily into the rudder and steer us wide around a boulder furred with moss so thick it's almost black.

"Realistically?" I huff. "Probably stand trial for stealing a boat, and then...I don't know. Just keep living."

Uli sniffs a little, amused. She isn't a woman who does anything by half—her head is shaved, her gaze is huge and brown and always lingers for a little too long on things she watches. My favorite thing is when she throws her head back and laughs heartily, even at the least-funny jokes, if she's eager enough to impress the person telling them.

I frown at her and keep the rudder straight against a fussy battery of the current. "What?"

"It's something I've always admired about you," Uli says loftily. "That you're content to just *live* and not aspire to anything."

She can bruise an ego as easily as she laughs at shitty jokes.

"Well, it's the best we can hope for these days," I grunt. I know she can tell I'm dodging the low grip of offense. "Just living."

Staring ahead at the water, Uli makes a sound, like the murmur she'd make turning over the flavor of a plucked herb muddled on the tip of her tongue. "It's kind of freeing," she says.

"What is?"

I watch Uli skim her knuckles over her shirt, against her ribs where the greenrot blooms hidden. "Dying."

She isn't looking at me when she says it. I don't dignify it with a response. I steer us carefully through a channel of rock, wondering how deep the river goes into its own murk.

I never considered myself a romantic. I didn't know how to be, nor did I understand that doggedly pitching myself from the heights of my own anxiety for Uli was just that: infatuation.

There was no incentive for anyone to point out that I was in love with her—or perhaps it only felt so outward to me, making itself known with a pitch and roil like a constant grindstone against my sanity. Pining had no place in the enclave. We shed sweat and shared in our collective desperation to cling to our humanity, our labor too precious for anything but surviving.

Although, I suppose romanticism could be its own sort of surviving.

We had jobs that suited our bodies and minds, but more often our bodies. Those of us with enough strength to hack and burn and build were the threshers—enclavers who beat back the growth from our walls like heroes from the moldering comic book issues kept in the frail rows of our library. Those of us who knew what a library used to be, people like Uli, were healers, solvers. Fixers.

We intermingled. Jealousy was almost ready to bloom.

His name was Sil, short for something I never bothered asking. Uli thought I was interested in him after he and I had been assigned to several excursions to the eastern quarry pit and struck a middlingly friendly rapport. She got herself into Sil's smallclothes less than a week after I noticed her glancing between us during an evening meal.

I caught them in the granary, my arms full of bonemeal sacks. In the low angle of the red afternoon sun, Sil's voice broke through his strokes with an *Oh, shit*—gasping, grunting, low and airy. Uli's legs were wrapped fast around his waist. She was on her back, balanced acrobatically across the vertebral stack of next week's rations.

Hey, Wren, she said, looking at me upside-down, victory flashing in her stare.

Two weeks later, Sil had been taken by rot. It started in his arms and made him useless, which was the most terrifying part: having your purpose taken away. Before his legs followed, we shepherded him to the grove where the rest of our dead had rooted. We held the customary vigil for him as he went rigid. Uli stood beside me and picked at the dry skin around her fingernails the entire time. She didn't even have the decency to shed a tear. I always lent at least one tear to the dead. It was bad luck not to.

If it ever comes for me, Uli whispered to me that night in our corner of the bunkhouse, *I don't want to stay in that grove. I want to root somewhere beautiful.*

I didn't have the energy to correct her *if* to *when*. I kept my mouth shut and shuffled under my blanket, staring hard at the patterns of stacked stones and mortar on the wall. I didn't say that I thought the grove was beautiful. Everyone who went there alchemized back into something that kept on persisting. It was the only way I taught myself not to fear the quiet stalk of its inevitability, coming for all of us.

Two weeks after that, Uli told me she was going to steal a boat. I never could say no.

We make it three days down the river before Uli gets bored of her own reminiscing and turns the exacting eye of her time-killing to me.

The rot has spread down the entirety of her right arm and part of her thigh. Sometimes when she wakes, I listen to her struggle briefly against the small roots that have sprouted from her skin in the night to seek the soil and bind her down. I pretend not to notice her fallibility every time.

"Remember Sil?"

I give a derisive snort along with the next pop of the small fire burning between me and Uli. "Yeah," I say, flicking my eyebrows up wryly. "How'd that dickhead's rot feel?"

Uli shifts awkwardly. A perverse twist of intrigue shoots through me at the idea I've made her uncomfortable, reminding her of such a simple mistake—although we all knew rot went from skin to skin by even the briefest touch. Perhaps she had done it on purpose.

"He didn't give me rot," Uli insists. Her eyes latch to mine in the dark, shining with an orange sheen from the flickering flames. "And I thought you liked him."

I shrug. "You're the one who fucked him."

Several minutes ooze long and drooly through the heat-heavy night. I feel Uli watching me with the same puzzling exaction she always gave to identifying the chattering sequences of genetic strings she tried teaching me to read once, just the two of us—*TAG, GTC, CAG, TCT.*

"Holy shit," she finally announces. I don't look up at her.

"Spreading?" I hum. I've watched her marvel at the mottling of her skin while the boat lazes through the water when she thinks I'm not watching. But Uli always knows when I'm watching.

"You like me."

When I finally let myself look at her, Uli is curdlingly smug. I squirm a little and poke at the fire. "Of course I like you. I'm risking my ass to get you all the way out here."

"No, no," she sings, leaning closer with her elbows on her knees. Her arm hardly bends, the scaling bark giving a creak that makes my skin crawl. "You *like* me. It was never about Sil, was it?"

Shame, hot and juvenile, rushes up my cheeks. "Whatever," I mumble.

Now Uli is grinning. The way the shadows lick across her face in the dark lends her a half-manic and afflictive glee.

"For how long?" she goads me. When I say nothing, she nudges me hard against the ankle. Her voice comes harder: "How long, Wren?"

"A long time," I snap, because it's the truth and I'm a terrible liar. How do you prescribe time to something that has always been there? From the moment I could perceive the warmth in me, I felt it looking at her. Uli, coaching me through the families and genuses of common flora. Uli, pointing out the specific vein patterns of blighted leaves. Uli, laughing when I reliably mixed up Asterales and Asteraceae. Feeling drawn to her was as natural to me as breathing.

I had never known anything different, and, if I had once, it was long overwritten by her magnetism.

"Hey."

I look up at Uli again and find mischief in her eyes. She quirks one thick, insubmissive brow at me. I wonder with a twisting sort of horror how her face will morph into grotesquerie as the rot takes it. I wonder if I'll have the stomach to stay with her and behold it. "You could've just asked to fuck me, you know," Uli says. "I'd have said yes."

In another small mutiny, the pit of my belly warms with a rich, achy coiling. "I didn't know that," I mutter in the safety of neutrality.

Uli keeps watching me. I don't have the guts or the resolve to demand that she quit it. "I'd still say yes."

"Oh," I grunt, turning the log on the fire again, as nothing else makes sense to do. She has always known me better than I know myself.

It happens later, when the fire has gone to embers and Uli and I have said nothing else of substance to one another. She puts her good hand to the shaft of my boot as I'm stepping around her to rinse out our tin plates in the river shallows. Uli looks up at me and I find her eyes so full of faraway promise that it makes me ache.

Maybe Sil had felt the same—her gaze has ever been her favorite weapon.

I am careful not to touch her rot. Beneath me, beside me, straddled above me, the animal parts of Uli still left free from growth quiver. She gives the last of her vibrance up to the dark, teeth bared; she knows she won't need it much longer. Not where she's going.

It's not nearly as transformative as I let myself dream it could be. I'm the same after as I was before we started, except now I'm quiet with knowledge I never knew before: Uli is breakable, average.

Sometime in the night, I hear her crying softly to herself. Maybe it's the fear she can't hide from me now that I've felt she's yielding.

She is unremarkable past the hardness of her handwrought armor.

We capsize halfway through the morning's final leg.

When I come up, kicking free of fluttering mooring as I heave myself onto the upended belly of the boat, my only thought is Uli. Breathing barely won out over the instinct to gasp her name: *Uli.*

The water is churning less now that we've passed the rapids that tossed us, but a splashing disturbance ahead of me draws my attention. I kick with a vital burn in my legs to reach her.

"Uli!" I plunge my hand out to grab at her and grasp the ankle of her boot. Patting upward, I wrap my fist in her shirt and haul her up until Uli's head breaks the surface. She makes a wrecked, sodden splattering sound. I drag her against the boat, holding the strap of her belt pack in the passing slippage of the current. Uli coughs. A bruised throb of relief beats through me.

"Fuck!" she chokes out. Another hideous, silty cough wracks her, and I wish I could wrap an arm around her and cling her close.

"Are you okay?" I ask. Uli keeps coughing as I angle us toward the nearest shore and kick with everything I've got.

Uli had told me to get some sleep and let her take the rudder. I wouldn't have taken her up on it if I'd known she would have been on her own with only one arm fully operable through the rocks.

I lug the boat up onto a bank slippery with moss and cakey dirt. I take Uli by the back of the shirt again and help steer her stumbling crawl, up out of the water and onto the ground. She heaves for air—the sort of gasping that the body drives itself, no conscious pitch to it besides the sometimes traitorous injunction to survive, survive, survive.

I lay down on my back and catch my breath. Let Uli be the first one to talk. She rolls her head to the side to face me. "You fucking cunt."

"Me?"

"Why the fuck did you pull me out?"

I stare at her. Through her, really. There have been countless times Uli has rendered me speechless before, but never like this. Her non sequiturs, her tangents, her rage, all of it before has shocked me with its ferocity. Never before has it shocked me with its timidity.

"Fuck you, Wren," she pants, her voice buckled and terrified.

Uli heaves herself up into her side, propped sideways against her claimed elbow. She inspects the splintering border of the bark against her shoulder, rigid and ashen.

I take slow breaths. My ears still ring faintly with adrenaline. I run a quick triage on my body and the pack still on my shoulders. The battening net only lost a few ration packs to the water. One oar is still knocked in its hinge.

Through my periphery, I look at Uli. The parts of her still made of flesh and blood are trembling while she cries. A spool of algae is stuck in her hair.

I realize with a lurch in my chest that Uli has become afraid of slow decay. Perhaps that was her plan from the beginning: to bring me along only to bear witness to her death, everything a performance.

"You're so fucking selfish," I announce.

Despite the swollen press of tears, Uli still delivers a glare that would have cut my knees out from under me had I not already been flat on my back. She never does anything by half. Disenchantment crawls through me from my soles to my skull in a cool trickle.

I steady myself into a sit. Wringing out the edge of my shirt, I will my body not to feel the light whiff of chill in the air beneath the damp. "Be a big girl and be thankful," I say, not looking at her.

"Fuck you."

I right the boat onto its hull and ease it back into the water. With my arm around the trunk of a bank-side tree, I hold in place and jerk my chin at Uli. "Come on."

She doesn't move. Fury licks low at the edges of my patience. I say nothing and watch her stew.

A bird calls from above. I imagine it—ugly and massive, feathers like steel wool, circling to see if it might snap up what it can grab of Uli before she goes entirely to green.

I wave at her this time with the arm not holding the tree. "Get in the boat, Uli."

Her face is held fastidiously down, too proud to admit to feeling cut low but not proud enough to wear it plain. Uli staggers to her feet and, catching on her instep, stumbles forward. She cradles her arm against her chest. When she makes it down to the bank, her left foot sticks.

I take the front strap of her foraging harness and tug her into the boat. Her foot comes free, but it doesn't give up easily—when I glance at the footprint in the soil while she settles herself on the prow seat, a small network of wriggling roots are retreating shyly back into the dirt. I look at Uli furtively examining her elbow, from which a ragged piece of bark is missing, torn away somewhere.

Being on land is an accelerant. It makes rot worse.

I cast a look behind me. I know with the barest inch of certainty there weren't any rapids on the course I had charted in those midnight hours when we were still preparing to leave the enclave.

Uli does not look at me again. I've run out of olive branches to extend her way. They were all cast into the river when the boat tipped.

We reach the beach an hour before sunset. The waves announce themselves far ahead of our emergence from the river vein, into the pebbly chase-and-rush of the breakers against their shores. Uli's tongue has been swallowed by rot, and I find myself relieved I never kissed her.

Uli limps and staggers from the boat. When I reach out an arm to help, wrapped thick with protective linen, Uli ignores it and does not balance herself against me even with her untaken hand.

She trips and picks her way over to the sand. At a spot where the water teases shallowly at a warren of rock pools, Uli lingers. She stutters down there into a kneel, facing the horizon. I can't see her face, but I can tell by the slouch of her shoulders that her eyes are closed.

"I can stay," I call out to her. A short silence covered only by the hiss of the current persists. I swallow. "I can stay through it if you want me to."

It's a mystery to me, the idea of Uli ever letting herself want something. The more likely fact seems to me that she has moved through life so brazenly that she has never *had* to want before. Uli has simply taken and seized and won whatever it is she has felt she deserves.

And what of the rot? Has she examined it? Turned over the blindness of fate when she can't sleep at night, listening faintly to the sound of her veins turning with slow purchase to mud?

Uli says nothing. She doesn't even turn and deign a nod to me, the only person who ever deemed her worthy of an end greater than the grove.

The last thing she said to me, when we had finally quit dripping from the capsize, was brief: *I hope I at least flower in the springtime.* She croaked it out before her tongue went wooden in her mouth's hollow.

A hard jut of incandescent rage rips through me. I remember we are not the same people, our differences many and painful and laborious as creation itself. It has always been like this.

Perhaps a braver coward would leave something on this beach—an *I love you,* or something else to offer poorly to the fucked-up altar of what Uli is becoming. But I am not brave. I only follow greater people into their dogged pursuits of ambition I do not have, and learn careful measures of what not to do along the way.

When I put the boat in again, it is a harder weight to heave, but the motion is familiar. Alone, my oar carves hard through the water with the pleasant burn of drudgery.

I look over my shoulder at the maudlin bleed of the sunset spilling across the horizon, the water endless and impotable, yet thick with the unique vitality of salt. Uli's silhouette is still and black against the sky—human, breaking strangely over the crux of flesh and bark.

I'll remember her laughter. I'll remember the way her thighs rocked arrhythmically as she flung herself from bliss beside me with a soft sound I hadn't known she was capable of making. I'll remember the way the moon painted her thieving arm lifting full from a bucket of water that tasted sweet for the rush of getting away with it.

I steer homeward to answer for my greatest sin, to pay my penance with labor that feels more home to my body than any roof and wall ever has. I steer homeward as Uli goes silently back to the earth in one final act of defiance.

I don't need to look over my shoulder at her again. She's gotten away with it.

Uli has had the final word. She's won. Like always.

EMMA

MORGAN SPRAKER

At the forest's edge, John shifted from foot to aching foot and adjusted the smart axe strapped across his back.

The sun suffocated him, the trees taunting. The heat would be more manageable if he could find shelter under the sweeping oak branches, even if the pollen made him sneeze. Yet none of the families picnicking between the winding river and tree line sought shelter, flush-faced children chasing each other and mothers mopping sweat from their brows while setting out food. John needed to seem just as comfortable in the soupy air and sunshine; just as comfortable turning his back to the woods, to the clusters of twisting trees that stretched for miles upon miles. Preferably, he'd seem even *more* comfortable.

That would show them what men from the city were made of.

A bearded man with dirty boots and a worn axe emerged from the trees, nearly bumping into him. "Oh, you again." He scrubbed a hand over his ruddy face, blinking his bright, tired eyes. "She might give you a chance if you mingle more. Patience is the game."

John could imagine little worse than small-talk with strangers—present company included—but if *she* emerged from the trees, he wanted to look genial, casual. The bearded man was right about one thing: there was always a game, and if he was caught waiting around for the most beautiful woman he'd ever lay eyes on, he'd lose.

"I couldn't intrude," John said, forcing a sheepish smile. The people here were friendly to a fault, smiling more often than not.

Even though the expression felt unfamiliar, he didn't want to draw unnecessary attention by not. "Say, though. You could help me along." A deliberate pause, giving the man's imagination time to run wild so John could ask for the tame. "You could tell me her name. I told her mine, but she wouldn't give."

The man tossed his head back and laughed. "You're on your own there, buddy."

Fair enough.

It wouldn't be much of a game if he cheated.

"Have you ever been out this way before?" the man asked. John stifled a wince. Didn't this man have a family? Someone, *anyone* else to talk to? "I thought when I first saw you that you looked familiar."

At the question, the trees seemed to hum, a wordless conversation to which John wasn't privy. Maybe *that* was worse than waiting—being excluded by the damn trees. Emma had always loved forests, always seemed to understand them more than she tried to understand John.

"Yeah," John said, for there was no use in lying. "Me and my wife, a long time ago."

"She didn't want to come this time?"

"Not this time." John turned his back to the trees, ignoring their buzz.

"Suppose that's why you have your eyes on the lady. But listen, whatever's meant to happen will happen. She's a good one."

The bearded man clapped a hand on John's shoulder, then went to a red-checkered blanket and kissed the cheek of the woman preparing sandwiches. A gentle smile on his lips, he took over preparing the food, letting the woman relax. John folded his arms over his chest, watching. Maybe that's what he should have done for Emma, even if it felt unnatural. Maybe then, things wouldn't have ended up the way they did.

He glanced over his shoulder, to the tree line. Relief pooled in his stomach.

There she was, and what a sight! Lithe and lovely. Dark hair tumbling loose down her back. He'd first spotted her a week ago, when he first arrived, tending to the trees. She'd taken the leaves in her smooth, pale hands, studying them with innocent green eyes. John had drunk in the elegant lines of her body, barely hidden in a white gown, and the tension of his circumstances ebbed from his shoulders. She was perfect. They were supposed to be together.

John only needed to learn her name.

"Hi," she said in her raspy voice.

"Marry me," he blurted.

Her eyes twinkled, catching the sunlight in a playful wink. For the first time that afternoon, John didn't mind the brightness.

"Marry me," he said again. "Come back to the city with me. Be my wife."

She let out an incredulous little laugh—one borne of wonder rather than withering spite. Emma used to laugh at him and mean it, but this woman in front of him, she wasn't like Emma. She understood the game they played and wanted him to win, too.

"Sure," she said. "I'll marry you."

John blinked.

I'll marry you.

She'd said yes. *Yes*, after asking only once. Disappointment prickled over his skin alongside the summer heat. Maybe she didn't understand as well as he thought she had.

"But before you do, I want you to meet my family."

There was his catch—he wasn't sure if he liked it. "Where does your family live?"

"The forest's center."

John peered over his shoulder at the trees, to the space where leaves and branches swallowed light. They swayed gently in the wind, snapping and crunching as green brushed green. Their hum ran hot over his hands, syllables dripping together until they formed words. *We know, we know.* "That's an awfully long way."

She pressed her index and middle finger to his chest and walked her delicate fingers to his collarbone. "Shouldn't my family meet the man who will sweep their daughter away?"

"Couldn't they come to us?"

"*John.*"

"Fine, fine." He could indulge her this once. "We'll meet them."

She smiled, her hand still resting at his jugular. "I'd like to go now."

"Now?" He squinted at the horizon. "Will there be enough light?"

"It isn't too far. Please."

At least she said *please* and recognized this inconvenience of her request. "Since you want to so badly, I suppose we can visit them."

It would be fine. She would never realize.

They wouldn't have to go to *that* part of the forest.

She took his hand as they started into the forest, calluses settling against his deflated blisters. He wished her hands were smoother, but that and her provocative dress could be fixed once they reached the city. For now, his main focus had to be the forest, with toothed light biting through the canopy. Golden strands of it twisted around trunks and tied clustered trees tight, creating mazes for the small creatures scuttling about.

John shivered. He hated small animals, always slipping between his fingers. Emma had a cat, and he'd hated that too—always hissing when he touched Emma—but it had been good for catching mice. She'd loved watching the chase.

"She could catch that mouse any time she wanted," Emma said, nodding at her cat. "But she's having fun, and soon, she'll have a snack."

John could have used the beast, now, to take care of at least one of his problems.

"You really can't tell me how long the walk is?" he called.

She stepped over a fallen branch, raising her skirt to reveal the defined plane of her calves. "Depends on how fast you move."

Suddenly, John had a new appreciation for the forest—every

damn branch could fall, if she had to navigate her skirt around them all. "You'll have to keep up with me."

"I assumed as much, John."

His name spoken in her sweet voice soothed his troubles. He could indulge her, this once. Besides, there was plenty to see. John took the smart axe from his back, swinging it in a circle, and stopped to trace a tree's grotesque shape. He'd seen a man with both arms and legs broken, once, and this tree reminded him of that shattered skeleton.

Everything breaks. Even this tree would, if John took his axe to it.

An upturned root caught his boot. He lurched forward, staggering. "Son of a bitch!"

She blinked with concern. "Are you okay?"

"Fine." He cleared his throat, straightening his jacket and slinging his axe over his back again. No need to drive it through his own chest. "Fine." He studied her open, worried expression, and an idea blossomed. "Nothing a kiss wouldn't fix."

Her lips curved upward as she started off again. "You'll have to wait for that."

John sped up to lead the way, passing her with a hand to the small of her back. Really, it was good she resisted his kiss. It made her respectable, not like the type of woman who sought out men for their own pleasure. Not like Emma, who sat with her blouse open at the window and watched the men walk home from work. They could toy with each other until the fun wore out.

He found the principle worked in a number of situations. He'd stayed with Emma until he could no longer. He'd stayed in the forest, away from the city, until he felt he could return without trouble. And now, he'd return with a new wife.

A wife whose heart belongs to the trees.

Jealousy gathered, warm and unpleasant, as she traced her hand almost reverently over each tree, caressing the branches and cradling the leaves like she should have touched him. It was a lover's path, borne from a feeling John didn't understand or, really, care about.

Trees were trees and people were people. Branches and leaves couldn't claim her heart like he could.

Couldn't they?

John couldn't shake the sense of eyes overhead, peering through the canopy, watching as laughter oozed down broken-bone trunks.

"All right, John?" she called.

Of course he was. John opened his mouth to tell her as much, but a rustling stole his voice. He flinched, whipping around. How had she distracted him so fully? How had he not remembered how many places there were to hide? In the brush. Behind thick trunks. Tucked under leaves. A chill ghosted the back of his neck as he studied the same trees he'd passed without incident. The sense of being watched remained, a pinprick, perpetual shiver he couldn't shake. He pulled his jacket tighter, the axe shifting with the fabric.

"John?"

Her voice echoed. *John, John, John.* She sounded like Emma: *I thought you would change, John* and *if you really don't understand why I'm upset right now, John, you never will.* Why did she sound like Emma, when she was so different?

Why did she look like a dead woman in this light, with her wide, surprised eyes?

"I'm fine." *Fine, fine, fine,* the word echoed, in his own voice, shouted at Emma in the middle of an argument. "What…" He wet his dry lips. "Tell me your name?"

He watched her honest face remain so as she said, "Emma."

Emma.

How could her name be Emma?

John curled his hands into fists, looking at her—*really* looking at her. Maybe she did bear some resemblance to his deceased wife. They both had dark hair and light eyes, but her mannerisms… maybe they shared mannerisms too. The tilt of their heads. The slow blinks.

It was impossible.

"Okay." He pushed his sweaty hair away from his forehead. "Okay, Emma."

They kept walking.

"Tell me..." John exhaled. *Emma.* "Tell me about your family, Emma."

Even if it was impossible, he could still gauge her intentions.

"We've lived here for centuries." Emma's voice had a dreamy quality, her words mingling with the lowering afternoon light and floating to intertwine with the leaves. "I'm sure we'll live here for centuries more. The people who live here are good."

"You won't leave?"

"Humans always seem to be searching for happiness. It usually leads them here." Emma turned her face to a sliver of light, a peaceful smile playing over her lips. "Why would we leave the place they come looking for?"

"You do want to leave with me, don't you? I'm not staying here." He shivered again, the chill sneaking under his jacket. "It feels..."

"Haunted?" She was pale, so pale, in the shadows, and her dress created a white haze. "I understand. Most people don't care for ghosts."

John's stomach plummeted. "No," he said. "No, they don't."

What are you? he wanted to ask. *Who are you?*

He feared the answer.

"You didn't answer my question about your family," he said, as casual as he could manage. "Do you have any siblings?"

John had a younger sister. He'd never gotten along with her and, frankly, blamed her for a lot of his problems in life. Much like the surrounding forest, she spoke a different language with their mother. It was exclusionary, full of knowing looks and uninterpretable silences.

Emma—his *other* Emma—had a sister. Allison. Before Emma and John visited this place together, they left the cat with Allison. He'd waited outside, arms crossed over his chest as he listened to Allison and Emma's muffled whispers.

...*never liked him,* Allison hissed, and he'd caught, *dangerous* and *worried.*

The trip will be good for us, Emma returned. *We need time.*

As they left, Allison had glared at him from the window, and when John returned, Allison made his life a living hell. Hopefully when he returned, she would be less hysterical—or ideally, just leave him alone.

This Emma showed no signs of slowing as she led him over a rickety wooden bridge. Clear water rushed over smoothed rocks. John ached for a sip, but he wouldn't stoop as low as kneeling in the dirty and sipping from the current. A kiss would be as good as a gallon.

"Emma," he said. "Won't you kiss me?"

Another coy smile. "Patience."

Patience.

John scoffed and kicked a tuft of leaves. The air around him hissed in an inhuman inhale. Who was Emma to tell him about patience? Wasn't playing along patience enough? He wouldn't wait forever—hell, he shouldn't have had to wait for this long.

But it was fine. Just fine, as he'd been swearing up and down for the past hours. He wasn't angry. His other Emma would have said he was. *Anger issues,* she spat at him in the heat of a fight. Her words filled the treetops, eyes tracking his every step. He ignored them. What did she matter, anyway? She was gone. The woman before him was here.

She matters.

John stilled.

She matters.

The words hadn't come from Emma, who walked ahead, oblivious to the deep voice.

She matters.

He turned, sticks snapping under his boots with a *cru-unch.*

The setting sun darkened the path they'd tread, soil shadowed in shades of green and gold. The hum swelled like the sea, louder, louder, like a memory of Emma tossing her head back and laughing bitterly.

The branches swayed, twigs splayed into fingers. They dipped down. Reached. John stilled as the leaves danced over his body, whispers of *soon, soon, soon* filling the air as they cocooned him. A scream built in his throat and he—

Blinked.

The trees had not moved.

John lifted a hand to the back of his neck. Palm met raised flesh. "Emma!" he shouted. "What the hell was that?"

Emma's eyes were feline in the low light. "I'm sorry?"

"What did the trees just do?"

"John, I'm not quite sure what you're talking about."

"Yes, you are! The trees..." He trailed off. *The trees tried to eat me,* he was about to say. If Emma had said as much, he would have called her hysterical. But he was right—he knew what he saw. "They were like arms. Reaching for me."

Emma offered a small hum, resuming her pace with an energetic bounce. "You must be tiring, darling."

"I'm not tired!"

The words came out petulant. He couldn't find it within himself to care. They hadn't stopped for food or water *all day,* and Emma showed no signs of slowing. No signs of thirst or hunger. Hell, she wasn't even sweating. Cold dread built in John's stomach.

What *was* she?

He could not find the courage to ask.

"You know what?" John pushed a hand through his sweaty hair. "Whatever. *Whatever.* Let's just find your damn family and get out of here."

"If you say so," Emma said lightly.

Miles blurred. Blisters opened in John's boots, soaking his socks with every step. All he wanted was the biggest meal of his life, water, and a bed with Emma in it. He'd demand the last thing once they reached her family's house, honor be damned. After everything she'd put him through today, he'd earned at least that. Maybe he could cash in early.

"Emma," he said, as calmly as he could manage. "I really would like it if you kiss me."

"When we get there," she answered.

"Get *where*?"

"Not much farther."

"You said that hours ago!"

Even at his raised voice, Emma's smile never left her face. "I told the truth. Come."

She broke into a run.

John sprinted in her wake—after the day he'd had, she wasn't getting away. He'd had enough of this cat-and-mouse bullshit.

"Get back here!" he shouted. "Emma!"

She darted between trees, her white dress fluttering around her legs and remaining pristine. She kicked off her shoes and ran barefoot, roots parting in her wake. John's lungs burned with the effort, but he wouldn't lose her, he wouldn't let her escape.

"Emma!"

She stopped.

John staggered to a halt, clutching a hand to his chest. He drew a ragged breath and raised his eyes to the surroundings.

Then froze.

He knew these oaks. He knew the copper-stained soil. He knew the way the canopy watched his back. He knew why one patch of earth had less greenery covering it than the rest.

He knew who lay in the makeshift grave.

John took the axe from his back. The long lines of Emma's body remained relaxed and tranquil—he'd change that. "Tell me what you're up to."

"I told you. I wanted you to meet my family."

"This isn't…" He glanced at the ground, where she was buried. "We're in the middle of nowhere. This place is *nothing*."

"It's my home."

"Oh, yeah? This is your home?" John swung the axe in a circle, the blade showing its teeth in the sunset. "Then you won't like it at all when I do this, huh?"

He struck the first tree he saw.

Emma's scream caught on the wind, burning in his ears. In the background, dishes crashed, shattering as he hurled them to the floor of his apartment in the city. Glass joined splintering wood, shards and slivers littering the forest floor, sticking to the sap like bone. He'd cut this forest down tree by tree. He'd break every dish. He'd teach Emma a lesson about looking at other men. He'd bring the world down around him until it resembled his insides, destroyed and raw and raging. It would match, and it would be right.

He reared the axe back, over his shoulder.

The blade caught flesh.

John turned on his heel. The axe nestled in Emma's chest, the blade splitting her pale skin open. John staggered back.

She made me do it.

She was just like the other Emma. She'd pushed and pushed until he had no choice. And just like the other Emma, he'd hide her body here. Nobody had to know.

Emma cocked her head at a broken-neck angle, studying the axe. Her eyes shone as she wrenched the weapon from her chest and hurled it away. It soared into the air, arching well above John's head, and vanished into the swaying trees. Sap poured from the wound. She plunged her hand into the cavity, rummaging around in her chest with a curious expression.

"You made me." Bile built in John's throat. "You made me do it! You've been trying to make a fool of me!"

Emma laughed. "I don't have to try very hard."

Oh, he'd show her. Maybe she was just like his Emma, smug and stubborn and sharp, much too sharp for a woman. He'd show her what happened to girls who tried to toy with respectable men, and then, he'd get the hell out of this haunted forest.

The ground held fast to his feet.

Thick, rooted tendrils locked around his ankles, holding him in place. John strained. Their grip tightened. Branches swooned to embrace him, curling over his arms and legs. Emma watched, expressionless, and the trees hummed.

"I saw what you did to her," Emma whispered.

There had been nobody there. "You couldn't have."

"I saw."

Skin peeled from her concave chest, revealing tree bark skin and dripping sap. Her flowing hair softened to cascading green leaves. John flinched back as her dress ribboned to the ground, her body filling out with a tree's naked and natural curves. She advanced with strong, solid legs, each easily as big as John's waist. John cowered back as she reached forward with twig fingers. Only her eyes remained the same, green and glowing.

When John killed Emma, there were no *humans*. But there had been trees, he realized.

Watching.

Witnessing.

Waiting.

As bark embalmed his ankles, hundreds of green eyes blinked to life. John strained for his axe. He needed a weapon—he was outnumbered. He stretched for anything, even a branch, but the wood locked his arm in place.

The creature who called herself Emma watched.

"Please," he whispered. Wetness trickled down his leg. "Emma, please."

She remained silent.

The bones in his wrists snapped. His shoulder. His ankle. With a mighty crack, his tibias and femurs, broken bones settling into bark. A scream tore from his lips, but the treetops silenced it, drinking in the sound and swallowing it.

Emma moved closer, leafy hair falling over her shoulder and

wisping against Jon's throat. Inches from his face, she smiled, showing sharp wooden teeth.

"We watch." Her voice was a chorus, deep, larger than herself. John's chest vibrated before bark closed over it. "We correct."

She ambled to the grave and planted her legs amongst the new growth. Slowly, her curves became gnarled, the soil turning darker and richer. Higher and higher she grew, twisting and curving into a senseless shape, until she reached the treetops, until only her eyes remained human. Life poured from her, into the grave, until the ground shifted.

Through hazy pain, John watched a hand emerge from the grave. As bark stole his lungs, the earth opened.

Emma drew new breath.

THE BOY WHO BECAME AN ENTIRE PLANET

NICHOLAS PEREZ

My parents died, leaving me with a mission.

Every generation of my family left the next generation the same mission before they all died from the Eco Spore Parasite. The parasite enters the body after coming into contact with the spores from the plant life of Cubanascnan, a planet discovered two centuries ago.

When Earth finally had the technological and scientific prowess, humanity decided to go even farther beyond the Solar System and the cluster it was in. Within the Milky Way they discovered more clusters, and within more clusters they discovered more systems, and within more systems they discovered more planets.

In the Tau Vita Nova Cluster was the Mundo System, discovered by explorers of mostly Latin American heritage. Every planet in the Mundo System was successfully colonized: Aztlán, Quisqueya, Borikén, Abya Yala, and Pindorama.

"RAFAEL!"

A hand smacks the back of my head. "Coño!" Rubbing my head, I turn to see Beatriz, a junior botanist like me, glaring angrily through her black-framed glasses. Her short, black hair ends just below her cheeks, and her light brown skin looks glossy under the lights of the lab.

"Were you listening to me?" she asks.

"Yes," I reply.

"What did I say?"

My mouth opens, but nothing comes out.

She shakes her head, glaring through her glasses. "I asked if you're ready. We take off in an hour."

"Yes," I say.

She nods to the table in front of me. "Is *it* ready?"

On the table is a containment box, a bulky thing with a metal lock and handle and inscribed with warnings in Spanish and English. What's in it is the most important thing in the world. The thing that my family died working on.

I place my hands on it. "Yes. It's ready."

"Good," Beatriz says. She looks at the containment box in awe. She leans closer. "Can I see it?"

I smile. "No."

"Oh, come on!" she whines. "Please! Both of our families spent decades working on this together!"

"I'm sorry, Beatriz. I can't expose it in public. Only back in the lab or on Cubanascnan."

"I have a right to see it!" Beatriz puffs out her cheeks.

She's technically right. What's in the containment box is a product of both of our families' scientific efforts—our families' efforts to live in harmony with Cubanascnan.

"Can you at least describe it to me?"

"It looks like a sunflower seed. I don't know if that's because of genetic modification or if that's actually what the seed is supposed to look like."

"Well, let's get going. I can see it in all its glory on Cubanascnan." She turns around and exits through the doors.

I take in the containment box one last time before picking it up and following Beatriz.

The docking bay is heavily crowded. I sway the containment box back and forth as gently as I can so no one hits it. Anyone breaks this open, then everyone on Borikén is dead. And both of our families' work goes to waste. Over near the docking ramp waits the space cruiser, where attendants pick up luggage and supplies and carry them onboard.

Beatriz hands her ID to the boarding attendant, who scans it with his arm tablet. The attendant scrutinizes the readings before taking Beatriz's luggage and letting her on board. The attendant scans my ID and approves me. When he reaches for the containment box, I pull away.

"No," I say. "This stays with me."

The attendant looks back at his tablet. His eyes widen, then he nods at me.

Inside the cruiser, I take a seat next to Beatriz. I put the containment box on the floor between my feet. Passengers go to their seats, and attendants store luggage. Beatriz taps away on her arm. I sit patiently, looking at the back of the seat in front of me.

"Beatriz," I finally say. She turns to me. I look down at the box. "It's all here. It could finally make Cubanascnan our home." She smiles. "My family couldn't have done it without yours, Beatriz. Your family caught things that mine didn't and kept everyone safe and alive."

Her smile dies. "We were never able to find a cure for the parasite though."

I frown. The memories of all the patients who couldn't be saved are painful. Especially of my family.

We don't know much about Eco Spore Parasite beyond the fact that it's caused by coming into contact with the plants on Cubanascnan. The spores enter your body and implant themselves into you. It affects every gland in the endocrine system, severing your brain's connection. After the spores plant themselves, they grow. They grow plants and vines in every gland. The last to go are the pituitary gland and hypothalamus; once they go, you're done.

That's how so many people died. My parents were luckier than the rest thanks to the treatments made by Beatriz's family. No cure exists, but a special pill prevents the plants from growing out of your skin. Unfortunately, we haven't been able to remove the spores entirely. Surgical removal is too risky. Removing that many glands is a death sentence.

I close my eyes.

"We won't have to worry about that anymore," I say. I put the containment box on my lap. "Cubanascnan will finally be colonized and its environment will be tamed. Our families spent years trying to genetically modify a seed from the mother plant so that we can grow a new mother plant that is not hostile. We got this." The mother plant is the head of the hive mind of the Cubanascnan vegetation. We don't know how or why. It's the strangest thing humanity has encountered. We believe Cubanascnan feels and acts like it is one, living organism. At the beginning of the colonization effort, deforestation was used to clear space. The deforestation "killed off" part of the planet, part of the mother plant. That's when the spores appeared and the plants became hostile.

Beatriz shifts in her seat. "But those plants are sentient. Their vines have hurt people."

I shake my head. "We'll do this. I know we will." I look at Beatriz until we both smile. We're uncertain of what's coming, but we will complete our mission.

The platform elevator takes our cruiser up to the runway. We're given the green, and the cruiser speeds down the runway with revving engines. We are all pushed into our seats under the force. Once past the docking bay doors, the cruiser takes off into space.

The planet Borikén gradually gets smaller behind us. Beatriz records a message on her arm tablet to send to her family and then says a prayer for our protection. I take in the stars through the window, wondering if there is another planet where the plants are sentient. Sentient, but docile. A planet where nature and humanity are in harmony.

A planet where the old beauty of Cuba can be reborn.

The Council of New Worlds designated Cubanascnan as the cradle for a new Cuba before they were aware of the plant life. After they learned about the plants, the Council merely told everyone "To master the new soil!" There were none left in the Mundo System, let alone the rest of the Tau Vita Nova Cluster, and resources needed to be rationed.

We have to fight for a new home, even when no one else is living there.

Beatriz feels the duty of her family, as I do mine. Our families worked together to make this happen. We've lost too many people.

I join Beatriz in her prayer.

Cubanascnan is a swirled marble of blue and green. I have seen it so many times in textbooks that seeing it for real is uncanny. I smile, forgetting about the danger the planet holds.

After we enter the atmosphere, we land in New Havana, the only city. Towers of metal and glass glisten on a flat plain with palm trees all over. Surrounding it is the towering forest of Cubanascnan. New Havana and the lakes and seas are the only things preventing the planet from being entirely forest.

After the cruiser taxis to the docking bay, we exit with the containment box and our luggage and are greeted by a man in a researcher's uniform.

"Rafael Silva? Beatriz Villaverde?" he asks. We nod. "I'm Enrique Ortiz. I'm here to escort you to base camp."

"Where's base camp?" I ask. "I thought we were doing everything in New Havana?"

Ortiz has us follow him out as he gives us the rundown. "We discovered that not all of the plants release spores. There's an area of the forest that we cleared out and set up camp."

My heart jumps when I hear this. I catch up to him. "You actually took down more of the forest?"

"Yup."

"Why!?" I cry out so loudly that everyone stops before the jeep awaiting us. "Tearing down the forest makes the vegetation aggressive! Even if the spores aren't in that area, the forest will retaliate."

"We're aware. That's why we uprooted them. That kills them. Now, get in." Ortiz takes the driver's side of the jeep.

Beatriz hurries past me to put her luggage in the trunk. I'm frozen and angry. Beatriz climbs into the back and waves me over. I'm seething because my family's warning has been completely ignored.

Beatriz comes over and drags me to the trunk. "Don't make him mad," she whispers.

As she puts my stuff in the trunk, I stomp into the passenger seat next to Ortiz. When Beatriz gets back in, Ortiz takes off.

The journey through New Havana is brief. We pass the city limits, and in less than fifteen minutes we're in the forest. The remaining trees and plants are of many different species. I grip the containment box as we get deeper into the forest.

Eventually, we arrive at base camp, which is just a collection of tents and makeshift labs. We take our luggage to a tent reserved for us. Putting our things away, we regroup with Ortiz and the other researchers around a table with equipment and three protection suits on it.

"Silva." Ortiz says my name firmly. "You still got it?"

I hold up the containment box.

"Everyone in the entire cluster has been waiting for this day. So, let's get to the point." Ortiz points to a path leading deeper into the forest. "Follow that path. After three clicks, you'll be with the spores." He looks at Beatriz. "Villaverde, you need to help Siva analyze the mother plant before planting the seed. You're also the medic. We've supplied you with a sealant in case any of the protection suits are torn. Apply it immediately."

He turns to the table.

"We've also supplied you with wilters. If any of the plants make a move on you, fire immediately. Any questions?"

"What if we fail?" I ask. Beatriz looks at me anxiously.

"Then Cubanascnan is done for."

As Ortiz glares down at me, a thousand questions run through my mind. Most of all, what will happen once we plant the new mother? Will it destroy the old mother? Will it really neutralize the spores?

We put on our protection suits and helmets and arm ourselves with wilters. Beatriz has her arm tablet and med kit, and I clutch the containment box.

Ortiz and the other researchers salute us as we set off down the path.

Deep in the forest, we can see the floating spores. Each plant has prehensile branches, roots, or vines. It's dark, save for some luminescent flowers and our lights. Beatriz scans the vegetation with her arm tablet while I shake.

"Amazing," Beatriz says.

"What?" I ask.

"All of these plants have genes related to the mother plant."

"Did every plant here come from the mother?"

"I think so," Beatriz replies. "I hypothesize that all their seeds came from the mother. We weren't ever sure because of how hostile the environment is, but this is the proof."

"Está volao," I say. "Just like the seed." I look around, wondering how it all came to be. Am I ready for this? Can I upend the natural order of an entire ecosystem? I'm so lost in thought that I don't notice the vine wrapping around my ankle.

"RAFAEL!"

I scream as I'm flung to the ground. My wilter flies out of my hand when I land, but I still have the containment box. The vine pulls me away. Beatriz gives chase while firing her wilter. She does not see the vines lowering behind her.

Beatriz fires at the vine while running, missing every shot. The wet debris of the blasts splatter against my helmet. The vine behind her grabs her by the leg and pulls her up. She screams my name, looking at me, eyes wide with fear.

Before I'm dragged through some bushes, I scream her name too.

The blasts from her wilter become distant as I'm dragged deeper into the forest.

The vine brings me to a glade heavy with spores and surrounded by bigger plant species. The forest's center. The place where people usually only go once.

The vines multiply, tearing my suit and helmet off. I reach for the containment box, but a vine snatches it.

I jump after it, but then stop immediately. I see it.

The mother plant.

It looks like a giant, blue king protea resting on a star of leaves surrounded by moving vines and thorns. The petals are closed. I feel like I'm standing before a primordial goddess, one who created everything.

The vines connected to the mother plant begin to violently break the box open. I reach out a hand. "Don't!"

The lid is ripped off. The seed drops to the ground. I dive for it. I catch it, but the vines grab me again and lift me up to the mother plant.

"Please! Let me do this! Let me plant this! I don't want anymore people to die!" The mother plant does not move. Is it listening to me? "We just want to live here! We have nothing back on Earth! Cuba lost everything centuries ago! We can't even call it home anymore!" The mother plant still does not move. Then I realize my own words.

Cubanascnan is the mother plant's home. She deserves to live here too. "I don't want this planet to die. I don't even want you to die. Even if you're responsible for my family's pain."

It hurts to say those words. I don't want to say them at all. The plants of Cubanascnan aren't predators. They merely live on instinct.

"We just want to live…"

My hands loosen. The seed falls and a vine catches it, bringing it closer to the closed petals. They open and the stigmas and anthers spread. The vines release me as the mother plant brings the seed closer. I watch the seed get taken into the flower, the vines pushing it in deep.

Why is she doing this?

A green light glows from the seed. I want to speak, but no words can suffice my feelings. The seed's coat breaks and the edge of a radicle seeps out as the flower closes. Vines and branches retract and the spores dissipate.

The light fades as the flowers on the mother turn brown. The petals collapse in on themselves and break.

She's dead.

"No…" I whisper.

I didn't want this. My family didn't want this. The seed was supposed to grow a new mother plant that would only stop the spread of the spores.

I drop to my knees. Without the mother plant everything else will die.

I've killed our planet. My warm tears come slowly. I've killed us all.

A petal falls to the ground. A young vine slithers out. Petals fall and vines replace them.

The light glows.

The petals fall faster, revealing something new. A bigger and more vibrant flower.

A new plant mother.

The new vines drag me to the yellow flower. As I get closer, I can feel her warmth; I bask in it. The stigmas and anthers spread and within is the shell of the seed—glowing. More vines wrap around me. I surrender to her.

For a moment, I think I hear whispering. Wait, I do hear whispering. A faint woman's voice. Is she speaking to me?

The vines push me into the flower, and my forehead touches the seed.

I see everything.

Me.

The mother plant.

My family.

Beatriz.

Every tree, plant, thorn, and flower.

I see all of Cubanascnan from above. I see below the ground and deep into the core of the planet.

I see both humans and plants living, growing, and dying.

I'm scared until I hear her voice again—stronger and louder. "What do you need to do?"

"Live," I reply.

"What do I need to do?"

"Live."

"You are me, but you are still you. You are of this world, but not the world itself. I am this world, but not of this world."

"I don't understand."

"You will. You must. You will live and so will I. But I must have a name. Please, my child, give me a name."

"You want me to name you?"

"Yes!"

"What do you want to be named?"

"I want a Cuban name. Just like everything else you've named here."

I think for a moment. I think over every story about Cuba my parents told me.

"So?" she asks.

"Atabey," I say. "I think it suits you."

"Atabey," she says slowly. "Atabey..." She's quiet for a moment. "Yes!" she cries. "Me encanta!"

And then the warmth makes me whole.

I find Beatriz. Dead vines lay around her, her wilter cast aside. She is tapping on her arm tablet but stops when she notices me. Her eyes widen and mouth drops.

Green markings like the vines cover my body. They all emerge from the same spot: a tattoo of a fern leaf on my back. My eyes are glowing green, and chalice vines and white mariposas adorn my head.

Beatriz continues to stare, speechless.

I swipe my hand and new vines break the wilter apart, awakening Beatriz from her trance. When the vines pull her helmet off, she jumps. She holds her breath until she's sure the spores are gone.

I walk and she follows.

I walk through the base camp, ignoring the shocked looks from Ortiz and the others.

I walk back to New Havana. Everyone stares. I reach the center of New Havana—a round park with kapoks bordering it. Everyone stays at the edge while I go to the center. Once there, I kneel down and put my hands on the ground.

I close my eyes and I call upon her. I feel all of Cubanascnan in me and around me.

Cubanascnan is home. A place of glass and metal, but also of vegetation. Of life.

The tree grows.

A royal palm. Long, high, and strong. Its leaves cast a shadow over the park. Vines swirl around it all the way to the top, flowers blooming on it. The royal palm glows green, warm and gentle.

All around us, every building is changed with some sort of plant growing around or through it.

It is up to those who dwell within those structures to live in harmony with nature. I help out. I teach everyone how to care for the plants. I make new ones grow and decompose dying ones.

Every so often she speaks to me. She tells me how she feels and reminds me that my parents would be proud of me.

I teach those who're worthy. I take them to the mother plant, and she gives them the understanding.

That they are not hostile, not invading.

They're living.

ALONE

ALEX BROWN

Legend has it that on a cold and stormy night, Laurie Santos went out for a walk and never came back. Rumor had it that she was supremely unhappy with her life. She'd left everything behind when she moved to America to become a nurse. And, even though she'd made a few friends in town, they couldn't replace everyone who loved her in the Philippines. She'd adjusted as well as she could to the harsh New England winter and the lifeless, barren trees that surrounded her. But, despite her best efforts, it still didn't feel like the place she was meant to be.

I could relate to that.

If you ask anyone in town, Laurie cried each day before she went to the hospital for her shift. Her agony could be heard from a block away. And, on that fateful night, as she walked to the bridge that connected her small town to the rest of the state, it's said that her wailing sounded just like wind carried into town by the blizzard that swirled around her.

Everyone heard her cry for help that night. And no one intervened.

She jumped off of the bridge, unable to cope with her new life. This town accepted this as fact. Another unhappy soul falling to an unhappy end. To this day, if you listen closely, right before it snows, you can still hear her crying.

There's another part of the story that every Pinoy in town knows:

ALEX BROWN

Before Laurie died, she promised to bring a great flood that would wash out the sins of our town's past.

We don't know when, or why, but we're certain it's coming.

On a similar cold and stormy night, Sidney Jackson sat on the bridge waiting for Laurie's ghost to appear—and I was right there next to her. It was an old habit. We'd been next to each other our whole lives.

I pulled my coat closer, shivering into it. All I wanted to do was scoot up next to Sidney and wrap an arm around her. I had the perfect excuse. It was cold enough to snow, and by the smell of things, it was going to. Soon. The air was crisp. Vaguely smoky. Like someone started a campfire nearby and forgot about it.

"Do you think this will really work?" Sidney asked, staring out at the water. Her feet dangled off the edge of the bridge. "Will we hear it?"

"I hope so. Otherwise we froze our asses off for nothing."

She reached over, swatting me lightly. "Not necessarily for nothing, Violet. We could always freeze our asses to this bridge and never leave. Spend the rest of our days looking at the same view. Listening to the same birds. Just you and me."

I sighed. I would've given anything to spend as long as I could sitting with her, watching the world go by. But once the sun came up, Sidney Jackson would drive out of my life to San Jose where her dad had gotten a new job. I wasn't sure I'd ever see her again. But that wasn't something I wanted to think about.

I grabbed the box of matches, turning it over in my hand. The bridge's steel beams were cold to the touch, even through all of our layers. We didn't have to worry about being interrupted—they'd built new ways to get in and out of town since Laurie Santos died. Most days, everyone forgot the bridge existed.

But nobody forgot Laurie.

Or, at least, who they thought she was.

Everything around us was eerily quiet. I'd sat on that bridge more times than I could count, watching the seasons drift by with Sidney Jackson at my side. There were always animals around. Even in winter. Burrowing, chirping, chattering accompanied our conversations about nothing and everything. Our fights. Our silence. Our laughter.

The times we could've told each other how we felt but hadn't.

I lit a match, ignoring how the world was so still it was almost frozen. Held the flame to the wind. Let it extinguish. And then I closed my eyes, waiting to see if we could actually summon a ghost.

"Let's do what we came here to do. We can figure out the rest of it later."

"The rest of it." Sidney sighed. "Okay. Hand me a candle?"

I found her favorite one. Her fingers brushed mine as I gave it to her. I let the touch linger for a second too long before I pulled away. "You remember what to do?"

"Wait until it sounds like the sobbing is right next to you. Light the candle without turning around. And then say the words."

I nodded. "And then say the words."

Since Laurie's untimely demise, the legend around her unhappiness grew. She turned into our town's version of Bloody Mary, with a few differences. You didn't need to look into a mirror and say her name three times to summon her. And she wouldn't kill you—or whatever it was that Bloody Mary was supposed to do.

Instead, whoever summoned her would be overcome with sadness. If one were to believe the legend, her despair was enough to drive someone mad. To plunge them into a darkness of their own making. They'd fall into an endless pit of hopelessness and never be able to claw their way out.

Why anyone would want to do this when they could just be murdered by a supernatural lady trapped in a mirror was beyond me. Especially when, if you failed to complete the ritual, your life basically fell apart. Some seniors at our school tried it a few years back but they didn't do things properly. They ended the ritual too early. And all died in a three-car pileup before graduation. Some people think they died because they didn't see Laurie. That avoiding her was its own kind of curse.

Of course, it could've just been dumb luck. Or fate. Or the world just being a cold, dark place. But everyone loved to use Laurie as an excuse. It was easier to accept that bad things happened when there was someone to blame.

A few things needed to happen before Laurie's spirit cursed you to a sorry existence. Whoever wanted to see her ghost had to be on the bridge she'd allegedly jumped off of. And it needed to be right before snow started to fall.

The summoners needed an even number of people to participate in the ritual. Mostly because no one would believe them if there were no other witnesses. But also because misery loved company. If they were successful—if they saw her—well. It wasn't fun being sad all alone, was it?

Once the summoners were on the bridge with the right number of people, they waited until 11:57 PM. This was the time—again, allegedly—that Laurie crashed into the water and died.

"It's 11:55," Sidney said. Her phone lit up the darkness around us for a moment before she shoved it back in her pocket.

There was one last piece of the legend. Summoning Laurie was only going to work if we heard her crying. If we lit the candle before that, she wouldn't appear.

Sidney and I weren't going to end this thing before we got the chance to talk to her. We had to know if it was real—if we could actually see her. Talk to her. If we did something impossible then our last night together wouldn't be a total waste.

"Are you ready?" I asked. I scooted closer to Sidney, not caring as much about the wall I'd put up between us as I had when we got here. Boundaries seemed like a silly thing when we were trying to speak to the dead.

Sidney looped her arm through mine. Her eyes shone in the moonlight as she looked at me. "Ready."

I struck another match. The wind blew it out before it had a second to breathe. I closed my eyes, taking in the silence one last time.

Footsteps sounded behind us, slowly shuffling closer. My eyes flew open. No one else should be on the bridge right now.

"Do you think that's—" Sidney started to say but sobbing interrupted her.

Sidney gripped my arm tighter. If it *was* Laurie, we had a small window of time for this to work. I struck a new match, shielding it from the wind as I lit both of our candles.

"Keep your eyes on the water," I said, staring straight ahead. "No matter what."

Sidney nodded. Wind blew around us, ruffling our hair. I cleared my throat before I began the incantation that was supposed to summon her.

"Laurie Santos, we call upon you tonight to reveal the depths of your despair." I paused. We'd practiced this so many times, but the words felt like sandpaper as they rushed out of my mouth.

"Share your secrets with us," Sidney said, picking up where I left off.

The wind was so brutal, it felt like someone was hitting my back. Sidney leaned into me and I did the same.

"Do you think it's working?" she asked as the wind rushed around us. We held onto each other as tightly as we could.

"Only one way to find out," I said, holding my candle into the air. Wind knocked into it, but the flame didn't even flicker. It stood against the darkness. Our only source of light. The sobbing swelled with the wind—so loud that Laurie might as well have been sitting right next to us. I held onto Sidney as tight as I could, finishing the incantation. "And help us find a way to set your soul free."

The world became still once more.

Sidney and I hung onto each other as if we were scared that the other was going to be ripped away. A few tense breaths flickered between us as we waited for something to happen. We'd done everything right. And now all we could do was wait.

Eons passed as we both stared ahead, not daring to take our eyes off of the water.

"Well?" Sidney asked, shifting a little next to me. "Is anything happening?"

"No." I frowned. We'd done everything we were supposed to. Followed the instructions like our lives depended on it. But too much time had gone by. Something was wrong.

"We messed up," Sidney said, defeat seeping into her words. "Maybe it's not going to snow tonight."

I shook my head. "Every weather app said it would. And it *feels* like it is. That can't be it."

"How do we fix it?"

"I don't know!" I winced. That came out sharper than I intended. "I'm sorry. I just… I need some time to think."

Sidney sighed, letting go of my arm. "Time. That's the only thing we don't have more of." She grabbed onto one of the bridge's posts. Hoisted herself up. "I've gotta get home, Vi. Can't be a zombie in the morning. Mom will flip if I'm not in move-out mode." She held her hand out to help me up, but I didn't take it.

"Five more minutes won't hurt anything."

"It's over, Violet. We tried. Nothing happened." She sniffled. "Maybe it's just a story after all."

I stared out at the water, blinking back tears. This wasn't how it was supposed to go. It would've been the one thing we had when everything else faded away. When I was nothing more than a distant memory in her mind.

It was impossible to forget summoning a ghost. But it was easy to forget me.

"Go if you want to," I said, not daring to look back at her. "I'm gonna wait."

"It's only gonna get colder, Vi. You'll freeze out here."

"I don't care," I snapped. Venom ran cold through my blood. "Just leave. It's what you're good at."

Sidney scoffed. "You think this was *my* choice? That I wanted any of this? God, you can be so damn—"

But whatever I could be was pushed away as something knocked into my back. "That's not funny, Sidney." I gripped the bridge's beam tighter, nearly slipping off of the cold metal that I was sitting on. Silence lingered between us for a moment. When Sidney spoke, her words were nothing more than a whisper.

"Violet. You need to stand up. Very slowly."

Someone sniffled next to me.

"Violet," Sidney said, her voice farther away than it should've been. "Look at the water. And stand up."

A soft sob came from my left. There was definitely something in the corner of my eyes. A silhouette that didn't belong to Sidney.

Or anyone who was alive.

"Laurie," I said, as calmly as I could. "We want to help you."

Laurie sobbed, gasping for air with each breath. She was so close, I could've reached out and touched her if I wanted to.

"We don't think you want to hurt us." I'd barely gotten the thought out when she started to wail. The sound made me grip the beam tighter.

Sidney cleared her throat. "Violet, I really think you should move."

"No. We came here to do this." I spat the words at her. *Unbelievable.* We agreed that we'd see it through, no matter what happened. But now that the ritual worked, Sidney just wanted to leave Laurie behind when she needed her the most.

Laurie screamed, freezing my thoughts in place. Wisps of wind wrapped around me, icicles dug through my clothes, grazing my skin. My blood ran cold as I turned to face her. I was breaking one of the rules, but it felt like the right thing to do.

I'd had so many days where the world felt less bright. Especially since I found out that Sidney was moving away. Now, as I sat on the bridge staring at Laurie, it felt like the only thing I'd ever known was darkness. Confusion. Searching for something but never quite finding it.

I gasped. Laurie's light brown eyes gleamed in the moonlight, brimming with tears. Her nose and cheeks flushed with red. Dark hair floating around her head as if it was getting tousled by an endless breeze that didn't exist.

"Violet." Sidney's voice shook as she spoke. "Run."

Every muscle in my body was screaming with agreement. But I couldn't go just yet. I had to know.

"Laurie?" I asked. She opened her mouth and for a moment I thought she was going to talk to me. Tell me about who she was before she became nothing but a ghost in a story.

But then the brown in her eyes faded away, overtaken by a white that was as pale as the moon's rays. A shiver raked its way down my spine. Icy white claws reached out from underneath the bridge, clamping around my legs. They dug through my clothes and broke my skin. Cold air rushed into my wounds, stinging them.

Laurie screamed one last time. Whatever was holding onto me pulled on my legs, yanking me off the bridge. "Sidney!" I screamed her name as I plummeted for the icy river below.

"Violet!" she yelled back. "I—"

I plunged into the water before I could hear what she was going to say. Frozen water forced its way into my lungs. The river wrapped me in an icy embrace.

Laurie was right next to me. Hair floating all around her. Eyes still as white as a fresh snowfall. Light surrounded her, as if the moon itself had decided to join us on a midnight swim.

I reached out for her. She tilted her head, blinking a few times. And then she reached back.

As soon as our fingers touched, warmth bloomed in my chest. Air flooded into my lungs. I was still in the water, but I wasn't drowning any more.

So much of my story is a lie, a melancholy voice sang in my head.

Laurie squeezed my hand. And the world came to life in front of me.

Two people were walking on a bridge, one going faster than the other. It was hard to see specific details, but one had a smaller frame and pitch-black hair. Both of them were shouting back and forth, as if they were in a fight. Then the first figure — the shorter one who was much too far ahead of the other — slipped. Plunged into the water just like I did.

Laurie held my hand while a different version of her sank into the river. She scrambled for a few seconds before she got her bearings and swam up to the surface. Somewhere above her, a car's engine roared to life. She called out for the other person on the bridge — a frantic *John* ringing out through the frigid night air — but he sped away instead.

The version of Laurie that was still alive slumped as the car vanished. She couldn't see it, because she wasn't under the water, but the same claws that had torn me off of the bridge wound their way around her ankles. She screamed as they dug into her skin. Writhed and jerked around, kicking at them. But no matter what she did, it wasn't enough. She yelled John's name one last time. And then the claws pulled her back under, down into the river's murky depths.

The vision faded. Laurie squeezed my hand.

I loved him. And I thought he loved me. But he left me behind. Never paid for what he did.

Her stark white eyes held my gaze as she continued.

That's why they'll all pay. The flood is coming.

Tears welled in my eyes. The claws reached out again, wrapping around the ghost's ankles. Laurie nodded toward it.

You see it too. Good. It knows when to find us. How to isolate us. We don't fight as hard for ourselves when we're alone.

She let go of me. Water flooded back into my lungs, choking me. *But we should.*

I reached out for her again, but she pulled away. Somewhere off in the distance, a car's engine roared to life.

When I came to this country — when I left everything behind — I thought I was giving myself the chance to find happiness. But there was only heartache and pain. How do you stand it?

Dark spots danced in my vision. I kicked, trying to get up to the surface. But I couldn't reach it.

I suppose you're different from me. I left my life behind. And this... this is your life.

Ice coursed through my veins.

I wonder, though. Don't you feel that pull — that longing for something you'll never truly know? Is there a part of your heart that's missing, too?

I closed my eyes. Water flooded my body, making it impossible to breathe. I couldn't stay awake anymore.

If you haven't figured it out yet, you will.

Something plunged into the water. Grabbed hold of my hand. And then everything faded away.

Our story went like this: Sidney pulled me out of the river that night and rushed me to the hospital. I was stuck there for a whole week after, slowly recovering from hypothermia and almost drowning. By the time I got out, she'd made it to her new life in her new town.

A month went by before I could bring myself to go back to the bridge. Sidney couldn't be with me in person, but she was there in spirit.

You'd better not fall off of it this time. Sidney texted.

I won't. I think we had the right idea, I replied.

Yeah. Miss you, Vi.

Miss you, too. I stepped out of my car and into the cold, crisp New England winter air, pulling my coat tighter. Even though I had four layers on, a chill still crept through, caressing my skin. I shivered. Maybe it was impossible to keep the cold out all the way.

The wind blew softly around me. I found the spot on the bridge where I'd been dragged off of it. Sat down. And closed my eyes.

Laurie came to this country full of hope. She died abandoned and alone. And then she became a monster. A ghost that haunted our town because they didn't know what to do with her memory. So, they warped it into something it never should've been. She was still grappling with the sadness she was filled with when she died. Now that Sidney was gone, I knew how she felt. Laurie and I were both alone.

But it didn't have to be that way.

"I had a lot of time to think," I said, rifling through my bag. I pulled out a letter. "I found your family. Sidney helped. A little." I laughed. Not the brightest idea, because that still made my insides feel like they were about to explode. I winced before I continued. "Actually, Sid helped a lot. We wanted them to know what happened to you. And that you weren't alone."

My hands shook as I looked out at the water. "I've gotta tell you something." I paused, tapping on a nearby beam. "My Great Aunt—Mary Beth Mendoza—she lived with you when you…well. You know. She never forgot about you. Tita Mary Beth hated what they turned you into. I hate it, too."

I stood, pulling one last thing out of my bag. A small plaque that Sidney and I decided to make. "I don't think anyone will mind if I put this here. Do you?"

I waited for a response that never came. Moved over to one of the bridge's vertical wooden beams. "This looks like the right spot." The sound of a hammer burst through the air as I nailed the plaque to the bridge.

"There we go," I said, admiring my handiwork. "Laurie Santos. Alone in life, but not forgotten in death. May happiness find her, wherever she is." I let my hand rest on the frozen plaque for a moment. And then I stood, tucking the letter back into my bag. "I'll be back to visit again soon. I promise."

I walked back to my car, wiping away at the tears in my eyes. The wind wrapped around me once more before it vanished.

I texted Sidney. *It's done.*

The world was still. And, for a moment, so was I.

I thought a lot about what Laurie said when she pulled me into the river. How there were so many pieces of me that were missing. But I didn't want them to define me. I couldn't live a life ruled by everyone who left me behind, or the things I wish I'd said.

In the distance, someone sobbed. A small, sad sound. Mourning everything that was lost. Everything that could've been, but never was. There was something else to it, too.

Something new.

My phone dinged. *You going to be okay?* Sidney asked.

Yeah. I exhaled, watching my breath vanish into the air. The water roared around me, slowly rising. *I think so.*

On a cold and stormy night, Laurie Santos died. Alone. There were whispers that she was unhappy with her life, but now I knew the truth: she could have been saved. Happy. Loved.

She deserved all of those things. But they were taken away from her. It was time everyone knew what happened.

The river spilled onto the bridge, soaking my shoes.

Laurie's flood was about to begin.

THE ROOTS CALLED US HOME

ONYX OSIRIS

This story features racist individuals who use bigoted slurs. Onyx Osiris is a Black and Indigenous Mexican (Durango Nahua) author, and his writing mirrors his own personal experiences.

Keep going...

Chimalli's stomach churned as they crested the final hill, his legs prepared to give out at a moment's notice. He could not remember the last full meal he'd had, despite the hours spent hunting and foraging in the past few weeks. He did all the hunting. The gringos did all the eating. That was how it went, he supposed.

The moon peeked over the mountains on the opposite edge of the valley, bathing the lush landscape below in an eerie pearlescent glow. It looked the way it had in his dreams: miles of trees huddled together, bracing against the outside world. Or perhaps they were bowed in worship, all their heads turned toward the tall peak in the center. Atop it sat not only Chimalli's solace but the source of all his ire—the Church of Remedy.

It had a longer name from another time, but it had since been lost. A year after the Scorch, rumors of a sanctuary deep in Mexico, where Mother Nature was a friend rather than a foe, were the only thing circulating throughout the suffocating Southwest heat. By then, much of Chima's town had been reclaimed by the onslaught of wild vines and thorned blossoms, helped along by more carnivorous stalks that no one could explain except the First People who still kept those tales. People like his Nana, who also told her grandchildren the tales of other things. Like how this church had not just been built on a hill, it had been built atop Tlachihualtepetl, the grand pyramid constructed by their ancestors.

Nana... His stomach turned again, and he forced her face from his mind. He could not think of her now, not when he was hungry and thirsty and tired and bloody and so close to breaking that he felt the fractures in his spirit. It might ruin him.

Still, her stories were the reason he had recognized the church the first time he dreamed about it, the voice in his head showing him the way with an ease that embedded itself in his bones. It was how he'd known exactly where to go and how to get there, even from all the way in Arizona. It was how he was going to save Nana and Tayanna and his unborn child. Until—

"Move it, Coyote," the Bear grunted from behind him, shoving Chima forward with the familiar jab of a rifle to his lower back.

Chima stepped down the slope some, away from the Bear, as they observed the valley. Chima called him the Bear because he looked like one—massive and malicious, yellow teeth always bared, even before the nasty sunburn burdening his skin had claimed most of his body.

Chima called the other one the Goose because he had a long neck and a big mouth, and all he did was talk about being king of a new world. Chima doubted he could be king of anything when an actual goose could probably snap him in half. But currently, the only acknowledged king was the one they *all* called the Snake, and it was fitting, too. He was tall and untrustworthy, and everything he said was out of hunger or warning.

And they all called Chima Coyote, but not because he looked like one. At least not the animal. It was an insult, a barb, a reminder that despite all things the Scorch had annihilated, bigotry was alive and well. Though it was the nicest of the names they called him, so…

There had been several others whose names Chima refused to remember or recreate, and considering only two of them remained, it had been a sound decision. Like Grant, the others had been claimed by the land along the way, a payment for their passage. All together, five gringos were left, but there had been at least a dozen in total who had broken into Chima's house and dragged him out of bed, leaving his pregnant wife and his grandmother screaming for him in the doorway. The men promised not to kill them if he came quietly.

You must go… Trust in me…

It was not the voice in his head that made him agree at first, soothing as it was. It was the fact that every step toward the church took them farther away from his family. Yet soon enough, he had kept going in hopes he would find an opportunity to kill Grant himself.

Grant. The two had been close friends since they were children. Chima had trusted him with everything he had, so much so that he'd named him godfather to his unborn child. But that was before Grant's girlfriend, Luna Zelnova, introduced him to Snake. Seduced by the momentary escape the Snake had apparently been selling in little glass vials to be inhaled or injected, had to go and run his mouth, telling the Snake he knew someone who could get them to the Sanctuary. For all of two vials, Grant sold Chima and his entire family out. Their friendship died somewhere in the drag marks outside Chima's front door the night they took him.

Grant tried to apologize several times, but Chima could not even look at him, much less hear him out. He died four days later, but not by Chima's hand. Instead, a winged coatl had flown down and pumped his neck full of venom before anyone could react. He'd writhed on the ground for twenty minutes before he went still, and Chima had watched silently, waiting for the sweet taste of revenge to grace his tongue and heal his soul. Instead, for a day or so after, he couldn't close his eyes without the memory rendering and sending bile up his esophagus.

Eventually, his anger overcame that. Though the memory still plagued him at all hours, it no longer made him ill. After a while, it became Chima's only comfort.

Since then, Chima had been driven by a single goal: getting the Snake and his band of bastards to that damned church and then getting as far away from them as possible. He refused to stay with them any longer than he had to. No sanctuary for him could exist within their presence.

Even in the old world, they'd been villains. These were the people who kept Chimalli's family down, drafting laws that put them in their place. The people who had put a pendejo in the highest office in America and let him build walls only they were allowed to jump over when it was time for Spring Break. As if colonizers hadn't ravaged both sides. There on the border, Chimalli had always been trapped between the home he could not return to and the home that had never wanted him in the first place. The sad truth was that it would be easier to raise his child in a wasteland than a stolen one.

Though, these gringos weren't that high up in their hierarchy, either. If they were, they would've been given seats on one of the get-away spaceships the billionaires had built to escape the mess they'd made. The Snake and his band were just the leftovers that used to vote for them—not quite bottom of the barrel but certainly not the top of the food chain. Before their paths crossed, Chima would say they got exactly what they deserved. But they certainly didn't deserve salvation amongst his people.

So it seemed like the world hadn't changed much at all. Even now, there was a fucking boot on his neck.

He took a deep breath and started down the mountain.

"Hold up. You wanna travel all the way tonight?" the Goose questioned warily behind him. "Shouldn't we wait for daylight?"

Now is not the time for rest.

"We—" the Snake started, but Chima answered quicker.

"We can't."

By now, Chima no longer questioned that voice, which had grown more distinguished over time. He suspected it had been with him since birth, but it only became louder when the rest of the world had finally gone quiet.

He pointed toward the stroke of moonlight painting a perfect line through the trees. His hand shook, his brown skin dry and withered by exposure. Before they'd reached the jungle's edge, they had been doing much of their walking at night, hiding from the hazardous sun. Though even in the few hours they ventured during the day, Chimalli had managed to avoid any notable damage beyond a bit of peeling and the blisters on his feet, but those didn't bother him much. They reminded him that he was alive. To his confusion—and delight—the rest of the group had not. In addition to the overall sunburn, they sported a decent amount of burns over their necks and shoulders. And those were just the ones Chima could see.

"If we lose the moonlight, we won't make it." The words left his lips of their own volition. "We would have to wait until tomorrow night, and I don't think the jungle will be generous enough to give us another day."

The Goose scoffed. "The church is right there."

"You won't be able to see it from the trees." And even if they could, Chima knew it wouldn't matter, but he left that part out. He inspected the moon, determining what time it was. "We have about seven hours before sunrise. That should be enough time."

And if it wasn't, at least the jungle would be swift with them.

The silence that settled between the trees felt purposely woven and spread over the vast expanse of growth around them like a net. Like a trap. Something waiting for them to hit just the right place before it clamped its jaws shut around them. And there was nothing they could do but keep moving.

At the very least, the silence was infectious, pacifying Chimalli's party at his back. He felt both comforted and concerned by the feeling of being watched, of being hunted. The foliage that served as foundation was thick and overgrown, plants that may have once only seen their ankles now towering above their heads or glancing over their shoulders. Every ruffle of leaves nearby was a threat, every ripple in the canopy above a warning, and yet…with each gasp and skitter of the men behind him, Chimalli felt more at ease.

"I'm telling you we should've waited 'til morning," Goose hissed, no doubt unable to help himself any longer. He had talked damn near nonstop since they'd left Sonora. It was a miracle he made it more than a half hour tonight.

"I told you we couldn't," the Snake shot back.

"No, the Mexican said we couldn't."

"Shut the fuck up, Benny, or you can turn your bitch ass back and wait all you want."

That shut the Goose up real quick. Chima gripped his staff harder, lengthening his stride a bit more. Every time they disturbed the peace, he felt ill. He was allowing these vultures, whose ancestors had stolen from his again and again, to do it once more. As he considered that reality, anger swelled in his chest. Because even though the world had ended, their sense of entitlement had not. Would his people ever find peace before death?

He contemplated it deeply, the idea of taking the slightest turn left and continuing on until they missed the hill entirely or the jungle found its appetite. He didn't care. And if it cost him his life, at least it would be worth something. He could face his family in Mictlan or wherever they ended up and tell them he didn't betray them.

No. Keep going…

The voice was so subtle that it caught him off guard, cutting through his treacherous thoughts and making him stop short. It was close, so close, like someone speaking in his ear. He was certain at first that it had been one of the Snake's boys. It sounded so real, but—no. The voice had spoken in Nahuatl. It was not them. And it was not *for* them.

"What is it?" the Bear grunted, lifting his gun.

Chimalli snapped out of his hypervigilant distraction, shaking his head. "Nothing, I thought I heard something, but—"

"Now, he's fucking hearing shit? Jeez, man," the Goose whined.

"What did I say, Benny?" the Snake huffed. "Keep it moving, Coyote."

Keep going…

It was the voice that he obeyed, not the Snake. Though it was definitely inside his head, it was the realest thing to him now. It was there, and it was beautiful, and it was thick with conviction.

And it sounded like his Nana.

I will protect you, tlazopilli. I will protect our people. Just keep going.

The assurance filled him with a sense of calm, of resolve, and the desire to do something foolish left him like a heavy breath. He pushed forward through the hungry jungle, following the thin path that cut through the treetops like a sharp blade the moon was dragging across the ground. He only made it a few steps before he realized that the ground had begun to move.

It was the faintest tremble, like those caused by a distant explosion or eruption. Chimalli could only discern it by the sudden imbalance he felt, as if a single step too far in either direction would send him toppling over. So maybe not like a distant explosion. No, no, it felt more like…like being on a boat. Or a very thin raft.

He stopped again.

"For fuck's sake," the Goose hissed, an acute frustration in his voice. He must have been on the verge of panic already. "What is it now?"

Chima held up a fist as he inspected the velvet green carpet beneath his feet, pushing aside shrubs and vines with his staff. Then, carefully, he pressed his foot down in a place that looked slightly darker than the rest of the moss around it. Water bubbled to the surface beside his toes.

He was right. They were standing on water. Though how deep or how large, he did not know. It was impossible to tell as it was buried under at least an inch of jungle.

"What the fuck is goin' on?" the Snake hissed in his ear.

"Water," Chima breathed, attempting to survey the path up ahead.

"What the fuck do you mean by water?"

"I mean, there is water underneath. Like—like this part of the jungle grew over it. Or—or water got trapped under the ground. I—I don't know. I don't know. It wasn't here in the...before. It—"

He could not recall a lake ever being here, but for all he knew, it could have been deep beneath the earth all this time, somewhere beyond the pyramid that the Spaniards had defiled with their church. Maybe it, like so many other things, had risen to the surface when the land was reclaimed.

"What the fuck are we stoppin' for?" one of the No Name gringos in the back called in a stage whisper. "Let's get the hell outta here!"

The Snake did not address him, instead speaking to Chima again. "Is it safe to cross?"

"I—I think so? The moss and grass is thick enough to support the plants, so I—"

He was cut off by the sharp shove of the Bear's large paws against his back, which nearly sent him crashing to the ground. He managed to get his staff in front of him to stop the fall, but the ground felt more unsteady here, and water pooling around the wood before him.

"Cross it, and find out, Coyote," the Bear said, and the others behind laughed. "That's y'all's specialty, right?"

Chimalli gritted his teeth but kept himself from turning around. He probably could've taken the Bear out of spite alone. Chima was shorter than him by several inches but solidly built, a fullback's form with some leftover footwork from the boxing matches that once sustained him when the world made sense. As for the hands, he still had those in full, so—

Keep going…

Chima let the voice take him by the shoulders and propel him forth anyway, taking a few cautious steps. He tried to determine where the water might end, but that was impossible. Apart from that thin strip of moonlight, it was pitch black, and he could make out nothing beyond it. Still, he moved, clinging to the promise this voice had made him, hoping it was not one of Huehuecoyotl's tricks. Or a sign he was losing his grip on reality.

At last, the ground seemed to grow sturdier under his feet. At the very least, no more water seeped through the moss in great quantities. Chimalli stopped and turned around, waving his hands. He could barely make out the Bear's pale forehead on the other side, but the moonlight glinted off of the Snake's green eyes.

"It's good here," he told them, as loud as he deemed safe.

They must have heard him, because he could hear them begin to move, and he turned back around to watch the dark for what else might be coming.

Behind him, the silence was shattered by a violent shriek.

Chimalli whipped around. All he could see was darkness, but the piercing screams of one—no, *two*—of the men filled the air, nearly bringing him to his knees.

The Snake and the Bear erupted from the dark, running at full speed toward him. The Goose eventually stumbled out of the din as well, yelling, but he seemed untouched by whatever had claimed his companions. One of the last two No Names broke out after him into the light, but Chimalli could tell he was not unscathed. He was limping.

"Run!" the Snake roared, racing right past Chima. The Bear followed, but he had enough presence of mind to throw his shoulder into Chima as hard as he could, knocking the air out of him and sending him sailing into a nearby tree before he crumpled to the ground. An offering to whatever was chasing them.

As the Goose ran past, Chima pushed himself up on his palms, shaking his head to dispel the disorientation just as something came out of the trees.

It was large. Larger than large, so large that it was impossible to gauge its size due to the way it bled into the black surrounding it. Chimalli thought vaguely that perhaps it was just part of that darkness, a material manifestation of its hunger. Then its head ducked into the light.

First came the antlers, a gargantuan spread with dozens upon dozens of points glowing golden. They were like sharpened glass, blood streaming down them, the body of one of the men still firmly skewered on its left side. Chima's eyes were still trying to process that when bright golden eyes flecked with green illuminated the darkness around them. And the man between them. There was blood all over him, his face painted in so much of it that it looked black rather than red. And—*oh*. His arm was missing. His entire arm was missing.

A forked tongue unfurled from the monster's wide mouth as Chima finally took in its full form. His breath caught. *The mazacoatl.*

Chima scurried back on his hands into the tree. He could not feel his legs, much less trust them to hold his weight. The man stumbled toward him, his screams echoing through the wood. Chima tried to shut his eyes, to look away, to shield himself from the inevitable, but he was far too afraid to lose sight of the serpent. He watched with bated breath as it descended upon the man, lowering its head once more before jerking it sharply upward.

The screaming abruptly stopped as a hole the size of a basketball opened up in the man's chest, his bloodied face contorted in shock. Every muscle in him went slack, his will to survive spilling out around the mazacoatl's glossy antler. Chima did not breathe. He did not dare. Death came in the quiet.

The serpent's eyes fixed on its newest ornament. Its antlers seemed to wilt, lowering the man down to eye level. Then, without further preamble, the snake began to eat.

Chima found the feeling in his legs with acute awareness. Shoving himself up, he scrambled around the tree, and once he secured his balance, he took off at a run, caring not for what he might be running toward. It could not be worse than this.

Even once he was sure he'd put a decent distance between them, Chima could still hear the echo of the serpent's powerful throat swallowing a man whole. He saw no sign of the others. Not that he could see much at all, but he contemplated his options once he caught his breath. There was still some time before sunrise, but if they thought he was dead already, he could go ahead on his own or he could turn back around. Not that he wished to have a second encounter with the mazacoatl, but he was less likely to come across the group again.

Yet, although neither option seemed altogether better, what might await him back home scared him more than what awaited him in these trees.

A sound from nearby snatched his full attention. He could not make out what it was, but it reminded him of a coyote's cry, high-pitched and helpless. Though the idea of a coyote felt so mundane now in comparison to what he'd seen on this journey thus far. And after being referred to as such for this long, it almost made him ill.

Yet his feet carried him toward it anyway, farther down the moonlit path. Chimalli felt a faint twinge of surprise that it remained after all that had happened in the past few minutes, as if he expected the deer snake encounter to scare the moon away as well.

He soon came to a small clearing where the cry was exceptionally loud, and after only a moment's hesitation, he continued toward it, stepping off the main path and into the thick jungle foliage, hoping he did not disturb anything else. Though as he drew closer, the sound became clearer, and he stopped short. Just as he did so, the leaves to his left ruffled, and out came the Goose followed closely by the Bear. Moments later, the Snake appeared, too.

"Maybe it's the Coyote," the Goose hissed.

"Who gives a fuck?" the Bear grunted. "He probably got fucked up by that *thing*."

"We might still need him," the Snake snapped. "I told you that, but you still had to fuck with him."

"We're right there," the Bear shot back. "We'll make it there without him."

"Yeah, but who knows if we'll make it *in*. Shit always seems to require blood with these Indians."

Despite the darkness that swarmed around the single flashlight in the Goose's hand, Chima could see them so vividly. He felt like a ghost, on the outside looking in as they passed him, completely unaware of his presence. Judging by their steps, there was water underfoot here, and that alone confirmed Chima's suspicions. He knew exactly what that cry was. It didn't even sound like a coyote anymore. It sounded human.

And maybe he should have said something, stopped them from progressing, saved their lives, because wasn't that what good people did?

No.

These were not good people. These were men far more monstrous than anything in this jungle. If anything, the jungle was only doing what Chima was meant to. Protecting his people. Because good people did not spare the threat. Good people protected the innocent.

Chimalli remained still.

The crying stopped.

Chaos erupted in the space of a breath, the sound of splashing water spooking everyone in the party. The Goose's flashlight fell—or was knocked—from his hand, tumbling along the ground just as he let out a blood-curdling scream.

"What the fuck!" the Bear screeched.

"Go!" the Snake bellowed.

Even in the dark, Chima could picture it. The ahuitzotl's catlike body coming out of the bog, its sharp claws claiming the Goose the moment he was near enough, its thick tail with the hand at the end clamping down on his skull. The tearing of flesh and snapping of bone filled the air in an insufferable song.

And more splashing. A lot more splashing. Not just from the thrashing of the Goose's body but from all directions. There were more.

Chima turned and raced back toward the path, using the clearing to reorient his direction. The sounds hardly faded, but he kept running, his lungs and calves burning with the exertion. Even once he reached the path, he kept running. He ran toward the church, toward the pyramid, wanting nothing more than respite. Something else drew him there, too, something he could not quite pinpoint, but it felt every bit like that voice in his head, soothing and sentimental in a way he deeply needed right now. Somewhere to put down his grief and sort through his joy, somewhere to parse victory and defeat.

Then he was flying through the air, his lungs emptied in a violent impact and his head spinning with confusion. And likely a concussion once it smacked against the ground. Something had tackled him.

No. Some*one*.

The moment he was flat, the blows came, fists making contact with his face, neck, chest. He threw up his arms, trying to shield himself, but the Bear's meaty claws were far too large and heavy for it to do much good.

"You planned all of this, you little bastard!" the gringo roared between blows. "You did this! You brought us here to kill us!"

"No, I—!" Chima tried, but a fist hit him square in the sternum, and any hope of speaking died in his throat. Not that it would have mattered.

The Bear kept hammering into him, and Chima tried to turn his body, but that only ended up in multiple shots to his ribs. He swore he heard one break under the force.

"We don't need you," the Bear growled, more to himself than to Chima. Punches landed with every word. "You're—a fucking—waste—of resources, you—fucking—wetback! I'm gonna—hang you from one of these—trees when—"

It all stopped. All at once, just like that, everything just—*stopped*. The punching, the yelling, the spit flying across Chimalli's cheek. All there was now a ringing in his ears and a pain in his chest. Even the Bear's weight was gone from atop him. Still, he tried to shield himself, to make himself smaller, just in case.

Until he heard the distinct sound of gurgling.

Rolling onto his back, he looked up to see the Bear's wide eyes staring back at him. But he was so far away, levitating in the air above Chimalli's head… Wait, no. Not levitating. Hanging.

Behind him stood a large tree, its roots gnarled and curled in on themselves. Well, most of them, but not all. Some of them were moving through the air, including the two now tangled around the Bear's torso and neck, their barbs cutting into his flesh like teeth. The Bear thrashed around in its hold, which only tightened further, dispelling one shrill shriek for help. Chimalli only watched as blood splashed near his feet.

He knew it then. The jungle was not going to harm him. It was not only protecting his people, the ones already within the sanctuary, it was protecting him, too.

When the Bear disappeared into the thicket of hungry branches, Chima forced himself to stand, looking around for anything to ground him. Ahead, the faintest flash of moonlight on the ground lit up the path. Night was dwindling. He had to be quick.

He winced with each step, clutching his side and spitting out the blood that had welled up in his mouth.

Go on, tlazopilli. You are almost there. Almost home…

He knew who the voice was now, and he knew from where it came. He let it wrap around him like a warm coat as he pushed forth, staggering down the path; the fears he had carried into the jungle were lost somewhere along the way. As darkness turned to gray mist, he could see more of his surroundings, too. There were more yateveo trees, their carnivorous branches spiraling out and up into the air. They creaked as he passed but did not attack. Instead, they bowed. Like they were welcoming him home.

Large, thick roots now lined the path, and he followed them without thought, leaning against them every now and again when he felt he could not keep moving. But he did it anyway, feeding off of them, wanting nothing more than to feel as alive as they felt with fresh blood seeping into the earth. He wanted to heal as they healed.

We will do it together...

He lifted his head after what felt like forever with his eyes fixed on the ground before him. Light was beginning to reach through the leaves. Beyond the trees, he could make out a large swath of stone. Even as his head pounded and his body ached, he smiled. He was almost there.

Chimalli slowed his steps, creeping forward to the edge of the tree line. Just beyond, the steep slope of the great hill greeted him, the ground sunken around the wide stone steps of the pyramid. High above, the church loomed just like it had in his dreams and in the pictures he'd seen before. Yet—unlike those pictures, its golden walls no longer glittered, its white dome no longer shining like a bright diamond atop its crown. And when he looked closer, he could see that the walls were draped in moss and vines, trees growing around and *through* its foundation.

It was as though the land were trying to devour it whole, to cleanse itself of this blight. One of the crosses that had no doubt adorned the top of a tower had long since fallen. It lay a few feet away from Chima, its color tarnished beneath the shallow waters. The others would follow suit soon enough, if they had not already. Chimalli was certain of it.

"Hey!"

The shout startled him. Looking further up the stairs toward a large stone door was the Snake, his face bright red and angry, his clothes tattered and mottled with blood. Chimalli took a deep breath he immediately regretted, the pain in his ribs flaring. Still, he approached with sure steps, something greater driving his body forth.

"Get me into this fuckin' place!" the Snake demanded, pointing at the door.

Chimalli climbed the steps until he reached the landing the Snake stood upon. Fear did not follow. Only contempt. His people, his land, and whatever lay beyond that door were not the Snake's to claim. And Chima knew that now it was up to him to make that clear. He and he alone stood between peace and a predator. The jungle had done its part. It was time he do his.

"Come on!" the Snake roared again. "Don't think I won't fuck you up, Coyote. Open the damn door."

"No."

His voice sounded foreign to him, to the point where he was almost convinced it was not his voice at all. But he owned it regardless, faithful in his response.

The Snake scoffed. "What do you mean no?"

"You are not welcome here. You will never be welcome here."

The Snake reached back with a quick hand, untucking his pistol from his pants and pointing it at Chimalli. Yet there was only calm in Chima. He did not flinch. He did not raise his hands. He merely stared back at the Snake, daring him. If he died on these steps, guarding that door, it would be worth it. And at least, if he did, he would soon see his family again.

"Maybe I get in by killing you," the Snake spat. "Isn't that what you people usually do? Human sacrifice?"

Chima felt a laugh tickle his throat. The Snake cocked his gun. Chima raised his chin.

A loud screech cut through the air.

Neither man had time to react. Before Chima could blink, his vision was filled with the majestic wingspan of a swooping eagle, its talons extended and his beak open. Each clamped down around the Snake, the pistol falling from his hand and over the edge of the stairs. He screamed once before the eagle's beak snapped shut around his throat.

Chima did not linger now. He moved toward the large door, resting his head against it, tears of grieving joy cascading down his face. He screamed into the stone. For his Nana, for his wife and unborn child, for his parents, for his gods. And as he did so, the door began to open.

He straightened abruptly, going silent as he watched the stone slide forward. Before him stretched a long stone path, this one lit by torches rather than moonlight. A breeze pressed upon his back, urging him forward, and he allowed it without question. The deeper he moved inside, the less his pain plagued him.

He could hear a waterfall somewhere in the distance, and although he wasn't sure, he could swear he heard voices amidst its song. At the end of the path were steps leading down into a vast, open space, sun streaming in from windows high above its floor. Chimalli's mouth went slack as he descended, awed by the towering idols of the many gods his Nana taught him about. He could recognize most of them. Tlaloc, god of rain, and Xiuhtecuhtli, god of fire. And in the center, larger than them all, stood Coatlicue, mother goddess of the earth, in her serpent skirt. Chimalli smiled. It had been her speaking to him. She, the roots of their people, had guided him home.

As he reached the foot of her totem, there was a loud roar to his left that startled him. Then another. And several more. He looked up, squinting toward the second level, where he saw shapes moving. Many shapes. When they came into the light, he could see the sleek and vicious forms of dozens of jaguars, their black and gold pelts glittering like precious gems. They descended the stairs with slow steps, their eyes luminescent in the shadows. The two leading them walked closely together, and one had something strapped to their chest, although Chima could not make out what it was.

Then they began to stand.

One by one, they morphed and changed, fur turning to skin and hair, paws turning to hands and feet. And Chimalli could not believe what he was seeing. He fell to his knees as he watched, overwhelmed with a raw relief. There, at the front of the pack, stood Nana, and she looked younger than she had in years.

Beside her stood Tayanna, and in her arms, she held a bundle. Chima now knew what had been strapped to the jaguar's chest. He wept without shame. They'd made it, too. They had all come home.

"How?" he breathed as Nana kneeled before him, cupping his face.

"The mother goddess led us here," she whispered, pressing her forehead to his. "Like she led you."

"We knew you would make it," Tayanna said, tears in her eyes. "We knew you would come."

Nana guided him up to stand, kissing his cheek before she stepped aside. Tayanna moved toward him, pressing the softest kiss to his chapped lips. Then she placed the bundle in his shaking hands. There, looking up at him, were a pair of shining eyes identical to his own.

Somehow, he needed not ask his name.

"Tlayolotl," Chima whispered.

Tayanna smiled. "That is what we named him. We thought it most fitting."

"I agree."

Heart of the earth. It was not the name they'd originally chosen, but after everything, what else could it possibly be? Chima glanced over at Coatlicue, watching from the center of the room.

"Thank you."

The voice did not answer, but he knew she was there.

MOTHER OF TITANS

DARCI MEADOWS

The dream always starts the same way— with the sound of sirens. She dreams she's a little girl again, playing by the sea. She's in the playground from her elementary school, only the layout has changed, shifted the way things do in dreams, the sand of the beach spread across the sun-bleached blacktop. She's drawing with colored chalk, the dust dry and clinging to her fingers. All across the asphalt of the playground there are chalk drawings just like hers: strange monsters, imaginary friends given form. When the siren begins to wail, she looks for the other children, but they're never there, just the scream of the sirens echoing plaintively across the empty beach. The sound grows louder and louder, even as the dream shifts, compelling her back toward the edge of the playground.

Her legs feel heavy, and yet she's traveled. She's inside of a storm drain now, the concrete tunnel turning the siren into a repeating echo, like a whale song bouncing off the cement walls of her makeshift shelter. In the distance figures move near the horizon but she can't make them out; she can never make them out except for the pink sweater— her sister Heather's sweater. She can always see it, even as the sky darkens and the sun disappears and the vast black shape in the clouds coalesces into a singular form. It's like a huge flying wing, passing over the playground and the coast. Everything in its shadow instantly turns to putrid waste. The sea bubbles and churns as fish corpses rise to the surface and flop helplessly on the sand. The chalk drawings melt away in acid rain that burns the play structures. The pink sweater turns to fiery ash in the distance. Alice Jensen begins to cry in her tiny safe haven— and then she wakes up.

Alice's mornings also always start the same way— bleary eyed and greeted by the soft rhythmic hum of countless electronics. The metal of the deck plates vibrates under her feet as she claws her way out of her rest pod, hugging her thin blanket tighter as she does. She doesn't care how thick the walls of the *Robohemoth* are— she swears she can feel the cold of space right through the titanium. Her quarters are big enough for the pod and a few personal possessions; it might be tolerable if not for the staleness in the air that seems to haunt her these days. In the dark of the morning, her morning at least, the walls seem so close, and the dream becomes so real it's almost like she really is back in that tunnel, watching the whole world burn away right under her feet. But that's only for a moment before she dresses and heads to her lab. There's work to do after all.

The lab is a solitary place, but it's hers. That's all anyone really has on the *Robohemoth*, their own private spaces. Most of it is whatever equipment they could salvage in the exodus— microscopes from middle schools, a spectrometer carried in an unmarked cardboard box, personal laptops daisy-chained together. Each object carries its own backstory, its own tokens of the people who willed it onto humanity's last best hope for the future. Alice's own items are scattered across the lab as well, just something to mark it as her place: old photographs and memories of better days, an mp3 player with just enough charge for a few more plays and no power cable, her mom's old hairbrush. The odds and ends of a life interrupted and hurriedly packed into a suitcase in the midst of disaster.

Things were so different then. Not better, just...different. When the news to abandon Earth reached what was left of humanity hiding in their burrows, there was sadness but at least there was hope too. A new life among the stars, a sense of everyone coming together to do their part for one last great endeavor, one last human achievement. But that was seven years ago— seven years of floating in space, patching problems, waiting for something to break that they can't replace or repair. Hope is in short supply on the *Robohemoth* these days.

Alice sat in front of her makeshift computer terminal, the machine huffing and puffing as it collated the soil samples and air analysis she'd fed into it. Her long auburn hair was pulled back in a ponytail, greasier than she'd have liked, but the water-free shampoo never seemed to help. As she waited, she fiddled with her glasses, a nervous habit. Letting the frames slide off her face, she held them at a distance, examining the glass. Somehow, even in space, they managed to get dirty. She smudged the lens with her thumbs before rubbing them against her shirt.

The computer pinged as she busied herself. She looked up, squinting through the blur of her eyesight to try and read the charts the machine had spit out, her fingers still idly cleaning her frames when the left lens slipped out of its socket. It hit the ground and cracked, not breaking, just a long obvious split running through the lens as she picked it up. Alice swore under her breath as she started working the glass back into place in frustration.

Finally, she resituated the glasses on her face, the crack running through her eye-line. Looking back at the monitor, she saw her own reflection and let out a laugh, even as the plunging graphs and red numbers confirmed what she'd feared. The ship's hydroponics were failing; the plants weren't able to thrive anymore, strangled under artificial sunlight. They weren't going to have enough air— not without some other option. Through her cracked lens, her eyes fell upon the sealed biohazard vault at the end of the lab, the piece of masking tape plastered over the front with thick handwritten marker reading "PROJECT TRIFFIDON: DO NOT OPEN TILL DOOMSDAY."

Alice quietly moved to the box, her fingers brushing the dust on the lid. She knew that was her dust; the air circulation system wasn't that good, so any dust in the area you lived was made of the dead skin you shed, the bits of yourself you left behind just by existing like this. Quietly at first but getting louder, her wrist terminal began to beep, the orange screen displaying a reminder. Alice stood and sighed; it was time for church.

The butterfly sanctuary sat near the top of the *Robohemoth*, inside what had once been a hangar. It was one of the only places you could see into the void beyond the makeshift sanctuary of the war machine they'd converted into a space ark. That's where they found the egg, floating in space, the last remnants of Queen Monarch, soul of the world. It took converting all of hydroponics to care for it, and even then, it was only possible thanks to the butterflies that had sprung from its skin. Now it stood as the tabernacle of this place, the soft orange glow filling the whole of the sanctuary as the swallowtails flapped their wings.

Alice stood at the back of the crowd. They had gathered at the foot of the great egg like they always did, Oon standing atop the ornamental bridge she used as a pulpit. She was speaking about renewal and transformation, the chrysalis as a metaphor, the kind of thing that sounds good but gets harder and harder to believe with every bad year you suffer through. Behind her, she could make out the shape of Oon's twin sister within the egg, arm's outstretched, cytoplasm swirling around her. When they'd found the egg, everyone thought it was their second chance; that Queen Monarch would return to save the world. They said it couldn't be coincidence that she was found by Oon and Yumi, the twin prophets who'd first introduced her to the world as nature's champion. Even when the weeks turned to months with no sign of renewal within the egg, they believed— believed that she needed a sacrifice. That was three years ago, when Yumi went to be one with the Monarch. Pople didn't believe as much anymore.

Oon's words rang clear across the assembled crew. "It has been said that, in the arts of life, man invents nothing; but in the arts of death, he outdoes the titans themselves. When they built the *Robohemoth*, he had but one purpose—to kill. He was not built as a spaceship, but as a weapon. But look at him now! This war machine has been our home for so many years. He gives us sanctuary in an indifferent universe—he can change, he can transform, just as the Queen Monarch does. This egg is not merely a promise of her return, but a challenge to each of us: we must emerge from our own cocoon, spread our own wings, even as we pray for a resurrection. The wings of a single butterfly can reshape the world. Our very home is proof. May the Queen Monarch watch over you all."

As she concluded her sermon, miming the flapping of wings with her hands, the crowd began to disperse, and Alice made her way to the front. For a moment Oon turned back toward the egg, whispering in Korean as she reached a hand toward the shell, not making contact. The material within seemed to shift and stir at her words— but it was only for a moment. Soon she turned back and spoke.

"Dr. Jensen. Good news I hope?"

Alice looked at her firmly.

"Ah," the prophet acknowledged, "perhaps not."

"Is there somewhere we can talk privately Oon?"

"Come now, this is a sanctuary after all. Only the butterflies will hear us here."

"How long do we have before the oxygen runs out?"

"Not long," Alice answered. "A year at the outside?"

"Ah...we'll have to tell them gently. Prepare them to move to the other ships."

"You know that won't happen," Alice said. "*The Robohemoth* has always been the flagship. We're the only one who can handle this large a population."

"I know, but at least some can survive. That's better than the alternative."

"...there is another way."

Oon froze, just briefly, before she said, "Triffidon?"

"It could work," Alice insisted. "It could've worked on Earth if they'd had more time. I've found a biomass in Earth orbit that can sustain it, and the process will release enough energy to launch the resulting plant matter back to the fleet. It'll give us everything we need to keep going up here."

"Dr. Jensen—"

"Alice. We've known each other long enough."

"Alice," Oon repeated. "I have to ask...this isn't about her, is it?"

Alice stopped mid-stride, her fists clenching tight at her sides as she collected herself. The insinuation alone was bad enough, but she'd hoped Oon would know better.

"This has nothing to do with my mother, Oon. She's the past; I'm worried about the future."

Oon smiled tiredly at her friend, reaching out a supportive hand to touch her arm even as Alice flinched at the gesture.

"It's okay Alice, I understand. I'm sorry."

Alice turned away, her hand going instinctively to the locket around her neck with the picture of her sister.

"You know it'll be a one-way trip, don't you?" Oon asked as gently as she could.

"The human element is what's missing. It's why the original Triffidon didn't work." Alice spoke without turning, ignoring the question. "But I can fix it. I know what it needs. I've spent so long...I'm the only one who can do this." Alice finally turned to face Oon, wiping the hint of tears from her eyes. "I promise, it'll work."

Oon came to join her, simply standing together in front of the arcing metal wall.

"It's a good plan," Oon said softly before reaching her hand out to the wall. " Your family wasn't sheltered at Daisuke, were they Alice? You weren't there—the day Behemoth died? We all thought he'd live forever, that he'd save us. When he was alive, we called him the Lord of All Beasts. And then he died, and we built this effigy in his likeness, around the bones of the greatest monster the Earth had ever known. We wanted to pretend he was something we could control. But these bones still remember what it was like to stride the Earth as a colossus, to not be afraid." Oon took Alice's hand and placed it on the wall beside her own. "You can still feel him under the layers of metal and glass. We live among the dead, among the bones of monsters; their voices are always with us, no matter how deep we bury them."

In her mind's eye, for a split second, Alice saw the Behemoth in all his primal glory—the fire in his chest, the crack of the Earth under his feet. For a moment it was all true, it was all real.

But only for a moment.

The jump ship was hardly bigger than Alice's quarters. The cockpit was somehow even smaller, the rows and rows of dials and controls surrounding her like a womb or a coffin, the flashing-colored lights casting rainbow patterns across her enviro-suit. The *Robohemoth* didn't support a launch bay for the ship, so instead she was going to be shot out of one of the missile silos from his spine. As she sat in the cockpit, strapped into her seat and facing what felt like upward in the artificial gravity of the mecha, she looked to her side for the motion of mission control. Past the torpedo bay turned hangar, she could make out the shape of the command station; technicians in white hazard suits busied themselves at consoles, monitoring output. None of it had to do with running the ship, but rather with monitoring the vitals of the young woman sitting on the elevated control throne between them—Tomoko Honda.

She looked barely older than twenty-four, hair trimmed back and nails carefully filed. There was barely a sign that she'd been sitting in that chair for the past seven years save for the tubes weaving in and out of her abdominal cavity. Her skull plate had long been discarded, the fusion of circuit boards and gray matter that was her central processing system sat exposed as wires connected her to the *Robohemoth*'s systems. Her father's signature design stood on display for all to see, Japan's artist of cybernetics and the masterpiece he'd left behind. He always used to say that her most amazing features were how lifelike she was. She had a pulse like a real girl; she'd even blush and laugh and cry, but she hadn't done those things in a long time.

She couldn't even if she wanted to, as most of her facial structure had been removed to allow for more space to access the *Robohemoth*'s systems. The colossus was originally built to be run via a massive supercomputer, row after row of processing units all housed under a mountain of steel and concrete. Some of the older technicians who were there when the *Robohemoth* was still a weapon said the sound of those machines processing was deafening. When the *Robohemoth* was run, you could barely hear yourself think; but Tomoko has run him for seven years in silence.

Alice watched intently for some sign of recognition in the woman, some spark in her one remaining free eye as the engines of the jump ship began to rev; but there was nothing. Alice had known Tomoko when they were young; their parents had met at a conference in Geneva before The Fall. She was so full of life then. It made Alice wonder what they all could've become if they'd never had to lose a world. And with that, the jump ship engines roared to life, and she was off, into the blackness of space, sling-shotting toward her destination, toward Earth.

As the jump ship sped through the vast emptiness of space, Alice traced the fading lights of the human refugee fleet. There was the bright form of *Battler Z*, his red, blue, and yellow lights twinkling under the city dome he carried on his back like Atlas. Beyond him the deep emerald glow of *Kronos*, a repurposed alien mecha hollowed out and turned into a space arc like they'd done to the *Robohemoth*. Before long, they all blended together into a small soft pinprick of light amid the indifferent stars. By this point, Alice had retreated to the hold of the ship; it was about the size of a cargo container, outfitted with whatever materials from her lab would fit. The ship's navigation and flight path were fully automated, and her computers were set to look over her calculations on their own. There was nothing left to do but wait till she reached her destination. Ultimately, she decided sleep was the most logical next move, so she strapped herself into the tight sleeping space, resting against the hum of the engines through the exterior hull.

As she lay there, bathed in the soft red energy-saver lights of the ship, she waited for the dream to begin again; but this time, something was different. She was standing on a cliff, the sky a blasted slate grate with orange and red at the horizon; in the last days, the sky had always looked like it was burning. Far below her, the sea waters began to bubble and heave. Fish and marine life floated to the surface as they boiled alive and an unnatural amber glow emerged from somewhere deep. On the horizon, a blue light appeared, a vast shape moving at high speed toward her seaside perch as a huge creature lurched out of the sea foam—Behemoth, in all his glory. His gray rough skin was dripping with barnacles and salt, the famous blue jewel in his forehead pulsating with energy. His arms were massive, like an ape but on a lizard's body. He let out a roar that shook men to the bone, but it was not directed at Alice. Its aim was something beneath the waves. A vast amber shaft shifted under the water; a titan in equal form erupting out of the shallows— Megapod.

It was said the Megapod was originally a near microscopic form of life that clung to Behemoth. That they were harmless before the runoffs and the oil spills and the polluted waters, before it fed on the waste of mankind and slowly mutated into a thing that rivaled its former host. From the back it looked like a huge arching shell, its face a slurry of tendrils and hundreds of glowing red eyes above a burrowing, gobbling mouth that consumed everything it touched. The heart of Megapod produced the amber glow, a sickly yellow jewel embedded in the creature's exoskeleton. In an instant, the two were upon each other, Behemoth reigning powerful blows down on Megapod even as its horrible mouths bit and tore and burrowed into the lord of all beasts. And as they clashed, a new form began to emerge. A black stain spread across the ocean, spreading into a crawling putrid shape, like a living shadow huge and terrible—Hexane, the toxic titan.

No one knew where it came from. Some say it was carried on a meteor, an aberrant form of life, but others were more pessimistic. Others thought it was a new species of titan altogether, a living pollutant, not alive like the monsters of old, but possessed of a malevolent sentience, a will to devour life and spread itself across the world. In a single horrible moment, Hexane came down across Behemoth, a black wave crashing against the noble beast, enveloping him in its sticky mire, even as Megapod renewed its biting attack on his chest. Alice turned away at that point, even if she could still hear the screams of terror and pain from one of the oldest creatures on Earth echoing. She could hear the sound of the spawn of the new world oozing and biting and tearing pieces of him away. She knew that this place, this moment, was a lingering psychic remnant from her communion with the bones.

Standing at the edge of the cliff, she knew that this was the place where Behemoth died.

This was the place where the world went with him.

Alice woke with a start to the sound of the destination alarm beeping over and over from the cockpit. Groggy, she unstrapped herself and made her way to the console, flicking off the alert as quickly as she could to silence the incessant tone. As she worked at her terminal, having the ship scan the surrounding orbit and plot its new course, she allowed her eyes to dart momentarily upward toward the planet. She hadn't been hopeful, not really, but there was always the chance, however remote, that maybe Earth wouldn't look the same as how she left it, that if this was her last time, she'd finally see it green like it was supposed to be.

Some people thought Behemoth's son would take his father's place and save the world, or that Queen Monarch might have a twin of her own waiting to emerge. Someone said the Atlanteans had survived and were working on a biomech program that would save the world, assuming there was still any world left to save. The planet that greeted Alice was a smoldering husk: chemical fires still ravaged nearly one-third of the planet's surface, vast noxious clouds of acid rain covered the other third, and part of the ocean was permanently boiling. Even from this distant vantage point orbiting in space, Alice could see the paths left by the new titans like Hexane and Megapod and Cadavrex. The old world was dead and the new one was smothered in its crib. Earth belonged to the monsters now.

The computer pinged, letting Alice know her next destination had been established and that it'd take forty minutes circling the Earth to reach it. She returned to the hold and began to prepare; the computer's diagnostics all came back clean, and she knew she needed to make sure the delivery system was ready. They'd only had the fuel for this one trip, only the catalytic material for this one last attempt. Project

Triffidon was going to be a one-time shot; she couldn't afford to get anything wrong, no mistakes. As the words echoed over and over in her head, her mother's voice speaking to her from out of a long dead past, Alice picked up the hairbrush she'd taken with her from her quarters. It was so old now, practically ancient, a family heirloom passed down from one generation to the next. It was the last thing her mother ever gave her, as the crowds pushed and shoved and screamed their way onto the rescue arcs, her mother's hand slipping out of hers at the weight of humanity pushed against her.

When Cadavrex had been sighted near the evacuation point, there was no time for anything less than panic. This was right after Triffidon failed, her mother's brave new vision to turn the world green and make up for Heather. It was funny, Alice was older now than her mother or sister had ever been. It'd been so long she barely remembered them outside her dreams and the look in her mother's eyes that day. She was so broken, so defeated, as Alice had slipped away from her, hairbrush clutched in her hand. "I'm going to be with your sister," she'd whispered before the smoke and noise swallowed her whole. Sometimes, late at night when she would pretend to sleep, Alice wondered if things would've been different if she had died that day on the playground under Hexane's cloud and not Heather. Maybe both her mother and Heather would still be alive if she had been the one to die. She sighed and tried to bring herself back to the task at hand, running her fingers along the rough bristles of the brush and pulling away a single strand of hair.

The recirculated air of the jump ship was beginning to grow stale when the computer pinged Alice that she'd finally arrived at her destination. Carefully adjusting the ship's telemetry, it fell into a geosynchronous orbit with her goal, the two whirling around the Earth at high speed together in perfect harmony. Looking out the window, she spotted the massive skeleton that had once been Atomo and Nuklo. The two monsters had been brothers, a pair created when some scientist was caught in a binary fusion experiment gone wrong.

The massive forms rose out of the nuclear muck to bestride the Earth as part of the titans, albeit more minor members of their pantheon.

When the final war came, the twins turned against each other as the black toxic sea raged and rose and ate away at more and more of the world. Atomo fought for the survival of the Earth alongside his fellow titans while Nuklo sided with the new creatures born of pollution and the spoiled planet. They died in each other's arms, falling into the bubbling sulfurous remains of the Mediterranean before their scoured bones washed ashore, fused into one skeletal mass. The EU had shot their remains into space just to get rid of them, hoping they'd drift outward to the rim of giant bones just inside the asteroid belt, but they were too dense and cumbersome. Instead, the conjoined skeletons remained in Earth's orbit, a grim reminder of the cost of the final war. At least back when there were still people left on Earth to be reminded.

The skeletons' legs were intertwined into something like a spiral as the spines went off in different directions. Their rib cages were pressed against one another, fusing into the other while their arms were wrapped in what might've been an embrace or a death grip. Finally, their colossal skulls had merged right at the eye socket, conjoining to create a single huge socket with the two smaller ones on either side, their fractured joke of a maw yawning open to the vast vacuum of space. The skeletons were large enough they had their own low-level gravity and Alice could see that a handful of smaller bits of debris and untended satellites had become caught in their orbit.

With any luck, the energy released at the point of transformation would be enough to launch the former remains out of orbit and follow the trajectory of the jump ship back to the Earth refugee fleet. That was the theory anyway. The Triffidon samples would transform the assembled biomass and then hurl it off to where it could do the most good; all that remained was to see it through. Alice tightened her helmet as she checked over the last of her supplies. Everything was assembled—only one small step remained.

The air hissed around Alice as the cargo bay of the jump ship opened to the exterior vacuum. She tightened her grip on her pack, checking the magnet locks between her feet and the CO_2 canisters at her side. The recycled air flushed out of the compartment and into the space beyond, the rush of force around her sealed suit quickly subsiding as she waited at the opening into the abyss. Her ship was still spiraling, trying to time its rotational speed with that of the skeletons, lining up just right to allow Alice to leap from one to the other without risking the jump ship being drawn into the gravitational pull of their biomass. Alice held her breath as the two forms twisted in space, the sun peeking around the edge of the Earth near the corner of her vision. Finally, the two began to sink, the flat expanse at the top of the head where the two skulls had fused lining up with the cargo port of the jump ship. It was a straight shot from one to the other, across maybe five yards of open space, barely a quick jaunt, and she'd only have to do it once. Alice exhaled, allowing one more moment to make sure the orbits were synced before hitting a button on her wrist console.

A burst of CO_2 shot from the tanks at her legs, and in an instant, she was rushing across the void. The stars sprawled out before her, the Earth in all its rotten grandeur under her feet as she leapt toward the skull of the long dead gargantuan. For a moment, Alice was weightless, suspended in between the gravity fields of her ship and the skeleton, hanging in the vast emptiness that surrounded the planet she once called home, but as with all things, it was only for a moment. Before she knew it, she was being pulled toward the skull, falling, albeit far slower than she would've on Earth or the *Robohemoth*. Drawing her legs close together, she aimed her angle of descent toward the orbital ledge where the fused singular eye socket became the dome of the skull and flattened into a plateau; she could set-up there. She landed harder than she would've liked, feeling the vibrations through her suit; the added weight of her pack and CO_2 canisters created the feel of a hard thud against the decaying bones. Quick as she could, Alice was scrambling from her position to more stable ground, finding firmer footing on the bone plateau as she'd hoped, even as the ledge she'd landed on fell away into the orbit of the vast skeletal frame. She was almost there now, almost finished, and there was no room for error.

Slowly and deliberately, she unpacked the Triffidon project, bolting the mechanism into place on the skull with an electric drill. It was a large container, glass walls designed to be broken at a specific frequency, UV lights humming along at their own internal power, and inside the container was the greenest thing she'd ever seen. Triffidon had been one of the titans, a huge plant creature born from a combination of plant, human, and Behemoth DNA. It had fought and died decades before the final war—almost forgotten by the time of Hexane or Megapod. But Alice's mother hadn't forgotten. Her project was to be Earth's last hope—a way to create a new and massive supply of plant matter to reverse climate change. She'd spent Alice's whole childhood trying to solve it, trying to make something big enough and strong enough to finally turn back the toxic sky and poisoned sea. Trying to give her daughters a better world.

Daughter.

Ever since that day on the playground, when Hexane made landfall in Southern California, when Heather had run to the sea and Alice had run to the storm drain and only one of them made it home—her mother had never been the same after that day. Alice released the CO_2 canisters into the limited gravity well of the skeleton, a thin but sustainable atmosphere of carbon dioxide forming around the bones to nourish the incoming plant life. That was all it would take, enough atmosphere for the new Triffidon to be born. Then it would be able to produce its own air supply, even in space. Even with all that power, it wouldn't be able to fix the Earth below, but launched back to the fleet…maybe it could be a better world for someone.

Finally, Alice assembled her terminal, entering the parameters of the experiment. As she worked, her eyes fell on the polaroid taped to her monitor. She stared at the picture of her family, ignoring the crack in her glasses. It seemed like a thousand years ago, that day with her mother and sister by the sea in the sunshine. She smiled as she looked, the computer blinking its request for final execution. Alice reached into her suit pouch and pulled out the sealed hair she'd taken from the brush. She'd run the genetic analysis twice on the way here, just to be sure, and she was. One hair was all it would take, all it should take, to splice titan and plant genetic material into a viable organism. She carefully installed the strand into the Triffidon container and returned to the terminal, preparing to activate.

Sometimes it seemed like Alice had never really known her mother, that she couldn't even remember the person she was before her sister died. If she was kind or funny or stern, it was all wiped away in that one instant. She'd tried to look back and find something there, something to connect with, some hint of the woman behind the pain, but in the end, pain was all she was. But her sister...her sister she remembered. "She would've been the good one," her mother used to say whenever Alice failed at another experiment or another test. "Heather would've figured it out." Maybe she was right. Alice pushed the button on her screen and closed her eyes.

There was a blinding flash of the most brilliant green as the walls of the container cracked and the plant biomass within began to spread and grow. The human genetic material fused at a chromosomal level, becoming one with the plant matter as it breathed in the carbon dioxide and exhaled oxygen. There was a rush of vines and leaves across the expansive bone of the titan skull, stretching and bending faster than any plant as the green tendrils embraced the floating form until the entire structure was covered in plant matter. Root systems grew like veins through the long dead bones, grass and lichen sprouting along the rib cage, saplings and ferns flourishing at the arm bones. Alice was knocked back by the force of the impact, the entire station she'd erected swept away in an instant. The energy being released at the conversion was incredible; she could feel it pushing at her suit, emanating outward. In the corner of her eye, she saw the jump ship shake at the waves of energy before she was thrown again by the advancing plant matter. The vast skeleton was beginning to move.

It was just like she had predicted: the huge bones were being converted into a giant mobile humanoid plant form, launching themselves out into space along the trajectory path of the jump ship, out toward the refugee fleet. As the huge form shuddered to life, its first cries of limited awareness audible through the new atmosphere Alice had built, she felt the force of the titan's acceleration pressing against her. She was pulled down into the layers of grass and leaves and underbrush. Her vision started to dim now, her arms and legs pinned by the force she'd unleashed. But none of it mattered anymore—she'd gotten it right. The one time it actually mattered and she'd managed it. Alice closed her eyes as the green swarmed all across her.

The playground under the warm California sun. The chalk drawings of strange creatures scattered across the hot asphalt. The sound of the surf plays just out of sight. There's not a cloud in the sky as Alice, now a little girl again, finishes her chalk drawing of a smiling tree. Over her shoulder, she hears Heather calling and she runs, cresting the dunes of the beach. The playground and the drainpipes are left far behind as she takes her sister's hand. Together they walk along the shoreline between the blue of the ocean and the green of the world.

AUTHOR BIOGRAPHIES

Isa Arsén is a certified bleeding heart based in South Texas, where she lives with her spouse and a comically small dog. Her work has been featured in publications including *Stone of Madness Press, Not One of Us,* and the *McNeese Review,* as well as several independent anthologies and multimedia projects. Isa's debut novel is *Shoot the Moon* (G. P. Putnam's Sons, October 2023). Outside of writing, she is an audio engineer for interactive media.

Alex Brown is a queer, biracial Pilipino American writer who loves rooting for the final girl—especially if she's a monster. Alex's YA comedy-horror debut, *Damned if You Do,* was a Junior Library Guild Gold Standard selection. She is also the co-editor of *Night of the Living Queers,* a YA horror anthology featuring stories solely written by Queer Authors of Color, and will be editing *The House Where Death Lives,* a YA horror anthology about a haunted house and the people—and monsters—that are caught in its grasp. In a past life, Alex worked on *Supernatural* and Netflix's *Resident Evil,* though now she lives a quiet life in Los Angeles with her partner and their three chaotic cats.

D.C. Dador (she/her) is a science fiction & fantasy author whose stories are about finding love in dark places. She was a finalist on the reality TV show *America's Next Great Author* and has been selected for multiple competitive writing programs including Author Mentor Match. As a first generation Filipino American, she enjoys weaving her heritage into her tales. D.C. is also a contributor to the anthology

When Other People Saw Us, They Saw the Dead (Outland Entertainment, 2023). She resides in Virginia where she enjoys exploring historic (sometimes haunted) sites with her family.

Lauren T. Davila is a Pushcart-nominated, Latina author, anthologist, and acquisitions editor. She has edited multiple short story anthologies, including: *As We Convene: An Anthology of Time and Place* (Inked In Gray Press; May 2024), *When Other People SawUs, They Saw The Dead* (Haunt Publishing, May 2022; Outland Entertainment, May 2023), *Places We Build in the Universe* (Flower Song Press; February 2023), and *Where Monsters Lurk and Magic Hides* (Bee Infinite Publishing; Nov. 2022).

Her poetry and short fiction has appeared online at *Granada Magazine*, *The Paragon Journal*, *Ghost Heart Literary Magazine*, *Peach Velvet Mag*, *Voyage Journal*, *Second Chance Magazine*, *Headcanon Magazine*, *In Parentheses*, and *Poets Reading the News*. She is currently editing her debut adult novel, as well as working on poetry and short story collections.

Lauren has an MA in English from Claremont Graduate University and an MFA in Fiction Writing from George Mason University. Besides her personal creative work, she is the Acquisitions Editor at Inked In Gray Press and is actively acquiring genre fiction from historically marginalized writ-ers. She is also the Assistant Director at PocketMFA, an online writing and mentorship program.

She lives in the greater Los Angeles area where you canfind her swimming, walking her golden retriever, and drinking one too many rose lattes. She is represented by Susan Velazquez Colmant at JABberwocky Literary Agency.

Sam Elyse Snyder is a Jewish author who enjoys writing spooky middle grade stories and graphic novels. Her work encourages children to overcome mental health barriers and face their inner demons.

As a motion graphics producer, Sam has a passion for crafting bold, artistically expressive campaigns (www.samelyse.com/mograph). With experience in 2D, 3D, cel animation, and live action, she is honored to host a workshop at Camp Mograph 2023. Watching Godzilla movies in her Portland loft, sipping mint-cacao tea, and skiing (slowly) down Mt. Hood are a few of her favorite things. But nothing compares to collaborating with her husband and director, Nick Snyder, and traveling the world together.

Laura Galán-Wells (she/her) is a Mexican American author, improviser, and explorer living in Austin, Texas. She loves blending speculative fiction genres, including fantasy, sci-fi, historical, alternate history, dystopian, and horror. Her work is inspired by nerdy media, Mesoamerican mythology, and both Texan and Mexican folklore, history, and culture. She writes adult short stories, and YA and MG novels/novels-in-verse. Her comic book origin story *Molt* is releasing July 2024 as part of *The Thirteen*, a Latinx superhero universe launched by Chispa Comics, a Scout Comics imprint. Laura's literary agent is Samantha Wekstein, and the Gotham Group represents her novels for TV and film. Her website is at lauragalanwells.com, and you can find her on Bluesky, Instagram, TikTok, and Twitter (aka X) as lauragalanwells.

Alyssa Grant is a reader, writer, and educator from Vancouver, Canada. After spending a good portion of her twenties living abroad, she's happy to be back home exploring the world through stories. When she's not working, Alyssa can be found attempting to make new recipes or getting distracted online.

Rien Gray is a queer, nonbinary author of horror, fantasy, and romance. Their short stories have been published in the anthologies *Shredded*, *Unreal Sex*, *Opulent Syntax*, *Sapphic Blooms*, and the upcoming *BRUTE* by Lethe Press. They have an ongoing romantasy series starting with *Valerin the Fair*. You can follow their work at https://subscribepage.io/riengray and on Twitter @riengray.

Mallory Jones writes spooky stories with a dash of romance. When she's not making her characters investigate that creepy noise in the basement, she's in the kitchen baking countless loaves of bread. She lives in Oklahoma with her husband and two dogs. You can connect with her on Instagram at @__malloryjones.

RJ Joseph is the award winning, Stoker and Shirley Jackson awards nominated author of *Hell Hath No Sorrow like a Woman Haunted*. RJ is also an English professor and editor of a novella series with Raw Dog Screaming Press. She can be found on various social media platforms under @rjacksonjoseph or in these spaces: https://linktr.ee/rjacksonjoseph. RJ is represented in film/television by Karmen Wells at The Rights Factory.

Mari Kurisato is an award-winning Nakawē niizho-manidoog kwe (Saulteaux aka Western Ojibwe person) writer and poet. They are a disabled nonbinary trans femme parent, artist romance book reader, and otaku. She/they/IT to the haters Their stories have appeared in *Apex Magazine, Absolute Power: Tales of Queer Villainy, Love Beyond Body, Space and Time,* the Lambda Literary award-winning *Love After the End,* in *Things We Are Not,* and in *M-BRANE SF* magazine. Their latest short stories and novels can be found on patreon.com/wordglass. Find them on Twitter @wordglass. You can also find their work on Goodreads.

Wen-yi Lee is Clarion West alum from Singapore whose work has appeared in *Nightmare, Strange Horizons* and *Uncanny,* among others, and in anthologies such as *Year's Best Fantasy 2* and *We're Here: The Best Queer Speculative Fiction 2022.* She likes writing about girls with bite, feral nature, and ghosts, and her forthcoming debut novel *The*

Dark We Know (Gillian Flynn Books, 2024) has a bit of all three. Find her on social media at @wenyilee_ and otherwise at wenyileewrites. com. She is represented by Isabel Kaufman at Fox Literary.

C.M. Leyva is a speculative fiction author and registered nurse who enjoys writing character-driven fiction in all genres. Her passion for science and medicine is often seen in her stories while exploring the what-if's around them. When she's not working on her next short story or manuscript, you can find her attempting home improvement projects, losing herself in a good book, or playing video games. Find out more at linktr.ee/cmleyva

Rachal Marquez Jones graduated from Pepperdine University, and currently works as a copy editor and copywriter in California. She always thought she'd be writing fiction, until a creative writing class showed them all the wonder to be found in poetry. Their current work includes fiction, poetry, and creative nonfiction. As a queer person with mental illness, she is drawn to themes of connection, shared humanity, and living in one's mind. In her free time, their hobbies include failing at gardening, succeeding at baking, and any excuse to be near the water. Their work has been published in *Currents*, *Expressionists*, *Dodging the Rain*, *So to Speak*, *Pleiades Magazine*, and *Musing the Margins: Essays on Craft*.

Darci Meadows is a disabled queer horror author specializing in short fiction. Her work has previously been published in *Decoded Pride Issue #3*, *Cosmic Horror Monthly* Issue #37, and the flash fiction anthologies *The Flash of Fang*, *Flashes of Nightmare*, and *Invasion: Dark Side of Technology* Volume 2. All this and more can be found on her link tree: https://linktr.ee/darcimeadows

Amparo Ortiz is the author of *Blazewrath Games* and *Dragonblood Ring*. She was born in San Juan, Puerto Rico, and currently lives on the island's northeastern coast. She's published short story comics in *Marvel's Voices: Comunidades* #1 and in the Eisner-award winning *Puerto Rico Strong*. She's also co-editor of the upcoming *Our Shadows Have Claws*, a young adult horror anthology featuring myths and monsters from Latin America. Learn more about her projects at www. amparoortiz.com.

Nicholas Perez is a writer of Cuban heritage from the Louisville, Kentucky and southern Indiana area. He holds a BA from Indiana University Southeast where he studied history and religious studies and a MA from Louisville Presbyterian Theological Seminary where he studied Biblical exegesis and theology. He currently works in a hospital. When he isn't working, he's writing countless Adult and Young Adult stories ranging from fantasy to sci-fi and to even horror. "The Boy Who Became an Entire Planet" is his debut sci-fi short story. He is currently un-agented. He can be found at the following social medias: Twitter: @ZephonSacriel; Blue Sky: @zephonsacriel. bsky.social; Instagram: vanezzania.

Laura G. Southern is a fantasy writer and an associate agent at Wolf Literary. She has a BA in English Literature from Baylor University, as well as an MS in Publishing from New York University. Her speculative work can be found in *Abyss & Apex* as well as a viral app called BetterSleep. Originally from Mesquite, Texas, Laura and her cat now call Brooklyn home. Laura is represented by Chelsea Hensley at KT Literary. Laura's twitter handle is @LauraGayle77.

Morgan Spraker is a writer and recent graduate of the University of Florida, where she earned her BA in English and Sustainability Studies. Her academic work focused on the linked portrayals of gender and the climate crisis in 2010s young adult science fiction. While she hasn't encountered the elusive Florida Man or wrestled an alligator, she's a lifelong Floridian with a love for the beach. When

Morgan isn't creating worlds of her own, she's usually exploring others—namely, *Star Wars*'s galaxy far, far away—and playing Taylor Swift's discography on repeat.

Onyx Osiris is a Black Indigenous 2S/transmasc author of fantasy, sci-fi, and horror. As a practicing polytheist and self-proclaimed son of the old gods, mythology, fairy tales, and folklore play a major role in his stories, which feature marginalized characters fighting to reclaim worlds held hostage by revisionist pens. When not writing, Onyx can be found watching horror movies, playing fantasy video games, or indulging in all-you-can-eat Korean BBQ. He has an MS in forensic psychology, and is on track to complete an MA in English Studies in 2023 before he goes on to pursue an MA in Ancient Religions. He currently lives in Nevada on unceded Southern Paiute land with his Funko Pop horror collection, his siblings, and his dog-nephew, a porgi named Koda. You can currently find him on Twitter @onyxedosiris or Patreon @onyxosiris. He also writes romance under the pen name R.M. Virtues.

Katalina Watt's writing is represented by Robbie Guillory at Underline, was longlisted for Penguin Write Now 2020, and awarded a 2021 Ladies of Horror Fiction Writers Grant. As founding Audio Director for khōréō, they won 2022 Ignyte Award for Best Fiction Podcast and were longlisted for 2023 Hugo Award for Best Semiprozine.

SJ Whitby is a nonbinary author who lives in New Zealand, where they see few hobbits despite their fondness for snacking. They've always loved telling stories and they've finally put themselves out in the world with the sprawling *Cute Mutants* series of novels (ten books and growing) about a group of queer superheroes. They're passionate about increasing diverse sexuality and gender representation in fiction.